THE LAST ALCHEMIST

And the Love of His Life

POE HAWKINS

thelastalchemistnovel.com

BALBOA
PRESS

A DIVISION OF HAY HOUSE

Balboa Press books may be ordered through booksellers or by contacting:

Balboa Press
A Division of Hay House
1663 Liberty Drive
Bloomington, IN 47403
www.balboapress.com
1 (877) 407-4847

Because of the dynamic nature of the Internet, any web addresses or links contained in this book may have changed since publication and may no longer be valid. The views expressed in this work are solely those of the author and do not necessarily reflect the views of the publisher, and the publisher hereby disclaims any responsibility for them.

The author of this book does not dispense medical advice or prescribe the use of any technique as a form of treatment for physical, emotional, or medical problems without the advice of a physician, either directly or indirectly. The intent of the author is only to offer information of a general nature to help you in your quest for emotional and spiritual well-being. In the event you use any of the information in this book for yourself, which is your constitutional right, the author and the publisher assume no responsibility for your actions.

Any people depicted in stock imagery provided by Thinkstock are models, and such images are being used for illustrative purposes only.
Certain stock imagery © Thinkstock.

Print information available on the last page.

ISBN: 978-1-4525-9655-6 (sc)
ISBN: 978-1-4525-9657-0 (hc)
ISBN: 978-1-4525-9656-3 (e)

Library of Congress Control Number: 2014907321

Balboa Press rev. date: 6/15/2015

ACKNOWLEDGMENTS

First, I extend my sincere love and gratitude to my wife, whose love and feedback throughout the writing of this novel was essential.

TRUE FRIENDSHIP IS PRICELESS

My special thanks to my friend, Lori Inman, for the countless hours of proof reading and selfless devotion to this novel.

The following friends, each living a full and busy life, refused to receive any compensation for the valuable time and talent they expended doing the rough edits of this book.

"Wise blond Leslie"
"Amazing Tish"
"Professor Cat"
"Same old Frank"

Final professional line edit by Dean Hurtt.

CHAPTER ONE

THE LETTER AND THE LAW

As Chicago Detectives go, Joe Costalino was a patient man. The job made him that way. His eyes no longer registered emotion and the lines creasing his face made him appear fatigued. In his twenty-six years on the job, he had seen the raw madness of mankind. After you witness enough criminal insanity, you throw in the towel on disgust and outrage. You just do the job and bear it.

Joe was doing the job and bearing it as he listened to Father Henry Dorcus ramble on about his missing friend, Ken McAlister. Finally Joe broke in on the ramble.

"I'm sorry, Father Henry—" he couldn't remember the priest's last name—"but no crime has been committed here, know what I mean?"

"Not yet perhaps," said the priest, "but soon, if we don't do something!"

The detective looked over his desk at the priest with the ruddy complexion and wavy white hair. He felt a twinge of embarrassment as he considered the drab, untidy office surrounding the gentle old man in the immaculate black suit. Joe concluded, from what he had heard already, that the priest had himself witnessed more tragedy than his mind could handle and was suffering delusions.

"With all due respect, Father, what you are reporting is unbelievable. Even if your friend is harboring some weird fantasy, that's not a crime. Tell you what, your friend, what's his name...?"

"Ken McAlister."

"He's also a priest?"

"No, detective, not anymore."

"He's missing, that's all you really know, and that's out of my jurisdiction. You can see Sergeant Coulter down the hall. He handles missing persons."

"Please, Detective Costalino, allow me to read Ken's final letter before dismissing me. You will realize he is in serious trouble. I'm asking you as a human being to hear his letter."

Joe, because he was a Catholic of sorts, and because he thought the letter would be short, smiled and consented to the priest's request. Immediately Father Henry removed the letter and began reading.

"Dear Henry, beloved friend, I apologize for being out of touch for so long, but I have been truly lost. This will be my last letter to you, and I ask that you receive it as my last confession."

"Forgive me, Father, for I am about to sin.

I am planning to steal a young man's body—not the dead body of a young man but one fully alive, healthy body. This is not a kidnapping as the law defines that crime. In fact, there isn't a name for the crime I'm about to commit. What would you call it if a man administers an ancient potion to cast a spell on someone in order to dispossess his soul and replace it with his own?"

"Nuts!" Joe interjected. "Wacko, off the charts! Father, if this is a letter from your friend and not something you made up, your friend is certifiably insane. Either that or he's pulling your leg, know what I mean, joking with you? Some priests do that, don't they?"

"He is no longer a priest, detective. But he is not joking, as the rest of his letter will verify. May I continue?"

Joe decided to endure the rest of the letter. He thought the old priest might be right and that his friend, if he really existed, might be seriously dangerous.

Father Henry raised the letter closer to the desk lamp and continued reading.

"Frankly, Henry, I don't know why I'm confessing this to you. It has nothing to do with cleansing my soul of sin, for I no longer believe in *sin as the church defines it. I chose to confess to you because you are my dearest friend and may actually understand why I am about to take over another person's body."*

"Politely put, wouldn't you say?" chuckled the detective.

The priest paused, unsettled by the comment. The detective's tone waxed serious.

"For your sake, Father, I need to tell you, giving false information to an officer of the law is a crime. What I'm saying is, if you wrote the letter, now's the time to tell me. No real harm has been done; no crime committed yet, know what I mean?"

"I know," the priest stated emphatically, as he searched through his briefcase, retrieving a photo and handing it to the detective.

"This is Ken McAlister. He's not a figment of my imagination, as you can see!"

Joe looked at the photo of Father Ken McAlister seated in a wheelchair. He looked to be middle age, with a full head of close-cropped black hair, graying in places. He had a masculine face, strong chin, but his cavernous eyes and sallow complexion revealed a man who looked more like a weary warrior than a priest.

"He's what, paralyzed?" asked the detective.

"From the waist down," responded the priest. "He was born that way. Actually, he was born out of wedlock to some street urchin, a dropped out teenager. I think her name was Ilene or Arlene. McAlister, was one of the assumed names she used in the dark world she inhabited. It's hard to imagine how this girl managed to care for an invalid child for eight years without a husband."

"She was probably a prostitute," said Joe.

"Ken never said that."

"Well Father, unless she was a trust-fund brat, there's no other way she could cover the tab of a paralyzed kid."

Father Henry scowled, "Ken always spoke of her with the highest regard."

"Considering the circumstances, who wouldn't! How did she die?"

The priest shook his head despairingly. "In jail, in Las Vegas I think. Ken never gave the details."

"Probably suicide," offered the detective.

"I don't know," said the priest, choking back tears. "I only know he loved her beyond words!"

Joe reached across the desk and patted the priest's hand.

"Continue your letter, Father."

The priest blotted his tears with a tissue, then resumed reading. As Detective Costalino listened to the rest of the letter, the missing person, Ken McAlister, was less than three miles away preparing dinner for the man whose body he planned to inhabit.

CHAPTER TWO

ONE LAST USELESS GOOD DEED

Classical music wafted through Ken's one-bedroom apartment in a well-kept brownstone in an impoverished neighborhood. The time on the copper pyramid wall-clock was quarter to seven. It was still an hour or so before his guest, Joel Ellendorff, was scheduled to arrive, and Ken couldn't break free of his depression. The classical music he enjoyed only added to his gloom, and preparing the meal of Beef Stroganoff wasn't demanding enough to sufficiently distract him. He was planning to take a young man's life. "What madness!" he thought. Shaking at the thought of murder, Ken managed to open a bottle of wine. He poured himself a glass and while he sipped it he considered canceling the whole plot— "I can still just have dinner with Joel, talk about his plans to open his own repair shop." The thought brought him some solace. But how could he abandon his plan, unless he was willing to kill himself? It was one or the other, he knew that. If he backed out now, with an almost perfect candidate, he would never regain the confidence to go through the painstaking process of culling another. Perhaps he'd been lying to himself all along. Maybe deep down his own soul knew he never would, never could do the terrible deed. All the work, the planning, the lying, for what! Ken reviewed the months of stalking that led up to this night of unrelenting anguish.

He'd met Joel Ellendorff in a Spanish Language class six weeks ago. Attending night school was a ploy he incorporated to find suitable young candidates for the switch. Joel was twenty-three and appeared to be physically fit. Except for his mother, who lived in England, Joel had no close family ties, and was more or less a loner. He worked as a handyman, another small advantage, which provided the ex-priest the opportunity to employ him and gather the necessary information in the process. It didn't take Ken long to forge a friendship with the young man, and after a month of intense research, in the guise of friendly conversations, Ken decided to make his move. That was the day he wrote his last confession and mailed it to Father Henry Dorcus.

Ken continued to review the many calculations leading to the rejection of several other candidates and the choice of this most likeable fellow, Joel. One thought kept intruding on his calculations: "Are you sure you're not crazy? Are you sure that this entire plot, all the planning and stalking and lying are not just the contrivances of your deranged mind?" Ken sipped his wine as he contemplated the nagging question again. This time, instead of trying to drive it out of his mind he chose to review the events that led him into this diabolical situation.

Ken's reflections began with the Las Vegas gun shop. The brightly lit glass cases that displayed the handguns were vivid in his memory. Then he was there having to listen to the sales clerk with the Justin Bieber haircut who looked too young to be selling guns to people.

"What kind of hand gun are you looking for, Father?"

"Oh, something with the fire power to blow my brains out at close range," thought the priest, who said, "It's for an anti-war display we are setting up at the church."

Immediately, he flushed with embarrassment, having told his first full-blown lie since becoming a priest. The young man behind the counter responded by removing an Army .45 from the case and handing it to the priest.

"This is an authentic military issue forty-five, Father."

The priest examined the weapon in hand, as though he knew something about guns. Handing it back to the clerk he said, "This is exactly what I'm looking for. I'll take it."

With that, the clerk leaned over the counter and whispered, as though there was someone else in the empty store, "This gun will cost the church two hundred and eighty-nine dollars. You can get a plastic one that looks totally authentic at K-Mart for six bucks."

"Thank you, son, but it has to be the real thing. And I need the real bullets also."

Upon exiting the store, Ken maneuvered his wheel chair through the parking lot toward his van. He had been concerned that there might be a problem buying the gun, and there might have been, if it weren't for the naive young Catholic behind the counter.

As Ken approached the maroon colored van he pressed the unlock button on his automatic key. Immediately the driver's side door slid back and the entry ramp slid out until it rested on the pavement. As he had done a thousand times before, he guided his wheelchair up the ramp and maneuvered it into place behind the steering wheel. Satisfied with his position, he then hit the button on the extended dashboard which triggered the metal device that latched the chaise of his chair to the floor of the van. Ken concluded the entry ritual by pushing the "Driver Ready" button on the dashboard which withdrew the ramp and closed the driver's side door. Placing the gun on the passenger seat, Ken fastened the remote seat belt and checked the time on the dashboard clock. It was nine forty-five. Depending on the cross-town traffic he could be at the cemetery in two hours or so.

The fatigue he experienced on the long drive from Chicago began to subside as feelings of relief flooded his consciousness. His ordeal to stay alive was over. For the first time in his life he had a personal advantage over other people still striving after life. He alone, in this city of blazing lights and excitement, was seeking peace, a peace he would have before the night was over. Scanning the menu on the CD player, Ken selected one of his favorites albums. "Requiem" performed by the New York Philharmonic Orchestra.

The drive went without incident. It was a little past midnight when Ken turned off the highway onto a two-lane blacktop that lead to the town of Appaloosa. The road soon narrowed to one lane as it snaked through the barren prairie land. Five miles later he came to a large beautifully carved sign:

APPALOOSA
POPULATION 1258
HERE JESUS REIGNS

Except for the single street light above the sign, the town was dark, everyone asleep or huddled around a late night TV movie. For certain, no one was out dancing or night-clubbing in this town of "the most righteous." Ken chuckled at the thought of the commotion his suicide would create. The pious population would be talking about it for decades, especially when they found out it was his mother's grave on which he shot himself, and how she lived and died a sinner. Not one of them, mused the ex-priest, could ever imagine that this poor girl, this sinner, had more love in her heart than their precious Lord. Ken drove past the huge Church of Our Savior, behind which was the cemetery of 'the saved.' He had to drive a mile beyond the town, and half a mile on a dirt road to reach the Cottonwood Cemetery where "the unsaved" were buried and forgotten. His mother was buried among the poor and the destitute. Decades ago the Las Vegas power brokers funded the remote cemetery to inter the paupers. In their minds, paupers were those who lost the game of life. When it was cheaper to just cremate "the losers" they stopped funding the cemetery.

The iron gate surrounding the defunct cemetery was rusted out and large sections of it were missing, probably the work of some ambitious junk dealer. There were a few weather-worn tombstones spread out across the property. Most of the rusted metal grave markers were hidden by the prairie grass which overran the place. The only building on the cemetery was a large prefab metal shed, where the grave digging equipment used to be stored—just a few yards from his mother's grave. The rusted shed doors hung open and bent, resembling a giant gapping mouth with crooked teeth. Ken drove his van behind the shed, running down the grass leading to his mother's grave before he parked.

He switched on the light in the cab, removed the gun from the box and opened the carton of bullets. The ex-priest proceeded to load the clip as the instruction manual illustrated. Not that he was anticipating more than one shot, but he was mentally adrift in the faded, all but lost memories of his mother. If life existed after death, he would gladly give all of it for just a couple of minutes with his mother, to thank her for the love she lavished on him.

With the gun loaded and lying on his lap, Ken removed some snapshots of his mother from his wallet. The one he cherished most was taken at Disney Land. She was holding him on a white horse on the merry-go-round. She looked so young and beautiful, too young to be his mother. Ken placed the photos in his pocket. Removing a pad and pen from the glove box, Ken wrote,

Dear Henry,

My only suffering at this moment is the thought of the grief my death will cause you. Please don't blame yourself, for there's nothing you could have done to stop me. I know you will pray for my soul, fearing I have sinned, though I no longer believe in sin as the church defines it, or Heaven or hell, which are determined by a most arbitrary fate. I learned that in a coffee shop where I witnessed several high school kids involved in a kissing contest. Their full hearted laughter captured my attention because in my whole life I never laughed like that. That thought triggered a revelation that the Kingdom of Heaven is literally in our midst, right where Jesus said it was. Heaven is right here, right now, Henry-not for everyone of course-not for me, not for the handicapped-but certainly for the blessed young, healthy and beautiful people-for those kissing kids it's here and now. And here's my take on hell, Henry, "Been there done that!" I have never had happiness like those teenagers were sharing, or peace, as a priest in the service of God should have. I faked it, dear friend, for there never was a day in my life that I didn't experience some pain, some discomfort, in this disabled mess of a body which continually claimed my attention. So, grieve not for my passing, dear friend. Rather, be glad that I have finally escaped from hell.

With Love and Gratitude,
Ken

Ken put the pad on the dashboard, placed the gun on his lap and pressed the buttons that released his chair and opened the door. Maneuvering his chair around, he rolled down the ramp onto the ground. The night was pitch black, no moon, no stars, just darkness. No sound but crickets. Ken thought about returning to the van and switching on the headlights but didn't want to expend the energy. He felt weak now, an all-consuming fatigue, no doubt brought on by the long drive and the emotions he experienced in the last two days. Instinctively, he motored the few yards to his mother's grave. He wouldn't see her nameplate tonight. It didn't matter. On previous visits he would pull up the grass around her name and place f lowers down. Tonight, he just wanted to die, to forget everything and be himself forgotten. With some trepidation but no regret, Ken cocked the gun and placed the cold barrel into his mouth, the way he had seen it done on television.

Out of the blackest night headlights flashed and the sound of a car approaching shocked him. Immediately, he pulled the gun from his mouth, as though he didn't want to get caught committing suicide. Before it dawned on him how absurd he was acting, a car pulled up on the far side of the shed, the motor and the headlights turning off simultaneously. Ken just listened as the car door opened and shut. A moment later he heard the sound of the car trunk opening, followed by some scuffling sounds along with the grunts and strident voices of two men.

"Don't, Bobby! Please, please give me a chance to explain!"

"Shut the fuck up! You were all over her in my bed! What am I, a fucking idiot! Start walking, asshole. I said, walk!"

Ken heard the men approaching in the dark. He glimpsed the broken shadow of a man walking in the beam of a flashlight. He was stymied, frozen in a state of total confusion as he listened to the men rage on.

"We lost our heads, Bobby, just drank too much! It was the first time. You've got to believe me! She loves you, man—she loves you to pieces!"

"Wrong response, asshole! Keep walking… She's seventeen, for Christ's sake! And you raped her, you low-life motherfucker!"

"No, Bobby, I swear to God! We just drank too much!"

The two men drew closer and closer to Ken until they were but one grave site away. When the flash light went out Ken felt no fear. So what if he was about to witness a murder, or was about to be murdered himself!

"What a world," he thought. "You can't even check out in peace! And how in Heaven's name will the 'righteous morons' down the road ever figure out what happened tonight? Did they even have a police station, or would that be an embarrassing indicator that Jesus didn't really reign in Appaloosa?"

Ken's thoughts were interrupted as the men's voices reached a fever pitch.

"You see that grave in front of you, that's—"

"I can't see shit! Bobby, listen—"

"That's your final resting place, scumbag!"

"Just listen a second. I can give you the secret to eternal life. I know it sounds crazy but—"

"Admit it! You drugged my wife and took advantage of her!"

"I swear to God! It was just a drunken mistake! Look, Bobby, this is premeditated murder. It's the end of your life too!"

"Not really, scumbag! This is no man's land! They don't bury people out here anymore. Nobody's ever going to find your fat ass! How does that make you feel?"

"Look, I swear—you want me to admit it—all right, Bobby, I owe you that as a friend—all right, I did it. I drugged her and I'm sorry, man. You're my friend—it was totally wrong—and—and I'm going to leave town. You'll never see me or hear from me again. I'll go to Europe— Brazil—I swear—I'll be out of your life and hers forever!"

"Sorry, Taulb, you're just a fucking creep! You drugged the wrong girl. Molly is so messed up in her head she thinks she loves you!"

"It's the drug I gave her. It will wear off in a few days. I'll be gone, in Brazil by then!"

Ken sat in the darkness coming to his senses, not ten yards away from the two men. Up from the depths of a past seminary sermon came a thought shared by Buddhist monk, Tully Boccti: "Even if one believes there is no God, no purpose to life, that one should more logically seek to alleviate suffering."

"Why not one last, useless good deed," Ken thought, when he heard the distraught man cry out as he was shoved into the grave, followed by the sounds of dirt being shoveled in on top of him. The condemned man kept shouting,

"No, please, Bobby! For God's sake, just think about this! I have some money."

"Enough of this! I don't want this to be my last memory," thought Ken, as he fired his gun in the air, and heard himself shout. "Drop the gun, or I'll shoot you!"

Ken barely got the words out before the pain in his wrist from the recoil claimed all his attention. The warning drew a volley of gunshots, the bullets whistling past Ken's head.

"Holy smokes," Ken thought, "this is my ticket out of here! Lifting his gun in both hands and firing wildly into the air, Ken waited for a return volley to take him out of the world. It never came. In spite of the ringing in his ears he was able to hear the shooter scurry off, jump into his car and drive away. After a long silent pause Ken collected himself enough to speak.

"Mister, are you there? Are you okay?"

"Yes, I'm okay. He missed," came the raspy voice of Ebizer Taulb.

"That's good," said Ken, at a loss for anything else to say.

"Can you help me get out of this hole, buddy?"

"I'm sorry, but I can't," said Ken as he motored carefully toward the voice in the dark.

"You can't help, or you won't? I have a few hundred dollars on me—"

"I can't. I'm paralyzed, in a wheelchair."

"You're joking, right!"

"No, sir, I'm not."

With the perseverance of a man who knows his life may still be at stake, Ebizer Taulb clawed his way up and out of the grave. In the blackness he was just able to discern the priest in a wheelchair two feet away.

"You saved my life…"

"I know," said Ken, aware that he was speaking to a tall man but unable to make out his face in the dark.

"Well then, let's tackle the big question," said Taulb. "What the hell are you doing out here in a wheelchair in the dead of night?"

"It's a long story," responded Ken.

"I don't suppose you have a car or anything?" inquired Taulb as he continued to brush the dirt from his head and shoulders. Holding out the van key, Ken said,

"I do. It's right there beside the shed.

"What, you're not coming?" queried the bewildered Taulb.

"No. Go ahead, take it. It will require a few minutes to figure out though. The controls are all around the steering wheel. Click on "help" then "controls" on the dashboard screen and the computer will talk you through it. Oh, you will have to unlatch the passenger seat and slide it over beneath the steering wheel."

"What's going on, dude? Are you a priest?"

"I'm going to end it tonight, my life," responded the ex-priest.

"Why?"

"Well," said Ken, "I've been paralyzed all my life, and ah, well, I'm…I'm just tired."

"No way, my friend! I'm going to do you a favor that's going to change your life forever."

"Thanks for the kind thought but I don't want to live anymore."

Instantly, Taulb snatched the gun from Ken's lap.

"My friend, you and I are going to have a beer together."

As Ken motored his wheelchair to the van, he thought, "What does a man have to do to escape this insane world!"

Once in the cab, Ken got a good look at Ebizer Taulb, a huge bear of a man, with a receding hairline and a "salt & pepper" goatee. The goatee provided the only definition on Taulb's well-fed face. It wasn't until they were on the road that the huge man spoke.

"My name is Ebizer Taulb, and you don't know it yet, but this is the luckiest night of your life. What's your name, Father?"

"Ken McAlister, and I'm not a priest anymore."

"That's cool. I always hated that 'Father' bullshit anyway. Now we can just get down like a couple of real men."

"Don't you think you should call the police? That guy tried to kill you," interjected Ken.

"You got a phone, Ken?" asked the huge man, who was still brushing dirt from his clothes.

"There's one in the glove compartment."

Taulb retrieved the cell phone and dialed the operator.

"Operator, put me through to the Las Vegas police department," Taulb said in his commanding, raspy voice. "No, I don't want the number. This is an emergency! I tried 911, it's busy! You want to keep your job, 'operator,' put me through to the Vegas police!"

After a brief pause, Ebizer Taulb spoke to the Vegas police.

"Sergeant, my name is Patrick Calhoon, and I just had a guy named Bobby Gallagher try to sell me some crack cocaine...Bobby Gallagher. He's in room four twenty one at Caesars Palace...What? No. He's got a gun. He said he's going to kill a cop tonight...Take every precaution, Sergeant, he's a drug-crazed maniac!"

Taulb closed the phone and erupted with laughter. When he settled down, Ken asked why he lied to them.

"I didn't want to get involved," replied the huge man. "You understand..."

"Look," said Ken, "I can drop you off wherever you want."

"No," replied Taulb, "I am going to buy you the best steak dinner in Vegas. Then, I'm going to get you a room at the Vallencia. You ever stay there?"

"No, sir."

"Have you got any other clothes beside that priest costume?"

"Not with me".

"Okay," said the big man, "there are shops still open at the Paris Hotel Casino."

"Mr.Taulb, I am physically exhausted. I need a bed and a bathroom as soon as possible."

"Say no more. We'll paint the town tomorrow!"

On the way to the Vallencia Ken couldn't help but think that Ebizer Taulb was some kind of con man who was going to try and use him for some scam. "I mean," thought Ken, "what does he want with a paralyzed priest, ex-priest? If it were my money he was after he could have taken that at the cemetery. Maybe he's just a crack pot? Of course he is, making insane statements about eternal life!"

While Ken was contemplating his situation, the odd, disheveled giant was on the phone booking Ken a room at the Vallencia. In the process, he turned and asked,

"Do you have a credit card I can use to book the room?"

Ken wasn't surprised in the least and handed him his wallet which contained a Visa Card.

"This good for a hundred and twenty, Ken?"

"Yes. Tell them I need a 'non-smoking, handicap room."

When Taulb concluded the reservation, he reached in his pocket, pulled out two one hundred dollar bills and stuck them in Ken's wallet before returning it to him.

"What's this for," asked Ken?

"The room," replied Taulb. "This whole excursion is on me. There's only one stipulation, my friend— you check in on your own and make no mention of me, or anything that went on tonight. Can I trust you to do that?"

"What kind of game are you into, Mr. Taulb?"

"To you the proper title is, Master Taulb. I will explain it all over a late breakfast tomorrow. Tell me I can trust you until tomorrow."

"You have my word, Mister Taulb. I just want to sleep,"

"Me too," said Taulb as he pulled the seat lever, lowering the seat to a reclined position. Minutes later the huge man was snoring, with the gun still clutched in his hand.

Only in an emergency would Ken ever use a public bathroom because it was a breeding ground for germs. Nevertheless, his urine collection bag was full and he had to stop at a gas station to empty it. This is something he did several times on his drive from Chicago, only because he thought it was the last two days of his life. When he returned from the bathroom, Taulb was still sleeping. Before locking his wheelchair in place, Ken ever so gently tried to remove the gun from the giant's hands. Without opening his eyes, Taulb just whispered, "Forget about it." and continued snoring.

Upon entering Vegas city limits, Ken woke Taulb to remind him that he was holding a gun. Taulb immediately sat up and put the gun in his jacket pocket. The giant proceeded to direct the ex-priest to the Vallencia Hotel, making his exit before they reached the entrance. Ken was trapped. Taulb took off with his gun. His body, wracked with exhaustion and pain, Ken ignored the valet parking because it would take too long to explain the controls. Fifteen minutes later

Ken had parked his van, picked up his room key and was in his room stripping for a shit and a shower. Too tired to think, he just concentrated on taking his required medications, three in all, and went to bed.

CHAPTER THREE

YOU AIN'T SEEN NOTHING YET

Ken paused in his reverie to turn down the Beef Stroganoff and fill his wine glass. While he hadn't yet confirmed his sanity, his journey into the past provided a welcomed distraction and peace. Thus, he settled back in his chair and returned to his memory of the room in the Vallencia Hotel. He remembered waking up to a phone call from Ebizer Taulb. Reluctantly, he took the call from the weird man, whose raspy voice triggered a rush of anxiety.

"Good afternoon, Ken. How'd you sleep?"

"Like a dead man," was all he could think to say, as he slowly awakened to the mess he was in with this man he perceived to be a nutcase!

"Don't dress, my man. I've got a new wardrobe for you. I'll be over in fifteen minutes."

Before Ken completed his morning bathroom ritual, Master Taulb was knocking at the door. Ken hit the room remote that opened the door and finished brushing his teeth. In the bathroom mirror he saw Taulb drop an armful of signature shopping bags on the bed. Taulb, himself, was wearing a silver sport jacket over a green golf shirt and white pants. Was it by accident that this weirdo was dressed in the exact colors of the room! The pale green and white striped wallpaper matched exactly Taulb's golf shirt and pants. Taulb's silver sport jacket could have been made from the silver bedspread. The long drapes framing the balcony window were also silver and white. Fortunately, the mauve carpet didn't match Taulb's tan sandals or he would have disappeared altogether. The light and airy room was beautifully accented with driftwood colored furnishings, and a miniature crystal chandelier.

When Ken rolled out of the bathroom, Taulb was on the phone to room service.

"The sirloin, with eggs over easy, a side of biscuits and gravy. Throw an order of pancakes in—large orange juice and a pot of coffee," said the huge man.

Looking over to Ken, he asked, "And what would you like for lunch?"

"A scrambled egg, with an English muffin...Earl Grey tea," replied Ken.

"That's it!" exclaimed Taulb. "No wonder you can't walk!"

The quip sparked a hearty laugh from Ken, who hadn't experienced that kind of laughter since he was a child. While Ken was laughing, Taulb placed the order, expanding Ken's order to three eggs with bacon and home-fries.

"Here, try some of these new rags on," suggested Taulb, as he dumped the new clothes all over the bed. "I've got some research to do."

As Ken began to dress, he realized that this strange giant of a man was one clever character, crazy perhaps, but clever. The underwear, jeans, shirt and tan sport jacket fit like they were tailored for him. The sandals were also a perfect fit. When he finished dressing he called to Taulb, who was absorbed in a Victoria Secret fashion show on TV.

"This stuff fits like it was made for me! How did you know my size?"

Without removing his eyes from the TV, Taulb responded, "I'm an alchemist, dude."

Ken began to understand why someone as clever as Taulb could wind up in a life-threatening situation. He appeared to live a life of unchecked passions and lunacy.

Taulb, slapping his hand to his forehead, exclaimed, "My God, Ken, check out these babes, these swimsuits! Every year they get younger and prettier!"

"That's not something I can indulge in, although I recognize the sheer beauty of their physical bodies."

"I thought you weren't a priest anymore," said Taulb, with his eyes still riveted on the babes.

"I'm not, but I have this small problem with my body. Nothing works below my waist."

With that, Taulb turned from the television to behold the ex-priest in his new garb.

"So, you can't 'get off,' no way, no how?"

"No way, no how," Ken repeated with finality, smiling as though it never mattered.

"Wow! Now that really blows!" exclaimed the mysterious giant. "We'll just have to remedy that, won't we?"

A knock at the door interrupted their discussion. As Ken motored to retrieve the room remote and open the door, Taulb ducked into the bathroom. Once the waiter was tipped and made his exit, Taulb re-entered the room. Together the two men spread the food out on the table by the balcony window and Taulb sat down.

"Do you mind if I say grace?" asked Taulb.

"Go ahead," responded Ken somewhat baffled, "whatever you want."

Looking quite serious, Taulb put his hands together, bowed his head and said, "Grace," followed by his own unique style of hearty laughter. Ken chuckled, not wanting to cause the giant any embarrassment, though he inwardly bristled at Taulb's childish prank. Even though Ken had given up the idea that God existed, specifically the God of Catholicism, he didn't like ridicule of any kind, not even of the faith he rejected.

"By now, I'll bet you've got me pegged as some kind of nutcase," said Taulb, while wolfing down a chunk of steak topped with eggs and gravy.

"Let's just say, I've never met anyone as unpredictable as you," said Ken while dipping his tea bag. "Do you mind telling me something about yourself, and what you want from me?"

Taulb worked half a pancake, dripping with syrup, into his mouth and just about swallowed it whole. Next, the huge man seized a piece of steak, buried it in a gravy-covered biscuit, and pointed the forkful at Ken.

"I don't want anything from you. You saved my life and I'm going to return the favor. For that to happen you'll have to trust me until tomorrow night. Can you do that, my man?"

Just as the last word left his mouth the mess impaled on his fork entered.

"What's going to happen tomorrow night?" asked Ken, venturing a fork full of eggs.

"If I told you now, you wouldn't believe me," responded the Master, chewing while he spoke. "You'll have to see it to believe it."

Ken nibbled at his muffin while watching Taulb wrap a pile of eggs in the remaining pancake, drown it in syrup and take it down in two gulps.

"Have you had your cholesterol checked recently?" Ken chuckled, "I think you gobbled the placemat with that last mouthful."

Taulb rushed his napkin to his mouth and roared with laughter at the insult, as he took hold of his large orange juice.

"Don't worry about me," you skinny prick. "I've got more lives than the Devil's cat!"

"Do you mind my asking what you do for a living?" queried Ken, enjoying the last of his muffin.

"I'm sort of a psychologist by profession."

"Sort of?"

"Well, people hire me to help them improve their game of poker, usually professionals. Right now I've got a movie star in the World Series of Poker. You ever hear of Zackary Taylor?"

Taulb, anticipating the time a response to his question would take, dropped the rest of the sirloin and bacon into the bowl of biscuits and gravy in preparation for a gastronomical finale.

"No, I don't watch movies that often," related Ken, "but I'm aware of the recent poker craze sweeping the world. I sometimes watch the High Stakes Poker games on television."

"Cool," said Taulb. "Then you know what a 'tell' is," stated the eating machine, while masticating the mess in his bowl.

"That's when a player unconsciously does something that gives away his hand," responded Ken.

"I couldn't have defined it better myself. 'Tells' are my specialty. Every poker player, I don't care who he is, harbors tells—Kid Poker, The Brat, The Magician, Phil Ivey, Johnny Chan, even old man Doyle Brunson. I can read those guys like a book!"

"That begs the question, why aren't you playing in the World Series?"

Taulb flashed a wry smile. "Because I'm involved in a game with much higher stakes."

"And what game is that?" asked Ken.

"You'll find out soon enough," replied Taulb, as he reached out and patted Ken's cheek.

Taulb then looked at his Rolex and walked toward the door.

"I've got to check on my guy, Taylor, at the Rio. He's presently third to the chip leader. I would invite you but we can't be seen together."

"Why?" asked Ken, perfectly aware that he wasn't going to get a straight answer.

"You'll know why tomorrow night, my man. Didn't I promise you a whole new life, with legs that walk and a cock that works?"

Ken was convinced that Taulb, if that was his name, was some kind of lunatic living out his fantasies.

"Mister Taulb, I wish you would just give me back my gun," pleaded Ken, hoping his heartfelt plea might persuade the deranged man to release him from whatever fantasy he was concocting.

"Master Taulb," corrected the giant. "I plugged your cell phone in by the lamp. Just stay out of trouble until I call. And we can hang together, off the beaten path, later."

"Master Taulb, please, I don't need any more games! I just want out of this world."

"Okay, contemplate this until I call you," said Taulb, as he plucked a rose from the vase on a pedestal by the window. Handing the lovely flower to Ken he asked, "What makes this flower beautiful?"

Ken, going along with the game, responded, "Its color...Its fragrance..."

Taulb stated emphatically, "Its life, dude!" With that Taulb raised the lovely rose close to his face and said, "You're ugly! No one cares about you. No one wants to see you anymore. You're disgusting and useless—now die!"

Ken watched in horror as the rose wilted instantly and died. Taulb flung the flower to the floor, with a wry chuckle. Before Ken could respond, Master Taulb was out the door.

Ken, on the verge of tears, rushed the dead flower to the bathroom, where he placed it in a small pitcher of water, hoping to revive it... but it just hung limp and lifeless over the side of the pitcher. The ex-priest, though momentarily mystified, concluded that Taulb must have dropped some poison on the flower when he snatched it from the vase. "What a weird and heartless character," thought Ken, as he went about cleaning up the table.

His next thought was whether the distance between the balcony and the ground below was enough to kill him if he jumped. He decided it was, but he would clean up the table first, where he would write a note of apology to the Vallencia owners and management for his suicide.

It was just about ten minutes later that Taulb called, interrupting Ken's suicide note.

"Hello, Ken, this is the Master."

"Yes," replied Ken into the phone, perturbed by Taulb's intrusion on his plans.

"Do you trust me, my man?"

"You didn't have to poison the flower."

"Oh, yes, the flower. Put her on the phone."

"What?" asked Ken, at the strange request.

"I want to talk to the flower. Put her on the phone."

Ken just paused, holding the phone away from his ear, waiting for Taulb's belly laugh. When it didn't come Ken decided Taulb hung up. Then Taulb spoke in his raspy commanding voice, "Put the fucking flower on the phone! Humor me, my man."

Bristling at the thought of being drawn back into Taulb's idiotic games, Ken fetched the dead rose from the pitcher in the bathroom. With the limp flower in hand, Ken mocked the obnoxious idiot.

"The flower is six inches from the phone, but it's not saying very much. It may have something to do with the fact that it has no vocal cords and that it's dead."

"Just hold the phone so she can hear me," responded Taulb.

Ken obeyed the request, putting the phone two inches from the rose. He was barely able to hear some gibberish Taulb recited to the flower, and felt his upper body flush with shock, as he watched the flower in his hand come back to life. In utter amazement, he stared at the rose standing strong, straight and beautiful in his hand. Stymied,

Ken returned the phone to his ear. He heard the Master's belly laugh. When the laughter subsided, Master Taulb said, "Pretty fantastic shit, wouldn't you say, coming from a fat guy with atrocious table manners? As the saying goes, you ain't seen nothing yet! I'll call you later."

CHAPTER FOUR

OUTSIDE THE REALITY BOX

Recalling his time with the alchemist was so vivid in his memory, it took Ken a good thirty seconds to become acclimated to his actual surroundings in his Chicago apartment. How could it all be an hallucination, some psychotic episode he was caught up in? Still, who would believe you can steal someone's body and not be insane? As he had many times before, he motored to his desk in the bedroom to remove the Army .45, which was still loaded. The gun was real. Placing the weapon back in the draw, Ken went to the kitchen pantry to check the potion the alchemist gave him. Ken placed the plastic vile containing the potion in his sweater pocket and went about setting the elegant cherry wood dining table, placing a candle in a crystal holder on the lace doily in the center. His remodeled kitchen had the ambiance of a dining room, with electric sconces that resembled Egyptian oil lamps gracing the walls of beige, woven wallpaper

The time was seven twenty five. With thirty five minutes until Joel's arrival, Ken still hadn't made up his mind. He still wasn't even sure he was sane. With that realization stoking his anxiety, the ex-priest covered the pot of Beef Stroganoff, turned the electric jet down to simmer and returned to the memories of that outrageously bizarre night.

He was getting ready for bed in his luxurious hotel room in Vegas when his cell phone rang. He knew who it was. He was tired and didn't want to deal with Taulb, or his games. Still, he had no choice but to see the whole thing through. He answered the phone.

"Hello, Ken."

"Yes?"

"Is this Ken McAlister?" inquired the raspy voice of Master Taulb.

"Of course," responded Ken. "Who else!"

"You sound different."

"I just gargled," said Ken, checking the clock on the bedside table.

"There's a change of plans. My guy, Zack Taylor, just busted out of the World Series…"

"Hold on, hold on!" Ken broke in. "I have to close the windows." Ken had the balcony windows open, and the music from a Marimba Band on the Vallencia patio was filling his room. Ken closed the windows and returned to his conversation with Taulb.

"Can you get over to my room at the Rio, in say a half hour?"

"You're staying at the Rio?" asked Ken, surprised at the fact.

"Yes," said Taulb, sounding a tad agitated.

"I can try. What's the traffic like?"

"Forget the traffic. I'll call for a taxi to pick you up. My room is on the second floor, 216. Come in the main entrance. Don't stop to talk to anyone. Come directly to 216. You got that, my man?"

"I've got it, but make sure the taxi has a handicap lift."

"You're talking to the Master, remember? See you in thirty."

Taulb hung up. Ken stared at the phone, speculating on what charade Taulb was setting up which would require a man in a wheelchair. At this point Ken had reasoned away the possibility that the flower resurrection was a miracle. It was a flawlessly performed trick by Ebizer Taulb who was probably a Vegas magician. Ken's best guess was that he was being lured into some kind of new reality show, involving magic. Nevertheless, he had no choice but to see it through and hopefully be on his way to the cemetery before the night was over.

Of all the memories that Ken reviewed, none was as vivid as the half hour he spent in the alchemist's room at the Rio Hotel. People talk about life-changing experiences but usually are exaggerating. Ken had already had his share of life-changing experiences, and heard about numerous others in the Catholic Seminary. His curriculum included regular spiritually-oriented encounter groups in which student priests would bare their souls, so to speak. He also heard enough personal confessions to know that life was an uncertain affair at best and often as weird as a Fellini film. But nothing he ever experienced, no miracle or fiction he ever heard tell of would come close to the half hour he spent in room 216.

Master Taulb must have been waiting for him at the door because it swung open before he knocked. With a mock flourish Taulb ushered him into the room, a posh one-bedroom suite with elegant dark wood furnishings, inset mood lighting and a gold carpet so plush it all but swallowed the rims of his wheels.

"Good evening, Ken, glad you could make it," exuded Taulb, while leading him to an alcove in the living room which contained a wet bar. The ebony wood bar was positioned several feet out from a wall of gold veined mirrors also framed in ebony wood.

"What's your poison dude?" asked Taulb. "I'll bet you fancy a Seven and Seven. Zack and I are drinking Margaritas, would you like to try one?"

The word "dude" sounded odd coming out of Taulb's mouth, for every time he said "dude," he emphasized it, like someone trying to fit it into his vocabulary. A few minutes later Ken would be given the reason for Taulb's use of it, along with a slew of other irregularities in Taulb's speech and eccentric demeanor.

"Why not?" replied Ken, to the offer of a Margarita on what he assumed would be the last night of his life. For he was certain that whatever grand theater Taulb had devised, it would be finished before the evening was over and he would be done with him.

As Taulb prepared the drink, Zack "the movie star" Taylor stepped out of the bathroom to the utter shock of the ex-priest. While he was not an avid moviegoer, he recognized the star's face immediately, probably from magazine covers at the check-out counters in the super market. This already surreal day reached new heights with the entrance of Zack Taylor. For of all the tall tales Taulb told, the one least plausible in Ken's mind was the one about restoring his body functions. But after that, the line about being a movie star's poker coach seemed the most unlikely, far-fetched, way the heck out there.

"Zack," said Taulb, "this is Ken McAlister, a friend of mine and a fan of yours."

Zack, who was clearly drunk, or stoned Hollywood fashion held out his fist and said, "Cool." Ken immediately tapped his fist against the star's, a hip acknowledgement he understood from his ghetto parish days. Zack Taylor was wearing a dark blue and gold silk Tibetan style shirt, which made his dark blue eyes appear like gems beneath his long black lashes and brows. The star's presence so completed the reality show scenario that Ken began to scan the room for hidden cameras. Surely, he was an unsuspecting guest on a TV show.

Following the introduction, Zack immediately reached into the East Indian man-purse slung over his shoulder and withdrew a small stack of 2x3 photos of himself. The laminated photos bore his autograph. Handing one to Ken, the star said, "You want an extra one or a few for friends?"

Looking at the photo in his hand Ken said, "No, this is great! Thanks."

"Those new?" Taulb asked, taking one of the photos.

"I got them in the mail this morning from the agency. You want to dig some wild PR," chuckled the star, "check out my hand in the photo."

"What is that?" asked Taulb, "it looks like a thread, or a—"

"It's a hair from my head, dude," interjected the star, laughing.

"Not really!" Taulb laughed.

"Yes, really, EB!" exclaimed the star. "Is it the shit, or what!"

"Absolutely, dude. Your fans will probably sleep with that photo in their underwear," commented Taulb.

"But it's not really hair from your head, right?" asked Ken.

"Absolutely dude, every single photo contains one authentic Zack Taylor hair," chuckled the star, "The agency hired a private barber to trim my hair and save the clippings. It's so totally Hollywood I can't stand it!"

Leaving the photos on the bar, Zack stepped behind the bar and chugged down a glass of ice water.

"Whoa, that Margarita has me whirling!" exclaimed the star, his face no longer a healthy tan in color.

"I warned you," Taulb said jokingly.

"No, EB, I'm really feeling sick," stated Zack.

Looking down, while grabbing one of the bar stools to steady himself, Zack blurted out, "Sorry, guys, I'd like to hang with you tonight but I feel like homemade shit! My stomach! E.B., walk me back to my room."

"E.B." was obviously the abbreviated version of Ebizer Taulb's first name. Taulb came around from the bar to help his friend.

"Why don't you crash on my bed for a while," suggested Taulb. "I'll have room service send up some Pepto."

The star just murmured, "Cool," and stumbled toward the bedroom, crashing to the floor half way across the living room.

"No, get a doctor!" the star groaned in pain. "Oh, shit..."

Zack Taylor contracted into a fetal position, gasping for help. Ken expected Taulb to grab the phone, but instead he just stood there sipping his drink. At this point Ken figured that this was all part of some horrible prank contrived by Taulb. But it was too real and Ken shouted at the huge man, "What's going on?"

Taulb just placed his drink on the bar, walked casually over to the fallen star, who was now unconscious, and nudged him with his foot. In the most matter-of-fact manner Taulb informed Ken,

"This is the hard part."

"What!" Ken responded in a state of panic. "He needs a doctor!"

"Take a good look at him," stated Taulb, as though he was referring to the star's photo instead of his contorted body on the floor. "This is the hard part of the process. You'll have to endure this yourself sometime if you want a new life."

"What are you talking about? Call a doctor!" Ken insisted. "This charade has gone too far!"

Ken raced to the phone beside the divan and grabbed the receiver, but Taulb stated, "It's unplugged. Chill out. It's all going as planned, my man, trust me."

"I can't be party to this, whatever it is!" Ken exclaimed.

"Relax, he's not dead, just missing right now," Taulb continued in his aloof manner, as though he was giving a discourse on choosing the proper wine for a meal.

"I gave him a potion that induces a coma. Specifically, it shuts down the endocrine gland system, forcing the soul out of the body. It's similar to death, only not quite death yet. Most of that stuff you penguins learn in seminary about the soul is horseshit. Your church, actually most of the half-ass religious societies that ever were, have their roots in the ancient science of alchemy. That sacred science became diluted and lost because it takes balls, real balls to experiment with the ethereal energies of life and death. The ancient alchemists were the only true scientists, fearless seekers after the mysteries of life! For instance, how many of your research scientists have ever mixed cobra venom with pureed starfish and the urine of a newt and shot it into their rectums?"

The question left Ken speechless, convinced that Taulb was stark raving mad.

"Sounds crazy doesn't it? But the greatest alchemist that ever lived, my father, performed that very procedure on himself, and many other dicey procedures on my mother."

"For what purpose?" asked the ex-priest, feigning interest in the madman's discourse while slowly backing toward the fire-alarm box on the wall.

"To reverse the aging process, of course!" exulted Taulb.

"Did it work?"

"No, but he found a cure for acne."

"Acne!" Oh God, tell me you didn't give that young man cobra venom!"

"That's my craft, Ken, alchemy."

"Tell me that the potion you gave him isn't poison!"

"If you knew what went into making the potion, you would fear me even more than you do right now. You would fear me the way your predecessors feared and murdered the alchemists down through the ages. The church declared them sorcerers, witches who served the devil and opposed the church's foolish god. Fact is, your Jesus was an alchemist! My friend, you are going to be so glad, actually ecstatic that you saved my life. I alone can free you from that wheelchair, so chill the fuck out and show me some respect—for I am the last alchemist! After tonight you may even want to worship me, but I don't want any of that. In fact, my friend, after tonight I want you to forget me. I'll explain all that shortly. Right now you are going to witness first hand a bona fide resurrection."

With that, Taulb handed Ken a small pad bearing the hotel's logo and a pen.

"Trust me now," stated Taulb emphatically. Your own resurrection depends on it. Write down exactly what I say and do. At some point I will recite an incantation, just a few words that will be unintelligible to you. They will sound like gibberish. Don't be concerned with the spelling, it's the sounds that do the trick. Just write them down phonetically so you will be able to recite them clearly. Are you with me?"

Ken's mind was reeling. Until the entrance of Zack Taylor he managed to maintain a logical line of reasoning in spite of the bizarre circumstances of the last two days. When the movie idol stepped out of the bathroom Ken was left clinging to the possibility that this strange giant, who probably drugged and raped an under-aged girl, was in fact a high-paid entertainer involved in producing a reality show. But where are the cameras, Ken wondered, as he scanned the room, searching for any sign of a hidden camera. Zack Taylor might be a great actor but no one can turn the color of his skin from tan to ash gray on cue. Was Taulb merely a raving lunatic who just poisoned the Hollywood actor? Would I be next, Ken thought, taking a big swallow of his Margarita in hopes of perhaps speeding up his exit from the mad, mad world swirling around him. In the midst of the madness Ken was forced to release any reasonable speculation and give some small consideration to the impossible scenario being espoused by the weirdest human being he ever met.

"Try to understand," Taulb continued his resurrection monologue, "what I'm about to reveal to you is something few, if any on earth, know about. This is not an experiment I'm just now attempting. I have switched lives more than forty times in the past thirteen centuries. This body you know as Ebizer Taulb was just twenty years old when I took it over thirty five years ago. He was a foreign exchange student at the University of Colorado. Most of his family lost their lives in the Bosnia Holocaust. Besides that, he was physically fit, a gymnast I believe. Take note, Ken, searching out the right body to inhabit is not an easy endeavor. You must gather all the information you can on any possible candidate before you choose. I'll relate more about that later. Later will be better because then you will have no doubt that soul transfer is possible. You will know what I am saying is true in a few minutes. For the sake of eliminating a lot of unnecessary questions after the switch, write something on that pad that Zack Taylor and I couldn't possibly know about you."

His mind spinning beyond reason, he merely complied with Taulb's request, still certain that Taulb was either a maniac or the host of some kind of reality show. Ken wrote, "My mother's name was Arlene McAlister. She hung herself in a Las Vegas jail."

Taulb glanced at the pad. "Very well. And I will tell you something that might ease your Catholic conscience. If Zackary Taylor were me, had my alchemist knowledge, he wouldn't hesitate a nanosecond to take another's body."

With that, the alchemist Taulb went about straightening out the young star's body on the floor, so that he was lying fully face up with his legs straight and his arms down at his side. Ken discerned that the young man's body was now limp, like a recent drowning victim, though he was still breathing, shallow breaths in and out. Next, the alchemist loosened his own shirt collar and belt before lying down on the floor face up with the top of his head touching the top of Zack Taylor's head.

"This position is essential for the switch, head to head exactly as you see us right here," Taulb stated. "Now I take a few granules of the potion on my tongue. Not even a tenth of a teaspoon."

Ken watched the alchemist take a small silver vial from his pocket and remove the cap. He proceeded to wet his finger and dip it carefully into the vile. When he removed his finger it had a miniscule amount of yellow powder stuck to the tip. The alchemist closed the vile and placed it on the floor beside him. He then put his finger in his mouth, transferring the powder to his tongue.

"I will now chant the incantation," stated the alchemist, "which is crucial in drawing my soul into Zack's almost dead body. As I do this I am envisioning myself as Zack Taylor."

Then, the alchemist began to chant:

"EEELOLI, EEELOLI, ZACK TAYLOR HAS DIED.
EEELOLEE, EEELOLEE, ZACK TAYLOR IS ME.
EEELOLI, EEELOLI, ZACK TAYLOR HAS DIED.
EEELOLEE, EEELOLEE, ZACK TAYLOR IS ME."

The alchemist repeated the chant just twice when his body started shaking from head to toe. A moment later Zack Taylor's eyes popped open and Ebizer Taulb's body stopped shaking.

As convincing as the bizarre drama was, Ken couldn't help expecting that at any moment the two men on the floor would jump up laughing, shake his hand and point out the hidden TV cameras in the room. Instead, Zack Taylor struggled to his feet, stumbled to the bathroom sink and vomited. Through the open door Ken watched the star as he washed his face and hands. For almost a minute Zack stared at his face in the mirror. Then, turning from the mirror he smiled his million dollar smile and exclaimed,

"What do you think, dude, am I the shit or what!"

Nothing more needed to be said to convince the dazed ex-priest that Master Taulb had indeed entered Zack Taylor's body. For only Taulb could pull off the greatest miracle ever performed and exult in it like a total adolescent. Ken was so awe struck that he couldn't speak.

Zack, alchemist Zack, walked up to Ken, stared into his eyes and said,

"Your mother, Arlene McAlister, hung herself in a Las Vegas jail. Let's go eat."

"What about the guy on the floor…Taulb? Shouldn't we wait for him to come around?" asked Ken.

Zack Taylor howled with laughter. "What about—him! Shouldn't we—shouldn't we—wait for him? He's dead, dude. Let's catch a mouthful and then I'll report it."

"Excuse me for sounding stupid," said Ken, "but what has become of Zack Taylor, his soul I mean? Doesn't he take over Taulb's body, or something?"

The alchemist, still chuckling, responded, "Ken, Ken, use your imagination. What the hell do you think would happen if Zack Taylor woke up in the body of that old, fat, fuck on the floor"—more laughter—"and he sees me across the room wearing his gorgeous body?"

"So he's dead. Zack Taylor is dead," sighed Ken ruefully.

"Here's the skinny, my man. I mean, here's the edit, dog. The body of Ebizer Taulb is dead. The coroner will find the cause of death was a heart attack. The authorities will ask me if my poker coach has any relatives that I know. I'll say, 'Not that I know of.' They'll do the required online search and close the case. In the meantime, I'll arrange for a cremation and an upscale funeral, which will grab some good press for me. Just hang cool, my man. I know you're probably brain-blown right now. I know that from your life experience, this soul transfer mojo appears devious and horribly mean. But it's the way life is, my man-dude. This hip lingo is going to take some time. It's all about survival, survival of the fittest. Sure, it's hard for you to grasp the obvious facts of life because you never had a life worth living. If you lived even one of my marginal lives you would have no remorse about any of this. You would know without a doubt that life in this world is the greatest treasure in creation—if you're young enough and healthy enough to enjoy it. Knowing this, you would do everything in your power to live on and on. Isn't that what everyone's trying to do anyway—taking all those vitamins, health tonics, face lifts, organ transplants?"

The alchemist sang the refrain, "And may you stay forever young," with more laughter. "And here's the really good news, dude. You will get to take such a life for yourself, a young healthy life! Get down with that a moment!"

The alchemist Zack Taylor retrieved his silver vial of powder from the floor and stepped back into the bathroom. He opened the medicine cabinet and extracted a small plastic bottle of aspirin. He proceeded to flush the contents of the bottle down the toilet. He then emptied his silver vial of yellow powder into the empty aspirin bottle.

"You know what," the alchemist chuckled, "You've got to call me the day you first get laid. That's the deal. But when you do, remember you don't know me, you never met me. You're just a fan, or some such fiction."

With that, the alchemist Zack Taylor handed Kenthe bottle containing the potion. Ken held the bottle in his hand, while some remnant of the priest in him demanded that he hand it back. He wondered, "What on earth am I involved with here? Surely, I'm dreaming!"

"Do you know what I have just given you, what you're holding?" asked Zack. Then without waiting for Ken to respond, Zack reached to grab the bottle back, but Ken pulled it quickly to himself, realizing he never wanted anything more in his life. He clutched the bottle containing the potion in both hands, experiencing a twinge of shame as the alchemist laughed. The ex-priest knew he would never give it back, for here at last was the answer to his life-long prayer to get out of his God-forsaken wheelchair.

"You, my friend, are now in possession of the most valuable thing in the world," stated Alchemist Zack. "Guard it with your life. There's enough in that bottle for two or three lives, if you use it right—a heaping teaspoon to eight ounces. The potion never deteriorates over time, so you have enough for a couple of long wonderful lives. And, what am I asking in return for this priceless gift? Just your word that you'll never mention tonight to anyone, not even to your children should you have any. After dinner and a few more instructions, you will go your way. You'll forget me. If asked, you'll swear that you never met me. You may have heard of Zack Taylor, seen his movies, but you never met me. Don't call me, not even after your first lay. I shouldn't have made that foolish suggestion. You saved my life, and I have given you two lives in return. I've done no such favor for anyone in thirteen centuries. Do I have your word that you never met me?"

"You have my word," said Ken without hesitation. "Just for the record, if you don't mind, what happened to the soul of Zack Taylor?"

"I don't know for sure. Souls never die or dissolve, so to speak - they live on. That's what my mother told me when my grandmother was captured and beheaded. As far as Zack Taylor's soul, where it is or what it's doing now, I haven't a clue. Alchemy is a courageous science, not an exact one. Hell, Zack might actually be better off than he was here on earth! Though my Father, the greatest alchemist who ever lived, said often enough, 'Heaven is a fool's hope. Don't ever die son, unless you have to. There is no sex after death.'"

"Maybe he will take on a new body, reincarnate. What do you think?" asked the ex-priest.

"Would it make you feel better if I said I think so?"

"Millions of people believe in reincarnation."

"Millions of people believe in an almighty, benevolent God," retorted the alchemist. "Well, he's either not almighty, or he's not benevolent, or he's not at all—pick the one most reasonable. Oh, I forgot, you already picked the one most reasonable," laughed the alchemist at his revelation.

The face was Zack Taylor but the laugh was unmistakably Ebizer Taulb.

"Hey," said the alchemist, "let's finish this conversation over some steak and lobster at Delilah's Bistro. Why don't you head over there and I'll meet you in twenty. The cab driver may not know of it. It's a little joint where Knoll Street and Mayflower intersect."

Alchemist Zack then opened the door, checked to make sure the corridor was empty and motioned for Ken to leave. As Ken motored toward the open door Zack said, " Wait. Call me if they're out of lobsters. Sometimes on a Friday they run out, and this is a steak and lobster night, dude!"

With that Zack scribbled his cell phone number on the hotel pad still on Ken's lap. Zack watched the bedazzled Ken motor down the empty hallway to the elevator. And the rest of the world spun slowly on in ignorance, supposing that such alchemy never did exist.

CHAPTER FIVE

A BIRTHDAY TO REMEMBER

E
x-priest, Father Ken McAlister had made up his mind. His review of the events that led him to this amazing night convinced him that he was quite sane, that Master Taulb, presently Zack Taylor, was an authentic alchemist. Ken gripped the aspirin bottle in his sweater pocket and knew he possessed the most valuable thing on earth. He would carry out the switch.

The liberated ex-priest poured himself another glass of wine and toasted his release from the anguish of indecision. He proceeded to lower the heat beneath the boiling pot of egg noodles, as he recalled some of the instructions the Master imparted over steak and lobster.

According to the Master, who said he'd been alive since the ninth century, in no less than forty-two different bodies, only the physical qualities remain once the soul has been dispossessed. The personal memory, he explained, resides in the soul not the brain. "Science is way behind the curve on this shit," said the Master. The alchemist was even flippant about the switch, using computer terminology to jest about "downloading your memory and personality into a stiff." The Master, however, did seriously caution him, saying, "Some small residue of cell memory does remain for a few hours, so it's prudent to remain alone until you're comfortable in your new body. In your case, Ken, you will have to learn to walk, and that may take some time also. Above all things, be sure there is no interruption in the process once you have administered the potion because it can have serious consequences, even cause memory loss or schizophrenia."

Ken's torso jerked at the sound of the doorbell, jarring his reverie.

He checked his watch. Joel was early. So much the better he decided, disappearing his wine in the refrigerator on the way to the door. Get on with it, the inebriated priest thought, as he let Joel in.

The young man appeared taller and more handsome to Ken than ever before. Was it the slightly curly blond hair that fell almost to his shoulders, appearing combed for the first time? No, there was something else—of course! Joel had shaved off his awful scraggly goatee. Maybe it was the wine, but the uncouth, usually unkempt handyman looked quite handsome. He stood at least six feet two, bearing broad shoulders under his jean jacket. His smile was compromised by a slight overbite, but his sculptured masculine face nullified the minor imperfection. Then Joel spoke, dispelling the wine-gauzed image in Ken's mind.

"Sorry, sir, I'm early—got done with a lady's fridge quicker than I thought."

"You forgot," chided Ken.

"My bad! You don't want me to call you 'sir'—"

"—or Father, or Reverend, or any other such presumptuous titles," said Ken. "Just call me whatever you call your other friends."

Placing a bottle of wine on the table, Joel asked "This the stuff you like?"

"Black Opal Shariz, perfect dog," responded Ken.

Joel proceeded to remove his jacket, revealing a tan and white cowboy shirt with white fringe accentuating the two breast pockets. Ken was aware that his young candidate liked western style clothes, but in spite of Joel's powerful physique such shirts made him appear immature.

"Dude, dog, man, or doofus—which means 'airhead'—that's what I call my friends. Take your pick," chuckled Jole.

"Dude, that's cool," responded the ex-priest. "Just call me dude."

"Okay then, happy birthday, dude!"

Joel leaned down and gave his friend a hug, handing him a small package in the process.

"What's this?" Ken asked, already knowing it was some kind of gift, and feeling guilt and remorse all over again—not just because of the gift, but because he lied about it being his birthday. It was all part of the plot to trap the young handyman.

"No gifts, remember?" Ken said, attempting to hand the gift back, realizing in the process how absurd the gesture was.

"Like, it's nothing, dude! Just open it," insisted Joel.

"Later," replied Ken, "when we have the cake."

"That's cool," responded Joel, hanging his jacket on the back of the chair.

"There's a closet next to that sofa, remember dude?"

Joel complied with the gentle instruction and took his coat to the closet. Upon sliding the door open, he spotted the laminated photo of Zack Taylor lying on a shelf amidst some food coupons, keys and scattered pocket change.

"What are you doing with Zack Taylor's photo?"

"Oh," lied Ken, "Came in the mail, with a Netflix ad."

"You're sure you're not a secret fan?" quipped Joel.

"Honestly, I've never seen a movie he's in!"

"Mind if I keep it? I've got a friend in the Guard who's gaga over this dude!"

"Keep it. It's a girlfriend, I hope."

"Yes, dog. She's all girl," said Joel, tucking the photo into his shirt pocket. "Wow, that stuff you're cooking smells good enough to eat. What is it?"

"Beef Stroganoff. Let's allow it to simmer in the gravy, while we have a glass of wine."

"I'm down with that."

"Is that a yes, dude?" Ken quipped.

"It most certainly is, dude," Joel chuckled.

"Certainly, my dead foot! That street slang changes with the weather, you dog."

Joel burst out laughing.

"What, did I say it wrong?" questioned the ex-priest, who was actually intent on grasping the young man's slang, which he might need after the switch.

"It's how you say it, dude," replied Joel, "like you need to put some edge on it. 'Dog' is like a friendly put down."

"Okay, get the wine glasses, you dog."

Joel, struck with more laughter, walked to the sink for the glasses.

"No, not 'you dog.' Just say 'dog,' the way you would say 'dude.' Hey, dog, grab the wine glasses."

"Got it, dog," responded the ex-priest, who was practically incapable of getting any edge in his voice.

"Way cool," said Joel, "You nailed it!"

Ken already had the wine uncorked, as Joel placed the glasses on the table.

"Can you do me one more favor and turn the pot of noodles off?"

"I'm on it," Joel said, as he went to the stove.

"And drain them, okay?"

"Sure, dog, but I'm not washing these pots after the meal!"

"Chill, dude, I never wash the pots. The Rottweiler next door licks them clean."

Joel laughed out loud, causing the ex-priest a deep stab of guilt, for in his mind genuine laughter was the only thing that held out hope for there being a benevolent creator. One of the insights in Ken's coffee shop revelation was that he never really laughed. He could manage a smile for the children he sometimes worked with, but spontaneous laughter was a rare experience for the ex-priest.

Feelings of guilt took hold of him. Thoughts of calling it off filled his mind. He had to get it over with, now. He would forego dinner and end it with the first glass of wine. While Joel was busy with the noodles Ken withdrew the plastic bottle containing the potion from his pocket, the bottle Master Taulb had given him almost a year ago. Ken knew nothing about the deadly yellow powder in the bottle, except that it was tasteless, required only a teaspoonful to work, and took effect in five to ten minutes.

His heart pounded and his hands shook uncontrollably as he tried to unscrew the safety cap. How foolish, he thought, not to have loosened it beforehand. Ken was so involved with the bottle he didn't notice Joel looking at him from the stove.

"So where's the noodle strainer, chef," asked Joel?

Ken audibly gasped, his heart pounding wildly.

"Oh, oh, the strainer…it's in the cabinet…below the sink."

Then more horror as Joel placed the pot of noodles down and walked up to him with his hand out.

"Here, let me open that for you."

Ken, at a loss for words, just stared as Joel took the bottle containing the potion and unscrewed the cap.

"This one of your meds?"

Ken's mouth was so dry he could barely speak.

"My meds? Ah, yes…thanks."

"You take aspirin with wine," Joel asked in a concerned tone.

"Always—dude. I can't get—get them down otherwise," Ken stammered.

Joel went to the sink for the strainer as Ken tapped the powder into the empty wine glass closest to him.

"What's it for?" Joel asked from the sink.

Ken cleared his throat before answering.

"What, the aspirin? It's for, well, it's for my heart…"

Joel was involved in finding the noodle strainer under the sink when Ken poured the wine into both glasses, the one with the yellow powder foaming up and running over. Ken's brain on tilt, he could think of nothing to stop the foaming wine, except to stick his finger in it and stir, which seemed to quiet it down. It looked more brown than red, but at this point he was so freaked out it didn't matter. He merely wiped the glass on the sleeve of his sweater and blotted up the spill with the other sleeve. Checking to see his prize candidate was in the process of straining the noodles, the ex-priest quickly sucked down a gulp of wine from the bottle. In a swift and unexpected move, Joel was at the table snatching up a glass of the vino, before the flustered ex-priest had a chance to grab the right one. Raising the glass high Joel made a toast.

"Happy birthday to you, my friend! May your wishes all come true."

Ken, bewildered and beyond caring, just grabbed the remaining glass without examining it, held it high and said, "Cheers," chugging it down in two swallows. Joel, also chugged down his wine, and let out an Indian war whoop,

"EEeeeouwww! Let's party!"

Ken scanned the glass in his hand for signs of the deadly powder… nothing. When his young friend placed his glass on the table the ex-priest felt his upper body flush from the heat of his own blood, for he could see that he had just committed murder. "Oh my God, my God, my God, have mercy on me!" The prayer exploding spontaneously in his mind and echoing on and on like a shout in a nightmare canyon. He had to look away from Joel, who momentarily morphed into an angel, his blond flowing locks shimmering like gold. It would take a while before the ex-priest could purge his mind of the Catholic images and indoctrination he absorbed over the years. For now, though, he had to bite his lips to keep from crying. Joel refilled the glasses.

"Okay, dude, like what's your birthday wish?" asked Joel.

"Isn't that supposed to happen when I cut the cake?" he heard himself say, his voice quivering and sounding far away.

"Depends on your family tradition," Joel responded. "I had to tell my wish when I first woke up on my birthday. And it had to be like my true heart's desire because my mom would know. She's like totally psychic! Let's have it, dude," Joel insisted, as he straddled the chair across the table from Ken.

Under the circumstances there was no reason for Ken to cloak his heart's desire, though he pretended for years that his heart's desire was just to be the best possible servant of God he could be.

"Well, my friend," Ken said, "I am forty-six years old, and every day of my life one wish has exceeded all others, and that is to stand up and walk away from this God-forsaken wheelchair."

"I'm sorry," said Joel, looking down.

Ken, intent on dispersing the negative atmosphere he just created, quickly added, "And my second wish right behind that is to get Julia Garnet in bed."

Joel faked a chuckle and responded, "Dog, you can't really think she's still hot! She's got like two or three kids!"

"Okay, dog," countered the ex-priest, "who's your number one fantasy girl?"

Joel momentarily flushed at the question, but then the blood started draining from his face.

"Wow, I never thought I'd be getting down with a priest like this."

"Ex-priest," Ken corrected.

"Okay, for the record, I would give anything to ride Scarlett Johannson. Has she got a rack or what!"

Joel was beginning to slur his words. Every moment seemed like an eternity to Ken, who was himself sweating profusely.

"I met her once, at a fundraiser," Ken responded, hoping to keep the frivolous conversation going so there would be no space for any more dreaded reflections on the deed.

"Hey, I gotta eat something soon. Man, this wine is really kicking me!"

"Okay, okay," responded the ex-priest, with no little panic in his voice. "You stay right in that chair, I'll serve the food."

Ken motored to the cabinet beside the stove, his mind racing with thoughts of dialing 911 for an ambulance, or screaming to Joel,

"Throw up now, the wine is poison!"

"Why," he thought, "is this so terribly painful?"

Watching Master Taulb's switch with Zack Taylor in Vegas seemed so matter of fact, although back then he thought it was all a charade, until Master Taulb did the final incantation. "Five minutes," Taulb said, "five minutes and then he would enter the coma from which he would never return."

"Jesus Christ," Ken prayed, "please let me wake up from this nightmare!"

Methodically, unconsciously, Ken withdrew a large serving tray from the cabinet which he placed on his lap. It was too late to turn back, though one thing was certain to the ex-priest now: if he still felt this terrible grief after the switch, he would just commit suicide. On top of the tray he placed two large plates, all the time continuing a conversation that was so calculated and hollow it sounded fiendish.

"So, what have you been up to? I missed you in class last week."

"Oh yeah, I'm like done with the class," Joel slurred, as he got up and weaved his way to the sink. "Man, I need some water!"

Ken just stared at the young man who had been his closest friend for the last six weeks. In all of his careful deliberations regarding the switch he never envisioned Joel in the throes of death. Ken forced himself to look away from the angelic image of the young man who was gulping down water directly from the faucet. Then, between gulps Joel related a fact that struck the ex-priest like a brick .

"Yeah, dude, no more school for me...my company has been called up."

42

"Your company," Ken repeated, on the verge of fainting.

"Yeah, you know, my Army reserve company has been ordered to active duty," Joel stated clearly, the water possibly delaying his doom.

"But it's over in Iraq. No reserves are needed," Ken pleaded.

"We're going to Afghanistan, dog, to the front, I'm guessing. I'm not supposed to tell you that," Joel said, sounding as clear as a fire alarm.

The ex-priest was suddenly consumed with a rage he never experienced before. The thought of going through all the heart-wrenching agony of murder to gain a new life, and for what! To go to war! To kill more people! He felt unmitigated hate for the God he knew couldn't possibly exist. Yet, it seemed to him that some unseen power had to be conspiring against him, to keep him crippled until the day he died.

"Surely there's a way to get out of it." Ken's said, his voice sounding desperate.

"Who wants out, dog? I want in," said Joel.

"Why? It's crazy!" Ken shouted, unable to hide his rage.

"Benefits, dude," Joel said, slurring again. "Why are you pissed?

Man, I'm really sick! You got any Pepto—ahhhhhhh …"

Ken watched in horror as Joel clutched his stomach and slumped to his knees, looking to him for help.

"My stomach…help me," were Joel's last words, as he fell to the floor gasping for breath.

Ken felt himself whirling in a vortex of negative emotions, from grief to rage.

CHAPTER SIX

A STOLEN STAR

When the verse, "I want to take my clothes off," played through the Blackberry for the third time, Kylie Bolinger answered it.

"Who's calling?" she asked in honey-coated tones.

"Is Zackary Taylor available?" came the reply of a faint male voice.

"Who's calling?" asked the personal secretary as per her instructions.

"My name is Ken McAlister..."

"What is this in reference to, Mr. McAlister?"

"I'm an old friend."

"I've got your number. I'll tell Mr. Taylor you called."

"No, you don't understand, this is an emergency!" came the anemic-sounding plea of Ken McAlister through the phone.

"Mr. Taylor is not available at this time. I'll tell him you called, Mr. McAlister."

With that she hung up, having fulfilled the phone procedure outlined by her boss. Such calls usually came from fans, who through some devious means acquired the star's private number.

Kylie was more than a personal secretary to Zack Taylor, she was his longtime girlfriend, though of late she was just one of many. Wearing jeans and a plaid lumberjack shirt, Kylie walked barefoot through the star's posh trailer. She enjoyed the feel of the mohair carpet as she made her way to the small lounge where she fixed herself a Pina Colada. Drink in hand, she sat on the red velvet loveseat and contemplated whether she wanted to watch her boss on the set. Watching him act had become a painful ordeal for her these last few weeks.

Kylie had been through thick and thin with Zackary Taylor, having been his partner long before his career took flight. Then he got his big break in the film, *Indelible,* and it wasn't long after that when everything between them changed. Her fantasy of becoming his wife faded in inverse proportion to his growing fame. These days she had to admit that she hardly knew the movie star she still slept with. At age twenty-nine; tall, trim, and gorgeous, with sky blue eyes and pixie cut black hair, she still inspired the eye-rape of every normal man. And she was savvy, as they say, too savvy to walk out on her womanizing boss. "No way, Jose!" she thought, while sucking on the plastic straw submerged in the Pina Colada.

She knew the Hollywood scene: if a woman her age wasn't yet on the glamorous inside, she was usually history. No, she thought, this old girl likes the glitzy inside and she will do whatever it takes to stay there. Sorry, Zack, she mused, you can sleep with every nymphet in Hollywood and I'll gladly keep track of their numbers for you but I'm not dumping your unfaithful ass or my fat paycheck until hell calls you home.

After enriching her Pina with another shot of rum, the personal secretary powered up the on-location video camera. When she was done pressing the pan button on the remote, the screen revealed the exterior glacier set of the movie, *Arctic Storm.* Her boss, who resembled a young Gregory Peck, wore a hooded fur parka while braving a manmade blizzard. The twenty-eight year old star was involved in yet another argument with the director, two-time Academy Award winner, Barry Mendelson, who wore a leather flight jacket and a Yankee's baseball cap. Lying at the feet of the men arguing in the blizzard was a blood-covered Husky whose trainer kept yelling, "Stay Timber, stay!"

"Goddammit, Taylor, can't you just say the lines as written," Mendelson pleaded, repeating the lines for the star: "You crazy fool! You sent that bear packing. Yeah, Timber, you saved my life!"

"That's what I said, doofus!" shouted the star over the sound of the hollowing blizzard.

"No, you said, 'You really scared that bear away.' And you walked on the line. Don't say a fuckin' word till you get to the dying dog and drop to your knees."

Turning from the snow-covered star, the snow-covered director shouted through his bullhorn, "Will somebody shut off that fucking snow machine!"

"Why am I dropping to my knees?" queried the star.

"Because I said so," replied the director sharply, his jaw muscles tightening with subdued rage. "Look, Zack," the director said, softening his voice, "we're thirteen takes into this scene. I'm losing the daylight. I apologize for losing my shit on you. That's not cool. We're professionals. Let's just put this shit behind us and move on— cool?"

"I'm cool," responded the star.

"All right," said the director through his bull horn. "Let's nail this scene down!"

With those words the snow and wind machine were turned on. The trainer sloshed more blood on Timber the Husky. The mic grips took up their positions and Mendelson's assistant director took his place before the cameras and waited for his cue to slate the scene.

Meanwhile, Kylie, watching the altercation on the lounge video, took a deep swallow of her Pina Colada and crossed her fingers. When the Blackberry started up with, "I want to take my clothes off," she checked the number and silenced the phone.

The budding star was hardly visible beneath the hooded fur parka, which covered most of his gorgeous face and black hair. It was the Hollywood Reporter that first dubbed him the reincarnation of Gregory Peck. People Magazine picked up on the Peck look-alike angle when he was nominated for the Academy Award for Best Supporting Actor in his first feature, *Indelible*. He didn't win, but he was immediately catapulted to the A-list of Hollywood actors.

Now the lead in the epic feature, *Arctic Storm*, Zack was experiencing all kinds of frustration, which was affecting his concentration. Kylie turned up the volume on the video just as the assistant director slapped down the scene slate, stating, "Dying Husky, Scene 22, Take 14."

Then she heard Mendelson's voice through his bullhorn over the howling blizzard.

"Roll sound…roll camera…and action!"

Kylie watched Zack get up from the blood-covered snow, walk to the blood-covered husky and kneel down. "So far so good," she thought. Then came Zack's lines.

"You crazy fool! You sent that bear packing. Yeah Timmy, you saved my—"

With that Mendelson erupted like a maniac.

"Cut! Cut! Cut! Who the fuck is Timmy! The dog's name, for the tenth fucking time, is Timber! Timber! Do I have to write it on a fucking board?"

"Fuck! Every time I speak I get a mouthful of fur from this goddamn hood," shouted the A-lister, Zack Taylor. "Who designed this fucking thing anyway?!"

"Pull the hood back off your head, for Christ's sake! I gave you that direction how many fucking times now?!" screamed the director.

It doesn't feel natural, it's snowing. Who removes their hood in the snow, asshole?!" shouted the A-lister.

"A man whose beloved Husky just saved him from the jaws of an eight-hundred pound polar bear and is now bleeding to death! Or a man who keeps getting fur in his mouth from the goddamn hood. Pick one!"

"Fuck you, Mendelson! Your direction sucks ass!"

As he had a number of times before, Zackary Taylor stormed off the set of the movie. Immediately, private secretary Kylie Bolinger switched off the video and awaited the arrival of her boss and bed partner. She knew the argument between the star and the director was not just about the dog's name or the hood. Along with the cast and crew, she had seen the dailies, the film footage shot each day for the last three weeks. Though no one said anything, they all knew it wasn't really about the dog's name or the hood. It was that budding star Zack Taylor, who looked like he was cloned from Gregory Peck, couldn't act to save his life. The movie thus far was such a disaster Mendelson seriously considered making it a melodrama. No one could figure out what the hell happened to Zack Taylor, whose portrayal of a homeless soldier in his first film was so compelling that audiences left in tears. It was as though Zack lost touch with his innate talent; which is exactly what happened when Ebizer Taulb stole his body in Las Vegas.

When Ebizer Taulb switched into Zack Taylor's body almost a year ago, he had never in all of his forty-two lives done any acting, except for his piss-poor performances as the people whose bodies he had stolen. His acting was so bad that on eight separate occasions, in eight separate lives, he had to fake amnesia to escape disclosure by relatives of the people he dispossessed.

It's not that Alchemist Taulb was some sort of fool, anything but. The fact is Alchemist Taulb always did an intense amount of research and study of the person he planned to replace. He spent weeks in front of mirrors practicing the speech patterns and mannerisms of his prey. Nevertheless, it was impossible to recreate all of the nuances of personality and character collected by a soul over the years, which was the excuse the Master fed himself for lifetimes. The fact was he couldn't act for shit! In most of his past lives, following the switch the alchemist would immediately cut ties with close family members and friends. He would usually concoct a reason to travel abroad and never return. In lives when the communication technology was practically nil it was easy to escape and live the new life without the maddening concerns of exposure. This is why he never sought to replace a prominent person or aspire to a position in life that would expose him to public scrutiny, for being found out meant certain death as it did for his father and mother. Notwithstanding, in his one and only life as a woman, he inadvertently became the most famous whore in Europe. His last few lives, however, were encumbered by well-meaning relatives tracking him down and all but demanding he stay in touch. This is the reason he changed tactics and switched into the up-and-coming movie star Zack Taylor. Ultimately, the alchemist had to admit to himself that the motive for the Zack Taylor switch was two-fold. First, as a movie star he could control who gets close to him and who doesn't, by virtue of legal restraining orders and body guards if necessary. The second reason was beautiful starlet, Rachael McAdams, whom the Alchemist wanted to bed more than anything in the world. Every thought of her sent the alchemist's libido into hyper-drive. Though he hadn't met her in person yet, he already had his agent working to get him in her next movie.

Alchemist Taulb's life as Zackary Taylor was golden, as they say in tinsel town, but trouble entered the day *Arctic Storm* went into pre-production and hadn't let up through three weeks of shooting. Zack's ego never allowed him to consider that the root of the trouble was his piss-poor portrayal of an angry but heart-driven environmentalist. The alchemist's soul was simply devoid of any real feelings for the environment or the endangered polar bears and Artic wildlife. That soul deficiency plus the fact that he had no acting talent put *Arctic Storm* on the endangered movie list.

Unlike the original Zack Taylor, who was a devout environmentalist with a natural empathy for all living things, the alchemist believed that life in any era was a rat race, the best of life going to the biggest rats. Besides that, 'The Master' just never considered acting any kind of art requiring study, practice, and devotion. He thought that anyone who could speak could repeat the lines in a script. The alchemist never got the lowdown on his lack of acting ability, couldn't receive it actually, not even after William Shakespeare confronted him, prior to his seventh failed audition at the Globe Theater.

"Speak the speech, I pray you, as I pronounced it to you, in the manner of one who is not reciting horseshit from a tabloid!"

Notwithstanding, the alchemist, formerly known as Taulb, never took an acting lesson or sought the guidance of an acting coach, which would have really benefited him on his journeys from life to life. However, upon inhabiting the dashing good looks of Zack Taylor, he did seek out plenty of young Hollywood ass to assuage his carnal passions. Though he was an alchemist the likes of which the modern world had never known, he had become a willing slave to the pleasures of the flesh.

When Zack entered the trailer, Kylie was waiting for him with a hot rum-toddy.

"How ya hangin', boss?" Kylie quipped, acting oblivious to the latest confrontation on the set.

"Help me off with this goddamn parka. I can't take much more of this fucking gig!" Zack snapped, as he kicked off his snow shoes and boots.

"What, is Mendelson on the rag again?" asked the secretary.

"He's an asshole! Is the hot tub up and running?" inquired the star, "I'm freezing! That fucking fake snow is colder than the real shit!"

"It's hot, babe. I checked it a few minutes ago. You hop in and I'll capture some treats."

Ten minutes later Zack and Kylie were submerged in the hot tub. On the fake marble rim of the tub was a fresh tray of assorted cheeses, crackers, and drinks. Kylie purposely filled the Bose CD player with

Zack's favorite hip-hop selections (which the impostor was learning to enjoy). However, before a single drink could be sipped or a cracker nipped, the impostor's foot was in Kylie's crotch. She knew there would be a bout of seduction before anything else. Zack would ravage her like some angry Neanderthal, something he did whenever he had a personal confrontation. This brute intercourse baffled Kylie because Zack use to be so considerate of her in their lovemaking. Back before Zack hit the A-list in Hollywood, she would look forward to their sexual encounters, but now she took no pleasure in them. Even when the star was in a good mood his approach to sex was filled with all kinds of exotic foreplay, weird maneuvers he employed and required of her that would make her cum but without any feeling of mutual love. In describing it to her shrink, she referred to such sex as a mechanical manipulation of her biology that would elicit a cold orgasm, that even when it happened during full-on penetration was devoid of passion for her. "Frustrating" was the word she used to describe the experience. Her exact words were, "It was like watching someone else cum."

Out of desperation one night she brought up the subject of sex between them, gently asking him if the new foreplay worked for him? He responded, "Of course it works for me! And it will work for you when you finally get over your tight-assed Quaker upbringing!" Kylie never brought it up again. She just wondered if what they say about fame wasn't literally true, that it somehow destroys the art and nobility of the soul.

When the rape was over, Zack, who never used to smoke, lit up a cigarette, inhaling deeply and filling the atmosphere with smoke.

"Did my agent call?" asked Zack between drags.

"No, babe, no calls except your mom," replied the secretary.

"What did she want, 'To come and see me?'" Zack screeched in a shrill female voice, mocking his mother.

"Why don't you bring her out for a couple days? She so loves you and misses you."

"She'll be a first class pain in the ass, trust me!" spewed the star in a cloud of smoke.

"Not necessarily. I'll keep her out of your way. She was no problem on the *Indelible* shoot," cajoled the secretary.

"What!" exploded the star, "I don't have enough bullshit to deal with here! I'll see her when we wrap the movie. Tell you what, send her a big box of candy."

"Zack, she's diabetic," stated the secretary.

"Oh, yeah, forgot that. Send her a fruit and cheese basket," responded the star, looking to the secretary for a sign of approval. "She can eat fruit, right? And cheese?"

"How about some flowers, with a nice card?" suggested Kylie.

"So she can't eat fruit either? What the hell is wrong with her!"

Before Kylie could answer, Zack's Blackberry was singing, "I want to take my clothes off..." and Zack handed it to his secretary.

"If it's her, I'm not here."

"Who's calling?" the secretary inquired.

After a brief pause, she covered the phone.

"Do you know a Ken McAlister?"

"No...yes...I'll take it. Why don't you restock our goody supply while I talk to this guy.

Zack Taylor was far from pleased to hear from Ken McAlister. The stipulation Zack made for the life he offered the ex-priest was simple and clear as he recalled: *"Forget all about me! With this potion I have given you a new life. Actually, there's enough potion in this bottle for two lives, if you use it right. I have never done this favor for anyone else in all my lives. I know you appreciate that, Ken. I ask nothing in return but this: never try to contact me. Never mention my name, not even to your children should you have any. From here on out you don't know me. You've heard of me, seen my movies perhaps, but never met me. Enjoy your future lives...ciao."*

Zack's stomach churned with fear as he listened to the pleas of Ken McAlister coming through his phone.

"Zackary, Zack, are you there? Zack, it's Ken...the ex-priest... please answer. I need your help. You know I wouldn't call if it wasn't an emergency. You know that, Zack."

Zack's fear increased with every word McAlister uttered. Considering the possible consequences if he just hung up, Zack answered, hoping that McAlister would just relate the situation in a way that wouldn't incriminate him. Hell, it was over a year ago! Maybe the ex-priest just lost the words for the incantation required for the switch. Maybe the situation wasn't all that bad, the alchemist consoled himself.

"Shit," Zack thought, "I should have tattooed the words on his arm!"

"This is Zackary Taylor, but I don't know who you are. Just state your business, Mr. McAlister, that's all."

"What?" asked the shallow voice. "It's Ken McAlister…you know, from Las Vegas…"

"I'm sorry Mr. McAlister, I don't recall ever meeting you. Just state your business and perhaps I can assist you in some way."

Zack had good reason for employing all the subterfuge in his conversation. There was trouble. That meant possible exposure, which could put an end to this life and possibly any future lives. For all he knew, the police were sitting right beside McAlister, recording their conversation. Zack became increasingly angry, not just at McAlister for screwing everything up, but at himself for ever giving him the potion. Struggling to keep from blasting McAlister with profanities, Zack tried to figure out how to get him to just state the situation. One thing the alchemist knew, McAlister was not a rat. If he was in trouble with the law he wouldn't cop out on the man who tried to help him. However, when your life and future lives are at stake, "probably" is too big a gamble. Still, if it wasn't a trap, he wanted to know the exact trouble the ex-priest was in, as he might be able to keep it from spreading to him. Avoiding any possible incrimination, alchemist-Zack gave McAlister a final opportunity to respond appropriately.

"Just state your business Mr. McAlister, so I can feel safe, you're not some fan stalking me."

"What are you talking about?" responded McAlister. "What is it you want from me?"

"Think about it," snapped the angry star and hung up.

CHAPTER SEVEN

VOICES IN THE HALL

Ken McAlister just stared at the cell phone in his hand. It was the phone which he retrieved from Joel's unconscious body. The ex-priest contemplated the last words the alchemist said, "Think about it." He knew that the Master was a mysterious character, who had every reason to deny knowing him. He also knew he was extremely wise, having the experience of more than forty lifetimes under his belt. The new Zack Taylor wasn't mincing words when he said, "Think about it." He remembered the parting admonition never to contact him. But this was beyond anything either of them ever anticipated. He knew calling back wouldn't work, unless he figured out what the alchemist wanted from him. Ken delved into his memory, as he motored into the bathroom to retrieve some towels. He gave a thought to continuing the arcane process, which would initiate the switch but dismissed it. He would not go to war; he would not take another life except possibly his own. Placing the towels around the head and shoulders of the man on his kitchen floor, Ken took the pitcher of ice water from the table and dumped it on Joel. There was not even a flinch, a blink, nothing. Now that his emotional state was bordering on panic, Ken's keen memory produced the answer to his quandary.

"Say you're a fan or some such fiction," were the alchemist's exact words a year ago. "Of course," Ken thought, "I should have realized it immediately. Create a fictitious relationship to insulate the alchemist from any possible incrimination should the phones be tapped."

It took a few moments for Ken to fabricate his story before he dialed the movie star's number, a number he was more thankful than ever that he saved.

Ken quickly canceled the call when he heard a knock at the door. The kitchen light was on. He wondered if Joel's body could be seen through the keyhole. Fortunately, the CD playing earlier had long since ended. He had to be careful. He couldn't move, for the noise of his motorized chair would certainly be heard in the hall. Who could be knocking on his door at this time of night? His life for the last year had been purposely isolated. Except for the few people he approached as possible candidates for the switch, he related to no one. He always paid his rent and other bills early by mail to avoid any personal contact. Maybe the building custodian was at the door. A few weeks back he shared a brief conversation with him regarding ice on the walk way. There was no ice on the ground now, and from Ken's point of view not a person in the world should be looking him up, or could, because he had meticulously arranged his exit from his church life.

Three times the person in the hall knocked. Then he heard a voice on the other side of the door that was the unmistakable voice of his longtime friend, Henry Dorcus.

On the other side of the kitchen door, in the hall stood Detective Joe Costalino and Father Henry Dorcus, each dressed in the stereotypical fashion of his profession—the detective in a tan trench coat, the priest in a black overcoat accentuating his white hair and priest collar.

"He's not in. What should we do?" asked Father Dorcus.

"What do you mean, Father, what should we do?" responded the Detective. "We wait or come back some other time."

Father Dorcus tried the door but it was locked.

"Do you think we should force it open, with a credit card or something?" asked the priest to the detective's astonishment.

"What? I don't have the authority to do that," stated the detective. "He hasn't committed a crime, remember?"

"Of course," said the priest. "I suppose we will just have to wait."

After checking his watch, Costelano suggested, "Why don't we grab a beer and come back later. You do drink beer or something sometimes, don't you Father?"

"A glass of wine perhaps. It's been a long day," responded the priest.

"There's a place down the street," said the detective. "It's more of a bar and grill, know what I mean?"

"It will be fine, Detective."

Ken listened as the footsteps receded from his door. Still, he waited several minutes in silence, bemoaning the stupidity of sending the letter to Henry Dorcus.

"How could this friend, this Catholic priest, divulge his confession to the police!" reflected Ken. Now his thoughts ran on about being arrested, prison, death in prison.

"Why," he thought, "did misery single him out from birth. Or was there some truth to the absurd notion of karma from past lives?"

At this juncture, Ken realized nothing could be labeled absurd, not after what he had experienced with the alchemist. Could you just call it bad luck and move on? There was a dying man on his kitchen floor, a man he poisoned. His best friend, Henry, brought a detective to his door and was now going to a bar to wait him out. Out of options, Ken had no choice but to call the alchemist again. The time in Calgary Canada was eight-thirty. Just ten minutes had elapsed since the dreaded phone call from McAlister. Zack Taylor, draped in a turquoise and gold terry-cloth robe, sat on the red velvet lounge staring at the snifter of brandy in his hand. He couldn't shake his gut-churning agitation, not even after a joint of the best weed money could buy. The star was freaked out and drunk, and as was his nature after forty-two lifetimes of self-centered living, he vented on whoever was in the vicinity. His beautiful, t-shirt clad secretary was his present scapegoat.

"Why do you answer the fucking phone to every yahoo that calls?" snapped Zack.

Kylie had learned to adjust to Zack's verbal abuses, often triggered by the most outrageous shit under the sun.

"It's my job, remember?" countered the secretary.

"But why do you always bring me in on it? Why can't you just hang up on the assholes and leave me the fuck out of it!"

"Is that what you want? You want me just to screen out everyone I think is an asshole?"

"Is that what I want?! That's what I pay you for, to screen my fucking calls!"

The secretary held back from verbalizing her next response, regarding the brainless nymphets who called constantly seeking the star's company, who weren't bright enough to be categorized as assholes. She was clever enough to back out of arguments, which put her lucrative job in jeopardy. She was indeed stoned, but not crazy.

"I'm sorry, babe. That guy just sounded like he was in trouble, you know… I thought maybe he was a friend."

"He's not a friend," shouted the star. "Where did you get he was a friend?"

"He had your private number."

"He's not a friend! I never heard of the asshole before tonight!"

These outbursts were also a new development in the young man she used to love. Supposing he might be suffering from a brain tumor, she once suggested he see a neurologist for an exam. The suggestion provoked such wrath that she never broached the subject again. She knew the call from McAlister had really rattled her boss. At the risk of enticing another sexual bout but intent on quelling the argument, Kylie slid in behind her boss on the lounge and began massaging his shoulders.

"You're right. I should challenge these yahoos more. Well, I'm going to shit-list this McAlister dude for sure! No more calls from him!"

"Don't shit list him! Stop anticipating every fucking thing I want done! What am I, some kind of cretin!"

"I got it, babe," responded the secretary meekly.

Then, the worst of all things that could happen, happened. The star's phone sounded with the refrain, "I want to take my clothes off." The secretary glanced at the number on the screen before her boss snatched the phone from her. Zack held the phone face down on the cushion while he dismissed his mistress-secretary.

"Make some French toast, will you, babe? I've got some business to wrap up with my agent."

"Sure thing, babe."

With that, Kylie left for the kitchen, only too glad to escape the star's shit-faced mood. Zack Taylor touched the screen on his cell phone, put it to his ear, and waited. A moment later he listened to the quivering voice of Ken McAlister.

"Hello… hello, is Zackary Taylor available?"

"This is Zackary Taylor."

"Are you really! I mean, am I really speaking to Zackary Taylor, the movie star?"

"That be me, dude."

"Mr. Taylor, you don't know me. My name is Ken Smith and I've really admired your work, especially in the film *Indelible*. I understand you wrote some of the scenes in that movie, is that true?" Alchemist Zack breathed easy now that McAlister had gotten the critical point about contacting him. Settling back on the lounge while lighting a cigarette, the alchemist Zack responded,

"I did some writing on that film," said Zack. "I didn't think that was public knowledge."

"It's on the Internet site 'Star File Hollywood.' Mr. Taylor, screenwriting is a hobby of mine and I'd like to get your advice on a particular scene I've written. Do you mind?"

"No, go ahead, pitch it to me," said the star.

"Well, it's a science fiction film that revolves around this young man who is in a coma. And I don't know how to get him out, you know, wake him up before he, well, dies—I mean write him out of his coma. I tried dousing him with ice water but I—I mean my lead character—doused him to no avail."

McAlister's information made the inebriated alchemist's blood boil. He surmised that McAlister had used the potion on a young man but decided not to go through with the switch. Why, the alchemist thought, did I ever abandon my own iron-clad rule to do this idiot a favor! Favors are for ignorant mortals!

"Why bring him back? Why not just let him die?" said the alchemist into the phone. "He will surely die, you know. I mean, most coma victims die in sci-fi films, at least in the ones I've seen."

"No, Mr. Taylor, he has to live or it will create problems for the whole film."

The drunk alchemist considered McAlister's last remark a veiled threat and he would have told him to fuck off if everything he valued wasn't at stake.

"Look, dude, I've never written anyone out of a coma. Any time you deal with this coma crap it opens Pandora's box, writing wise. Anything could occur in a science fiction film. I mean, anything! Your coma character could wake up with serious brain damage, amnesia, or worse—some mad discarnate could jump into his body and have you for dinner—I mean, the main character who wakes him, have him for dinner! How long has he been out, Mr. Smith, according to your script?"

"About fifteen, maybe twenty minutes," stated McAlister.

"That's a short coma for a feature film, dickhead!"

"It's a science fiction short."

"Okay, then, it's best to go way out with some weird antidote to break through the coma. What I'm about to suggest could be a tad dangerous."

"It's not cobra venom or anything like that, is it? Because venom is hard to come by, according to my script."

"Forget venom! Does the character who will wake the coma victim have cayenne pepper or oregano available? Can you write that in? Maybe there's a supermarket in the area, in the script."

"No, nothing like that," replied McAlister, "What about the flower resurrection? Remember that Twilight Zone when the guy talked the flower back to life? Think that would work?"

With that idiotic suggestion the stoned alchemist went postal into the phone.

"Twilight fucking Zone?! Listen, you chuckle head! A flower is a fragile, brainless plant. It's nothing but an overgrown protozoa, for Christ's sake—without a brain, a nervous system, or organs, or glands, or bones, or a thousand miles of blood fucking vessels! And here's the real kick in the cock, a flower has no fucking soul flying around who knows where in the infinite goddamn universe! Why don't you just do the fucking switch, there's still time!"

"I'm sorry. I'm really sorry, but the coma character is in the Army. I know it's probably bad writing, but he's scheduled to go to war in a few days."

"The Army! Fuck! They're bound to come looking for him!"

"I know…"

"In that case, Tabasco sauce!" shouted the irate alchemist movie star. "Surely you can score a bottle of Tabasco sauce! I mean write it into the script somewhere!"

"I've got Tabasco sauce in the pantry, I mean, in the script. But it's that really hot stuff, with the volcano on the label," responded the amateur writer.

"Perfect," said the alchemist. "Pour it down his fucking throat, the character's throat!"

"All of it?" inquired the amateur writer.

"Every flaming drop! If you've got two bottles, fire that one in too," raved the alchemist. "And by all means have your gun in hand and cocked, because I haven't got a clue as to who or what might show up!"

"You mean in my film," said the amateur.

"Of course, in your ass sucking film! Who else's film have we been discussing?"

"Thanks for all your help, Mr. Taylor," said McAlister.

"Anything for my fans. I love you guys!"

CHAPTER EIGHT

A NIGHT TO REMEMBER

Ken McAlister placed Joel's cell phone on the table and rolled to the kitchen pantry, a small closet whose shelves were crowded with cooking supplies. Ken was a fair chef, though he himself ate very little food. Changing his rubber briefs and catheter device were such ordeals that he regulated his life around them. Over his lifetime he had disciplined himself to gauge the time it took for every kind of food or drink to move through his system. He was, through all his adult years, never embarrassed, for every activity, every meal was calculated to get him home in time to relieve himself. Though he was seldom on the road, the back of his van was designed with a state of the art compostable toilet and medicine chest, which accommodated his many handicap needs away from home.

Ken searched through the shelves of herbs, spices, canned fruits, nuts, cereals, syrups, olives, anchovies, salsa, and at last found the unopened bottle of Volcano Tabasco sauce. With the bottle on his lap he rushed across the room to the refrigerator where he extracted the bin of collected ice cubes. He quickly made another pitcher of ice water and placed the remaining bin of ice cubes on the dish board beside the sink. They were now in easy reach. Unfortunately, Joel had finished his convulsions on his side. In this position Ken might manage to pour the Tabasco sauce into Joel's mouth, but it wouldn't run down his throat, which is what the alchemist prescribed. On the other hand, the ex-priest understood you can't pour anything down an unconscious person's throat without choking him. Unless the person swallows, the liquid will run into his lungs. Maybe that was the idea, to get the comatose body to choke and thereby draw the lost soul's attention back to the body. Ken didn't mind dealing with the consequences when Joel woke up, as long as he woke up. Sweat was dripping from every pore in Ken's upper body as he contemplated his options. Right now he could let Joel die, and an autopsy would conclude that he had a heart attack. Ken wouldn't necessarily be suspect. Things wouldn't be that clear cut, however, if Joel drowned in Tabasco sauce. He chided himself for not getting enough information from the alchemist. He was tempted to call back but decided instead to blow his brains out if the Tabasco sauce remedy failed.

As the ex-priest rolled into the bedroom to fetch his gun, he thought about the final warning from the alchemist: "Be sure to have your gun in hand and cocked because I haven't got a clue as to who or what might show up!"

Ken checked the weapon to make sure the clip was full. Just having the gun in reach provided some additional comfort, because throughout the year he possessed the potion, he never fully rejected the option of suicide. With the gun resting on his lap he rolled to the kitchen and placed it on the dish board beside the ice cubes and water. Next, Ken motored to the bathroom where he removed the long flannel belt from his bathrobe, a useless piece of apparel considering his circumstances. He returned to Joel's body and proceeded to tie the belt around Joel's upturned shoulder. It required a great deal of concentrated effort to secure the belt and keep himself from toppling out of the wheelchair. His hands wet with sweat, Ken tied the other end of the belt to the chassis of his wheelchair. Putting the chair in reverse, he backed up slowly. The maneuver worked perfectly. Joel was gently pulled over onto his back, his head almost straight up with his mouth wide open.

After untying his belt from the chair, Ken opened the Tabasco sauce and began shaking the contents, drop after drop, into Joel's throat. There was no immediate reaction, as Ken hoped there might be. Dutifully, he continued, shaking the red hot sauce into Joel's mouth, realizing as he did that it must be running into his lungs, and that he must have stopped breathing.

When the bottle was empty and Joel apparently dead, he threw the bottle against the wall, shattering it. In rage more than despair,

Ken grabbed the gun and put it in his mouth just as Joel coughed and coughed and coughed violently, grabbing his throat and thrashing wildly around the floor, slamming into Ken's chair. Ken grabbed the pitcher of ice water yelling at him,

"Joel! Joel! Here's water! Water, Joel!"

Eyes open and wild, red sauce mixed with blood all over his face and chest, the young man gagged, puked and thrashed simultaneously for a couple of minutes. Throughout, Ken tried to pour ice water on his contorted face, while yelling his name. In the throes of agony, the photo of Zack Taylor flew out of Joel's pocket, becoming soiled and inconsequential in the ensuing melee. The horrible choking and gasping seemed to go on forever, with Joel periodically glancing at Ken like a terrified animal. When Joel finally felt the ice water on his face, he grabbed it from Ken's hands and poured it into his burning mouth, coughing most of it up. When the pitcher was empty, Ken held out the bowl of ice cubes, which the young man seized, crushing ice cube after ice cube in his teeth like candy. At last Joel's coughing began to subside and he pulled himself to his feet at the kitchen sink where he opened the cold water tap and continued to swallow and cough for several minutes more. Ken just watched, his emotions alternating between guilt and elation.

When Joel turned from the sink to face Ken, he looked like a monster in a horror film, his swollen face covered with bloody puke, his hair tangled in blood soaked strands all over his face. His eyes were mere slits in his bloated face. He stared at Ken but said nothing, still struggling to breathe, for his throat was almost swollen shut. Concerned that he might take some hostile action, Ken picked up his gun. Then he rolled up to the frightened man and took his hand. After a moment, Ken led his blood-spattered friend into the bathroom. Handing him a bottle of castor oil, he said,

"For your throat. Swallow some of this. It will soothe your throat. Clean up as best you can. Sleep here tonight. If need be, we'll go to the hospital in the morning."

Ken looked into the young man's eyes. There was no recognition in them, no nod that he understood what he said, nothing.

"Look, Joel, I've got to leave you alone for a while. Can you take care of yourself, you know, clean up and go to bed? The bedroom is to your right out of this bathroom."

The ravaged young man just kept nodding as though he understood. Ken watched him insert two fingers into his mouth to depress his swollen tongue in what appeared to be an attempt to get his tongue situated so he could speak. Only gagging sounds came out. Again, Ken offered him the castor oil.

"No Joel, don't try to talk. Just put some of this on your tongue. Swallow a little bit. It will help."

The ex-priest was relieved when Joel took the bottle of castor oil into his hands and dripped some on his tongue.

"Okay Joel, I have to run. Take as much of this oil as you can. You're going to be all right. Just wash your face and go to bed, or shower if you like. Get some sleep. I'll be back in an hour or so."

With that, Ken motored out of the bathroom, not bothering to turn his chair around to close the door. There wasn't time. It was an act of faith leaving Joel alone in his apartment, but he had no choice. He had to get to Father Dorcus and the detective before they returned to his place. The kitchen was a bloody mess, no time to clean it. Before leaving the apartment Ken checked himself out in the coat closet mirror. There was blood or Tabasco on his face and hands, which he washed off at the kitchen sink. Then he rolled up the cuffs of his sweater to hide the red stains on them. Fortunately, his black trousers didn't reveal much of the blood and sauce. However, he had to wash his white and silver running shoes with a washcloth.

While he was involved in cleaning up, he didn't hear the disoriented young man climb out of the bedroom window.

The ex-priest removed his fleece-lined leather jacket from the coat closet and put it on. Before leaving, Ken yelled back to Joel, "Hang tough, dude! I'll be back in a little while."

CHAPTER NINE

RUNNING ON EMPTY

When the Tabasco spattered young man jumped out of the bedroom window, he hit the ground running and never looked back. All he knew was that he was running for his life, looking for the first cop he could find. Not absolutely certain he wasn't having a nightmare, he ran down the middle of the street, terrified that at any moment the psycho in the wheelchair might come out of a doorway to set him on fire. He ran through the deserted streets, cutting around corners, changing direction randomly to lose the psycho should he be following him. "Where am I?" he questioned, while racing through the cold night. He kept looking for a street sign that might answer the question, give him some direction, but none of them were familiar to him. "Try to find a cop when you need one!" he thought. There were no stores open, no place to get help. "Where the hell am I?" he kept screaming internally, the neighborhood becoming less and less desirable as he ran. His eyes blurred, and dripping with sweat he ran past dilapidated housing projects, broken-down cars with smashed windows, bags of garbage torn open along the curbs. His inflamed lungs gasping, his legs leaden on the verge of collapse, he came upon a McDonalds glowing like a neon comet that somehow landed in the worst slum on planet earth.

Having no thought of what he looked like, the Tabasco spattered man entered the abandoned McDonalds. At least it appeared to be abandoned, until a slender black girl wearing a yellow and white uniform stepped out of the kitchen. Her nametag had "RUBY" embossed on it and she looked to be the only person on duty. When Ruby recoiled at the sight of him and grabbed a pot of hot coffee to protect herself, he realized that he must have looked like he felt, horrible.

"Don't you come no closer! Ain't no money in the draw—we closed!" Ruby shouted while brandishing the hot coffee.

Through swollen lips, sounding like the Golem with laryngitis, he croaked out the words, "Caa! Carr...rum me...over...need help!"

"Ain't no help here, mister! You got to leave right now!" responded the frightened girl.

Pronouncing any single word with his swollen tongue was near impossible, "Pleece...call...da...pleece!"

"Sorry mister. My battery is dead. You got to go some place else."

His throat parched and burning, Joel pulled his wallet from his pocket and removed a twenty dollar bill, which he held up for the girl to see.

"Mill-thake...ice...cleam...pleass."

"Man, you are really fucked up," declared Ruby, lowering the pot of coffee to the heating unit. "What kind a shake?"

"Virmella," growled the distressed man as he moved toward the counter.

"No! Stay back there," shouted Ruby, grabbing the coffee pot again. "Throw me the money! You just stay there—sit down!"

Joel crushed the twenty into a ball and tossed it to Ruby behind the counter, who caught it with her free hand.

"You want a vanilla frosty shake?"

"Yeth...ice cleam...too...big cup."

Ruby waited until he sat down before she went about pouring the shake, never taking her eyes off him in the process. The distressed man was glad to find an additional hundred and sixty three dollars cash in his wallet, though his hands began shaking uncontrollably when he realized he couldn't remember his name. Frantic, he emptied the wallet on the table, but none of the identification was his. The garish neon atmosphere enhanced his belief that he was in fact dreaming, only he couldn't wake up. His neck was black and blue from pinching but he couldn't break out of the nightmare. He was becoming more and more freaked out, trying to remember his name, while checking the door in case the wheelchair psycho showed up.

Ruby placed the shake and ice cream on the far end of the counter, along with the change from the twenty. Picking up the steaming coffee pot, she called out to him, "It's ready. You can come get it, but be real cool, or else!"

The blood spattered man retrieved the shake and ice cream but left the change on the counter. Back at the table, he downed the shake slowly, each swallow a painful chore in the beginning. After a few swallows the cold shake felt good in his mouth, providing more pleasure than pain. Even while he enjoyed the cold ice cream sliding down his throat he could taste only Tabasco sauce. After a minute the burning subsided and swallowing became something wonderful. Upon finishing the frosty shake, he ordered another cup of ice cream and a large container of ice water, getting closer to the correct pronunciation of each word. While he alternately chewed the ice and gargled the ice water, Ruby never took her eyes off him, all the time praying he would leave or another customer would show up, preferably a cop.

When he felt his vocal apparatus might be functional, he ventured a question, "What part...of L.A... is this?"

"This ain't L.A.," replied Ruby. "This is Chicago."

"Jesus, I can't remember a thing!" the man eating the ice cream thought before asking another question, still sounding like he had laryngitis.

"Is there...a police...station...near here?"

"Not near here. I don't know where one is. You bout finished eaten and stuff? Cause I got to be closing down."

"Ruby, please...is this all a dream?"

"Look mister, whatever you into, ain't my business. If you got run over, I'm sorry. Please finish your ice cream and go on out, okay?"

"I just...need to use...the john and...I'll go."

"Okay, be quick though."

All through the night he had the creeps, typical of nightmares, but when he looked into the bathroom mirror and saw a strange face, he started screaming. Totally freaked out of his mind, he crashed out of the bathroom, running into Ruby, who was also streaking for the exit door. Outside, running again, he started crying and praying to wake up. "Maybe this whole insane episode was drug induced," he thought, while wiping tears from his face. "It's just a bad trip. I must have taken a hit of acid, some weird dope at a party? With who? Maybe some bad ecstasy or crack — with who—where? What's my name? Who the fuck is Joel Ellendorff? What am I doing with his wallet, in Chicago? This is so fucked up! I just have to wait it out—relax till the shit wears off."

The crazed man ran until he came to a small church. The front doors were closed but unlocked. It was dark inside, except for a couple of electric candles on the altar casting an eerie light on a large crucifix between them. He searched through the chapel and the adjoining rooms for a priest. There wasn't anyone around. His energy spent, and shivering from cold sweat, he wrapped himself in the organ cover and stretched out on the front pew. He fell asleep praying.

"Please God, help me out of this nightmare."

CHAPTER TEN

DAMAGE CONTROL

There was only one bar and grill in the neighborhood, "The Dive," a beer joint that catered to college students. Ken occasionally went there with Joel after class because it was close to his apartment. Now Ken raced down the deserted street, avoiding most of the dilapidated asphalt and pot holes and just missing a cat who jumped in his way.

Since he renounced "The Faith" it occurred to the ex-priest that ordinary people spend most of their waking hours involved in damage control. At least that's what his life seemed to be all about as he rolled madly down Grant Street toward the Dive.

"What's that lunatic in the wheelchair doing?"

"Damage control, dear. He was probably in the process of hijacking someone's body when it all unraveled, as things have a way of doing."

"Hey, slow down," Ken thought to himself, "count yourself among the very fortunate, because Joel is at least alive. Right now you could be running from the police instead of just doing damage control. Slow down, there's no reason to panic. Joel may be suffering from some inflammation in his mouth and throat, perhaps a touch of disorientation, but he will recuperate," the ex-priest consoled himself.

He knew, from his seminary studies, that people awakening from traumatic circumstances often suffered some disorientation, which usually subsided in a few hours. With a little luck he would encounter Henry and the detective in the bar, and convince them that his letter was just a foolish prank, and that would be the end of the matter.

"Not in a million years," he thought. That will never fly with Henry, who knew him too well. Pranks were something Ken would never be party to, having suffered more than his share of ridicule as a child. Lying wasn't Ken's strong suit either, even though he did a lot of it in his recent quest for a healthy body to inhabit. In the process, he was amazed at how susceptible people were to lies. It clarified for him how the political system became so totally corrupt. Under the present circumstances, however, he felt he had no choice but to lie, and it would have to be a whopper. Ken slowed down and took to the sidewalk, needing some time to devise a more convincing story than he first anticipated.

Cringing within, he thought, "What am I becoming—a liar, a con-artist! Still, I can't tell them the truth without going to jail or an insane asylum!"

Thus, the ex-priest rolled slowly along, conjuring up the tallest tale he would ever have to tell. When he finally rolled into The Dive, it was crowded, noisy and wreaked of beer soaked sawdust, which covered the floor. The subdued lighting was provided by plastic mermaids hanging from the ceiling, whose breasts lit up as they turned in place. The bar furniture and the rest of the décor resembled a pirate ship in the seventeen hundreds.

Father Dorcus spotted him first and stood up, waving his hand in the air. Ken waved back as he motored to the table occupied by his old friend and a detective he wasn't looking forward to meeting.

"What are you doing here?" asked Henry, crouching down to hug his friend.

"I sometimes eat here when I'm low on grease," quipped Ken. "What are you doing here?"

"We stopped by your apartment to see you, my friend. But you weren't in, so we came here. Oh, this is detective Joe Costalino. We were worried about you. Detective Costalino, this is my best friend in the whole world, Ken McAlister."

The detective reached over the table to shake Ken's hand.

"What is going on with you?" queried the old priest. "I've been trying to locate you for almost a year! You canceled your phone, e-mail, your regular doctor, then this strange letter comes to me with no return address. It's not really a letter, but a final confession implying suicide."

"I'm sorry Henry, I went through a really bad spell in my life."

"You don't say!" exclaimed Henry. "From your letter I didn't know if you were seriously considering murder or if you just went raving mad! That, dear friend, is why I am sitting in this rank bar with Detective Costalino here. So, what happened to you?"

Ken paused, presumably to motion to the waitress, but he really needed to catch his breath, as he was seized with the anguish of telling his tall tale to the detective. The waitress, a twenty-something in torn jeans and a t-shirt inscribed with the words "**THEY'RE REAL**," made her way to their table. She seemed uneasy under Father Henry's gaze, while taking Ken's order of a bottle of Perrier and fish and chips. Ken ordered the Perrier merely to facilitate the story he was about to tell. Looking to the two men, he added,

"How about you? Are you hungry?"

The detective said, "No, I'm good." Father Dorcus just shook his head and held up his half full glass of wine.

When the waitress left, Father Henry commented, "That's what's wrong with our country. Today's youth are over sexed, and it's undermining the whole system of education! I mean, how can a young man focus on his studies when he's got that in his face all day?"

When no one responded, the elderly priest turned to his friend, "So, Ken, what happened to you?"

"Well, I certainly understand your concern over that ridiculous letter," responded the ex-priest. "The fact is, I was out of my mind when I wrote it. Forgive me Henry, but I reached a breaking point with the hypocrisy of the church—and myself as a priest. I just had to get out of it, free myself from all that the church has become. In saying this, I'm not referring to the devoted servants of the Lord such as yourself, Henry."

Ken reached over and squeezed Henry's forearm reassuringly.

"I hope my letter at least made that clear. Long before writing that insane letter, I started drinking and doing drugs. I lost the faith—I didn't care about anything—I just wanted to die."

Ken hoped his periodic pauses to catch his breath would be taken as mini bouts of emotion brought on by his painful confession.

"The irony is," Ken continued, "you can't really drink yourself to death—at least I couldn't—I just got horribly sick—oh, it didn't stop me from drinking. I just got sicker and even more depressed."

"Why didn't you call me, talk to me?" interjected the white-haired priest.

"Because Henry, I couldn't bear the burden of drawing you into it, into my pain."

Ken reached over and patted the back of his friend's hand.

"Anyway, as I related in the letter, I bought a gun— with the intention of ending it all on my mother's grave. As you know, a good Samaritan rescued me."

"A good Samaritan!" Detective Costalino exclaimed, "You said he was a god of sorts, with a magic potion!"

"I was insane, hallucinating when I wrote that—what he turned out to be, this good Samaritan—Ken faked a chuckle—was a down and out drug addict. The whole thing was so bizarre! I guess he once worked as a magician, or a magician's assistant in Las Vegas. But he was just an unscrupulous drug dealer! He exploited me. He got me hooked on narcotics—so he could finance his own habit."

Strangely enough, as Ken got deeper into his fantastic story he required fewer pauses for breath. But his mouth was as dry as boxed cotton and he was glad when the waitress delivered his Perrier. Ken took a long drink before continuing.

"The guy knew some tricks, simple stuff with cards and flowers, but he was a charlatan—he got me started on some kind of narcotic laced pastries. They certainly relieved my depression! Well, it wasn't long before he had me main-lining some really expensive dope."

Ken had no trouble recalling the drug terminology he had picked up during his stint as a prison chaplain. The ex-priest was beginning to marvel at how seamlessly he told the tall tale.

"That's when I began having hallucinations, really strange episodes involving magic potions and, and—well, you read the letter. I mean, I was literally out of my mind! Out of my mind for months! Didn't even know it."

"What kind of dope was it?" asked the detective.

"I honestly couldn't tell you, probably heroin. I never asked," responded Ken. "At the time I actually didn't care!"

"Did you pay him for the drugs, the dealer?" continued the detective.

"Of course I paid him. He was a con man, a drug dealer!"

"And the money?" pressed the detective, "Where did you get the money to go full on junky for months?"

Ken paused to sip his mineral water, searching for the best way to end the interrogation. He could feel his heart racing in his chest and he was beginning to sweat beneath his leather jacket. He hadn't actually contemplated such details when hastily devising the story. The truth was that Ken was never broke and never would be broke because he was a world class chess player. He actually coached those who aspired to the game on line. Henry knew his friend was a good chess player, but Ken, who was not one to brag about himself, never told Henry that his World Federation Chess rating of 2500-2599 placed him among the top five hundred players in the world. As a priest whose physical needs were met by the church, Ken donated his winnings from online tournaments to the church, tens of thousands of dollars every year. Still, having confessed to being a full-on junky for months on end, he could hardly tell them that he made money playing chess. Thus, the canny ex-priest was forced to improvise as he went along.

"The money, yes—at first I lived in a hotel, off the Las Vegas strip—but when the money ran out I lived in my van," said Ken, hoping the detective would drop the inquiry and allow him just to finish the story as he devised it.

However, after twenty five years as an investigative detective, inquiry was an ingrained habit with the detective, who pressed on.

"When you ran out of money, how did you pay for the narcotics?"

"Hey, is this some kind of interrogation, Detective Costalino?" asked Ken, as he removed his jacket, hanging it on his chair. "Because, if it is, don't you have to advise me of my rights", said the ex-priest, with a chuckle.

"No," lied the detective. "I'm just curious."

"You have to admit, Ken, it's a fascinating story!" added Father Dorcus. "How did you pay for the drugs?"

Ken was up against the wall. There was nothing left in his bottle of Perrier to sip. The arrival of his fish and chips provided a much needed pause. Ken ordered another round of drinks for everyone, while contemplating his options. He was about out of lies. If it wasn't for the delight that radiated from their faces he would have dropped the agonizing subterfuge and confessed his crimes right there and then. But his well-meaning friend, Henry and the detective appeared so goddamn smug it made him angry.

There they sat, upright and whole in body and mind, tearing him down like vultures—enjoying their life-long superiority over such unfortunate prey as him. They found their comfortable perch in life, from which they could look down upon the lost and desperate losers of the game. What did they know of real suffering, real desperation, the kind he dealt with every day! What were their great concerns, running out of shaving cream, gas prices going up, the flu? Whole people can hardly imagine the life he had to live, a life plagued with aches, pains, and pus-dripping infections—a life without mobility, filled with physical restrictions, and never a moment free of the anxiety that you might befoul yourself in public! And now they wanted to bring him down even further below their smug faces!

It would be the most difficult lie he would ever have to tell. It just wasn't something he would ever admit and Henry at least would know that. And perhaps the two whole men would take pity on him.

"After the money ran out, well, well, I went out on the Vegas strip—and started begging. Drugs will do that to you."

It wasn't anticipated or planned as part of his lie, but when Ken spoke of begging, he naturally began to choke up and cry. His tears were not for the reasons the two men at the table might assume, but because he was begging, actually begging them to take pity on him, to leave him alone. The elderly priest immediately bent to one knee to hold his friend in his arms. Ken assumed the interrogation was over. Surely the detective would stop questioning him, just out of human decency.

Ken looked over at Castalino's resolute face and knew that the cop in him ruled over any human empathy, that tears were no substitute for the cold hard facts that this cop thrived on!

"So," asked the detective, "You wrote that letter, with the perfect spelling, perfect punctuation when you were strung out on drugs?"

"Yes, quite out of my mind, really!" responded the ex-priest.

"In perfectly legible handwriting," smirked the detective.

"I guess so, detective."

"And how long ago was that?" pressed the detective.

Ken's face was wet with sweat and he felt a sick churning in his gut. He had unwittingly erred regarding the time frame of his story. He paused to chew on a piece of deep fried fish, while contemplating the answer.

When he fabricated the story he neglected to consider that he sent his ill-fated letter just a week ago. That fact, that he was a total drug crazed addict seven short days ago, and now he was perfectly free of the addiction, was beyond belief. Even Henry, a most trusting person, gullible really, would have a problem with that part of his story. There would be no end to their continued intervention into his life if he tried to bluff that one through. Besides, the detective would laugh at the notion that a "full on junky" kicked his habit on his own in a single week. As a prison priest, Ken witnessed firsthand the long painful struggle of addicts trying to kill "the monkey on their backs." Here goes nothing, Ken thought, as he launched once again into damage control.

"I wrote that insane letter many months ago—maybe seven or eight months ago in Las Vegas—I probably addressed it, and stamped it back then too—who knows! But in my delirium I neglected to mail it—not too long after that I broke ties with my dealer—and worked on getting clean and sober. I joined a Narcotics Anonymous group which met at the Salvation Army. I went through a living hell kicking my habit."

"But you mailed the letter a week ago when you were perfectly clean, sober and sane. Why would you?" asked the detective?

Squirming inwardly, and on the verge of throwing up, the ex-priest looked directly into the eyes of his interrogator and said, "The letter was posted by mistake. I didn't even know it was still in my possession… when I moved back to Chicargo. It must have fallen out of my stuff when I was moving in…and some good Samaritan must have found it—"

"And dropped it in a mail box." added the detective sarcastically.

"Imagine," Father Henry concluded, "all this worry over a letter you never meant to mail. Well, I for one am happy to hear that you're out of the woods now. We have an excellent Narcotics Anonymous group meeting at the church, if you are planning to continue…which I hope you are."

The interrogation was over. The detective fired no more questions at him and whether he believed the story or not didn't matter. Somehow, Ken had survived the most extreme bout of lying he would ever indulge in. Through intense intimidation, through tears of humiliation, through the greasiest fish and chips he would ever consume he put this ill-fated night to rest. He took no pride in the whole devious episode; he was just relieved to the marrow of his bones that it was over.

Father Dorcus, possibly sensing the tension between the two men, segued into a comment on the perils of drugs and alcohol, after which the three men attempted to make small talk about police work and religion. But it wasn't long before Detective Costalino checked his cell phone for the time and called for the check. Before leaving, Henry made his old friend promise to visit him for a game of chess at his earliest convenience.

"The time you spent in hell notwithstanding," said Henry with a smile, "you are still going to spot me a rook."

Henry leaned down and kissed his friend on the cheek while the detective patted him on the back saying,

"Do you want a ride back to your apartment?"

"No thanks, Detective Costalino, you would never fit this contraption in your car anyway."

With that, Costalino led the elderly priest out of The Dive. On the drive back to the church Detective Costalino and Father Dorcus conversed about Ken's fantastic story, the priest believing every word, the detective believing none of it.

Ken remained at The Dive for another half hour before rolling home. Concerned as he was that the detective and his friend might have lingered around, Ken went a block out of his way so he could enter his apartment building from the back alley. It wasn't until he was back in his apartment with the door locked behind him that Ken felt the tension ebb from his neck and shoulders. Exhausted, he rolled immediately to the bedroom to look in on Joel. But he was gone. Ken rushed to the open window, pulling himself out as far as he could. There was no sign of him, but he could see Joel's bike, which was chained to the front gate.

More trouble! More tension! "It never ends," thought the man in the wheelchair, as he raced to check the bathroom. Empty—Ken could not endure any more stress. "Enough!" he shouted out loud. "Kill me God!

Kill me and get it over with! Kill me for contemplating murder—for hating this life you gave me! Just kill me-kill me-kill me!" reiterated the distraught ex-priest, as he tore off his sweat soaked clothes and overflowing urine pouch. Then he pulled himself onto the stationary chair beneath the shower and let the warm water cascade down on his body.

While he languished there, he settled it in his mind that he would go to bed with his gun and let the chips fall where they may. If the police showed up, he could still blow his brains out before he answered the door. After a while Ken dried off, took his meds and went to bed.

CHAPTER ELEVEN

SLEEPING IT OFF

The church janitor reached down to shake the blood spattered vagrant sleeping on the pew. The vagrant shrieked, shoving the janitor so hard he tumbled backwards onto the altar. The janitor laid there, silent, with the morning sun beaming through a stained glass window on him and his cleaning supplies strewn all over the altar. It took the bloody vagrant a moment to realize it wasn't the psycho in the wheelchair.

"I'm sorry, I thought you were someone else," apologized the vagrant

"How did you get in here?" asked the janitor struggling to his feet.

"The door was unlocked. Are you okay?"

"I'll live! You have to go. There's a Catholic mission on Franklin Street, where you can get help."

"Can I use the bathroom first?" asked the vagrant, as he neatly replaced the organ cover.

"Follow me," replied the janitor, leading the blood spattered man up the aisle to a men's room off the sanctuary.

In the bathroom the disoriented vagrant relieved himself at the urinal, then went to the sink to wash. He was aware of the blood stains on his hands, and the awful taste of Tabasco sauce in his mouth, which made him feel sick and angry. He washed his face and hands vigorously but he was afraid to raise his head up and look into the mirror. A nauseous feeling in the pit of his stomach was taking hold of him as he dried his face, knowing before he even looked in the mirror that the face he was drying wasn't his. Then he looked in the mirror, fear and nausea consuming him as he saw the strange face looking back at him. The face was odd, unfamiliar, frightening, and it proved that he was in fact insane. His heart pounded wildly and the room started spinning. Hanging onto the sink with one hand, he splashed cold water on his face and head until he regained some equilibrium. Then, stepping back from the mirror, he staggered out of the bathroom. The janitor was waiting for him, grabbing his arm to steady him.

"Are you stoned or something—sick? What's all that blood from?"

"I'll be alright. Can I just sit down for a minute, just one minute," pleaded the disoriented vagrant.

Helping him into a pew at the back of the chapel, the janitor asked, "Should I call an ambulance or something?"

"No. I just need to catch my breath."

As he sat, waiting for his heart to quiet down, the dazed and disoriented man began to accept his circumstances as real, not a dream. Contrary to what he felt or believed, he was forced to consider that he was indeed suffering from amnesia. He flashed on the film, *Memento*, in which the lead character had amnesia. Like the character in the movie, he knew he was in danger but couldn't recall from whom specifically. "At least the guy in the film knew his own name!" he thought.

Okay, so he had amnesia—but he'd never heard of someone with the disorder forgetting what his own face looked like. Anyway, in most cases people regained their memory a short time later—a few days or weeks. With that realization, he dismissed the idea of going to the police, just like the character in the movie. It occurred to him that all the blood on his clothes may not be his own. Maybe he killed somebody and the wheelchair psycho was trying to get revenge. As alien as the idea was to him, he couldn't just disregard it. In his insane state of mind anything was possible. Reconciled to the possibility that he was suffering from amnesia, he searched through his pockets. The janitor just watched, as the vagrant emptied his pockets on the pew—a key ring with three keys on it, a pocketknife, Zippo cigarette lighter, a comb, and a wallet. More closely now, the vagrant went through the contents of the wallet, knowing that it might actually be his, and could provide some insight into his predicament. There was no driver's license, only a laminated military ID card bearing PFC Joel Ellendorff's name, photo and fingerprint. The photo was of the strange face, possibly his face. The information below the photo read:

UNITED STATES ARMY RESERVE
32ND INFANTRY DIVISION, CHICAGO, ILLINOIS

On the back of the card was Ellendorff's address, blood type and signature. Beside the ID card, there were a couple of receipts from Home Depot, a photo of Scarlet Johansson in a wet t-shirt, and a dry cleaner's receipt listing two shirts, a sweater, and a pair of pants. And there was the hundred and sixty three dollars cash.

Joel thought the best thing to do would be to check out the address on the ID card. Perhaps returning to his digs would break through the amnesia. With nothing else to go on he stood up, thanked the janitor and left the church, but not before turning his bloody shirt inside out.

Riding in the cab, it occurred to him that the psycho in the wheelchair might be lying for him at his digs. He instructed the driver to go to the Empire Dry Cleaners instead, at 2112 Fillmore Street. After picking up the clothes, he stopped at a Walgreens in a mall two blocks away, and bought a toothbrush, toothpaste, and mouthwash. Next he walked into the Big Bear Pancake House in the same mall and sat down at the counter. An older waitress, with frizzy bleached hair, showed up to take his order.

"Been in a fight, have ya?"

"Kind of…I'll have the granola cakes, with the fresh fruit and vanilla yogurt."

"Anything to drink—coffee, tea, OJ?" asked the waitress.

"Orange juice, large."

When she turned away, the man with the swollen face went to the bathroom. Inside, he locked the door and bathed in the sink, using paper towels and his stained clothing to dry himself. His mouth wasn't quite as sore as it was the previous day, but brushing his teeth and gargling with the mouthwash caused a burning pain which forced him to stop and rinse with cold water several times. It was no easy task to wash the blood and crud out of his hair using the liquid soap in the dispenser and drying it under the hand blow dryer. He did his best to scrub the red stains off of his running shoes but threw the ruined socks in the trash.

He proceeded to put on the pants he picked up at the Empire Cleaners, hoping they wouldn't fit. His hope faded immediately when he put on the powder blue bellbottoms.

"Powder blue bellbottoms!" He cringed. "Jesus, what kind of bozo am I? I must be gay!"

Someone started knocking on the door.

"Be out in two minutes," he shouted in response.

The bellbottoms were disconcerting, but when he opened the package containing two cowboy shirts with the smiling arrowhead pockets, he began to seriously question the amnesia premise. "No fucking way!" he said to himself, "What grown man would walk around in clothes like this! Chuck Norris? And what would demure Scarlett Johansson think!"

Finally, the sweater, a green and yellow football jersey bearing a large number 2 caused him to consider tossing it in the trash even though it was really cold out. In the end he put the jersey on over the cowboy shirt, looked in the mirror and said, "How do you do. I'm the quarterback for the Chicago morons."

The pancakes and fruit were waiting for him at the counter when he returned from the bathroom. Eating the food was such ecstasy it had his utmost attention. He didn't even notice the pretty Asian waitress staring down at him from the other side of the counter until she spoke.

"How come no spam today, Joel?"

"What," responded the man who was probably Joel.

"You always have spam and eggs, what's up?"

"You know me?"

"Duh??? What's going on Joel?" responded the pretty waitress with shoulder length black hair and brown almond eyes.

"You know me. Like how? I mean, are you a friend?"

"Are you putting me on? No, you're really weirded out!"

"I hit my head. I can't remember squat! I need your help."

"I thought you were called up—to active duty or something."

"I'm in the Army reserves, right?"

"Like yeah dude! You need to see a doctor, Joel—like right away!"

"Relax okay. Please, just tell me how you know me."

"I've got food in the window. I'll be right back."

Joel finished his breakfast while the pretty waitress served her customers. The cakes and fruit were delicious with no Tabasco after-taste in his mouth. The idea of being Joel Ellendorff...dressed like a total bozo was an ordeal all its own, but he felt some real comfort meeting this cute friend. When the cute waitress returned, she was very understanding, telling him that her name was Samantha, Sammi to him. She informed him that he ate breakfast at "The Big Bear" almost every morning and that he got around on a bike since he lost his license—for driving under the influence. She told him that he worked independently as a handy man, and that he was going to night- school to learn Spanish. She very quietly related that they dated for a while in high school, nothing serious—and that she was married to an attorney named David Thorn but they couldn't have children because he had a vasectomy. Joel had no awakening, no recognition regarding anything she related. When she paused, he asked if she recalled his being in trouble of any kind, and did he have any dealings with a man in a wheelchair who had black and grey hair.

"No," she said. "I never saw you with anybody in a wheelchair. Actually, I don't remember seeing you with anybody, except that skank, Tonya, you hung with for a while. Like you're kind of a loner, Joel."

"What about family or a roommate? Do you know if I have any family in town?"

"No family that I know of—no roommate either. You live with turtles, that's all."

"Turtles? I live with turtles?"

"They're your pets. Look babe, you should see a doctor right away."

"I will. First, I want to check out my digs—see if I can jog my memory that way."

"That sounds cool," said the waitress. "If you want, I could meet you when I get off."

"That would be really cool, Samantha."

"Sammi," corrected the waitress.

"Sammi," repeated the man with amnesia.

"Gotta run, I'll meet you at your place at six. Oops!"

"Sammi! You and I are more than friends."

"Shushh. Keep your voice down. Yes, we had a little thing for a while, but not for the last three months."

"I had a cell phone, right?"

"Of course, why?'

"I need that number."

"I don't know it—we never called each other. It wasn't that kind of thing. I love my husband. I've gotta go."

"Wait! Where do I live?"

"You don't remember where you live?"

"I have the address, but—"

"Out the front door, go to the corner, that's McKinley Street. Go right down McKinley three blocks. Turn right there on Ninth Street. There's a red brick apartment complex in the middle of the block. You're in 201 South—on the top floor—3B. See you at six."

Sammi scooted away. Meeting her alleviated some of the tension in Joel's life. He probably didn't kill anyone. He wasn't a complete bozo, attending night school to better himself. He worked for a living and he probably wasn't gay, having had an affair with Sammi. Just thinking about her meeting with him at his apartment turned him on.

CHAPTER TWELVE

WAITING FOR THE ENDGAME

The sun was blazing through his bedroom window when Ken opened his eyes. The digital clock on his nightstand clicked to 11:14 a.m.

Before getting dressed, he looked out the window to see if Joel's bicycle was still chained to the front gate. It was. Ken dressed and motored to the kitchen where he put on the teakettle. He couldn't call Joel because the young man's cell phone was still on the table. As he proceeded to clean up, Ken wrestled with two questions: Why would he leave? Where could he go?

Though Ken had never been to Joel's apartment, his "ruins," as he referred to it, he knew it was on the east side of town, miles away. The young handyman traveled mostly by bicycle, which was still chained up outside. The nearest hospital was also miles away. If that's where he wanted to go he certainly wouldn't walk. He would bike or call a cab… or maybe he called 911. If that's what he did, Ken speculated, call 911 for an ambulance, then it wouldn't be long before the police would arrive. Deliberately, Ken removed the loaded gun from the coat closet and placed it in the leather glove case on his wheelchair. He decided to wait and finish cleaning up before calling the hospital. It was two in the afternoon when Ken was done cleaning his apartment. He paused to wolf down a fried egg sandwich and a second cup of tea before calling.

He called Chicago Community Hospital first; it was the closest. He inquired about a young man named Joel Ellendorff with long blond hair, who suffered from inflamed lungs and throat, perhaps some disorientation. The receptionist put him on hold for a minute but then told him that no one fitting that description showed up at their emergency room, and no one named Joel Ellendorff was registered at their hospital. Ken went on to call every hospital in Chicago, only to get a similar response. If Joel went directly to the police, they surely would have arrested him by now. Nothing made any sense. He had no choice but to wait things out, while resting his hand on the glove case that held the gun.

To Ken's surprise the day passed without incident. And the next day, and the next, though he never stopped calling hospitals, homeless shelters and the local morgue. It seemed Joel had vanished without a trace. Ken had already purchased a cell phone charger from Radio Shack to keep Joel's phone operating, just in case he called. Except for two inquiries from people seeking Joel's services as a handyman, there were no calls.

Father Henry paid him a brief visit on day ten. They played a couple of games of chess, which were for the chess master, Ken, an exercise in in utter tedium.

Chess started out as a hobby for Ken in seminary. Several of his instructors recommended it to the student body as excellent mental training. At the St. Paul Seminary it was always a favorite pastime for many students. For Ken, however, it became an addiction, a way to escape his limited social life, his boredom and his unspoken physical misery. He didn't know whether he had a photographic memory before he got into the game or whether it developed with his daily discipline of analyzing and memorizing opening, middle, and end game strategies. By the time Ken was ordained he had gained a professional ranking inadvertently by defeating other professionals in online tournaments. He never discouraged or belittled the students he played with at school, but the fact was he could foresee the end game for them after only eight or ten moves.

Eventually the young priest preferred playing professionals online, where he could lose himself in the contest. Developing the level of skill Ken achieved in seminary was a testimony to his superior memory, without which he never could have met the academic demands and service projects required of student priests along with the countless hours devoted to chess.

By the third match with Henry, the game was approaching the definition of torture for Ken. He was about to make up an excuse to leave when Henry said something that unsettled him to the core.

"Has detective Costalino talked to you recently?"

"No. Why would he want to talk to me?"

"Oh, I don't know." replied Henry. "He called me a couple of times, asking about you."

"What did you tell him? I mean, what's he asking about me?"

"Nothing, really. I think he's just curious. I told him to drop in on you, that you wouldn't mind. You know, you really should get a phone."

Ken finished the third match and begged off Henry's dinner invitation, telling him he had a dental appointment. Ken hated lying to Henry, who was more like a father to him over the years than a friend. Obviously, the detective didn't believe his story. Just when the ex-priest was beginning to relax he now would have to deal with a "curious" detective. He made up his mind to move out of town the moment Henry mentioned the detective's inquiry about him.

There was no telling what became of Joel. Waiting for him accomplished nothing. Worrying about him accomplished less than nothing. Why continue to worry? Maybe he was physically okay. Maybe he just shipped out with his company to Afghanistan.

CHAPTER THIRTEEN
ACTORS WITH GREAT SMILES

When the man, suffering from amnesia, left the Big Bear Pancake House, he had no problem finding his apartment complex.

However, the place was beyond disappointing. There were no late model cars in any of the parking spaces. The brick buildings, six in all, looked like they hadn't been cleaned since Columbus discovered America. Beside most of the brick being stained and mottled, there were buildings with sections of brick missing altogether, exposing mildewed particle-board. The landscape around the buildings looked like a war zone. Some dirty-faced kids were kicking a soccer ball around a barren area that use to have grass. The man with amnesia stepped into the dust storm, holding up two dollar bills, as he called out to the biggest kid.

"Hey son, want to make some green?"

"Clue me in," replied the kid, a Latino maybe thirteen, wearing a Cubs baseball cap backwards on his head.

"I need a favor. I need you to knock on a door for me—see if someone is home."

"What then?"

"Nothing. just clue me if someone is home," responded the man, using the kid's lingo.

"What do I say if somebody's there?"

"Tell him Joel owes you money, money for, ah, for the newspaper you deliver."

"Who the fuck is Joel?"

"Nobody. Just ask for Joel, if anyone answers the door."

"Sounds risky, homey. I need twenty green."

"I'll give you five."

"Twenty green or no deal," said the kid, holding out his hand.

"Get lost homey! I'll get another kid."

"Which building? What's the door number," asked the kid reaching for the five.

"Building 201-door 3B—knock hard."

The man with amnesia gave the kid the five and stood beside a trash dumpster where he could see the entrance to 201. Suddenly he remembered himself, wearing torn Army fatigues inside a dumpster scavenging for food. Clinging to the flashback, he tried to expand his memory of it. As tragic as it was, he knew it was him. He was wearing remnants of an Army uniform. He was dirty and desperate. He was wearing Army dog-tags around his neck. He strained to remember the name on the tags. His memory dispersed like a soap bubble when the kid lunged out of the building, yelling,

"Run, run, he's got a gun!"

The man with amnesia started running, but the kid called after him through gales of laughter.

"I'm shittin' you! Ain't nobody home— Just shittin' you dude!"

When the man stopped and turned around, the kid was doubled over with laughter.

"Look at you homey", gasped the kid through laughter, "you bout to piss those faggot pants you wearing!"

The frightened man went to smack the kid who ducked and ran off. As he walked to building 201, he tried to recapture his vision in the dumpster but it revealed nothing new. He was happily surprised to find the vestibule of 201 was almost clean. Except for some smudged graffiti over the mailboxes, the hallway, unlike the exterior of the complex, seemed to be maintained. He stopped to consider the name Ellendorff printed unevenly on one of the empty boxes, probably with a magic marker. Walking quietly up the three flights to apt 3B, he paused and listened at the door for at least a minute before knocking. When he was certain no one was there, he tried the door—it was locked. He proceeded to try the keys on the key ring he found in his pocket. The first key worked and he counseled himself before opening the door,

"This is probably my place. It's okay. Just be cool."

His personal resolve was challenged the moment he stepped into the apartment and saw a life size poster of Vladimir Klitchcoff, the boxer, on the wall above a dilapidated green couch. Two smaller portraits, one of Faith Hill and one of Elvis, hung on either side of the champ. The portrait of Elvis was one of those exquisite velvet renderings that continue to collect dust until Elvis looks like Santa Claus. Sitting open beside the couch was a well used La-Z-Boy recliner. And beside the recliner was a giant bowling pin lamp, the kind one usually sees half buried in garbage at a dumpsite. The two windows in the far wall were covered with yellow plastic blinds that were turning an interesting shade of brown. All of the walls were painted an uneven salmon pink, accentuating the ragged blue shag carpet and the orange work boots and grey socks scattered over it. Fastened to the wall across from the couch was a flat screen TV. But the item that brought the whole "early crap- hole motif" together, the master stroke of sheer elegance, was the giant aquarium under the TV, containing two foot-long, shit-covered turtles trying to climb up the glass.

The man with amnesia, who was probably the occupant of the apartment, stood frozen in disgust, unable to reconcile his confusion.

"I know that Joel, who might by some freakish act of nature turn out to be me, had sex with the Asian chick in this sty, but he must have required her to wear a blindfold or agree to be chloroformed before he carried her in."

Absolutely nothing in the room sparked a memory for the man with amnesia, and for that he was beginning to be thankful. Still, he had Joel Ellendorff's face, and that fact overruling all others compelled him to continue his search.

The kitchen wasn't all that disgusting, just a basic "single-guy" kitchen, cluttered with newspapers, beer bottles, and handy-man projects lying on top of everything with a flat surface. There were dishes piled up in the sink and a pair of Army boots, polish, and rags sharing the kitchen table with a book titled, *Combat Zones*. So far, only the Army boots seemed to suggest that he had some connection to Joel. Everything else just violated his sensibilities. Notwithstanding, the amnesia scenario was the only rational explanation. Thus, with fearless resolve, he opened the refrigerator to find four bottles of beer sharing a shelf with an open package of Velveeta cheese and a jar of mayonnaise with a table spoon sitting in it. On the shelf below was a baking dish of something resembling road-kill, a wilted ball of lettuce, two cans of spam, one open with a knife protruding from it, as though the thing in the can had to be killed before you could eat it. The freezer compartment harbored foil covered TV dinners and packages of an inferior blend of chopped meat, which, from the amount of fat exposed in the meat, he hoped was used to feed the turtles. Nothing made any sense to the man with amnesia, though of one thing he was certain, Army chow would seem like fine cuisine to Joel Ellendorff.

The bedroom—there was only one—wasn't all that bad. It had a matching dark fake wood bedroom set, a couple of snarling tiger lamps, some more of the blue shag on the floor, and a small Sony media center on the dresser. Also on the dresser was a digital clock and a framed photo of Joel with his arm around a twenty-something woman, who fit the description of Tonya, the skank. The bathroom needed a cleaning, along with the towels. It was probably the maid's day off! The medicine chest on the wall contained Band-Aids, aspirin, toothpaste, a large jar of Vaseline, Schick razors, and a photo of a nude woman on skis taped to the inside of the door. From the look of things, this might have been Joel's—favorite room!

The man, who was most likely Joel, searched the whole apartment thoroughly for a cell phone or any documents that might have the number to his cell phone. It was a good bet that the cell phone was left at the psycho's place; if he could come up with the number, or even what company issued the phone, the police could trace it back to the psycho. No such luck.

Under the circumstances, going to the police would only complicate matters, and possibly get him committed to an asylum. That was his posited rational. Actually he wouldn't go to the police, not yet anyway, until he got with Sammi, for the prospect of shagging her was the first shinning possibility his mind entertained since last night.

It was only one-thirty in the afternoon. Anticipating the arrival of Sammi at six, he took up the impossible job of cleaning the apartment. He started with the aquarium, placing the turtles in the bathtub and using a hairbrush he found in the bedroom he scrubbed them clean.

After scouring the aquarium and all the turtle toys and ground cover, he had had enough. He needed some fresh air, decent clothes and incense to prepare for the possible seduction of Sammi.

Leaving the apartment, he walked back to the mall where he remembered seeing an Urban Outfitters store. Figuring his remaining hundred and thirty dollars wouldn't cover the food, wine and clothes he needed, he took his first advantage of being Joel Ellendorff. He signed up for the Urban Outfitters credit card. Using his military ID card, and telling them he just got back from Afghanistan worked like a charm. The credit card allowed him three hundred on his initial purchase, with a ten percent discount. An hour later he left Urban Outfitters wearing clean underwear, socks, tan leather half boots, Levis, a crew neck black shirt, and a leather flight jacket. He stopped at Walgreens again for some deodorant and cologne. He hadn't anticipated seeing a movie but as he passed the movie emporium at the mall, he felt compelled to see George Clooney's film titled *Melt Down*. While no particular character in the movie triggered his memory, it was like deja vu. He knew the plot, with all its twists and turns, from the very first scene when a high school teacher, played by George Clooney, takes his class to tour a nuclear plant. When he left the theatre, he wrote down the names of the writer and director for future reference.

It was five-fifteen and he hadn't finished his shopping. He hurried through the Whole Foods market and emerged twenty minutes later with a shopping bag containing wine, cheese, crackers, olives, stuffed dates, fresh strawberries, ice cream, and condoms, all at a discount of ten percent for veterans. The Joel Ellendorff ID was proving such a benefit to him, he decided to accept the name, live with it and see where it takes him. He walked to the pancake house to meet Sammi but she left work early. Bags swinging from side to side, he hurried, almost ran down to the apartment complex. There was a new cream-colored Lexus in the parking lot. It had to be hers.

Sammi was sitting on the third floor steps beside her tote bag, waiting for him. The Asian beauty greeted him with a very friendly hug.

"Wow," she said, "you're all spiffed out! How are you feeling?"

"I'm cool, but the apartment—I don't know. Have you been inside lately?"

"Joel, please! Snap out of it!" She snapped her fingers. "You call your apartment, 'the ruins' for good reason."

With that, the man who accepted the name Joel opened the door and followed her in.

"Sammi, nothing in this place feels like it belongs to me."

"Okay, babe, start with this. Your turtles are named Hugo and Grace, but don't ask me which one is which. Hey, you cleaned the aquarium!"

"An act of mercy."

"Did you use your buddy yet?"

"My buddy?"

"Your recliner chair, you call it 'your buddy.'"

"You're joking, right?"

"No," chuckled Sammi. "It's your favorite chair. See if you can remember the song it plays."

"That chair plays a song?!"

"Your buddy, Joel, plays your favorite song when you sit in it. Come on," the Asian girl insisted, nudging him toward the recliner.

"Sammi, if I sit in that chair and it plays a song I remember, I will have to admit I'm fucking retarded!"

Sammi walked over, kicked the chair and violins played, "Over the Rainbow." "Remember?"

"No, thank God! How many times do you have to kick the chair to shut it up?" asked Joel.

Sammi shoved the footrest and the chair closed, ending the song.

"Don't worry about anything, babe. I'm going to break into your memory banks big time! Why don't you open the wine?"

With that, Sammi trotted into the bedroom, while the man with Joel's face went to the kitchen to find a corkscrew. When he returned to the living room, Sammi was standing in pink silk panties bordered with black lace and a matching bra.

"Anything look familiar?" asked the Asian beauty in a sultry voice.

"Let's see," responded the man with Joel's face, taking in the scent of her rose perfume, and gazing at her beautiful olive skin.

She was standing four feet away but he could feel the warmth of her engulfing him. As she stepped into him, Sammi unhooked her bra, which clung momentarily to her protruding nipples. Gently, his hands started toying with her warm perfect breasts, as he leaned down and kissed her full on the mouth. She tasted like toffee and mint. Shaking with passion, Sammi unbuttoned Joel's shirt, caressing his body as she slid to her knees, unzipping his jeans on the way down. Joel helped her slide his jeans, along with his briefs, down to his ankles. As her hands deftly teased his extended manhood, causing him to groan and his legs to tremble, something odd caught his attention—something was happening in the usually dull and motionless aquarium. One of the turtles had climbed onto his partner's back and was pushing its way up the glass. The man who was probably Joel watched, transfixed, until the top turtle had its front claws gripping the rim of the aquarium.

Joel thought to himself, "Nice try turtle, but it's physically impossible to pull yourself up and over the rim." But then, the turtle on the bottom started to push up with his back legs, nudging his partner higher and higher up the glass. The man who was probably Joel was stymied, thinking, "This is impossible! It's Cirque de Soleil with turtles. Any second now buddy is going to start playing 'Over the Rainbow.'"

Meanwhile below, Sammi was wondering why the man's anatomy shrank right before her eyes. The situation had gone weird and the man with Joel's face was caught on the horns of a dilemma. If there was time, he could interrupt this new treatment for amnesia and yell down to the Asian waitress, "Stop, my turtles are in trouble!" But the top turtle was already teetering on the rim, and under the circumstances the waitress below probably would take it all wrong.

The man with Joel's face watched the bottom turtle, probably Hugo, give one final shove upward and he had no choice but to launch over Sammi's head and catch the stupid turtle before it hit the floor. Sammi screamed, "What the fuck! What are you doing with that stupid turtle?"

There was some initial squabbling about what just happened, which led to a debate regarding the Buddhist principle of "right action." The couple made up over wine and cheese. When the wine was finished, Sammi introduced a wood and brass pot pipe from her hair. She then fetched a zip-lock bag of cannabis from her tote bag, saying, "If this shit doesn't jog your memory, nothing will!"

Thus, the man with amnesia and the pretty Asian waitress smoked two bowls of the weed, aptly labeled "Joy Jump." They spent hours in bed, eating strawberries with ice cream, giggling and making world-class love. They were asleep in each other's arms when Sammi's cell phone jingled in her tote bag.

"Oh shit!" she yelped, grabbing her phone. "It's my husband."

Sammi said into the phone, "Hi babe," and scurried into the bathroom to finish the conversation. When she emerged from the bathroom she bent down close to Joel, who was still half asleep.

"Gotta go Joel."

"Isn't there any way you can stay?"

"Can't, babe. Maybe next Thursday again."

With that, she grabbed her purse from the floor and raced back into the bathroom. While she was waiting for the shower to heat up, she stepped into the doorway. With the bathroom light accentuating her flawless body and long black hair glistening from the steam, she was one memory Joel wouldn't lose.

"I don't know much about amnesia or any of that mind stuff," Sammi said, "but whatever happened to you, Joel, has made a huge improvement! You want my advice, babe, don't go back, don't remember who you were."

Saying that, she stepped back into the mist. The man with amnesia got up and joined her in the shower. With the warm water flowing over their bodies, he asked Sammi what specifically she was referring to when she said he had improved.

She said, "The way you make love, your hands, the way you move. Even the way you talk, the way you say things is way different, Joel. You sound like that actor, who was in that soldier movie…I can't think of his name."

"What was the name of the movie?" inquired the man with amnesia, while she began to lather him up with shampoo.

"I can't remember. The actor who talks like you has black hair and blue eyes, I think."

"What's his name—think!" implored Joel, rattling off a list of actors, "Johnny Depp? Tom Cruise? Ben Affleck? James Franco? Vince Vaughn? Any of them?"

"No babe, he has a killer smile."

"All the actors I just named have a killer smile! What about Robert Downey Jr.? Ben Stiller? Adrian Brodie?"

"You're amazing! When did you become so interested in movie stars?" asked Sammi. "The guy in the soldier movie isn't as famous as Tom Cruise and those others."

After grilling her during a final bout of sex in the shower, their attempt to cure his amnesia failed. Sammi dried off with a towel from her tote bag, jumped into a different set of panties and bra, and proceeded to brush her gorgeous hair. Meanwhile, the man with Joel's face stood next to the Asian beauty, offering a list of excuses she could use on her husband. At the door, tote bag in hand, Sammi kissed him on the cheek, and dashed down the stairs into the night.

The next morning the man with amnesia took a long walk to the State Street Police Station. He told his story about his escape from the man in the wheelchair to Detective Alihondro Gomez, who sat there cleaning his nails. When he got to the part about seeing the strange face in the mirror, the detective stopped the recording and asked him if he would submit to a drug test. Of course, he couldn't. He probably had enough marijuana still coursing through his system to toast the guy giving the test. When he declined the test, the detective said,

"You don't need a detective, Mr. Ellendorff, you need a psychiatrist. Let me give some advice. Lay off that shit you're smoking and get a job, while you can still spell your name!"

"Look, could you just find out what company my cell phone was purchased from?" asked the man with Joel's face. "Then you could trace it to the maniac's digs, his apartment. I'm not crazy!"

"Officially," responded the detective, "I can't take any action until you submit to a drug test. How about it?"

"Okay, okay. I'll be back after lunch."

"Sure you will," smirked the detective, as the man with Joel's face walked out.

It was at that point that he decided to go to California. It was just too scary to hang around Joel's digs, his ruins! After leaving a key for Sammi at the restaurant, with a note to feed the turtles, the man in search of himself started hitchhiking to Hollywood. Two days later he was picked up by the California Highway Patrol and booked for possession of an illegal substance, Sammi's bag of weed.

CHAPTER FOURTEEN

SHARKS IN THE PARK

Ken McAlister had been settled in New York's Greenwich Village for a month and had all but forgotten about Joel Ellendorff. He was enjoying a game of chess in Washington Square Park with a young hustler named David Heightly. Since Ken's plan was to lose the game, he was free to take in the beautiful park, teaming with people of all ages. At some distance, in the center of the park, children frolicked in the gushing water of a huge fountain. Fathers and mothers took turns leaving the surrounding benches to snap photos on their cell phones. A short distance from the fountain, people occupied benches in the shade of towering maple trees, listening to an acoustic jazz combo. In every direction young students sat on the grass eating lunch or flirting with each other. Ken couldn't help but admire the wonderful integration of the many races and cultures mingling so freely together. The park was like an enchanted place where people shed their petty fears, gripes and prejudices at the entrance for a day of peace.

Ken loved this park and his Village apartment six blocks away. Here he sat every sunny day at one of the three stone chess tables with a bench full of easy marks, also known as "fish," waiting to test their skill. With David Heightly it was different. He was a full-fledged "chess-shark" in hippy garb. So was Ken, but their personal attitudes toward the game were very different.

Not yet thirty years old, David was, as the saying goes, tall dark and handsome, with a face more stoic than friendly. Except for his curly black hair, which softened his visage, his features accurately portrayed the cold, calculating gambler that he was. He was fairly well read, able to paraphrase Plato, Neitzsche, Karl Marx, and Bobby Fisher, but he had scant insight into human nature.

Unlike Ken, the young Shark played for higher stakes in several places around town, usually Central Park. Most of the money games at Washington Square Park were for small stakes, twenty-five to a hundred dollars. However, when David Heightly was around he would invariably sucker some college kid into raising the stakes, either by pretending to be a college kid himself, new at the game, or by spotting the fish a rook or a bishop, or one double move—he was that good.

On a couple of occasions Ken watched the Shark cash a student's tuition check and win it all from him in several games. Of course, the young student was devastated and tried to borrow some of it back, but the Shark just put his earphones on and listened to music until the fish stopped pleading and walked away. In one instance, when the Shark suckered a student out of his rent money he turned to Ken smirking, "Don't worry, his mommy and daddy can afford it."

Ken looked forward to the day he would break the Shark, but that wasn't today. Whenever Ken took up a money game with college kids he always warned them that he was a pro and he didn't need their money. The smart fish learned to take him seriously, while others, along with many newcomers, donated foolishly. Ken viewed his fish as students paying for their lessons. And he never allowed any fish to gamble his rent or tuition. He would say to them, "Look, I don't care if you have to live on mustard sandwiches this week! Just pay your tuition and your rent first—then come back and donate to me."

Ken really didn't live on the small stakes he won at the park. He made most of his money playing professionals online. Those games, hosted by a Chinese Internet company, were played for thousands of dollars a match. Ken's online pseudonym was "Uncle Sam," which was fitting, for unlike many of the international money players, he paid the taxes due on his annual winnings. The ex-priest's prowess as a chess player wasn't the result of endless study of the Grand Masters and their strategies. He had a photographic memory and uncanny intuition at divining his opponent's strategies. Because of his keen memory, with some research into their previous games he could just about predict the trusted strategies of most of his opponents. With that advantage Ken was able to lure them into one of his elaborate traps. Ken also researched his opponents carefully, avoiding games with truly gifted players. Even as skilled as Ken was at the game, he lost a match on occasion, usually when his body was giving him such discomfort and pain that he wanted to get the game over with. All things considered, he made a good living playing chess.

David the Shark knew nothing of Ken's online chess prowess. Nor did the elder Shark ever let him in on it, just as he never let anyone in on the fact that he had been a priest. David thought that Ken's altruism toward the fish was born of his handicap, that he lacked the necessary ego strength to claim what by nature he was entitled to. Such subjects never came up between them because they rarely met, and when they did play, Ken's game plan was always to lose a hundred or so and lead the younger Shark into believing Ken had a deficiency in his attention span. When David played chess, on or off the clock, he talked to himself incessantly, which further distracted his opponents. Away from the game, while waiting for a fish he was usually as quiet and stoic as a stone. The only time Ken heard the Shark in any extended conversation was at the sandwich truck, where he got into a debate with a theology major. The Shark challenged the student to reveal God's hand anywhere in life. With every response from the student, the Shark countered with such clear, logical rebuttals that it impressed the ex-priest and left the student crestfallen. The debate ended with the student walking away and the Shark calling after him, "Life's a crapshoot, dude, with more crap than shoot! Face it and get a job that'll pay you enough to offset the pain of it all!"

A couple of co-eds at the truck applauded the victory. The Shark was, as the younger generation would say, "way cool." However, Ken sensed that there was a festering rage boiling beneath the cool, handsome exterior of the young hustler. After that debate, the Shark got involved with one of the co-eds and they walked off together. Ken was fascinated by the dubious young hustler, wondering how someone as young and advantaged as he was could have become so cynical. This is especially rare, thought Ken, in someone with such an insufferable ego.

Once, when he won a couple of hundred from Ken, he commented, "God, you're easy!" never realizing the bankruptcy Ken had planned for him. When the Shark wasn't around, Ken could enjoy the lessons he imparted to his opponents. Even when playing on the clock Ken could carry on small talk with people watching the game, because none of the park opponents came even close to Ken's level of play.

Ken knew better than anyone that the game of life wasn't fair in the least. Even when he was a priest he didn't believe that God somehow interceded in the affairs of people to establish justice or fairness—not in this world! All fairness resided in Heaven, where it awaited the faithful upon their physical demise. Today, in the ex-priest's mind he could understand what hope the idea of Heaven provided the ill-fated poor and handicapped. But he could no longer be party to it. Life, as he saw it now, was like a hand of showdown poker, where everyone is dealt just five cards from a shuffled deck. There is no option to receive more cards, as in Draw Poker. The deck is not stacked for or against anyone. Your hand may be anything from great to terrible, but you can only play the cards you were dealt. The young Shark, along with every person on earth with just two exceptions, was doing just that, playing the hand dealt to them.

The two exceptions, of course, were Zackary Taylor (formally Ebizer Taulb) and Ken McAlister. Each had the power to choose a new and much improved hand in the game of life.

And maybe it was this most unfair advantage that kept the ex-priest from being just as cynical as the Shark. When Ken first met David at the park he never thought of him as a candidate for the switch. He had already chosen a college senior majoring in sports medicine, named Timothy Gales. Gales was a twenty-three year old Caucasian, six foot two, whose biological parents put him up for adoption at birth. He carried some heavy psychological baggage, even suicidal tendencies, all having to do with abusive treatment at the hands of his foster parents. Of late, however, the school shrink cut Gales back to one session a month. He really was becoming a friendly, well-adjusted person, while maintaining a B average. Besides that, he was in excellent physical health, which Ken bore witness to while watching him play in the impromptu rugby games at the park. Ken also knew that any psychological damage would disappear with the soul after the switch. Gales also liked to play chess, which is how Ken met him. Ignoring numerous requests for lessons from other students, Ken took Timothy Gales under his wing, giving him inexpensive private lessons at his apartment. Ken knew everything he needed to know about Gales for a successful switch, including the fact that he wasn't involved with any military programs. Another small advantage was that the young switch candidate's favorite drink was orange juice, which would completely conceal the yellow potion. However, the perfect candidate had accepted a six-week student internship at Texas A&M. That Gales would be out of town for six weeks was but a minor imposition for Ken, whose life could be defined as one imposition after another. Besides, he would have no problem waiting in the interim, for something new and refreshing had entered his plans. Her name was Bethany Burton. She was just nineteen and unspoiled by the world.

CHAPTER FIFTEEN

IDENTITY THEFT

While ex-priest Ken McAlister had all but forgotten Joel Ellendorff, the man with Joel's face was still dealing with his identity crises.

It was the fantasies that caused most of the trouble for Private Joel Ellendorff. Now, Major Bifford (Biff) Galloway would take a crack at them; at least that was the good doctor's intention. Galloway was the Army's Chief of Staff at the Psychiatric Wing of the Fort Cluster Medical Center.

Joel was let into Major Galloway's office by an M.P. wearing large yellow earmuffs, to preserve the confidentiality between doctor and patient. The M.P. told Joel to sit and remain seated in a large leather chair facing the Major's desk some fifteen feet away. The purpose of the layout was obvious. Should the mental patient leave the chair without express permission, the M.P. stationed beside the chair could subdue him before he reached the good doctor.

The office décor spoke volumes about the Major's world view. Large framed photos of President Truman and General MacArthur hung on either side of an American Flag on one wall. On the opposite wall hung a huge painting of the Japanese Admiral surrendering his sword to MacArthur aboard the battleship Missouri. Several feet away on the same wall hung a painting of the "Enola Gay," the B-29 that dropped the first atomic bomb on Hiroshima. Between the two large windows behind the Major's desk was a grandiose painting depicting the U.S. hockey player draped in an American flag on the ice after the U.S. defeated the Russians for Olympic gold at Lake Placid.

Major Galloway was seated behind his desk perusing the patient's medical records which included words like "paranoia," "schizophrenia," and "amnesia." Joel really didn't look deranged when the military police took custody of him at the L.A. County Jail. Notwithstanding, less than four hours in U.S. Army custody and he looked quite deranged, with his head shorn and wearing yellow Army fatigues. Perhaps it was the Major's age and his thin hair brushed back on the sides beneath his receded hairline that reminded Joel of Jack Nicholson in *A Few Good Men*.

"It's all in now," Joel thought, with no little trepidation, as the Major slid the computer aside and addressed him directly.

The following is the complete transcript recorded at Major Biff Galloway's first session with Private Joel Ellendorff.

FORT CLUSTER MEDICAL FACILITY 6/4/2011
TRANSCRIPT OF PSYCHIATRIC EVALUATION FOR
PFC JOEL ELLENDORFF, SERIAL # US51459412
CONDUCTED BY MAJOR BIFFORD GALLOWAY

GALLOWAY: Why do you really want to get out of the Army, son? Just tell me the truth—no flimflam, no screwy-looey, no BS. Consider this before you answer. I have no ulterior motive, no earthly reason to keep you in this man's Army at the cost of good taxpayer money. I can, with the stroke of this pen get you discharged. And all you have to do is tell me the truth.

ELLENDORFF: It's not the Army, sir, I swear it! If you discharge me I will never blame, sue or talk smack about the Army. The Truth is I don't belong here. I never enlisted, sir. I'm not who everyone thinks I am.

GALLOWAY: Okay, Private Ellendorff, you've decided to waste my time. Let me clue you in up front. This session is being videotaped. See those tiny cameras in the ceiling? In the next few minutes I'm going to ensnare you in your own words— sink you in your own bull feces and send you out of here an honest soldier! Yes, to that dreaded bunker in Afghanistan—that bunker which is presently the cause of the only trauma you are suffering. You're shit scared of war, Ellendorff! And that doesn't count in this man's Army. Now admit it. Look right at that camera and say, "I'm shit scared of war."

ELLENDORFF: Are you serious, sir? GALLOWAY: Of course I'm serious!

ELLENDORFF: Well, all right, I'm scared of war. GALLOWAY: Shit scared, shit scared!

ELLENDORFF: Shit scared! I'm shit scared of war.

GALLOWAY: Now that the real trauma has surfaced, let's examine the story that you contrived to shirk your responsibility to America, and the oath you took when you enlisted.

ELLENDORFF: I never enlisted, sir. Why would I enlist if I'm shit scared of war?

GALLOWAY: You never enlisted… ELLENDORFF: No, sir.

GALLOWAY: According to your records, Private Ellendorff, you enlisted on September 11, 2010. Surely you remember something about that date. It was the anniversary of the 9/11 attack on America.

ELLENDORFF: No, sir, I don't. I don't relate to anything regarding this Ellendorff character. I told the MPs that the day they picked me up.

GALLOWAY: A tad convenient wouldn't you say,

considering you were AWOL for two weeks, you pathetic excuse for a man!

ELLENDORFF: I was in a Los Angeles jail for two weeks. I wasn't knowingly AWOL, sir.

GALLOWAY: Are your testicles sweating, Ellendorff?

ELLENDORFF: My testicles?

GALLOWAY: Are your testicles sweating? Recently, a couple of Harvard researchers discovered that when a man lies repeatedly his balls sweat profusely.

ELLENDORFF: My balls are dry.

GALLOWAY: I'll bet they're sloshing around in your panties as we speak, you spineless turd! You had orders to show up at Chicago's Army Induction Center on April 27th, at 10 a.m. Is that the day you went bonkers, Private?

ELLENDORFF: I had no awareness of such orders. Those were Joel Ellendorff's orders, not mine.

GALLOWAY: Let me be perfectly clear here, Ellendorff. No plea of insanity has ever succeeded in an Army court martial on this base. I'm your last chance to avoid one. Now, man-up and admit you're a lying sack of excrement! Man-up and I will spare you from any court martial proceedings. I'll clean-slate you, Private Ellendorff. You'll be able to stand up like a man and join your unit in Afghanistan.

ELLENDORFF: Major Galloway, I swear I'm not Joel Ellendorff. It sounds crazy, I know, sir. But I can't recall anything about this, this Ellendorff guy. I don't know why his ID and shit were in my possession when I woke up.

GALLOWAY: And it's just a matter of coincidence that you look exactly like him, right down to the kangaroo-shaped mole on your ass! We're talking about an eight-inch kangaroo on your butt cheek, Ellendorff!

ELLENDORFF: I can't explain any of it, sir, not logically.

GALLOWAY: Don't insult my intelligence, you lying, anemic turd! Your own mother flew all the way from England to identify you—to comfort and assure you. She told us about the kangaroo on your ass.

ELLENDORFF: Honestly, I never met that woman before in my life!

GALLOWAY: Then how did she know about the kangaroo, Joel?

ELLENDORFF: Can we forget the freaking kangaroo for a goddamn minute! What about the—

GALLOWAY: No problem, Joel. You've probably spent your whole life trying to forget that kangaroo. Bet you never once took a shower with the other little boys at summer camp. Isn't that why you went AWOL in the first place!

ELLENDORFF: What the hell are you talking about sir?

GALLOWAY: The kangaroo on your ass, Ellendorff. Tell me you don't have a phobia about getting naked with other men—and that's why you're shirking your military duty and why your testicles are dripping with sweat!

ELLENDORFF: Look, I don't know anything about the mole on my ass. I didn't even know it was there until Lieutenant Bosley showed me a photo of it.

GALLOWAY: What about your fingerprints, blood type, shoe size, past photographs? What is all that, some kind of government conspiracy!

ELLENDORFF: Right now it seems as reasonable as anything else.

GALLOWAY: Really, Joel! The CIA slip you a micky— kidnap you—do plastic surgery on your face— tattoo an eight inch marsupial on your hiney!

ELLENDORFF: You're really obsessed with the kangaroo, Major. Do you want to talk about it?

GALLOWAY: Better bridle your tongue, soldier. You're already looking at some fat time in the stockade!

ELLENDORFF: I'm not Joel Ellendorff!

GALLOWAY: Then, who are you, for the record?

ELLENDORFF: For the record, I don't know.

GALLOWAY: Then how do you know you're not Private Joel Ellendorff?

ELLENDORFF: You're not going to like the answer to that question, sir.

GALLOWAY: Try me.

ELLENDORFF: My gut.

GALLOWAY: Your gut! So, your gut is running the show, not your brain.

ELLENDORFF: Everything about this guy Ellendorff just doesn't feel like me. He's a plumber or something, a handyman! He owns turtles! His favorite food is Spam, for Christ's sake!

GALLOWAY: What were you doing hitchhiking in California if not running away from the Army!

ELLENDORFF: I don't know. I was trying to get to Hollywood, to figure things out. I think I was involved with the film industry.

GALLOWAY: I'm well aware of your movie star fantasies, Private. Your file is filled with them.

ELLENDORFF: Why is it then, in my dreams I hang with actors, directors, agents?

GALLOWAY: Why is it then, that no one in Hollywood knows you?

ELLENDORFF: Of course they don't. This is not my real face.

GALLOWAY: You steaming pile of excrement! Are you aware that it's not humanly possible to be as crazy as you're pretending to be?

ELLENDORFF: What about the psycho who drugged me?

GALLOWAY: The spooky guy in the wheelchair, whoooo…

ELLENDORFF: Yes, did anyone check him out? He's the one who did this to me!

GALLOWAY: Listen to yourself, how ridiculous you sound, how ridiculous your whole story sounds! Don't tell me your testicles aren't swimming right now!

ELLENDORFF: Read the whole report. Army doctors verified that my throat and lungs show signs of being severely chafed.

GALLOWAY: The Army lab found no trace of poison in your system—just a hell of a lot of taco sauce in your lungs.

ELLENDORF: Tabasco sauce!

GALLOWAY: Well, that couldn't have felt wonderful, Joel! What did you do, choke on a tamale?

ELLENDORFF: You're hilarious. You ought to try stand-up.

GALLOWAY: Look, Private Ellendorff, I've taken an adversarial approach with you because…well, you have to admit, your story is beyond belief. What do you say, we call a truce. I can accept that you're not faking, that you actually have some memory loss, some form of amnesia. We can work with that—it's treatable. But you have to agree to accept the irrefutable evidence, that you are Joel Ellendorff. How's that sound?

ELLENDORFF: Okay, I'll try. I'll try. I really want to get my head straight, sir—believe me!

GALLOWAY: Excellent! Let's start with your very

first memory; tell me everything that happened up to this present moment.

ELLENDORFF: Sir, I already did that. Lieutenant Bosely recorded it when I first arrived.

GALLOWAY: I know, I reviewed it. But I'd like to hear it again, directly from you so I can monitor any subtle inflections in your speech, which could reveal a tiny ray of light into your memory. Tell your story Private.

Major Biff Galloway wasn't really looking for a tiny "ray of light" into Private Ellendorff's memory. No, the canny Major was looking for great big discrepancies in his story, which he could use to nail his "lying anemic ass" to the wall at a court martial.

Ellendorff, on the other hand, still wasn't a hundred percent sure he didn't have amnesia. When he finished telling the Major his story, he was dismissed and escorted back to his windowless room with the padded walls.

CHAPTER SIXTEEN

A NEW LIFE IN A NEW WORLD

H er name was Bethany Burton. Her family still called her Bethany, but to all others she was Beth. Like David, the Shark, she had dropped out of the mainstream of life, choosing to live each day as it came to her. Unlike David though, she celebrated life, danced in the miracle of it, and believed, as many in her generation did, that "God is love."

She was only nineteen, but her delicate features and delightful countenance made her appear even younger. She left home after high school to find the meaning of life, on her own terms. She was an artist and a folk singer, but she lived on the money she made hosting children's birthday parties. Her handcrafted advertising flyers could be found on bulletin boards throughout the downtown area. The flyers included pictures of the face paintings she did for the children, which were extraordinary. However, most of the area parties were hosted by "Birthday's Inc.," a huge company offering everything from clowns to midgets who did magic. Sometimes the company would hire Beth to do face painting when their in-house artist couldn't make it.

Ken met her when he first moved into his ground floor apartment on Bleeker Street. To get the apartment, he was required to foot the remodeling bill. It cost him nineteen thousand plus for the entry ramp, the changing of all doors to sliding doors, the lowering of the sinks, stove, cabinets and closets, as well as the installation of an entire handicap bathroom. He spent another sixteen hundred for a beige and maroon living room carpet and white drapes, which went with his beige wallpaper and accentuated his dark walnut furnishings. All this was provided by his online chess victories.

Beth lived behind him on the same floor, but she paid half as much rent because she cleaned the yard and hallways. In the winter she shoveled the snow. The building owner, a somewhat gruff character, Attos Albaniack, introduced Ken to her the day he arrived.

The following day, Beth knocked on Ken's door holding a kitten. She invited him to come down the hall to the backyard where Cleo, the alley cat, had her kittens, just seven weeks old. Ken was delighted by the lovely girl, who had violet colored angel eyes and long chestnut brown hair which sparkled with highlights of auburn and gold. She was tall and slender, Ken estimating her height to be about five-nine or ten.

Pausing in the doorway, Ken looked out at the backyard where Beth was playing with Cleo and the kittens. He wasn't about to motor into the yard for fear of cracking what appeared to be very thin flagstone. Beth, standing at the cardboard box containing the kittens, called to him,

"Come on over, the flagstone won't break."

That was the first of numerous occasions when Beth would know exactly what was on his mind.

"Oh, no," Ken protested, "you have no idea what this contraption weighs!"

"Don't be silly, Mr. McAlister, I had an elephant back here last week."

The way she said it, with a whimsical smile that mocked reason thoroughly, made Ken laugh.

"Please call me Ken."

"Not unless you come over here and see Cleo's kittens. You're making her sad."

"Well, all right. I hope the owner has good insurance."

Thus, Ken, overruled by her contagious caprice, motored out to the box of kittens. He watched the angel girl gently lift each of the six kits up to display them.

"Aren't they the most precious sweethearts you've ever seen?"

Ken just nodded. Then Beth placed one, a typical grey and black tabby, right in Ken's hands. In an exaggerated male voice she said, "He's the man! 'Top Gun' of the litter! Did you ever own a cat, Ken?"

"No, Beth, my situation doesn't work for pets."

"Oh, right," she said, as though she just became aware that he was wheelchair bound. "I guess dealing with a cat box would be a problem in your situation. If you're up for a little experiment, I'll take care of the cat box. Let's just see if it works out, okay?" Then she hugged Ken, as though he had already agreed, and he agreed. In his whole life he never met anyone who disarmed him completely, who dissolved the many subtle defenses he unconsciously relied upon to feel secure. She was an enigma to him. Most people, especially in her age group, steered clear of handicapped people. Ken knew first hand that people felt uptight around the handicapped, not knowing how to relate appropriately. Ken could sense their thoughts— *"Geez!, I'm sorry God fucked you up like that. I can't tell you how glad I am that it wasn't me."* Paradoxically, this girl Beth was quite at ease around him from the get-go. Ken wondered, "Does she really live without guile, without the self-conscious fears that inhibit most people?" He wanted to know about her, but even more, he wanted to bask in her infectious personality, her open hearted presence.

Within a few days Beth showed up with Top Gun, a newly purchased bag of kitty litter and a half dozen cans of cat food. As she poured the litter into the box she said, "You probably won't need this. If you leave your front window open six inches he will do his duty outside."

Then she removed a supermarket receipt from her woven shopping bag.

"Top Gun's supplies came to $26.34."

Ken immediately removed the money from his chair wallet and thanked her. Placing Top Gun on Ken's lap, she said, "You can have him neutered if you want, but I wouldn't."

"You wouldn't, why not?"

"So he can mate when he wants to, of course."

"Of course," responded Ken, "but isn't there an overpopulation of cats in New York ?"

"There's an overpopulation of everything in New York," Beth countered with a grin.

With that, she pointed her finger at Top Gun and said, "Did you get that? Don't overdo it! This nice man is concerned about the cat population. So, what I suggest is—"

Beth burst into laughter before she could finish her speech. Ken joined her. Her natural delight was contagious and something entirely new to the ex-priest in his wheelchair.

After getting Top Gun and Ken acquainted with some cat rules, Beth went to Ken's state-of-the-art media center.

"We need some music around here!" she remarked as she ran her hand over the cream-colored Sony cabinet, which opened with a touch.

"This cost a bunch! What do you do for a living?"

"I play chess."

"You make a living playing chess? You must be really good!"

"Not really," quipped Ken. "I cheat."

Beth laughed her delightful laugh, as she continued to peruse his collection of CDs.

"Hmm, *New York Philharmonic, Boston Symphony, The Best of Pavarotti, Best of Enya—Norah Jones,* what's she doing in here? *Les Mis,* oh, I love *Les Mis!*"

"One of my favorites too, play it," suggested Ken.

"No, it makes me cry. Oh, you've got Sting. He's cool!"

As the music filled the room, Beth remarked, "You dig Sting, or was his CD a birthday gift?"

Ken never heard of Sting or the album. It was the birthday gift from Joel.

"Sometimes I like a change of pace, you know..."

Ken just stared at the delightful creature standing in his living room. She was dressed in jeans over black Army boots. A yellow stretch halter outlined her beautiful upper body, while her luxuriant hair was pulled back into a haphazard cluster behind her head and held in place by a butterfly hair clip. She wasn't wearing any makeup. She didn't need any. Ken watched as the angel girl removed a piece of string from her pocket and said, "Look, Top Gun wants to dance!"

Teasing Top Gun with the string, she had him up on his hind legs, twirling and dancing around the room with her. In the middle of the song she tossed the string to Ken.

"It's your turn, dude."

Obediently, as though in a trance, Ken started playing with his new roommate. Beth was only in his apartment for a brief hour but the atmosphere remained charged with her presence all day. Several times that morning, while listening to Sting, Ken sniffed the air to see if her faint scent, possibly of Dove soap, was still around. He really had no experience with people like her, people he politely dismissed as "drop-outs." They sometimes crossed his path when he was a priest, but he never considered them as "purposeful people." In his orthodox mind they were rootless adolescents, choosing a hedonistic lifestyle because it afforded them the most freedom and pleasure for the least amount of work. Such was not the case with Beth. Every day she swept down the entire building, and twice a week she put in a full day mopping the halls and steps and waxing the woodwork. Along with that job she hosted children's birthday parties. She also understood cats. Top Gun seldom used the kitty litter, preferring to use the window and do his duty outside. Even so, he managed to be a pain in the ass in numerous other ways. Every now and then he would take to scampering around the room, bouncing off of the furniture and shelves. In his scampering he would occasionally bounce off of Ken, scaring the hell out of him in the process. "The Rascal," as Ken nicknamed him, also preferred human food, and given any opportunity would snag food right from Ken's plate. There was also his repulsive habit of coming in the window with a mouse he caught. Ken would try to escape but the Rascal would usually run him down and drop the mouse on his lap, as if to make the point. *"Hey, I'm not out there chasing tail all day! I'm doing my part to rid the city of vermin—you want this?"*

When Beth showed up each day to check in on "the experiment," he only praised his furry roommate, never wanting Beth to think Top Gun was too much for him to handle. He would never risk losing the one link he had to this delightful girl who brought sunshine into his shaded life.

On the second Friday after he moved in, he found a note taped to his door inviting him to a house party Saturday evening in the backyard. There was a ten dollar donation required to cover the cost of the alcohol and finger food. Beth spent most of Saturday decorating the backyard for the party, stringing multicolored lanterns on a clothesline tied to poles surrounding the yard. Folding tables were set up on the perimeter of the yard to hold the refreshments and sound equipment. In preparation for the party Ken bought some new clothes and spruced up his wheelchair, waxing the vinyl and polishing the chrome. He couldn't stop thinking about her.

CHAPTER SEVENTEEN

GOOD THINGS HAPPEN WHEN LEAST EXPECTED

t was just six days since his session with Major Galloway when Joel was escorted from his room to the Major's office. Private Joel Ellendorff immediately sat in the brown leather chair he occupied on his previous visit.

"Stand up, Ellendorff," commanded the Major. "Come forward and salute me!"

Ellendorff complied and remained standing before the Major's desk, prepared to bare his soul to the good doctor. The last six days confined to his room gave the hapless soldier some fresh insights into his untenable situation. Something terrible had happened to him. A psychopath, assuming there was only one involved, somehow rendered him unconscious and tried to drown him with Tabasco sauce. Those were the facts. The experience seriously damaged his mind because he couldn't remember who he was and didn't believe he was Joel Ellendorff, though the evidence against that supposition was irrefutable. He could spend forever trying to convince the authorities and himself that he wasn't crazy, but to what end? Crazy people are only considered crazy as long as they insist that their illusions are true. To return to sanity they must realize that their illusions fly in the face of reason. It only made sense to accept the fact that he was Joel Ellendorff. So what if his brain cells got rearranged in the Tabasco sauce incident—shit happens! So what if he felt disgusted by the person he actually was, a turtle-loving, spam-eating moron. All that could be changed. Hell, Sammi already said he was a new man between the sheets! So where's the real pain in starting out from scratch, as the new and improved Joel Ellendorff? In time, maybe his memory would reveal who the wheelchair psycho was, and then he could pursue having him arrested and put away. In the meantime, he would accept his military obligation, succumb to whatever fate was in store for him. It made perfectly good sense to plead with the Major to clean-slate him and ship him to Afghanistan, kiss his tight ass and avoid the court martial.

The fact was that Major Glenn Galloway had already signed Private Ellendorff's discharge papers. Not because he believed it was the right thing to do—far from it! He knew for certain that Joel's cowardly testicles were drenched with sweat during the evaluation but needed time to prove it. Unfortunately, he wasn't the final word in such situations. He could only make a recommendation to General Eugene Cox, the base commander.

FORT CLUSTER ARMY BASE 6/10/11
EVALUATION OF PFC ELLENDORFF US51459412 (NOT PRESENT)
PRESENT: GENERAL EUGENE COX AND MAJOR BIFFORD GALLOWAY.

COX: Major, I'll get right to the point. Your recommendation regarding Private Ellendorff seems unreasonable to me. You say, and I'm reading directly from your evaluation now, "Private Ellendorff is a clever and devious individual, who is faking a whole host of mental illnesses to get out of the Army." And that, Major Galloway, is your professional diagnosis?

GALLOWAY: Yes, sir. If given a few more weeks I'll be able to prove it.

COX: I beg to differ with you, Major, but his profile depicts a total fruitcake, a psychopath who is not only a danger to himself, but given a weapon could become a danger to everyone in his vicinity.

GALLOWAY: Sir, he's faking as sure as I'm standing here!

COX: Really, Major! Would any sane man inhale a bottle of Tabasco sauce?

GALLOWAY: Please sir. Let's just court-martial this spineless turd! A few weeks in the stockade and he'll come clean as a bleached bed sheet!

COX: He's nuts, Major! He's got amnesia. He's never going to be fit for duty. Section Eight him immediately, before he adds himself to the list of suicides around here!

GALLOWAY: Okay, forget the stockade—let's just pen him up, sir, in a padded room for a few months and break his lying wet balls!

GENERAL COX: His lying wet balls! Is that what you said?

GALLOWAY: It's just an expression sir. It doesn't connote any medical relevance. But given a few months in an isolated room, with no windows and an occasional visit from me, and this lying sack of excrement will own up to his military obligation!

COX: A few months! Who's got the fucking time for such shit!

GALLOWAY: General, can I be frank? I mean, can I make an honest soldier-to-soldier recommendation, sir?

COX: What is it, Major?

GALLOWAY: We don't need a few months, sir. Let

me quietly and secretly water-board this candy-
ass and—

COX: Major Galloway, this is a direct order.
Give Private Ellendorff a medical discharge
immediately! I mean today! Is that clear?

GALLOWAY: Yes sir, but—

COX: You're dismissed, Major!

Thus, Major Galloway wrote his signature on Ellendorff's medical discharge, never knowing that had he withheld it five minutes longer he would have been vindicated, would have defeated the anemic turd! Thus, Major Galloway looked up at the turd standing before him and said, "Here's your discharge, Ellendorff. You are officially designated medically unfit to serve in the United States Army. You're free to go! Pick up your belongings at the Quartermaster's office on the first floor. But know this, you lying sack of excrement—I'm not that far away from retirement. I just might be looking you up."

Joel didn't hesitate a moment. He turned and ran directly to the base Quartermaster's storage facility, retrieved his civilian clothes and a check for six weeks' pay. After cashing his check at the PX, the ecstatic ex-soldier hopped a bus to the Greyhound station in town. Not pausing to eat or drink, Joel took a bus to Los Angeles, feeling like a bird who just flew free of his cage.

CHAPTER EIGHTEEN

WALKING IN FIELDS OF GOLD

On the evening of the party Ken waited until it was in full swing before he rolled down the hall into the yard. He was surprised to see so many people. Obviously some of the tenants brought friends. Even Attos, the "owner dude," as Beth referred to him, was there with his wife and two young children. He was the first to say hello and introduce Ken to several of the tenants. Such parties were rare in Ken's experience. People don't invite priests to parties, especially priests in wheelchairs. He planned to have a quick glass of wine and exit the scene.

Attos was pulled away by his six-year-old daughter, who insisted he dance with her. Ken made his way to the refreshment table, being extremely careful not to run over anyone's foot. Cleo the cat was under the table wearing a festive yellow bow around her neck. Ken was pouring himself a glass of Black Opal Shiraz when he felt a pair of hands clasp his shoulders from behind.

"How are you doing?" Beth said in his ear to counter the loud music.

"So far okay. I haven't run over anyone yet."

Close to his ear again she said, "Better drink up. The place is packed with freeloaders."

Though he hadn't sipped his wine yet, her angel voice in his ear made his heart beat faster.

"Come," she said as she poured herself a tall glass of wine. "I'll introduce you to our family."

Ken gently tugged on her delicate wrist and she bent down to hear him.

"Please, don't worry about me. Go and enjoy yourself."

"Hey, dude," she quipped. "It's my party! If I want to hook up with the hottest dude in the mix, that's what goes down!"

Ken had all he could do to repress the emotions he felt. If only for one evening in his life he could actually be the "hottest dude," it would be this evening with her. He managed a chuckle and dutifully accompanied her through the crowd. She made sure he met all of the tenants. Most were professionals, his age or older, who worked either in the arts or on Wall Street. There were two younger guys her age, who were roommates, Duncan, an Afro-American, and Jeff, a blond Caucasian. When introduced, Duncan quipped, "We make salt and pepper shakers for a living." Everyone laughed. Actually, they were aerial performers in the Broadway musical, *Spiderman*. Neither was the star of the show but they easily shared the award for "hottest dude at the party." Ken could sense their uptightness as Beth introduced him. And why shouldn't they be uptight, Ken thought, as Beth went on to explain that they were aerial acrobats who performed the stunts as Spiderman in the show. Each was wearing a form fitting t-shirt that revealed bodies fit for a comic book hero. Ken was quick to dissolve the strained atmosphere.

"What a great gig!" Ken chimed in. "You dudes get to fly through the air every night to the thrill of the audience! Wow! I actually auditioned for the show and the producers were amazed by my aerial gymnastics but, alas, we couldn't figure out how to fit my wheel chair into the costume."

There was a heart-stopping pause, before everyone simultaneously erupted with laughter. The ice was broken. The evening belonged to the new guy in the family, for a little while anyway. Toward midnight, with the Attos family and half the crowd gone, Duncan turned off the music and insisted that Beth sing. She declined, claiming to be too wasted. But the crowd would not take no for an answer. Even though Ken's catheter was close to full, he would stay to hear her sing. Everyone waited while Beth went inside to get her guitar. Jeff, the Spiderman double, turned to Ken. "Have you ever heard Beth sing?" Ken shook his head.

"Get ready for the highlight of the evening."

When Beth returned, she sat on a folding table and tuned her guitar. Looking down on her instrument she had to sweep her long hair back over her bare shoulders cresting like white caps above the ruffles of her mint green blouse. She was wearing white shorts, and her long elegant legs were gently crossed at the ankles below the table. She looked like one of those porcelain figurines just too beautiful to be real. Ken lifted his cell phone from his pocket, positioned it in the clip on the arm of his wheel chair and pressed the video icon. When her guitar was tuned she sang her first song, a modern folk song written by Sting, "Fields Of Gold," the verse of which would remain an indelible refrain in Ken's heart:

> You'll remember me when the west wind moves
> Upon the fields of barley
> You can tell the sun in his jealous sky
> When we walked in fields of gold

Ken had his perfect night. While everyone applauded, he left quietly, tears running down his face. They were not tears of self-pity but tears that flow when you experience something just too beautiful to be real.

Something new and extraordinary was happening to him. His thoughts between chess games no longer ran on and on about the coming switch. Instead they ran on about her. Just the sight of her sent warm feelings flowing through him. He would listen for her door to close in the morning so that he could accidentally run into her before he went shopping or to the park. On such occasions they would exchange a quick chitchat about Top Gun or some other trivial matter. He knew she enjoyed his sense of humor, typically exaggerated cynical barbs about New Yorkers or super insensitive remarks about his handicap which would get her howling . More than anything he loved to watch her laugh. He would use every possible device to extend her visits when she stopped in to check on the experiment with Top Gun.

As his new life in New York progressed, Ken made trips to the Music Station, where he elicited the aid of a young clerk to educate him in the music of his generation. As suggested, he bought the recommended folk, rock and country rock tunes: Melissa Etheridge, Adele, Eva Cassidy, David Gary, Sting, Christian Sweetland, Dave Matthews Band, The Loners, and Lady Gaga. He also ordered some vintage classics of Stevey Wonder, Michael Jackson and Joan Baez. He purchased a subscription to *Mother Jones* and *The Village Voice*, which Beth quoted from a couple of times. He also purchased the *Harry Potter* film series on DVD, watching one flick faithfully every night before going to bed. In his quest for a new life, Ken had taken up the arduous task of retraining his soul in the ways of the youth culture of the day. In the process he would let his hair grow long and bought his clothes at shops like The Gap, Banana Republic and Urban Outfitters. During his shopping sprees he bought Beth things too, like "super cool" barrettes, bandanas, earrings and the like, but he never gave them to her, for fear it might offend her. On occasion he would admonish himself "to drop this insane infatuation—wait until you've completed the switch." However, every resolve to postpone his pursuit of her dissolved each time he saw her. One day in a hallway encounter he invited her and her boyfriend to a home-cooked dinner. Her response was music to his ears.

"What boyfriend? I'm between boyfriends right now."

"All right then, bring a girlfriend, or anybody you like. Bring Cleo; I'll cook up some salmon steaks."

"I'm a vegetarian."

"Okay, veggie burgers it is!" proclaimed the man who never walked in fields of gold.

She smiled and said, "Cool. I'll bring the dessert."

"Oh no, not tofu ice cream!"

"No way dude. We are going to have some mouthwatering goat curd in frog froth."

They laughed together.

CHAPTER NINETEEN

HOLLYWOOD, THE HOME
OF GIFTED WAITERS

On the bus he reviewed his plan, to accept himself as Joel Ellendorff. All of his recent insights still made the most sense. True, he didn't have the threat of the stockade to deal with, but why waste his life trying to find the wheelchair psycho? Just accept the new life of Joel Ellendorff and "follow your bliss." If your memory reveals the psycho, nail the fuck—otherwise get on with the rest of your life. By the time the bus reached the terminal in L.A. he had resolved his identity crisis. He was Joel Ellendorff, a young man in pursuit of an acting career.

Getting started wouldn't be easy, with only fourteen hundred dollars in his pocket, but he felt inspired. It would not be just a foolhardy venture either. The first thing he bought when he got off the bus was a push button knife to protect himself. Later, as his economic conditions improved, he would buy a gun just in case there was a personal factor involved in the attempted Tabasco sauce drowning. First, he had to find an apartment and a job.

Upon questioning the ticket agent in the terminal, he received directions to the cheapest digs in town, the YMCA. Joel walked the eight blocks to a five story gray brick building bearing a sign above its entrance, "Young Men's Christian Association." He entered the less than upscale lobby which reeked of Clorox and cigarette smoke. A huge window that looked out on the street let in plenty of light which over exposed the threadbare, once green carpet. A dilapidated set of over stuffed chairs was situated with a couple of standing ash trays beneath a sputtering neon light. Joel walked to the check in desk at the back wall displaying numbered boxes. He hit the bell on the desk and a very old man stood up who had been asleep on a beanbag behind the desk.

"Do you have to be Christian to rent a room here?" asked Joel.

"This ain't the YMCA no more," responded the old man. "But you can rent the room for sixteen bucks a night…or a hundred a week."

"I'll take two weeks to start," said Joel, removing his wallet.

"Don't you wanna see a room first?"

"No, as long as it's clean…oh, do you have a smoke free room?"

"They're all smoke free…no one can smoke except in this here lobby."

While checking in Joel asked, "What's the name of this place? This registration card still has YMCA on it."

"That's still the name, far as I know…though it's not the YMCA no more…hasn't been for years."

"Cool!"

After checking in Joel went out to buy a cheap cell phone and some writing supplies.

On the outside chance that he might actually possess some skills as a handyman, he printed up some flyers advertising himself as "The Fix All, Go-To-Guy." After two weeks of zero calls, he landed a job waiting tables at Caminos Italian restaurant, which required buying a secondhand bike to get there. As he quickly found out, waiting tables was the preferred occupation of most aspiring actors because you're always guaranteed to have something to eat.

Joel lived on the meager four dollars an hour salary and invested two months of tips, twenty-four hundred dollars, in some clothes and an acting class with the not-so-noted screen actress, "Sonia Ammonia." Sonia was a younger looking fifty-something. Her real name was Sorrenson, but she used the ridiculous pseudonym, Ammonia, because she worked more as a stand-up comedienne than a film or TV actress. Naturally, she emphasized comedic acting, flip, tongue-in-cheek stuff that was presently the rage on TV sitcoms and commercials. After just six of her classes, however, she assigned Joel the principal role in two scenes from a dramatic play.

Joel never heard of the play, but upon reading it through, thought it was brilliant. His character was a young drifter who returns home for his mother's funeral and has to deal with his womanizing father. Sonia told him to be ready to perform the scene in three days. He was somewhat baffled when he asked which classmate would play the father and Sonia said the playwright himself.

"This is not an audition, is it?" asked Joel.

"Oh," replied Sonia, "Now you went and spoiled my surprise."

"Hey, thanks, but I'm not ready for this."

"Trust me, dude, you are, or I wouldn't have recommended you. Be here at six on Friday."

"Shoot, I'm working Friday night."

"Take off, dude!"

"I can't really. I just started a couple of months ago."

"Take off, Joel. The director and the playwright are flying in to audition three people, and you're one of them."

"Oh, no pressure there! Why me?"

"You've got levels, kid. And, hey, there are no guarantees."

Joel was thrilled at the opportunity. He arranged to switch shifts with another waiter and got a down-and-out actor, Julian Moore, at the YMCA, to cue him. Julian, an African American in his sixties, didn't mind cuing Joel as long as he supplied the beer. Julian was of average height and surprisingly muscular for someone his age. He had short, hardly combed black hair, tufted in places. His eyes were bloodshot, as one would expect of someone who drank and smoked all day. But he didn't mumble, or stumble or dress in shoddy clothes like an unfocused derelict. In fact, he was well read and articulate even though he harbored a rather cynical outlook on life. In his own words, Julian referred to himself as a "diamond in the rough."

As agreed upon, Joel brought a six pack of Bud and joined Julian in the equipment room of the YMCA gym. Julian was good for the first fifteen minutes of cuing, but then he looked at the title on the script, *Don't Call Me Son*, and decided to get something off his chest.

"You read the trade papers, bro?"

Joel replied, "No, bro, I can't afford it."

"You can't afford it!" repeated Julian mockingly.

"Is that a crime? I can barely afford my cell phone!"

"Well, then, tell me something. Have you stepped in a pile of dog shit recently?"

"Of all the many mishaps that Murphy has tossed in my path lately," Joel replied, "that particular one missed me!"

Julian continued his aside, "It's just an old superstition, that it's good luck if you step in dog shit. And the deeper the shit the greater the luck! It never worked for me, though. I've stepped in dog shit so deep I've had to leave my shoe behind. No, it never worked for me! And I'm the most talented goddamn actor on this fucking planet!" shouted Julian in the dusty room filled with ancient gym equipment.

"Why not take a moment to vent, bro. I don't think they heard you in Spain!"

"Fuck Spain!"

"What's going on, man?"

"This play we're rehearsing is bound for Broadway, you mindless cracker!"

"You're shittin' me!" exclaimed Joel.

"Jesus, man! You don't even read the trades and this fucking audition falls into your lap! Lady fuckin' luck! Do you know how many actors, who have been struggling for years to perfect their craft—washing dishes to survive, never get a shot at a Broadway show? I know actors who would sacrifice their genitalia for a part like this!"

"Chill, dude, I didn't get the part yet."

"God, I hope you don't! What are you, twenty-three, twenty-four… got off the bus last week with stars in your eyes! You don't go to New York and stand in line with a thousand actors waiting to read for the part! No, the director and playwright fly out here to see you! How does that happen? Please, somebody, before I check out of this fucked-up life, tell me how the dog shit trick works!"

"The playwright is my acting teacher's brother."

"Oh, you didn't mention that. Hey, I shouldn't have said that I hope you don't get the part. I'm sorry. What I really hope is that God dies and the world ends before you even get a chance to audition!"

Joel burst into laughter at Julian's diatribe. Joel bought another six pack and the two actors got drunk together. Before parting from the empty gym to their rooms, Joel invited Julian to join him on Saturday to see the new film *Arctic Storm*. Julian declined, saying, "I just know that film is going to be too white for me!"

CHAPTER TWENTY
DINING ON HOPE

On the evening of the dinner, Ken spent an hour and a half dressing himself. He went through several pairs of pants and shirts before deciding on khaki college trousers, a tie-dyed Nehru shirt and desert boots. Over the shirt he wore a crystal pendant which he discarded the moment Beth knocked on the door. He purchased a blow-dryer for his hair, giving it a hip tousled look, but became concerned about the quantity of gray it revealed. Several times in the course of his frantic attempts to shed ten years he stopped, looked directly into the mirror and said, "Idiot!"

Ken had better luck with the dinner, "Vegetarian Delight with Noodles," which he prepared from a cook book titled *Chinese Favorites*. Beth showed up with a covered dish of homemade brownies and Cleo the cat under her arm. When she released Cleo the evening took off in high gear, with Top Gun and his mom tearing around the apartment after each other. Upon releasing the cat she bent down and gave Ken a friendly hug. She was wearing a blouse, candy apple in color, buttoned up so that only a hint of her cleavage was exposed. While such sexual allurements didn't affect Ken the way they did healthy men, he was able to appreciate the sheer elegance of the lines, curves and shadows of her body, as one appreciates a stunning work of art. She also wore Levis and a pair of rope sandals.

With the opening greetings, Ken offered Beth a choice of wines, a chilled Kendal Jackson chardonnay or a San Geovachi Mole, Ken's favorite red wine. They started with the white. Their initial conversation centered around music and movies, though Ken took every opportunity to get her to talk about herself.

Thanks to the clerk at the music store and the Harry Potter DVDs, Ken came across as cool. Lady Luck was partially with him. Beth's all-time favorite movies were *Wedding Crashers,* which Ken did not see, and *Avatar,* which Ken saw and wrote a series of sermons on. Of course, he never mentioned his affiliation with the church, and he never would. He was well aware that Beth was not into traditional religion, which revealed her independent spirit. On a couple of evenings when he arrived home he heard her doing some kind of religious chanting, which had an East Indian sound. He thought it was beautifully weird but typical of the anti-establishment youth culture.

While Beth continued to carry the conversation, Ken said, "Please rap on," and rolled to the stove to fetch the appetizers, cheese wantons and spring rolls with duck sauce. When Beth realized what he was doing she insisted on helping, but he protested.

"Please sit down. This is the only exercise this wheelchair ever gets. Look at how fat these tires are getting!"

Beth chuckled and sat down. It was better this way, for in serving her Ken had every reason to move close to her, to feel her warmth, to breathe in her scent, to bask in her delightfulness. With her second glass of wine, Beth, the most unpretentious person Ken had ever met, did finally open up on a personal level. Beth was quite content to let Ken serve dinner, while she spoke freely about her strained relationship with her family. They were ultra conservatives, who made huge contributions to both of Bush's successful campaigns for the presidency and McCain's failed bid for the office. Beth, on the other hand, campaigned for Al Gore and John Kerry, and believed that George Bush stole both elections. At that juncture she threw in the towel on politics, but then Barack Obama came along promising hope for the downtrodden and poor. She joined his New York campaign organization and worked tirelessly to get him elected. At this point in his presidency she had lost hope in him. In her mind Obama wasn't at fault. She just accepted that his idealism couldn't prevail against the selfish interests of the multinational corporations who owned the politicians running the country. She believed the political system was so corrupt that nothing short of armed revolution could fix it.

Beth wasn't one to blame or complain. She just did "the next best thing," which was a phrase she used to define her core philosophy. In short, she would pursue that which seemed to her made for happiness, not just for herself but for everyone and everything sharing "Mother Earth" with her. If what she pursued didn't work out, she dropped it and pursued "the next best thing." She refused to entertain negative emotions. She saw life as an incredible, miraculous gift and lived it accordingly. In regard to her family and their conservative values, for which they ostracized her, Beth held no ill will. Nor did she harbor negative feelings for her older brother in the Air Force, who was presently flying sorties in Afghanistan. At one point Ken asked her what her plans were for the future.

"I don't have any right now. I'm sure I'll travel some more, "she said, sticking up her hitch-hiking thumb.

"What about a career, don't you want to record that beautiful voice of yours?"

"I don't know. I've written a couple of songs...Maybe someday. Okay, dude, it's your turn."

"My turn?"

"Yep, I've been blathering away for an hour. It's your turn to blather. Start with your childhood. Tell me about your parents, while I clear the dishes."

Ken had anticipated having to discuss his past and had concocted a whole new back story for his life. But now, eye to eye with the angel girl, he just couldn't bring himself to lie.

"My mother was a self-employed prostitute. I never knew my father."

Beth paused to see whether he was joking.

"Your mother was a prostitute?"

"Yes. Do you know any of the stories in the Bible?"

"I went to a Baptist Sunday school until I was fourteen," responded Beth, looking stunned by his opening remarks.

"Do you recall the story about the woman who was a prostitute but washed the feet of Jesus with her tears?"

"Yes."

"That explains the life and devotion of my mother. And the Lord said—"

"'Because she has loved much, she is forgiven much,'" Beth said, completing the quote.

"You really do know the Bible!" Ken exclaimed.

"Chapter and verse, dude. Tell me about your childhood."

Beth poured them another glass of wine as Ken told his tragic story. Beth shed silent tears and gently held his hand during the telling of it. But there were no tears from Ken, who knew he would be released from his torturous life in a few short weeks. Ken did wind up lying about his education and subsequent adult life as a priest, but he thought it was for the best.

At the first opportunity Ken inquired about dessert. Beth warmed her brownies on the stove, they opened the bottle of red and moved into the living room. They settled in, with her on the sofa and him across from her with the marble top coffee table between them. Ken was really feeling the wine. Never in his life did he ignore his carefully allotted intake of wine and food. Tonight, he was two brownies and a glass of wine beyond his intake quota. Beth chuckled to herself at his disjointed, stoned speech pattern, through her equally stoned ears.

"Do you …believe in miracles…anything like that?" Ken asked.

"What do you mean by miracles…like living, thinking, music, the birth of babies, sunrises, birds, flowers of every scent and color, oceans?"

"No…no, not that…not reasonable miracles…supernatural… you know, the unexplainable miracles. Do you…believe in them?"

"I believe in love…in the final analysis," she uttered almost to herself, "that's all that counts."

"What?"

"Love. It's all that counts."

"Well, it counts…it counts a lot…but I don't know," Ken stammered, wanting with all his heart to say, "I won't always be handicapped." But how would he say it so that it didn't sound insane, even cruel, even evil?

"No, Ken, love is the real miracle! Have you ever read the Dali Lama? The whole purpose of life is to live for love, from love, no matter what!"

"A wonderful sentiment…I agree…but it can get you…into a ton of trouble…trouble, my friend," emphasized Ken. "Where did love get the Dali Lama? The Chinese…took his country!"

"You're missing the point, dude."

"Which is, dude?"

"They took away his country but they couldn't take away his love for life, all of life!"

"I'll drink to that!" Ken said, raising his glass for a toast.

"Hey…is 'dude'…is 'dude' appropriate? I mean to use…in reference to a female…or should it be 'dudess'…or 'Ms. dude?'"

"'Dude' is universal and may be used in reference to anything," chuckled Beth.

Suddenly Ken was gripped with fear. He smelled something horrible, his own excrement. He couldn't tell how far along the bowel movement in his rubber pants had progressed.

"And this dude is drunk, my friend," Ken stated, his fear abolishing his inebriated condition. "What say we call it a night?"

"You talked me into it," Beth quipped, recognizing the panic in his voice, but thinking he was feeling nauseous and had to throw up.

Ken did not escort her to the door, but kept his distance while she searched for her sandals. He was overtaken with cramps. He couldn't wait for her to exit. He merely called to her from across the room, "Thanks for coming over," he gasped, as he motored full speed into the bathroom.

"No, thank you, Ken, for a fabulous dinner," responded Beth to the empty room.

She was torn between her kind-hearted nature and her intuition. She didn't go to the bathroom door but removed a tiny vile of peppermint oil from her purse and placed it on the kitchen table.

"Peppermint," she called out to him. "I left some on the kitchen table. It will settle your stomach…see you tomorrow."

Ken, bent over in agony, heard every word through the bathroom door.

"Thank God!" he thought. "She thinks I have an upset stomach."

Outraged at his "God damned" condition, Ken shoved himself out of his wheelchair on to the floor of the shower. He tore his pants off with his bare hands, all the time cursing himself for abandoning his life long regiment regarding food and drink intake. In the throes of anger his rubber pants filled with wet feces got hung up on his shoes. "And why, why, why," he grumbled, "didn't he induce a bowel movement before his dinner date! It would have been so simple, routine really, something he did every morning using a suppository."

Disgusted, sick, and whirling with vertigo, he turned on the shower and let the warm water wash the urine and shit from his legs. While he was accustomed to all kinds of pain and discomfort, the feeling of vertigo was something new. As he contemplated this new distress he began hallucinating—bottomless pits, out of which darted weird dreadful gargoyles striking terror in his heart—murky landscapes with severed heads and pieces of bloody anatomy strewn all over—

After an hour of self-loathing and horror, Ken pulled himself out of the shower, donned his bathrobe and climbed into his wheelchair. He carefully attached a new fluids collection bag to his catheter tubing before gathering his sopping wet clothes into a plastic trash bag. The hallucinations persisted as he motored into the living room where he took several of his prescribed painkillers. He then pulled himself into his stuffed recliner, picked up the remote that was stationed there and turned on the TV. He spent the night phasing in and out of strange hallucinations involving the Dali Lama, alchemist Taulb, Joel, and the ancient performer Carol Channing.

Ken was still in the recliner when Beth tapped on the door the following morning. He knew it was Beth and quickly mounted his wheelchair.

"Who is it?"

"Beth."

"Just a minute," he called out, while running his hair brush through his hair.

Ken rolled to the door, pretending to unlock it before opening to her. She was on inline skates, the additional height adding to her goddess-like visage. A white and gold headband circled her head, allowing her radiant hair to fall naturally about her bare shoulders. Her flawless upper body was accentuated by a gold and white tank top, which matched her short pleated skirt. From his lower point of view, if he looked, which he didn't, Ken could see the white panty brief beneath her skirt, a view that would have aroused the marble statue of St. Paul in the Vatican.

"Are you going outside like that?"

"Like what?"

"Beth, if you go skating through the streets in that outfit there will be traffic accidents all around you. Have you no regard for public safety!"

"Never mind me, how are you feeling?" she asked.

Beth was seriously concerned because she did a foolish thing; she had lightly laced the brownies with Cannabis flakes. When Ken suddenly took sick she wondered if the dope might have some harmful effect upon her fragile friend.

"I'm cool," responded Ken. "Come in."

"You looked a little green when I left last night," said Beth, as she rolled into the apartment. Top Gun was immediately at her feet. She took him into her arms.

"Oh, that was nothing, just a touch of nausea. I shouldn't have eaten the rest of the brownies, though," Ken said, waiting to catch her reaction.

Beth's eyes widened,

"You ate the rest of the brownies!"

"There were only four left."

Truly freaked out by the thought, Beth responded, "You didn't. My God, say you didn't!"

"Yes. I figured here's my opportunity to walk. But I couldn't pry myself loose from the ceiling fan to do so."

"So you were on to me," the goddess giggled with relief.

"Not right off. It hit me after you left. I realized you had drugged me sometime toward the end of *Hello Dolly*, the movie I watched on TV with the sound off."

Ken and Beth shared another hearty laugh.

"You have to try that, watch *Hello Dolly* with the sound off while you're stoned. It gives a whole new meaning to the plot."

Ken did sit through the movie with the sound off but not while experiencing a euphoric high. He was very sick with vertigo and cramps all night. He would never want his angel girl to feel bad, so he continued to joke about being stoned. He literally cherished their friendship. His high was her. He told himself that his love for her was pure friendship, while he fought the heart felt idea that he was in love with her—because he couldn't be—because it wasn't permitted by life's decree. Over and over again he dismissed the impossible idea of her ever being able to love him as a partner, though he knew for certain, that given the choice of a perfect physical life without her or a handicapped life with her, he would choose the latter.

CHAPTER TWENTY ONE

BOX OFFICE, BOX OFFICE, BOX OFFICE

K ylie Bolinger, personal secretary to the star Zack Taylor, sat in his palatial living room sorting through a bag of mail, mostly fan mail. Now at least she knew Zack could afford this Beverly Hills estate. After a month of delays on the shoot and twelve-million dollars over budget, the studio released *Arctic Storm*. As the byline in the Hollywood Reporter stated, "Arctic Storms the Box Office," cashing eighty-two million on its opening weekend. The fan mail was pouring in, the phones were ringing off the hook. The studio was already hot to trot out the sequel. And where was the star? His secretary didn't know but guessed he was in bed with some babe somewhere. She didn't call him, knowing he wouldn't want to be disturbed. She had waited up for him and was still wearing the black silk negligee she slept alone in.

"What a business," she mused, "it's not about talent—it's not even about who you sleep with any more. It's about what you look like blown up on the silver screen! Are people so mindlessly beguiled by Zack's perfect face and physique they can't discern the vast disconnect in his character's dialogue?!"

But the film's success wasn't all about Zack's face and physique. And the secretary, sometimes bed partner, realized it a few days after the premiere when she watched it again in Zack's private screening room. She realized the real talent came through its director.

Indeed, director Barry Mendelson pulled off some miraculous tinkering in the editing room. At the red carpet premiere, secretary Kylie

134

was a little too toasted to pick up on Mendelson's masterful diversions. A couple of days later in Zack's screening room she got it. Mendelson had added a narration, an over dub of the story in a voice that sounded like Zack Taylor but wasn't. Yes, the canny Mendelson had Zack record the narration but his secretary knew it wasn't him. The dubbing actor spoke with such genuine understanding and emotion that the passion of the Arctic saga was felt. Of course, Zack had some lines on screen but the crafty Mendelson enhanced them with a slight up-tic of the background music. The rest was easy, just keep the audience looking at the breathtaking Arctic scenery, the gorgeous husky, Timber, and Zack's face whenever he didn't look lost. At the second viewing Kylie scanned the credits to make sure of what she already suspected. Zack Taylor was given credit for the narration. This ruse had to cost the studio or Mendelson some big bucks under the table, because even a hint of such chicanery would start the law suits rolling. That the star, Zack Taylor, wouldn't recognize the vocal sham was the biggest chance Mendelson took. Certainly, the egocentric star would have objected to any other actor doing the narration. And if he found out after-the-fact he would sue Mendelson and the studio out of existence. This sham, thought the secretary, is money in the bank, my bank, should I ever need to retire. She wondered who the ghost narrator might be—it would be advantageous to find out.

In the meantime she had Zack's mother, Henrietta, to deal with. She arrived uninvited at the red carpet opening. A security guard and Zack's personal bodyguard tackled her after she broke through the barrier. Kylie's first thought at the skirmish was, "How did this sweet, reserved lady from Nebraska manage to muscle her way through a thousand fans and get through the rope barrier?" The whole fiasco was the star's fault. Kylie begged him to invite his mother to the gala opening but he was adamant. She was invited to come out the following week, when she could see the movie in Zack's screening room. Notwithstanding, there she was on the red carpet.

"Zackary, Zackary, it's me!" she cried out as she ran to embrace her son.

With every camera in Hollywood focused on her when the security guards submarined her, why did her chubby pink legs have to fly up and separate in mid-air? She came down on her shoulders, two guards wrestling her into a facedown double hammer lock. Thankfully, Zack had the wherewithal to grab the men by the hair and yank them off.

Taking his mother in his arms and wiping the blood off her cheek with her dress was both tender and stupid. Still, it played well enough and the reporters rushed in to get the story. Thanks to Henrietta's clever adlibbing the star didn't come across as the biggest asshole on earth.

Following the film, Zack escorted his mom to the ladies room, turned to Kylie and said, "Get that woman out of my life!"

"Zack, Zack, there are reporters everywhere. We've got to take her to the party!"

"This is not her night, goddamn it! It's mine!"

"Keep your voice down, babe. We'll take her to the party in our limo. When we get there I'll take her off your hands. Okay?"

"Okay, but she's not sleeping at the estate. Get her a hotel somewhere."

"Zack, we can't do that. She's your mom."

"What the fuck is she doing here, anyway! I specified next Tuesday!"

"She loves you, Zack. Let her stay at the estate."

"Okay, okay! But keep her upstairs."

"And how am I supposed to do that?"

"I don't know! Lock her in her room. Tell her there are snakes everywhere! Anything! I just want to celebrate when I get home!"

Fortunately, whatever bimbo Zack lassoed at the party brought him back to her place. Of late, Zack wasn't demonstrating a great deal of insight, but Kylie was sure he wouldn't be stupid enough to check into a local hotel with a bimbo. After Kylie tended to Henrietta's scrapes and bruises, she escorted her to a guest room on the upper level. Henrietta hugged Kylie before retiring for the night and said,

"My son is a star now, a real movie star, isn't he?…"

"Yes," said the secretary, "a real movie star."

Kylie had all she could do to keep from crying. She knew that this kind lady raised her son on her own, making all the countless personal sacrifices required of single moms. She deserved better.

After the gala opening night, Zack did come home to freshen up but he had an excuse every single day why he couldn't spend time with his mom. He did manage to kiss her cheek each time he took off but

Kylie was left to take care of her. The first day Henrietta delighted in the newspaper stories and photos of her on the red carpet with her son. In the afternoon she watched *Arctic Storm* again in the screening room. After the screening she got totally absorbed in creating her scrap book. The next day Kylie took her to breakfast at "The Hideout," a restaurant that requires an annual membership fee and caters to movie stars. Henrietta got five autographs and had to tell Penelope Cruz, Ben Stiller and Daniel Craig that Zack Taylor was her son. The personal secretary took her to the movies twice to see *Arctic Storm* on two different days in different theaters. After the movies Kylie took Henrietta, faithful mom, shopping until she was exhausted. Henrietta bought her son a silver buckle belt with her money, against the secretary's adamant protests, saying that she should put the gift on Zack's credit card, which he would never know about because he is rich and she does the bookkeeping. Henrietta bought the belt with her own money.

It was the fifth morning, a day before Henrietta's flight home. Kylie was trying to catch up on all the calls and correspondence when Henrietta came down stairs early, hoping to catch her son before he left. She was too late.

"Hey," Kylie said, "let's have breakfast at Paramount Studios. Zack has a meeting there at eleven. Maybe we'll run into him."

Kylie wasn't lying. Zack did have an eleven o'clock meeting at Paramount and she knew exactly where he would be having breakfast before the meeting. "Fuck the inconsiderate bastard!" she thought. She would see to it that he spent some time with his poor mom, who wanted nothing from him, no new house, or cars or money—just a couple of hours to talk with him, reminisce, and hold his hand.

CHAPTER TWENTY TWO

THOSE GIVEN TO PLAY IN THE FOUNTAIN OF LIFE

About a month into their acquaintanceship, Beth invited Ken to watch a birthday party being hosted by Birthdays Inc. at Washington Square Park. Beth was hired to do the face painting. It was scheduled for Saturday at 1 o'clock and Beth suggested they have lunch at the fountain beforehand. Ken was euphoric at the invitation.

On Saturday Ken left the chess tables early to keep his tryst with Beth at the big fountain. She was waiting for him, sitting on the end of a bench so he could back in right beside her. She ate a hummus and artichoke sandwich on whole-wheat and he had ham and cheese on rye with mayonnaise. She drank strawberry Vitamin Water and he drank bottled water, declining to remove one of the two cans of beer he had stashed in the plastic cooler slung over his chair. The conversation started with his morning at the chess tables but somehow segued into her rather scant outfit of short shorts and a white stretch halter that revealed more than it concealed. She laughed at his suggestion that every single eye in the park was on her, including the pigeons. She said it was just too hot to dress decently, and laughed. However, when Ken continued to quip about her "overexposure," the conversation shifted abruptly. Without any lead up, she just asked the big question, as though she was asking about his brand of toothpaste.

"Are you able to have sex at all?"

"Not at all," came his frank reply.

"Wow, that sucks big-time!"

The way she said it was so unexpectedly flippant Ken had to laugh. "What's funny?"

"Nothing. The way you say things sometimes just blows my funny bone."

"I wasn't trying to be funny."

"I know. But honestly, it's not that big a deal. What you never could have—I mean, when you know something is impossible, you don't think about it anymore. It just has no bearing on your life anymore."

"Are you sure, though. Did you ever give it that college try?"

Ken couldn't stifle his laugh. Beth joined him, but stayed on point. "Well, did you?"

"When I was seventeen, I hired a really pretty hooker, who proved all my doctors were right."

Ken finished his confession with a chuckle but the angel girl would not be put off.

"I'm sure something can be done, dude. You were seventeen, like what, a hundred years ago? My God, the medical sciences can grow human kidneys on pigs and transplant them in people!"

"But, the body parts I need might embarrass the pig, don't you think?"

Beth's face turned red as she laughed. Ken joined her, then leaned over and kissed her on the cheek, saying, "I love you."

The angel girl just looked down at the sandwich wrapper in her hand and said nothing.

"Forget I did that, okay?" pleaded Ken as he squirmed in his chair.

"No…it was nice." she whispered, patting his arm to reassure him. The subject shifted abruptly again and they went on to talk about the children and their carefree, spontaneous happiness. Their conversation was sparked by a big yellow lab who broke from his leash and plunged into the fountain with the frolicking children. It was wild fun for the kids, who tried to capture the ecstatic mutt, while the adults who joined in to capture him only succeeded in getting soaked. Finally, Beth couldn't resist the mayhem and rushed into the fountain folly, chasing the dog, getting soaked and laughing the way only children and angels can laugh. It was no small reward either for the men watching the event, their eyes riveted on Beth's sopping wet halter while silently praying for it to come down.

When the Birthday Inc. crew showed up, Beth gave up the chase and joined them for the set up. They began staking out about a thousand square feet of turf beneath some maple trees. The stakes resembled tall candy canes to which they attached sections of plywood painted with the different fairy tale characters, Snow White and the Dwarfs, the Wicked Witch, Shrek and his donkey, Buzz and the Toy Story characters, and many others. Connecting them together created their fenced in party area. About twelve kids between the ages of four and six along with several parents arrived for the party. Ken watched as Beth, still dripping, donned a long white smock and stationed herself in the open booth. She became very focused while preparing the different colors of paint and brushes. Then she hung out pictures of the many faces the kids could choose from: prince, princess, pirate, queen, wolf, space alien, and every type of monster imaginable. She was amazing at her art—and fast. The kids were also entertained by a clown who did magic tricks that backfired on him. The party lasted a couple of hours and Ken stayed to the end, hoping to buy Beth dinner when it was over. She had to decline because there was another party scheduled for 4 o'clock.

With less than an hour break, Beth suggested they go to the chess tables where she could watch Ken play. He tried to dissuade her, on grounds that watching the game was boring. However, her compelling nature prevailed and she watched Ken play against a student who admitted to Ken pre-game that he was a "money player."

Ken responded, "Save your money, son, I'm a professional."

"So am I," insisted the young man.

"Let's just play for a beer," suggested Ken.

"Sounds like a waste of time! Let's play for a hundred—you got the stones for that?" asked the young man, eyeing Beth, who was standing next to Ken.

At the taunt, Ken just proceeded to set up the pieces. Beth watched the game for a while but lost interest and lay down on a bench behind Ken, out of his sightline. Twenty minutes later, Ken collected the money and while his young opponent was setting up for a second game, Ken turned his chair around to see Beth. She was still behind him, on a bench across the walk, learning how to play on a small board belonging to David Heightly, the dashing young Shark. Ken experienced a moment of panic, accompanied by a blast of flaming hot jealousy. Beth looked up from the game at Ken.

"Who won?"

Ken managed a smile, saying, "I did." Then, like a jealous adolescent he checked his watch and lied about the time.

"Wow, we've got to go. It's a quarter to four."

Looking surprised, she said, "Are you going to the next party also?"

"Absolutely," stated Ken.

"What about our rematch, dude?" asked Ken's fish.

As Beth got up, the Shark rose with her and said, "Cool, where's the party?"

Ken didn't respond to the fish. His attention was riveted on the Shark as he stated emphatically, "It's a birthday party for toddlers."

"Over by the fountain," Beth added.

Before the Shark could invite himself along, Ken said, "The young man behind me at table one has a lot of money. He wants to play for a hundred a game."

As expected, the Shark was at the table in a heartbeat. Ken and Beth started for the fountain but not before she turned to the Shark and said, "See you around, chess guy!"

"Yeah, cool," replied the Shark without looking her way.

Ken watched the second party, finishing his two beers in the process. A little excitement broke out between the party leader, costumed as Captain Hook, and several of the fathers attending. It centered around Beth. One of the fathers sat down to have his face painted and two others lined up to do the same, when Captain Hook stepped in. He told them they would have to pay extra to have their faces painted. The contract only included the children. There was some blustering and posturing from the fathers but it subsided peacefully, as party manager, Captain Hook, was one menacing looking dude. Ken understood why the men wanted Beth to paint their faces. They never took their eyes off of her for the first hour of the party. No such attention would have been paid a homely girl, Ken thought. The thought drew him back in time to when he served the church.

As a priest for most of his life and incapable of lust, he looked upon all women in the same way. Yes, he knew some were prettier than others but simply from an artistic perspective. What he learned during years of listening to confessions was that most attractive girls in the modern, sex-driven society are not in the least modest. Oh, they're wise enough, even in their early teens, not to overplay their beauty cards but instead feign modesty, while allowing their subtle glances or the flip of their hair to play their cards for them. The beautiful ones had an air of confidence and freedom about them that was missing in those not so fortunately endowed. One particular confession was very informative concerning the adolescent ego.

A high school senior, about sixteen, confessed that she was pregnant with her uncle's child. Ken asked if she had reported him to the authorities. She said she hadn't and wasn't going to. She wanted to know if getting an abortion was a mortal sin.

"It's taking a life," Ken said.

"So, I'm bound for hell if I do that?" she asked, not sounding overly concerned.

"If you don't repent, yes," responded Ken. "But at your age you were taken advantage of, by what I assume is an older man."

"No, Father," she pleaded, "I took advantage of him. For years this hunk of a guy, my uncle, did everything in his power to avoid my advances. I would lure him on every chance I got. I would go to his apartment after school and strip. He wouldn't touch me, but I knew he wanted to. He threatened to tell my father and I threatened to say he fondled me all the time I was growing up. He even begged me once to leave him alone—that's the day I wrapped myself around him and took him for my own. I know it sounds evil, but he's not married and I really am in love with him!" she concluded.

Ken said, "He should have told your father when you first started to tempt him. He's a responsible adult!" stated Ken, from a strictly doctrinal perspective.

Ken knew nothing about the allurement of the opposite sex. The teen, reveling in her power said, "Really, Father, no man can withstand a beautiful girl. We know the power we have over them! It's really no one's fault. Didn't God make us this way?"

Ken concluded that confession by telling the teenager to pray to God for the strength to break off the relationship, and to seek counseling with a Catholic psychologist, whose name he gave her. Recalling that confession all but destroyed his fantasies about Beth. He was just a confused old man, captivated by her feminine power—playing on her sympathy for friendship.

Ken had planned to invite Beth to dinner after the second birthday party, but chose to wave goodbye and roll away before the party was over.

CHAPTER TWENTY THREE
OF GOOD NEWS AND BAD NEWS

The auditions for *Don't Call Me Son* were held at the studio where Sonia taught acting, a huge room with three rows of theatre seats facing a small, six by twenty foot stage. There was a bank of eight stage lights focused down on the stage and a standing spotlight in the corner.

Sonia's brother, Stanley Sorrenson, along with the play's director, Clay Abbot, were late while the three actors to be auditioned, Terrance Lancaster, Martin Steikes, and Joel Ellendorff sat in the seats starring at their scripts. Sonia busied herself setting the stage with a coffee table and chairs. When the writer and director arrived they went directly to the stage to introduce themselves and explain what specific qualities they were looking for in the character of the son. Before they were finished, Abbot's cell phone rang and he turned upstage to take the call while Sorrenson continued the briefing. When Sorrenson concluded, the director proudly announced that he just got a confirmation from Russell Crowe's agent that Russell Crowe just signed to do the part of the father. Upon hearing the announcement, Joel's pulse increased as did the pulse of every actor in the room including Sonia.

Acting opposite a star like Russell Crowe was for any aspiring actor like hitting a lotto. Even so, and surprisingly to himself, Joel had no jitters. Upon meeting the other two actors up for the part of the son, Joel already released any hope of landing it. Both Terrence Lancaster and Martin Steikes had solid film credits. Even though neither was yet on the A-list, they were on the verge of "breaking out," as they say in film industry jargon. Beside those hard facts, Joel knew the character of the

144

son perfectly; he was confident he wouldn't come across as awful. For the young man, with no certain past and no certain future, the audition was just a cool learning experience. Thus, Joel didn't feel too bad when the director asked him to relieve the playwright and read the part of the father opposite the other two actors.

Sonia called the following day with the news,

"Hey, Joel, it's Sonia. I've got bad news and good news—which do you want first?"

"I didn't get the part. Fuck! Who got it, Martin Steikes, right?"

"Yes, but there's good news too. They want you for the understudy."

"Yeeoooowwee!" shouted Joel.

"You have to understudy both roles, the father and son. Are you up for that?"

"Hey, I love challenges!"

"Damn, I hope you never go on as the father. They'll have to put deep wrinkles around those beautiful eyes and a skullcap over those golden locks."

"Hey, I'll survive. Wow, I don't know how to thank you, girl."

"You can take me to dinner tonight. My brother left a contract for you to check out. I think they're low-balling you on the money. But that's for you and your agent to decide."

"I don't have an agent."

"You've got an appointment with my agent at the Lillian Tabor Agency in the morning."

"Thanks again. Where do you want to have dinner? It has to be in bicycle range of the YMCA."

"Let me decide. I'll pick you up at seven—that work for you?" "Yeah, cool. Do I need to dress? I don't have a tie."

"No problem. See you at seven."

The first thing Joel did was bike to Carminos to quit and pick up two days' pay. Next, he went shopping for a gift for his angel patron. He spent fifty dollars on earrings and thirty-five for flowers. He figured the dinner could run as high as two-hundred dollars and that would be cool. He would have about nine hundred dollars left to bus to New York and get settled in at the "Y." My God, he thought, what does an understudy make on Broadway? He could ask Julian, who was up on all such details, but decided to avoid him. It was a great day and he didn't want to make Julian feel bad. Though he'd only known the man a short time, he felt a common bond with him. Up until a few hours ago they were both down and out actors. The difference between them was that he, Joel, had many more opportunities to rise out of his "hand-to-mouth" existence, while all of Julian's opportunities were behind him, or were never available to begin with. Julian probably never did catch a break because in his prime black actors were still just struggling to get a foot in the Hollywood door. Joel got back to the Y about five and walked right into Julian sitting in the lobby, probably waiting for him. Julian didn't stand up, he just waved him over.

"My man, my man! I know those flowers aren't to brighten your room. Congratulations, dog," Julian said, motioning for him to sit down in the other stuffed chair.

"I didn't get the part. Martin Steikes did."

"What are the flowers for, your funeral?"

"My acting teacher. They want me to be the understudy. She and I are doing dinner tonight—kind of a celebration."

"Well, you didn't strike gold but you sure as hell struck silver, dude! Now all you have to do is figure out how to get Steikes sick as a dog on opening night," said Julian with a straight face before he erupted with laughter.

Joel joined in the laughter.

"I'm laughing, dude," said Julian, morphing serious again, "but the chances of you replacing him even once are as slim as an anorexic razor."

"You never know, dog. Life is an unpredictable affair," said Joel.

"In most cases, yes," conceded Julian, "But a straight play on Broadway has a one in seven chance of surviving a week. If the play doesn't get great reviews, you'll be waiting tables before you get your makeup off!"

"You're always such a bundle of cheer, Julian. Have you considered becoming a life coach for people who are too happy?"

"Hey, I'm not trying to down you, dude, just laying out some valuable heads-up. Be prepared—Boy Scouts' motto."

"I've got to get on my horse. I'll catch you before I exit L.A. I've got some furniture you might be able to use."

As Joel got up to go, Julian offered his fist for a parting fist connect, and said, "Take a box of condoms."

"What?" asked Joel.

"Condoms, you got any?"

"Hey, dude, I'm not putting any moves on my acting teacher. She's like, twice my age."

"Take this to the bank, young dude, there ain't no free lunch. Every favor in this business requires some skin."

"Some skin?"

"Pay back, my man. It's the unspoken factor in every Hollywood favor."

With that, Julian fished a couple of foil wrapped condoms from his wallet and tossed them to Joel.

"Don't be concerned about the pre-civil war date on the package."

"Thanks, but I really won't need these."

"Tell you what. If you don't, I'll eat them without removing the foil!" Joel took the condoms and proceeded to his room to get dressed. Following his shower he set about shaving. It was over four months since his living nightmare in Chicago but he knew he had changed. The face in the mirror no longer appeared like a stranger to him. It was his face. His hair had grown in quite a bit and some of the terror in his eyes had subsided. While his mind hadn't returned any concrete memories of his past, it had reconciled itself or realized he was in fact Joel Ellendorff. It now seemed to him that the whole weird episode wasn't insanity but likely an extended hallucination brought on by some drug, possibly LSD, given to him by the psycho in the wheel chair. His recent research on personality disorders online at the library revealed that acid trips often result in recurring hallucinations months or even years later. Who knows how much of that shit the fiend put into his system? Besides, the information on people with multiple personalities didn't jibe with his unique case of feeling like a stranger in his own body. But hell, he thought, he was adapting to his circumstances, which psychiatrists claim is the first sign of mental health. Every now and then during his Internet research he would be sent to "Occult Phenomena—Witchcraft." However, his life was just too busy to check out foolish superstitions. And all things considered, his new life wasn't going all that bad.

When he was ready he opened the closet door in his room and checked himself out in the full-length mirror. He had adorned his six-three stature with a cream-colored shirt designed with some black paint spatter running down the left shoulder into a shirt pocket. He wore Levis without a belt, and brown penny loafers without socks. He brushed his blond hair up from the sides and back from the front, giving it that stylishly unkempt look.

A couple of sprays of cologne and done. The face in the mirror smiled with assurance. He was young, healthy, and looking cool. Flowers in hand, he took the elevator to the lobby. He was a tad upset to see Julian still sitting there.

"Do you actually have a room, Jules, or do you sleep out here?" quipped Joel.

"Hey, the man cleans up pretty good!" said Julian. "Yes sir! You're looking very caucasian tonight."

"Thanks, I think I'll wait outside."

"What, you're not going to introduce me, the black friend that coached you to success?" chuckled Julian.

"Catch you later, Jules. Please don't be sitting here when I return. I might get the impression you don't have a life!"

CHAPTER TWENTY FOUR

HEART BREAKING WHISPERS

After the birthday parties at the park, the meetings between Ken and Beth dropped off to a few passing hellos in the hallway. Ken got involved in a week-long chess tournament online. The cash prizes for first, second, and third place were too enticing to pass up. If he finished in the money he could just hang out for the next year and concentrate on his new life as Timothy Gales. It would all be new and exciting but not without some immediate challenges, not the least of which would be how to get up and walk away from the dead body of Ken McAlister. The alchemist said that learning to walk might take some time. Ken planned to have three days alone after the switch to deal with whatever complications might turn up. However, from what he witnessed in the Taulb to Zack Taylor switch, there weren't any other problems to be overly concerned about.

Gales, being an orphan and a loner, left only minor details to deal with, like officially quitting school. Of all the elements involved in carrying on his new life, the one that occupied most of his conjecture was how to contact and court Beth. He chuckled sometimes at the thought of having the inside information on her, which he could use to come across as cool.

The level of competition in the "2500 Chess Tournament" would be fierce. Any player with a rating in the 2500 range could enter if he could afford it. The base entrance fee was five thousand dollars with an additional fee of one thousand dollars for every tournament he/she won in the last twelve months. First place prize money was three hundred thousand dollars. Second place paid one hundred and fifty thousand.

And third place paid fifty thousand. The field in the tournament included last year's first- and second-place finishers who were among a half-dozen others about to break out of the 2500 ranks. Ken never played at this level of competition before, but it was time to "get it on," as they say. He would have to be on his game and that meant almost total seclusion. His daily plots to encounter Beth in the hall were replaced by periods of quiet contemplation, study, and sleep.

For the first three days of the tournament each player was required to play three games, and on the fourth day and fifth day, two games. Ken was on his game, avoiding elimination and checkmating his second opponent on day five in twenty-eight moves, placing him into the semi-finals. He was just two opponents away from the championship when something cut painfully into his peace of mind.

It was eleven o'clock at night when Top Gun jumped on to the end table by his bed, knocking over a glass of water. Ken didn't get up to deal with it, he just removed one of the pillow cases and used it to blot up the water. While he was doing this, he heard Beth's voice outside his open window. She was with a young man.

"No," she whispered, "I don't have any coffee. Besides, I have to get up early in the morning."

"Tell me you don't like the way I'm holding you," said her male companion.

"Sure, but let's take our time, okay?"

"You know you're feeling the same thing I am right now," said the companion. "Admit it!"

"Admit what, that I'm turned on by you? It's basic biology, man! Please don't do that—people are watching," she gasped. "Nobody's watching, babe. The world's asleep."

Ken could discern their heavy breathing, the rustling of her clothes. He considered breaking it up. He wanted to with every fiber of his being but didn't know how. He could shout, "Quiet down out there, I'm trying to get some sleep!" But the consequences might be catastrophic. He had no choice but to either pull the pillow over his head or continue to listen. He would continue to listen, if for no other reason than to acquire some pointers in love making, which he could use as Timothy Gales.

"Please, please don't, oh, please, oh, oh, God!" Beth moaned.

"Come on," the companion said in a husky voice, trying to catch his breath. "We're going to get arrested out here."

There was a pause and then Ken heard the key in the entrance door.

"Be quiet, I don't want to wake people up," Beth whispered.

Ken listened to their footsteps; each step, each faint giggle in the hall engulfed him with emotional pain. He tried to go back to sleep; he had to, because he was scheduled for a critical game at 4 a.m. Such was the pain of international chess tournaments, where the leading player between the two opponents gets to choose the time of their match. He would be sitting down at his computer at 4 a.m. but his opponent in England would be Skyping in at 9 a.m.

It was no use trying to sleep. He could close his eyes, but it only sharpened the images in his mind of the woman he loved having intercourse with another man. He could actually hear the blood rushing in and out of his heart, while rage flooded his mind.

"God," he thought," is this what jealousy feels like? Is this what instigates crimes of passion?"

Ken made numerous attempts to reason himself to sleep. "What did you expect," Ken admonished himself, "that she was so beguiled by your friendship that she would restrain her youthful passions? She's a healthy, freedom-loving girl. She has a right to grasp whatever pleasures are there for her. Your problem is that you want to think of her as an angel, and in your Catholic mind angels don't have sex. Is it really that much of a problem? No doubt she's been with other men—no, not men, young men her age. Kids today know how to enjoy their bodies, without all the guilt the church and society try to heap on them. Just because these youths indulge in sexual relationships doesn't mean they are faithfully committed to their sex partners. Sex for her doesn't imply she's in love with this guy, whoever he is—probably an old boyfriend she bumped into. Who knows, this could be a one-time affair. The guy could even be married. Think about Timothy Gales. He's got what Beth would call a 'rockin' body.' That's the body you will be courting her in. 'Courting!' Do people still use that word? It sounds old-fashioned! Look, winning this tournament is everything! You'll have all the time you need to bone up on the lingo of this generation, soon to be your generation if you win. Just relax. It's all good—let it go—go to sleep. Get some female anatomy books too, idiot! Except for that hooker you embarrassed to death, you've never seen a naked woman. She got paid; she knew in advance what the deal was. She wasn't as pretty as Beth. Just got to let it go and sleep, just sleep. What am I expecting from Beth? After the switch it will be different. Why torture myself now? Just let it go and sleep. Books! You won't need books or a lot of research on sex—there's pornography all over the Internet. I've just got to rest my brain for the game! Pornography! How much sin does one have to absorb to get on in this world! Are you really getting back into the sin thing? No—of course not—no! Shit, am I ever going to doze off! Blah, blah, blah, blah, blah! Your eyes are open—close them—breathe easy. It's all going to work out. Pornography! Is that really necessary? Primitives had no pornography— maybe on cave walls. I'm done here. I don't care if Beth has sex! I've just got to get some sleep. Sex is a natural process. Primitives, who couldn't read or write, figured it out! What a terrible night this is! God, I have to sleep!"

Ken tossed and turned for another half hour before he pulled himself up and out of bed. He rolled into the kitchen to tap on his electric coffee maker, which he used exclusively for tea. It was 1:10 a.m. when he rolled into the living room with a mug of Earl Grey in his cup holder. He turned on the tube and watched a rerun of yesterday's evening news. He stuck to it for half an hour to catch the review of *Arctic Storm*. The reviewer lavished praise all over the film, a lot of it for "the rising star," Zackary Taylor. The commentator concluded his review, saying, "This epic film has Academy Awards written all over it!"

Ken turned off the TV and turned on his computer. He navigated his way to www.chinagaming/highstakes.chi. He scrolled through a list of games that ran from bingo to soccer. Keying in on chess, he proceeded to review the previous tournament games of Osgood Bentley, last year's second-place finisher and his semi-final opponent.

This was the second time Ken reviewed Bentley's tournament games. Bentley's style of play was similar to Ken's own. Both played what could be termed a French King-Pawn waiting game. Such a similar strategy between him and Bentley meant the game would go on for hours, each man making trap moves waiting for his opponent to take the bait that triggered the end game onslaught.

"Just what I need after a brain draining sleepless night!" figured Ken. He would never be able to maintain the mental advantage in such a game. He had no choice but to abandon his winning style and launch a Genghis Khan approach, which consisted of several capture and kill strategies. No doubt Bentley reviewed Ken's past tournament games and hopefully wouldn't be mentally prepared to trade pieces with a reckless maniac. At 3:45 a.m. Ken set his hot water maker, Earl Grey tea and honey dispenser on a table beside his computer. He had to lock Top Gun in the kitchen with a can of sardines to keep him from the honey dispenser. At 3:55 he Skyped into his match with Bentley and at 4:20 a.m., the shortest game in the history of the tournament was over. Ken lost. However, he wasn't eliminated yet. If Vitali Ikovich, a Russian, lost his game there would be a playoff between Ikovich and Ken for third place.

After his loss to Bently, Ken went back to bed and slept into the afternoon. He awoke to the good news that Vitali Ikovich lost and the playoff game between them was scheduled for 6 p.m. the next day, Eastern Standard time. It was only marginally good news for Ken in the wake of his loss to Bentley and his deflated expectations involving Beth. He wanted to see her, just to see her, so he fabricated an excuse to roll down the hall to her apartment. She wasn't home, which was usually the case on sunny afternoons. She was either working a birthday party or rollerblading somewhere, perhaps the park. He could call her cell number, which she gave him in case of an emergency. He decided not to call and blow his cool. Instead, he fed Top Gun and motored to the park. He wasn't interested in penny-ante chess with a fifty-thousand dollar tournament prize at stake the next evening. He searched the park for her, but she wasn't around. He purchased a sandwich and Vitamin Water from the fast food truck in the street beside the park. He motored to the fountain area to eat and "get clear," an expression he heard a Scientologist use in a speech at the park.

Getting clear was about being truthful to yourself. "Nothing new," Ken reflected. He studied all about personal deception in seminary. Besides, his own observations confirmed that most people felt justified in lying to others to advance their opinions and improve their situations in life. On a number of occasions, politicians lied to Ken when he was a priest, to gain the backing of the church. Back then, they were lying to the wrong priest, and it cost a few their jobs at election time. Politicians aren't alone, Ken mused, CEOs of huge corporations lie continuously to protect the interests of their companies, as is the case with every oil spill or distribution of a harmful drug by some huge pharmaceutical company. What once really disgusted Ken, were the network news programs that blatantly spun the facts to serve their sponsor's point of view. The big question on Ken's mind, as he ate his sandwich, was whether it had ever been different in any other culture or generation. Even Jesus was somewhat ambiguous, stating that "the world was inherently evil," while praying to God not to remove His disciples from it. He prayed only that God keep them from succumbing to the evil. So, Ken concluded, the world wasn't really evil, only the deceit which most people succumb to in conducting their lives. But, Ken thought, what chance did any human have being born into a world of deceit, where even the esteemed "holy men" of the different faiths are deceitful, twisting their holy writ to justify their personal shortcomings, self-interests, and points of view. These days, however, Ken spent very little time reflecting on the deviant beliefs of others, while his own personal beliefs were as deviant as deviant can be. Whenever Ken considered his quest to take another person's life, he rationalized that it really wasn't murder because he didn't kill any "body" but his own, and his own had been half dead since his birth. He would be willing to argue the case with Jesus should He actually show up a second time. The fact that there is no God and no Heaven actually made Jesus Christ the King of deceivers!

To prove his recent conversion to atheism was justified, he made a silent wager with the seeming "All-knowing God." From his heart he swore to repent completely and spare the life of Timothy Gales if God would use His power to make him lose the big game to Vitali Ikovich. From anyone else's point of view, such a wager was foolhardy, for Ikovich was not only favored to win but was last year's tournament champion. Ken always knew this showdown with Truth had to come. Would an Ikovich victory really be undeniable proof that God existed? No. To anyone else the wager would prove nothing, really, even though Ken swore to honor the outcome. And this he did because he was presently in one shitty mood. And because, over the last year he studied no contestant's games the way he studied the games of last year's tournament champion. Vitali Ikovich used no pseudonym online to hide his identity as Ken did. Thus, every game ever played was open to be analyzed. Ikovich was a devotee of the Russian methodology, which came to be called "Red Revenge." In short, Vitali Ikovich was an open book to Ken, who had a photographic memory and twelve ways to implement a flawless mid-game trap. And to lose to Ikovich, Ken thought, would indeed require divine intervention.

Ken remained at the park, watching the people who were drawn to the gushing, spellbinding energy of the fountain. They came to sit and stare, to daydream, to toss a coin and make a wish, to rest and forget their troubles for a moment. They weren't evil, regardless of the lies they may have succumbed to in their short lives. Most of them were hard working, helpless creatures trying to eke out a little happiness in a fearful and arbitrary world.

Ken did not run into Beth at the park or at her apartment, which he visited upon his return. He then went to his place to bathe and listen to music. As was becoming a regular occurrence, Top Gun came in the window to greet him. Ken had grown to love the Rascal and took time every day to play with his roommate. Their favorite game entailed Ken tossing a catnip-filled mouse connected to a string out on the floor. Each time the Rascal attempted to pounce Ken would jerk the mouse away. After a few minutes Top Gun would get wise to the trickery and fly into Ken's lap to get the string. Laughing, Ken had to surrender the string to avoid having his hands clawed to shreds.

After bathing, Ken put on some meditative music and went to his computer to review Vitali Ikovich's recent loss in the tournament. Ikovich was a cagey method player. He was capable of shifting from one strategy to another when an opponent made an unexpected move, but he was stymied whenever an opponent made two unorthodox moves in a row.

If you took Ikovich out of his method game he was incapable of spontaneous play. It's like someone who has memorized a speech but before he can finish reciting it you interrupt him with a question. He must go back to the beginning of his speech, for he cannot randomly choose a place to continue from. Ask such a rote speaker two or three questions and he will be so confused that his mouth will dry up. Ken watched the three-hour game, and only when it was over did he notice Top Gun purring on his lap.

Out of the blue he called Fandango to find out where *Arctic Storm* was playing and bought two tickets for the Sunday evening show. Hell, he thought, Beth could always refuse! Besides, he was interested in seeing the alchemist in his first acting role. To relax and continue his education he watched the fourth Harry Potter film, keeping the volume low so he could hear the front door. He rolled into the hall twice at the sound of someone entering. The first time he encountered Attos Albaniac, the property owner, who was himself looking for Beth. The second time he just cracked his door for a peek before committing to an encounter. It was the guys from *Spiderman* who entered holding hands. Their gay demeanor surprised the ex-priest because he believed, beyond a shadow of a doubt, that they were straight. He also thought, if Beth were to get crazy-involved with anybody it would probably be with one of these Adonises.

After a while Ken gave up his surveillance, finished the DVD and went to bed, but not before closing his bedroom window and sticking ear plugs in his ears.

CHAPTER TWENTY FIVE

TWISTS AND TURNS ON THE HIGHWAY OF LIFE

Just as Joel stepped outside, Sonia pulled up in a midnight blue Prius. He handed her the white roses as he got in the car.

"Thanks, Joel. How sweet. You didn't have to do this," she said, as she leaned over and kissed him on the cheek.

It was just a quick peck but he spied Julian at the lobby window giving him a thumbs up.

"No. Thank you, girl, for getting my foot in the Broadway door."

"I got you the audition, dude, you brought the talent," she said, turning down the radio and placing the flowers on the back seat.

Joel had never really checked her out before. There was a lot of makeup on her face, which read better at a distance. Her punk-styled black hair had a bright red streak running through it. She was wearing a tight red over-blouse which pressed hard against her ample breasts—plump breasts. Below the blouse she wore black stretch pedal pushers, with a gold chain belt and matching chains around her calves. Her plump feet were squeezed into a pair of black stiletto heels. Her perfume, however, was subtle, like the scent of lilacs on a spring breeze.

"This," he thought, "was Sonia Ammonia." Close up now she looked more like fifty than forty, and he feared that if Julian's prophecy came to pass he wouldn't be able to perform.

As they drove into a million red tail lights on Highway 405, they talked all about the audition, the contract and the difference between a film and live theatre. Sonia started out in New York, which was where

157

she grew up, on Long Island. Her acting career peaked with a couple of bit parts off-Broadway before she took a shot at "stand-up."

She confessed, "Stand-up was probably a big mistake. Once people see you, and everybody sees you on YouTube, they can't take you seriously—as a legit actress, that is."

"I don't know," responded Joel, "the few readings you did in class were amazing. The one you did from *Sophie's Choice* brought tears to my eyes."

"Tell that to my agent. And every casting director in town. For fuck's sake, my own brother wouldn't read me for the mother in his show! You know what he said, my own brother—what a dick! He said I was too young for the mother. Give me a break! Like with a decent make-up job I can't play fifty!"

"What about one of the other women in the show? I could see you as the father's main mistress, Felicia Phelps."

"I begged the dick for that part. I mean, give me that role, I'll not only wreck the marriage on stage, I'll wreck everyone's marriage in the audience! Fuck, what I could do with that role!"

"Your brother wouldn't even let you read for it," commiserated Joel, knowing full well she was way too old and plump for the serpentine Felicia role.

"Hey, life sucks for a while, and then you die," quipped the acting teacher. "You know what, I'm about done with this traffic! Let's can the Hideout tonight and go to my place."

The suggestion hit the young actor like a swarm of bees.

"You don't want to cook tonight," responded Joel, with an exaggerated frown that required no acting ability whatsoever.

"Cook? Hollywood babes don't cook. We order out, dude. You like Japanese?"

"I don't remember. I mean I don't remember the last time I had Japanese. Is it like Chinese?" Joel asked, searching his mind for some polite excuse to get out of the invite.

"Not really. But don't worry, after a couple of shots of sake you could relish the weeds from your fish tank without the plum sauce."

Sonia took the next exit, and two minutes later pulled into her driveway. It was hard to believe the whole thing wasn't planned. He was captured. He could hear Julian laughing.

"This is my place," Sonia said, as she led him to the door on one side of a modest duplex. Inside, the place was a typical actress's den, furnished with theatrical memorabilia displayed everywhere about the living room. Beautifully framed posters of TV shows she had done adorned the walls. Several scripts were piled up on a large white coffee table that sat in the middle of a semicircle of an off-white sectional sofa. There was a fireplace with a large artificial polar bear skin on the floor before it. High above the fireplace hung a large flat screen TV. A faint aroma of Jasmine incense permeated her digs throughout. Sonia went directly to the media center on one side of the room and played "Sketches of Spain," an album of sultry Latin jazz, featuring a muted trumpet.

"Take off your shoes—make yourself at home. You dig jazz at all?"

"Yeah, it's cool," Joel responded, feeling anxious and trapped.

The young actor removed his shoes and walked over the plush gray and red carpet to a cluster of photos of film stars on the wall behind the media center. While he checked out the photos, Sonia got on her cell phone and ordered the food. She was obviously familiar with the menu because she had none in hand while ordering.

Looking at a photo of Sonia with two-time academy award winner Steven Spalding, he called over to her, "Did you actually work with Steve Spalding?"

"Kind of," Sonia replied. "He produced a pilot for HTO that starred Bette Malter. I had the second banana part of her retarded sister. The thing was beyond hilarious! Bette's character was this flamboyant dike, while the retarded sister loved Jesus."

"What, it didn't get picked up?"

"Too hot to handle. Even HTO thought it was too controversial to air. Hey, are you up for some weed before dinner?"

"Sure. This is a celebration!" exulted Joel.

The captured actor figured there was no way out of the evening, without totally offending a wonderful lady, who really did him a solid favor. A little weed really stimulated his libido with Sammi back in Chicago, and might do the same for him tonight when he really needed it. After smoking a bowl of sensational marijuana, the food arrived. Joel went to the door to pay for it, but Sonia jokingly grabbed his ass and laughingly sputtered, "This is my party, dude!"

"Let me pay," protested the stoned actor, "I owe you big time!"

"No way! Just make sure they spell my name right in your Broadway bio!"

Sonia paid the delivery boy and slid the scripts to the floor while placing the containers of food down on the coffee table. She scurried to the kitchen and returned with an ice cold flask of sake and a bottle of plum wine on a tray. Unless sake and plum wine were her favorite breakfast drink, the whole evening was planned before she left to capture him. Bowing like a Geisha, she filled two Japanese mini cups with sake and proposed a toast.

"Here's to you, Joel. May your career exceed your wildest expectations."

Joel refilled the cups and returned the toast, "Here's to you, Sonia. May you go on to win more Academy awards than Meryl Streep."

After the second sake toast Sonia poured two wine glasses full of plum wine, giving one to Joel.

"See you in five," whispered Sonia, as she retreated into the bedroom.

Joel was already chopstick searching through the savory delights when Sonia returned from the bedroom wearing a white silk Japanese kimono. Joel paused to survey the pleasantly plump body of his teacher. The sheer kimono left little to the imagination.

"Hey, man, you're screwing up a thousand years of Japanese tradition," Sonia mockingly complained. "You can't dine unless you're wearing a kimono. "Here," she said, tossing him a duplicate black and white kimono which was draped over her arm. Joel immediately started to put it on over his clothes but she hit his knuckles with a chopstick. With a sake-slurring Japanese accent Sonia admonished him, "So sorry, must not dishonor ancestors—sacred kimono not worn over clothes."

Joel, doing his own sake impersonation, proceeded to strip while slurring, "Have often wondered why ancestors wear sacred kimono. Is so eyes can feast also as tongue does feast! Also, ancient proverb, man who close eyes when eat must fall on chopstick and die."

Sonia started giggling and Joel joined her, taking turns reciting stupid marijuana-inspired proverbs, laughing like stoned idiots. In the throes of the merriment Sonia started getting physically friendly, running her hands over Joel's body. He was indeed turned on but he was also starving, and offered a proverb, "Lao Tzu say, is bad luck to mate when food hot. Cold food make stomach angry, make stomach growl like lion."

No other proverbs were required. The stoned actors fell on the Japanese delights, killing a flask of sake and a bottle of plum wine in the process. Joel was no longer the innocent prisoner of his acting teacher. She didn't pull him to her but merely slinked down onto the white fur skin at the fireplace. Joel crawled to her, obsessed with passion. There was just something about the way she moved in the drunken midst of his mind. He ravaged her, but before the ravaging was consummated the young actor said, "Wait, let me cover up," as he reached to retrieve the condoms from his Levis.

Sonia pulled him back to her. "I've got you covered."

Not another word was spoken, not a proverb uttered, only moans and groans and sporadic shrieks of ecstasy filled the next half hour. Then there was silence, as they dosed off in each other's arms.

It was hours later. Someone was at the front door, no bell, no knocking, just a disturbing bumping, pushing sound. Joel stiffened, as the bumping got louder turning into a loud banging, banging, against the door.

"Where's the knife?" He cried out in panic. "It's him, it's him—where's the knife?" Flashes of the fiend ramming his wheelchair into the door—Joel frozen, unable to move—cold sweat dripping from his body. "Where's the knife?!" The banging louder, louder, deafening, door hinges breaking away.

"Where's the knife?!" Joel shouted, bolting upright—the door exploding open—the fiend rolling toward him.

"Help! Help!" Joel screamed at the top of his lungs. Sonia on her feet, pissing all over the place, as she scrambled and stumbled to reach the light switch. When the light went on Sonia saw a different Joel. He was sitting up, soaking wet, eyes wild, unfocused and darting around the room like a rabid wolf, once again trying to figure out where he was. Sonia, nude, still leaking, holding the Emmy she won for her cameo on the short lived sit-com "Mr. Potato Head."

"Joel, Joel, what happened? Are you okay?" asked the freaked out Sonia.

Joel couldn't respond. He just stared at her until she began to look familiar.

"Was it a dream, babe, a nightmare?"

"Yeah," Joel whispered. "Is the door locked?"

"Yes, always, it's automatic. You okay now?"

"I'm sorry I frightened you."

"No problem, babe. Do you want to talk about it?"

"No, it's all cool now. Can you get me some water, a lot of water."

Sonia replaced her Emmy on the pedestal and went to the kitchen for water. Joel looked down at the wet yellow stains all over the white fur and wondered if they were his. Removing his cell from his Levis on the floor, he checked the time. It was 5:35 a.m. After a couple of glasses of ice water, Joel and Sonia showered together, cleaned up the living room and went to the kitchen where she made breakfast. Joel devoured four eggs and a pile of home-fries, while Sonia had an egg and a piece of dry toast.

They talked mainly about the ten-page contract on Joel's lap.

"Don't break your head on that contract," stated Sonia. "Eddie Bracken, my guy at the agency, will give you the skinny on it. You didn't eat your bacon."

"No," Joel said, concealing the fact that it made him queasy. "I'm full. I thought you Hollywood babes didn't cook."

"It's a first! And don't you breathe a word about it to anyone!" Sonia chuckled.

"Hey, I'm really sorry about freaking you out."

"It's cool, dude. People have nightmares. Not usually sitting up with their eyes open and screaming, 'Where's the knife?' But hell, it was stimulating! Do you have nightmares often?"

"No, only on rare occasions when I follow a bowl of weed with a bottle of sake and plum wine."

Sonia laughed along with Joel. Then she reached across the table and took his hand.

"I'm seriously going to miss you, Joel,"

Joel remained silent, sipping his coffee to escape a response.

"Hey, it's not about the fun we had, the sex. I really like you as a friend," she confided.

"Oh, Hollywood babe," Joel said without looking at her, "we'll always be friends."

It wasn't the response she wanted, but it was honest, and it was enough. During the drive to the Lillian Tabor agency they talked about the play and New York Theatre. "Lillian Tabor Entertainment" occupied the top floor of the Berkshire building in Hollywood. Sonia drove into the underground garage, parking in one of the spaces stenciled "TABOR CLIENTS ONLY." On the way up in the elevator Sonia offered a couple of pointers.

"Eddie Bracken is a no-nonsense gay man. He doesn't bed his clients and hates bullshit, unless he's slinging it—so just be truthful. And don't be timid or self-effacing, which is something you have a tendency to do." When the elevator opened on the eighteenth floor, Joel surveyed the lavish layout of one of the top entertainment agencies in the world. Huge framed posters of movies, TV and Broadway shows lined the walls in every direction. Sonia introduced Joel to the two male receptionists, one of which escorted them to a posh lounge outside of Eddie Bracken's private office.

Joel did not sit down, for he was immobilized by the sight of the *Arctic Storm* poster on the wall beside Bracken's office door. There he was, Zackary Taylor, his name written in gold gilded letters beneath a stunning portrait of him in a fur parka beside a magnificent husky. The sight caused Joel instant confusion and fear. He was on the brink! He felt like he was slipping back into total insanity.

"Oh my God! Oh my God! Am I dreaming? This can't be! Am I crazy? What's going down here? What the fuck is this!"

His thoughts just kept crashing into the barrier of reason that protects people from irrational behavior. Now, nothing made any sense. He was about to meet a very important man, someone who could make a huge difference in his life but his mind was churning with confusion. The office with all the brilliantly colored posters morphed surreal. It was a dreamscape in which the details were blurred and the sounds muted like distant echoes. Tears filled his eyes though he knew he couldn't break down here, not with Sonia beside him, not in the top agency in Hollywood. There was nothing he could say that wouldn't freak them out. They would think him insane. They would call an ambulance and rush him to a hospital, or worse, to some institution for those demonstrating abnormal behavior. Sonia broke in on Joel's trance.

"What's going on with you? Why are you crying?"

After a pause Joel replied. "The dog in that poster—he's so beautiful!"

"You're crying because the dog is beautiful?"

Joel hadn't realized tears were rolling down his face. Wiping them away with his hand he responded.

"When I was a kid I had a husky—looked just like him."

Sonia pulled a tissue from her purse and proceeded to dry Joel's face.

"It's a good idea not to let Bracken see you in tears. Sentimentality is not his strong suit. So, stop looking at the freaking mutt already!"

Joel forced himself to look away and sat down. When the office door opened Eddie Bracken wasn't the first to step out. Sid Wycoff, the top news anchor on television preceded him.

CHAPTER TWENTY SIX

TO ERR IS HUMAN—TO BLUNDER IS INTOLLERABLE

In thirty-six moves Vitali Ikovich laid his king down, conceding the third place victory to Ken McAlister. Beside the fifty thousand dollar prize, Ken gained an even greater prize, a victory over his deeply embedded belief in God. During the entire match Ken never felt that he wasn't personally in control of his game. Likewise, he was assured the game of life had no secret power vying for or against anyone. You were on your own to play the hand you were dealt. There was no sin, no bad karma, as Buddhists define it, only the immediate consequences of your decisions and the fickle factor of luck. If it wasn't so, would not the alchemist, presently inhabiting the body of Zackary Taylor, have been stopped, penalized, punished in some way after centuries of defying God's command to love your neighbor? No, the Truth that made you free was the honest observation that life itself is a free-for-all. And he would be totally free in sixteen days when Timothy Gales returned from Texas.

There would not be a single delay in the process. He dropped Gales off at Kennedy Airport when he left and he was scheduled to pick him up when he returned. Gales loved orange juice, even when it wasn't laced with vodka. Orange juice would mask the color of the potion completely. Ken would stop at his apartment before dropping Gales off at the student dorm. Gales certainly wouldn't refuse a piece of cake and a toast to Ken on his birthday.

Still, life was not without problems. That very night, the night he defeated both Ikovich and the superstition of God, Beth showed up with her male companion. It had become a nightly occurrence which Ken had to endure. He heard them come in and share a few words at the mail box before their footsteps retreated to her apartment. With a whole new life just sixteen days away, a life with legs, and strength, and new dreams to pursue, the thought of Beth sharing herself with another man was still unbearable to him. He spent another sleepless night, not because he refused to wear earplugs but because Top Gun had eaten them. All night he thought of every possible scheme to intervene, to break up their affair, but there wasn't anything he could say or do without jeopardizing the fragile friendship he had with the girl he loved. He would ride it out until he could re-enter her life as the young, vibrant Timothy Gales.

In the morning Ken left his door cracked, while he had tea and toast for breakfast. Beth and her companion did not leave. He was washing the dishes when he heard Beth knock at the door. He called out, "Come in. It's open."

When he spun away from the sink he saw Beth standing in the kitchen doorway wearing practically nothing, actually a pair of sheer summer pajamas. Her hair was pulled haphazardly into a side ponytail held in place by a rubber band. If it weren't for her perfectly pert nineteen-year-old breasts, Ken thought, she would look fourteen years old. Such a false estimation testified to Ken's non-virile, celibate existence.

"Hey, Ken," she began, "do you have four eggs I can borrow?"

"Four?" asked Ken. "You must be hungry. Pull up a chair and I'll cook them for you."

"Thanks, but I need them to make pancakes—for me and a friend."

"Oh, a friend," Ken repeated, as he rolled to the refrigerator. "It better be a very special friend because I don't lend my eggs to just anyone."

"Oh, he is," responded Beth. "He's a chess player. David Heightly. He said he's played with you at the park. He's the guy we met when I did those birthday parties at the park…"

Her words caused Ken's upper body to flush full with heat and anger, leaving him speechless. Ken handed his angel girl the eggs. He wanted to shout, "Don't you know that I love you? How could you take up with that sinister bastard, that con-man!"

Instead, Ken made an attempt at playing her well-meaning friend.

"I know you're an adult and it's probably not my place to say anything—but, well—really get to know this guy before you get involved. He's kind of a drifter."

Beth bent and kissed Ken on the cheek. He felt her warmth. He inhaled the scent of her.

"Thanks for the fatherly advice," she smiled.

Before leaving, she stopped to snuggle Top Gun with her nose. "He misses you," Ken said.

"Oh, he's just a babe magnet," she chuckled.

His feelings for her, overriding his judgment, Ken, blurted out, "I miss you!"

Beth turned to her friend, but then looked away while searching for a response to his outcry. Had he made the statement as a matter of fact, Beth would probably have invited him to join David and her for breakfast. But the emotion that accompanied the statement conveyed the feelings of a man hopelessly in love. Beth was no stranger to such feelings being expressed to her. Hardly a man she met didn't want to bed her. And the ones she gave any attention to literally lusted after her. Throughout her life she had been mindful not to give any man false signals which could create fantasies she had no intention of fulfilling. With Ken, she wasn't that mindful, once she found out he was incapable of sexual arousal or fantasies. She knew this, not just from their conversations but because he "kept his eyes to himself," a rare discipline regarding men in general, who are forever eyeing a woman's carnal accoutrements. Even now, with her dressed in a pair of sheer cotton shorts, which were little more than panties with ruffle trim, and a halter top, euphemistically labeled pajamas, Ken only gave her eye contact. She understood fully that his cry for love was different. It was genuine, not a cry for intimacy but for friendship and companionship. She just then realized what a lonely life this handicapped man must lead and she felt sorry for him. She could turn and console him with promises that she would spend more time with him, but she knew it would be untruthful and terribly misleading. Since David had entered her life, her spare time was lavished on him completely.

"Oh," she said, "I miss hanging with you too, dude, but I'm really slammed these days—you know, with birthday parties, my cleaning chores, and David. He doesn't have a "job-job," so he's—well, hey, let's all have dinner this week. You can create one of your mouth-watering feasts and you can meet him up close and personal. He travels a lot but he's not a drifter. You'll see."

Feeling embarrassed to the core, Ken attempted a chuckle and said, "Cool. You supply the brownies for dessert. But we'll have to put a limit on them, like one per person."

Not one day ever passed in his life when his condition didn't require his utmost attention. There were painful days as a priest when he had to counsel with parishioners about their petty problems. He sometimes had to recite a silent rosary to himself to keep from telling them to throw themselves face down at the altar and praise God for their ability to walk to a bathroom and take a normal shit. At the next dinner with Beth and David he would be extra careful not to get intoxicated and reckless again.

Eggs in hand and still smiling her angel smile, Beth went to the door, Ken rolling behind her.

"Friday night work for you dude?" she questioned.

"Yes, but hey, I…it's," Ken stammered, "it's okay if you can't make it. I know you're busy and, and—well, I shouldn't have laid that guilt trip on you."

"I know that, most gentle friend. But you should know, I don't hang out with you out of guilt. I don't. You're—"

"I know," Ken cut in, "It's all—"

"No, Ken. Let me finish and remember who's holding the eggs," she threatened. "You're really an interesting dude, and you're funny—but friends are all we can ever, will ever be. As long as you—well, I just don't want to hurt you, okay?"

"Let me see—what I hear you saying is that you refuse to sleep with me and my wheelchair. How inconsiderate is that!" Ken quipped.

The off-the-wall humor missed but Beth let herself chuckle for her friend's sake.

"I'll see you and your wheelchair Friday at seven."

Ken yelled after her as she walked down the hall to her crib, as she often referred to her apartment.

"Don't show up without your brownies!"

Ken closed the door and retreated to his media cabinet where he played the Sting album that first united them. He made the lip-whispering sound that summoned Top Gun to his lap. As he gently stroked the fur of his closest companion, he reflected on the unexpected turn of events which caused him more emotional pain than he had yet experienced in life.

"So, this is the unpredictable factor of luck in life," he mused. "The luck of the draw, as they say…"

His handicap had so compromised his life, so worn on him over the years that this blunder with Beth made him angry, suicidal again.

"How selfish is that," he thought, "that you never take into account Beth's happiness? Be honest here. Do an unbiased evaluation of the situation. Isn't that what they taught you in seminary? Here's a beautiful nineteen-year-old girl who lives the life she was given, the hand of excellent cards she was dealt. And here is David, the Shark, who in truth is bright and talented with the features and physique of a Greek God. True, he is totally self-possessed, a swindler who will never have Beth's best interests at heart, but she doesn't know him to be that way. Maybe she'll figure him out very soon and break from him. Or maybe she will change him. Or maybe it's just a fling. So, chill out, dude, as Cameron at the music store would say. Or, as the Buddha would say, 'Everyone suffers.'"

"The Call To Suffering" was the title of one of the most memorable sermons Ken ever heard. It was given at the Catholic Seminary by Tully Boccti, an elderly Buddhist monk with a long white beard. He was born in America and gave his sermon in Christian terminology. Ken bought the CD after the talk. He listened to it often as a student because it brought him rare moments of peace. Even though there were sections in it he didn't fully understand he felt compelled to listen to it, so he dug it out of his collection of religious CDs and played it. He thought it might bring him the solace it used to so many years ago.

"*I am an old man,*" *the Buddhist monk began.* "*Perhaps you noticed,*" *he chuckled.*

"*I too was young once. Before I was a monk I also had a loving wife, who died in my arms. She was young and so beautiful—too young to die. It brought such pain to me that I wanted to join her in death. I* cried out, 'Where is God in this tragedy?' But there was no answer. No answer came to my mind. No sorrow was lifted from my heart. Then, that same day, a little girl, a Brownie Scout came to my door selling cookies. She was just so delightful, with her cute smile and big innocent eyes, like the eyes of a fawn. You see, she was practically brand new, a brand new person on earth. I thought, maybe the cruelty of life would not break her—maybe someday she will alleviate some suffering in our world. Maybe she will become a doctor, or a teacher, or a wonderful wife. Through her, God may be able to alleviate some of the suffering in our world. Maybe that's all that God can do, just bring His children into the world, children who grow up to alleviate some suffering— not all suffering. Even Jesus couldn't do that or possibly wouldn't do that. A case in point. Most of you are familiar with the story of Jesus and the paralyzed man in John's Gospel, chapter five. Allow me to paraphrase. There was this pool in Jerusalem around which lay a multitude of invalids, blind, lame, paralyzed. Jesus shows up and notices one paralyzed man who had been lying there for thirty-eight years. And he said to the wretched fellow, 'Do you want to be healed?' No offense intended, but that had to be the stupidest question ever asked. What paralyzed person wouldn't want to be healed? Except, this paralyzed man didn't say yes right off. No, he hemmed and hawed and made excuses why he couldn't be healed. Well, as you know, Jesus healed him anyway. But why did the man resist and forestall his healing? Because this is not strictly an historical event pointing up the miracle power of Jesus.

"That pool surrounded by a multitude of invalids is the world. Why do you think John emphasizes that the pool consisted of five porticos, five porches, in which were all these invalids? The porches are symbolic of the five senses. And all those invalids are us, the people of the world imprisoned in our five-sense world, prisoners in the physical life. The paralyzed man who didn't want to be healed reveals our own human dilemma. We worship our material existence, driven by our egos. And we prefer it to the Truth that Jesus represents, which is that we all have a divine origin, made in the image and likeness of God, the Bible states—born, each and every one of us, like the little

Brownie Scout, to love one another, and to do our part in alleviating the suffering of our world.

"In the story, John depicts the ego-centered world, the world of self-centered interests, as a sick world, which indeed it is. The Truth, which alone can heal our lives and our world, is the revelation that Mankind chooses to suffer. Did I hear some groans out there? Is it too harsh a truth to own up to? Mankind suffers at his own hand because he chooses to be self-serving instead of world-serving. Until we awaken and love our neighbors as we love ourselves, we are left to our own self-imposed suffering.

"Jesus didn't heal everyone around the pool because it's our world—we made it sick and it's up to us to heal it—"

The sound of Beth's song "Fields of Gold," Ken's chosen ring signal, interrupted the monk's sermon. Ken hit the pause button on his stereo remote and answered his cell phone. It was the Manhattan Bank seeking some personal verification concerning the money transfer from China.

Five days before, Ken established an account in seven different banks and credit unions, with a money transfer of a percentage of his fifty thousand dollar winnings. This was a necessary part of his plan. Prior to the switch he would have to withdraw all of his money from the banks and hide the cash somewhere. Keeping his deposits under eight thousand in each account, he would draw no suspicion to himself or a federal inquiry when he withdrew it. The Manhattan Bank had lost his personal records in a computer glitch and needed him to put in a personal appearance to fix the matter. They were very apologetic, but there was no way to handle it over the phone. Ken immediately called a cab, went to the bank and closed his account, taking seventy-three hundred in cash away with him. Through the entire inconvenience, Ken continued to contemplate the salient points of monk Boccti's homily.

The ex-priest had no problem with the idea that each of us is born to participate in the alleviation of suffering. It's an excellent ideal, Ken reflected. If such an ideal caught on, it would greatly benefit the human race—and the best part of it was that it didn't require faith in any imaginary God. However, Boccti's point, that God creates us in his image of love to alleviate suffering is obviously flawed, Ken concluded.

"Why would this God, this all-loving God whose purpose is to alleviate suffering, create paralyzed children, children like himself born to suffer—all just as innocent as the Brownie Scout—but deaf, blind, and crippled at birth? How can they feel His love and serve Him?"

The monk's sermon might work to inspire some people to love and serve, but not all. Ken certainly would do his share of loving and serving just as soon as he took over the handsome, healthy body of Timothy Gales.

CHAPTER TWENTY SEVEN
LEARNING A NEW LANGUAGE

On the return trip from the bank Ken had the cab driver drop him off at the music store, where he hooked up with Cameron, the young man schooling him on the present youth culture.

Cameron, an African American with a thick New York accent, looked older than twenty-one, his professed age. Ken told him he was doing research on youth culture so he could better identify with the young adults he was counseling online and on the phone. Cameron was only too happy to tutor him at twenty dollars an hour. Usually, they would have a conversation about the music of today, and the young man would not only educate him on the "tunes," as he referred to the music, but he would correct Ken's choice of words, revealing how someone cool would say the same things.

Today, however, Cameron was on his lunch break, and they walked and rolled together to "Mother Earth," a health food sandwich shop filled with college kids and leftover hippies from the sixties. Even before entering the shop, Ken was tantalized by the smell of freshly baked bread. Inside, the exposed brick walls and the floor of natural wood planks housed a décor that related "natural living." All of the tables and chairs were made of knotty pine, with green cushions and woven straw placemats. Here and there on the walls hung beautiful photos of golden wheat fields and vegetable gardens. The staff behind the counter of the open kitchen wore red aprons and green baseball hats with the Mother Earth logo. After receiving their order, Ken steered his wheelchair through the crowd to a corner table where he and Cameron relished their veggie burgers and fries.

"So tell me, Cameron," Ken began, "who are those older guys dressed in hippie attire?"

"Shit-can that uptown jargon, dude! Like, get down with some youth-speak. Rap it with cool, my man."

"Let me think a minute."

"No dog, that's your hang up. Like, you think too much," admonished Cameron.

"Like, I wasn't born and raised spouting youth-jive, dude!"

"That's getting down some, cool. Ask me about the gray-beards, dude."

"Clue me dude, what's with the gray-beards?"

"They hang here, like old paint, scoping the tender babes— I think some codger scored a chick here once and they think lighting might strike twice, dig?"

"Like, maybe some horny honies dig getting it on with older dudes."

"Horny honeys," repeated Cameron laughing, "That's so fucking white! Drop horny. Never say it again as long as you live! Now, check out these babes, my man. What do you see?"

"They're really hot, dude."

"No dude, they're smokin!'" corrected Cameron. "If any one of these smokin'-hot babes got down with a codger it wouldn't be for a motorcycle ride. No way! The old fart would have to be traveling in a chauffeur-driven limo with a trunk full of cash! Do you still record these rap sessions?"

Ken held up his pocket recorder, "Dude!"

The lesson in youth-speak continued on, from the sandwich shop to the music store into the late afternoon. It wasn't just youth-speak Ken was picking up from Cameron, but how he carried on with the male and female clientele. He checked out his "moves" as his young tutor would say. Cameron was way cool, but with the ladies he would always add some "come-on" no matter what their age. On rare occasions he would include a sexual innuendo which appeared to stimulate the woman's ego and her desire to flirt. Cameron had "game," modern day slang for charisma, specifically sexual charisma. "Game," according to his tutor, can't be taught—ether you have it or you don't! On the job, however, his tutor's game wasn't about "bagging chicks"—it was all about selling the albums, from which he scored a "sweet" commission.

Over the weeks of training Ken became familiar with most of the hip words and phrases, which he would practice at home using his tape recorder. Still, he knew just saying the words wasn't going to get it, so of late he focused more on conjuring up the sometimes aloof, sometimes sullen "attitude" of young people, along with their most popular idioms. Applying all this coherently in conversation required a great deal of practice. He got most of his practice over the telephone, calling to inquire about advertised youth outings, church groups, sport teams, rock concerts and Young Democrats and Republicans with whom he had a chance to spontaneously discuss politics in their cool lingo. Even though youth jargon was rich with phrases containing profanity, Ken found it difficult to even recite such phrases into his tape recorder. Saying things like fuck, fuck me, fuck it, douche bag, fuck this, fuck that, fuck off, and cluster fuck just rankled his sophisticated sensibilities. And he wondered what discontented adolescent first coined the term cluster fuck. He considered eliminating profanity altogether but his switch candidate, Timothy Gales, used it enough to warrant Ken's continued attention. Even so, Ken knew one term would never find a place in his vocabulary; he would never use the term "mother-fucker," no matter how much shit hit the fucking fan!

Time was becoming his enemy; with the switch only two weeks away he had to get on with his practice of spontaneous youth speak. Ken went online and printed out a list of pizza joints which he would call, knowing he would likely hook into a young person on the other end. So he dialed Dominos, the one closest to the university, but a girl answered and he couldn't launch his first nasty rap on her. Next he called Gigolo's Pizza and got his guy.

"Hello, Gigolo's—twenty-four seven delivery," came the voice of a young man.

Ken said, "Hey dog, you dudes deliver?"

"Yeah, twenty-four seven, like I just said. Whatta you want?"

"A pizza doophus, what else! And I want it to be hot when it gets here. The last fuckin' pie was so cold my tongue stuck to it!"

"Like sometimes our delivery dude gets lost. Usually people rave about our pies."

"They pay you to flap that bullshit?"

"No, they pay me to take orders. You gonna order or vent your sad ass all night?"

"My sad ass wants a large square pie, with the seven fuckin' toppings!

"We don't do square pies. And the most toppings is five. You want a round pie with five toppings?"

"Yeah, douche bag, if that's all you got!" responded Ken.

"Who you callin' douche bag, asshole?!"

"Unless there's more than one douche bag holding your phone, I guess you're it!"

"Tell you what, motherfucker, you come down here and I'll serve you your fuckin' teeth!"

"I'm busy, you fuckin' tool! But I'll send my little sister," fired back Ken, and hung up because he couldn't hold back his laughter another second.

Ken had never laughed that hard in his life. It brought sharp pains to his stomach and ribs but he couldn't stop. He tried to free his mind of the hilarious exchange, but it persisted. He wondered how Henry would respond if he sent him the recording of the phone call, and that thought rendered him hysterical. Of course, Ken thought, the whole pizza episode was contrived. It was beyond remote that he would ever allow himself to get involved in any such juvenile altercation. Even Timothy Gales wouldn't, although Gales let the expletives fly when he played rugby.

On Friday he would host a dinner for Beth and David. In the few days before the dinner he tried to run into David at the chess tables in the park. David the Shark once bragged that he not only furnished his entire crib with chess winnings but also had a cool seventy-five grand in winnings on which he never paid a dime of taxes. That made it clear that he never deposited the money in a bank. Ken wanted to further investigate the young con man before he suckered him in. Not that Ken had any concern about beating him, but he wanted to analyze the Shark's psychology in order to devise a scam that would relieve him of the most cash.

Ken already wrote an outline for the dinner meeting. He would play the fatherly frump role, looking after his young friend Beth. Sometime after dinner he would leak a bogus story about a recent inheritance, just to whet the Shark's appetite. He would attribute his three-hundred-grand inheritance to the death of a dear friend. The scam was not motivated by spite, though he was jealous of this lowlife character who stole his angel girl. Nor was the scam contrived just to avenge all the innocent students the Shark conned without mercy. From the beginning Ken planned to skin the Shark just to deflate his insufferable ego and then give back his money. However, now there was more at stake. Ken's revised plan was to return the Shark's money only if he agreed to break off with Beth and leave town. The ex-priest was naïve in the ways of young love, but he wasn't in the ways of the world. He received plenty of experience with con artists during his stint as a prison priest. He knew the Shark would have no qualms about breaking his agreement to leave town once he got his money back. Thus, Ken's plan was to only return a tenth of the money. The remaining nine tenths would be mailed in nine monthly installments to the Shark's out-of-state address. As long as the Shark didn't show his face within a hundred miles of Beth, or attempt to contact her in any way, he would get all of his money back in nine months. By that time Timothy Gales would at least have had a fair chance to win the heart of the girl he loved. As Ken thought about his future in a new life, Top Gun jumped on his lap meowing for his dinner.

CHAPTER TWENTY EIGHT

NO NIGHT IS AS DARK AS THE DARK NIGHT OF THE LOST SOUL

Joel's interview with the agent Bracken went well enough considering the circumstances. Joel's attention was not on the interview but racing through every possible explanation for the unshakable feeling that someone else was living his life. The one persistent explanation was that he was in fact insane. Insane people believe their totally irrational fantasies. Joel grappled with the idea of just going to New York and getting with a good psychiatrist.

When Joel stepped out of the agent's office he remembered speaking to the tall tan silver-haired Bracken but wasn't aware of anything he said. Sonia got up to join Bracken and Joel for the parting formalities. While shaking Joel's hand, Bracken turned to Sonia.

"This young man has a unique visage. He's got eyes, as they say— James Dean's eyes, right?"

"Yeah, like the eyes of a cornered cougar."

Turning back to Joel, Bracken said, "I'll take you in on a standard one-year contract. Mario, our receptionist will fill you in on it. And before you head to New York I need a reel on you. Sonia, sweetheart, can you shoot some footage of my new client?"

"Already have some. We videoed his audition for *Don't Call Me Son*."

"Send it over," said Bracken. "Wait, are you going to the *Arctic Storm* bash tomorrow night?"

"I wasn't invited," responded Sonia.

"The whole agency's invited. If you go, bring me his video."

With his request, Bracken kissed Sonia on the cheek, squeezed Joel's shoulder and disappeared into his office.

Sonia was obviously psyched at the thought of spending another evening with Joel. The party was all she talked about on the way back to the YMCA. Satirizing the invitation, Sonia quipped, "Party time, babe! Twist my arm, okay! I'll see if I can squeeze the hottest party in tinsel town into my busy schedule! The biggest names in the industry will be there, babe! Hey, no grunge attire for this one. Dress to the nines! Have you got anything in the nines category?"

Joel wasn't listening.

"Okay, we're going shopping. I'll lend you the cash. And you need cards. We'll have some made up—what's going on with you? You look like bad news."

"No, Sonia, I'm cool—like I'm a little blown out by all of it," said the sullen Joel.

"As well you should be, dude. Do you know how many people get a standard contract with Eddie Bracken at LT? Like about one in a hundred who even get to an interview!"

"Will we get to meet Zack Taylor?" inquired Joel.

"No doubt…what's the big deal with Zack Taylor! My God, every director in tinsel town will be there. It's the monster schmooze event of the year! Here's where connections are made, Joel—where movies are really made—at parties like this. There will be a mob of reporters, and casting directors, snapping phone photos—any one of them could jump-start your film career! And nix to that cologne your wearing! I've got some Richy Blaze at the house."

"Richy Blaze," queried Joel?

"What, you never heard of Richy Blaze, the cologne of the stars! The shit is two hundred dollars an ounce. It shouts money, my green friend. And that's what makes this business happen."

Joel pulled out of his sullen bag, taking Sonia's hand from the wheel and kissing it, "You're amazing, girl! I owe you everything."

"You're not the first guy to say that to me. Just promise me one thing, no more freaked-out nightmares."

Joel laughed, but picked up on her subtle hook. He was obliged to spend another sleepover at her place. As Julian would put it, "The skin required for the favor."

"Hey," Joel asked, "is it okay if I spend the night at your place after the party?"

"Sounds like a plan. What about tonight?"

"I wish I could, but my dad is flying in for a couple of hours tonight," Joel lied.

"I suppose he wouldn't be up for a threesome," Sonia quipped.

"He's a devout Catholic," Joel chuckled back, "He spends every Christmas at the Vatican."

"With your mother?" asked Sonia, with a wry smile.

"My mother passed away five years ago," said Joel, expanding the lie.

Joel didn't feel cool about lying to his generous friend, but he needed some down time to figure things out.

"Oh, sorry," apologized Sonia, "What's he do for a living?"

"He's a pilot for Continental—flies free and shit."

"So you were raised a Catholic, taking communion and all that ritual stuff?"

"Yeah, but it never took with me."

"So you don't believe in God, Heaven and hell, anything like that?"

"Not really. Do you?" asked Joel, trying to escape her inquiry into his past which didn't exist.

From his recent experiences, Joel wasn't certain that hell didn't exist and that he hadn't somehow stumbled into it. He finally got her talking about her somewhat unhappy past. She had been married twice, the first time for love which turned to hate, the second time for comfort. It was the second husband who bought the duplex before he ran off with a cocktail waitress named Bunny Baxter.

"With a name like that," Sonia laughed, "the poor girl had no choice but to be a first class cunt!"

They drove to an upscale men's clothing store named "Diamond Jim's." Sonia actually knew the owner, whose daughter use to study with her. She introduced Joel to the owner, chatting briefly about Jean-Marie, the daughter, who was married and expecting her first child. Then Sonia got down to business.

"Mr. Martinelli, I can afford to spend five hundred dollars. I'm going to rampage through your store grabbing things off the racks for my friend to try on. Stop me when I've reached my limit, okay?"

"If that's your budget, start over here with the Italian slacks. I've got some real bargains on them and a line of sport jackets that are just a tad way out!"

Thus, Sonia rampaged for a half hour, while Joel jumped in and out of the dressing room, modeling her selections. Sonia winked her approval as Joel stepped out of the dressing room for her perusal, wearing black slacks with pleated cuffs over black suede gaucho boots. On top Joel wore a black silk shirt with a diagonal sterling silver zipper. Over the shirt he wore a way-out silver-blue sports jacket, the upper half of which was conventionally cut but the lower section was cut in uneven jagged lengths that hung elegantly to his knees. With his gold locks curling around his neck and his gray cougar eyes accented against his black and silver attire, Joel looked more like a movie star than Zack Taylor ever did. Sonia was stunned by her own creation. Pointing to a swank array of men's jewelry in a nearby glass display case she said, "You need that silver watch and the turquoise ring next to it."

At this, Mr. Martinelli interceded, poking away at his cell phone-calculator.

"Miss Ammonia, excuse me but you are already three hundred dollars over your budget. Joel looks stunning! Believe me, he doesn't need the jewelry."

"How about letting us borrow the watch and ring for tomorrow night. We will have it back in that case Saturday morning. I'll polish it myself."

"But Miss Ammonia, if something unforeseeable happens, my insurance will not cover it. You understand."

"How much is the watch?" inquired Sonia

"Sonia, we don't need it," Joel broke in.

"Chill out babe—I'm cool. How much Mr. Martinelli?"

"Sixteen hundred and ninety-five dollars, plus tax."

"For the watch and ring?"

"No, just the watch. The ring is seven hundred and ninety five. But I can let you have the set for twenty-one hundred, plus tax."

Like a woman possessed, Sonia removed her diamond ring from the third finger on her right hand.

"Do you know what this ring is worth?"

Immediately, Martinelli removed a jeweler's glass and proceeded to appraise the ring.

Joel insisted, "Sonia, don't—we're cool. I don't need the jewelry."

"You want to trade this for the watch and ring?" asked Martinelli.

"Please, Mr. Martinelli, you know as well as I do that you're holding a ten thousand dollar diamond ring. You hang on to the ring for collateral until Saturday morning when I return your jewelry and I'll throw in a hundred for your trouble."

"All right, just for you, Miss Ammonia. But I will take a photo of all the jewelry involved. And you must sign a note agreeing to the deal."

Laughing, Sonia quipped, "What, you don't trust me Mr. Martinelli?"

"You, I trust. It's life I don't trust."

Thus, the deal was photographed and signed. The clothes were billed to Sonia's credit card and the world rolled on toward evening. The drive to the Y was relatively short, with one stop at One Day Printing, where Sonia had a hundred cards made up. The cards contained Joel's name scrolled artistically in silver across a black background. The rest of the information included on the cards was the Lillian Tabor Agency—Eddie Bracken—along with the agency's phone number and e-mail. It was six o'clock when they pulled up to the Y. After expressing his gratitude, Joel shared a long wet promissory kiss with Sonia, gathered bags of clothes from the back seat and waved to her as she drove away. When Joel turned to walk into the YMCA he saw Julian staring out from the lobby window. Once inside the lobby, Joel confronted his friend, "Jesus Christ, Julian! You're like a fuckin' spy!"

To which Julian responded, "Shit, brother, I'm just watching out for your young ass. My God, look at you with all that Diamond Jim apparel! Tell me she didn't fuck the shit out of you!"

"How do you know it's Diamond Jim apparel?"

"The signature, dude. Check it out on the suit bag. Looks like she's adopted you," continued Julian as he peeked into a couple of the bags. "All this is going to cost some more skin for sure!"

"It's my skin, bro!"

"Come on, sit down a minute. Tell your black buddy what's going down."

Joel wasn't about to discuss his sex life with his black buddy but he desperately needed some feedback on the escalating predicament of his life, so he sat down.

"Jules," Joel began, "can I trust you? I mean, like not to divulge anything I say to you now?"

"Whoa, sounds like serious shit!"

"It is. You'll probably think I'm crazy."

"Lay it on me, brother. No wait. Let me light a cigarette—helps to stimulate the brain functions."

Julian selected a half smoked butt from the ashtray beside his chair and lit up.

"Want one, Diamond Jim," chuckled Julian?

"No," responded Joel coldly, deflating Julian's attempt at levity. "Promise me you won't repeat a word of what I tell you."

"My lips are sealed. Shoot."

"I'm invited to a big party tomorrow night."

"And...?"

"And," said Joel, "I think the top dog at this party, put some kind of spell on me—back when—several months ago, before I came to L.A."

"A spell," repeated Julian. "Like a Voodoo type spell?"

"Something like that," responded Joel. I think he entered my body somehow. It's fuckin' weird, right?"

"You mean, he entered your body—and like talks in your head, shit like that?" asked Julian.

"No. No, not like that."

"Not like that?"

"No. I think he took over my body, my life."

"Hold on here," paused Julian, taking a deep drag on his cigarette and talking through the exhale, "This dude, who cast the spell, he's not talking through you right now, right?"

"No. I'm not schizo. I don't have multiple personalities—no one is talking through me! I think this guy took over my real body and is walking around in it—living my life, the life I should be living."

"Oh good," quipped Julian, "I was concerned that you might have some kind of mental disorder!"

"See, you think I'm a mental case."

"You're just fucking with me, right?" chuckled Julian. "Almost had me too—Jesus Christ, man, tell me you're fucking with me!"

"No, Jules, I'm not," insisted Joel, "I'm living a freaking nightmare!"

"You actually believe that some dude put a spell on you—took over your real body—and he is, like, walking around in it, someplace else. He's in your body right now, some place else?" questioned Julian.

"Yes, that's exactly it," confirmed Joel.

"Cool, we can clear this spell up right now. Let's just go look in the hall mirror. You will see what I see, Joel in his body."

"No, no! He's not Joel. He's Zack Taylor. I'm really Zack Taylor. He stole my body, my life somehow!"

"Just chill a minute, man, while I wrap my head around this, requested Julian... Are you talking about Zack Taylor, the movie idol?"

"Yes, the movie idol, Zack Taylor—the star of *Arctic Storm*," responded Joel. "I believe he, with the help of some ghoul, some witchdoctor in a wheelchair, stole my body when I was Zack Taylor, and he is living—"

"Joel, Joel," interrupted Julian, "did you do some weird dope last night, some acid, or meth, anything like that?"

"No, a bowl of pot, some sake. Jules, I'm not tripping out here. I've been in this nightmare for months!"

"Chill out a second! If some evil dude high-jacked your body, Zack Taylor's body, where did you get this body I'm talking to?"

"I don't know. For all I know it's the body of the evil fuck who stole mine!"

"Perfect. Listen... Do you believe that I am your friend?" queried Julian.

"Yes, I wouldn't be telling you this if I didn't."

"Cool. So you know I have no reason to bullshit you."

"Of course not. I trust you totally."

"I gather the party you're going to tomorrow night is the *Arctic Storm* gala," stated Julian.

"Yes," confirmed Joel.

"And you are planning to confront Zack Taylor about this body-snatching shit. Am I right bro?"

"Something like that, yes," stated Joel.

Julian looked directly into his young friend's eyes and spoke like a father to a son, "I don't know what's going on with you, man. But I know this. You are on the verge of flushing your career right down the toilet. Don't go to that party, Joel. Hang here with me. Better yet, grab the bus to New York tonight."

"Jules, I've got to go. I made plans with Sonia. She bought me all these clothes."

"Listen to me!" Julian insisted, as he leaned in grabbing Joel's shoulders. "Are you stable enough to grasp on here? You need help. Fuck, everyone needs help sometime. Don't go to that party! Go to New York—hook up with a good shrink and work it out… Just for the sake of pressing home the all-important point—even if this fantasy about Zack Taylor is true, which it can't be, but suppose it is—what the fuck do you think he's going to do when you confront him, give you back his star-studded life? No, Joel, he's going to have you arrested, committed—and what's worse, you will be the headline in every newspaper in the fuckin' world! 'Maniac Accuses Movie Star Taylor of Stealing His Body!' Kiss your Broadway show good-bye, bro—kiss your career good-bye! Am I getting through?"

"Yes, Jules. You're making perfect sense to me. I can't be that crazy, because everything you just said I've already considered. I guess I just needed someone to confirm it for me."

"Cool, then you're not going to the party?" asked Julian

"I have to go—but trust me, I am not going to say a word to Zack Taylor. If I run into him, I'll shake his hand and say, 'great party,' and go on with my life as Joel Ellendorff, opening soon in the Broadway show, *Don't Call Me Son*."

"Don't drink or drug all night. Just schmooze the directors, smile for the press and enjoy the entertainment. Just be cool," said Julian, holding out his fist for a confirmation.

Joel tapped his fist to Julian's.

"Thanks for the one on one."

As Joel stood up to leave, he held out a twenty dollar bill to Julian.

"Here, best buddy, buy yourself some dinner."

"Okay," said Julian, taking the bill, "but this is just a loan, until my check arrives."

"Cool," said Joel, as he gathered his bags and walked to the elevator.

Before the elevator doors closed, he saw that his friend had already left the lobby for the neighborhood bar.

CHAPTER TWENTY NINE

FATE IS A COWARD'S COP-OUT

t was three in the afternoon when Ken returned from the movie theatre where he saw *Arctic Storm*. Four hours remained before the scheduled dinner with Beth and David. He had spent a good part of yesterday making his own tomato sauce from *Old Europe's Cook Book*. Now all he had to do was to boil the flat noodles for the vegetarian lasagna, grate the cheese and make the salad.

It wasn't his best day. The back pain that began in the theatre stayed with him until he got home. His usual assortment of pain killers hadn't fully kicked in and he was tempted to have a glass of wine to speed it along. Better judgment prevailed and he decided to wait it out. He was so occupied with his cooking that he accidentally ran over Top Gun's tail, which happened once before, causing him no little guilt. It was unavoidable. Whenever Ken opened the refrigerator, even to just get some ice water, the cat would scurry around his wheels hoping to snag anything he dropped. Ken called the Rascal to his lap and after some cuddling and a piece of cheese he was happily playing around his wheels again.

During his cook-a-thon Ken flashed back on *Arctic Storm* and Zack Taylor, whom he hadn't seen since the "big switch" in Las Vegas.

"Such an idealistic film," thought Ken. Knowing the alchemist made it impossible for Ken to believe a word the actor said. Ken was not an avid film buff, but *Arctic Storm* seemed so chauvinistic that he was surprised it wasn't boycotted by every woman on earth. The major sub-plot had a pretty half-breed Eskimo, Migthump, tracking Gil Hammond, the alchemist's character, for days. Mile after mile she relentlessly pursues

Gil's dog-sled tracks over the vast Arctic landscape. Migthump is driven by the belief that Gil Hammond is in the Arctic poaching polar bears and she intends to kill him. That at least was plausible, mused Ken. But days of dog-sled tracking ensued, and though she never stopped to feed her dogs or tend to their bleeding feet, her faithful dogs who were trained to never bark, charged on over the tundra. Ken estimated that at least a half hour of film time elapsed during the tracking sequence, while the audience listened to Gil Hammond's voiceover, revealing the plight of the Arctic and the ice dependent creatures who live there. The narrative waxes poignant as Hammond, choking back tears, tells of his personal pain in watching the Arctic ice melt away, leaving the endangered polar bears to perish. Finally, with the audience on the verge of snow blindness, Migthump, the pretty Eskimo, finds Gil's camp in the moonlight. She removes a whale bone hunting knife from its sheath, sniffs the air and delivers her very first line with a New York accent, "Migthump can smell him."

Ten more minutes of Migthump sneaking up to Gil Hammond's tent, with one pause for her second line, she looks up at the moon and says, "Grandmother moon, forgive Migthump for what she must do."

With that, brandishing the whale bone knife, she rushes the tent and slashes it open. Surprise!—the super cunning Gil Hammond is hiding beneath a pile of his sled-dogs. Ken laughed out loud when the rest of the audience simultaneously gasped at Gil's surprise on Migthump. They tussle, fight, and roll over and over in the snow until Gil figures out Migthump is a woman and decides instead to bone her. That she goes along with "the boning" in sub-zero weather borders on science-fiction. Ken paused in his reflection to pride himself on spontaneously surfacing the slang phrase, "bone her."

What a movie, Ken mused. It should have offended every woman who saw it, but obviously didn't. *Arctic Storm* had already grossed over a hundred million at the box office. Ken thought, the pen is mightier than the sword, but sex is mightier than common sense.

With the lasagna prepared and in the oven, Ken set to making a delectable Greek salad, minus the anchovies. He decided to listen to some "tunes," as his young mentor referred to them. However, upon pressing the play button on his remote, he was greeted with the continuation of monk Boccti's sermon. Ken realized that the monk's CD must have been left in the player and the system left on for days. It's serendipitous, Ken figured, and decided to let the old monk finish his sermon.

"Do we want to be healed?" Boccti posed the rhetorical question to his audience.

"If you ask anyone that question, how many would sincerely say, yes? I suspect the majority would say yes, until you explained what being healed means. Well, you all know what it means, don't you? Shout out if you disagree with my position on all this. It means being whole in consciousness, expanded in a selfless awareness—an awareness that includes everyone and excludes no one. It means realizing that suffering anywhere is 'my' suffering. It means responding appropriately to suffering wherever we see it, in whatever way we can. To the degree that we have the ability and means to alleviate any apparent suffering we take up our divine calling. For in healing we are healed—not necessarily in the physical sense, but in our hearts. In taking up our divine calling to heal, our hearts are healed of selfishness. In the process—and most of you have experienced this or you wouldn't be here—in the process of helping, the love that is God rushes in, reminding us that it is in giving that we receive. I usually finish this talk with a statement that seems unnecessary to share with this audience of aspiring priests. But I will share it anyway. If we can't rise up to answer the call to alleviate suffering, we should at least be mindful never to cause any. Thank you, and may love be with you."

Boccti's concluding lines struck Ken so hard he couldn't believe he ever heard them before. Of all the times he played this sermon, he never heard the concluding lines. Well, he thought, certainly he heard them but it didn't register back then because he was an aspiring priest. Ken recalled how often he himself had preached such platitudes, on the basis that there was a God who rewarded you for serving His children on earth. Now, however, his circumstances were different. Now, with God and the promise of a future reward in Heaven removed from the equation of life, the call to alleviate suffering translated to "live a life of personal sacrifice and die, never having fully persued the personal pleasures of the world."

Then the ex-priest ruminated on Timothy Gales playing rugby, recalling the personal exultation he exuded whenever he scored a goal. Except for chess, Ken never competed for anything. He never experienced the personal exultation of winning, the rush of adrenaline happiness that accompanies every kind of human conquest. Even when he won his chess matches for thousands of dollars, he didn't feel the visceral high of winning for himself. Such personal pleasure requires a healthy ego which hasn't been compromised by religion. According to the scriptures, God frowns upon such pride and demands penance, humility from His children. Ken realized that he even felt a twinge of guilt upon winning his chess matches, as though he used his personal skill to take advantage of others. "No wonder there are so many anxious, frustrated people in the world," reflected the ex-priest. "They have been turned against their natural inclinations to strive and succeed for the sheer pleasure of it. "Or, was it just him, who was compromised from birth, prevented by his lot in life from ever knowing the pleasure of winning?" The alchemist said it all when he quoted the famous refrain from Bob Dylan's song, "And may you stay forever young." The monk's sermon faded from the handicapped man's awareness, as he put Dylan's album on and set the dinner table.

When he heard the familiar knock at the door, he was dressed like Timothy Gales would be dressed, right down to the Nike running shoes. He opened the door to behold the love of his life beside the young man he both disliked and envied. Backing up his wheelchair, Ken said, "Come in, come in. The white wine is on ice and dinner has fifteen minutes to go."

Beth and David were wearing Levis. Beth wore a white halter, leaving her tanned shoulders and arms exposed. Her beautiful chestnut hair was adorned with silver and white feathers. Ken thought, this girl could walk into any modeling agency and be signed before she opened her mouth. David wore a white silk shirt with the collar open, exposing his tan chest and accentuating his dark almond eyes. Ken's young adversary appeared younger now that his ample black hair was down to his shoulders and not pulled back in a ponytail. Ken thought, "The actor Johnny Depp has nothing on this guy!"

Placing her dish of brownies on the table, Beth said, "David, this is Ken McAlister, my friend who—"

"Save it, babe. Ken and I are brothers of the game. How's it going, old buddy? You still killing those fish at the park?"

"No," responded Ken, "I've lost interest playing the game for peanuts!"

"Well, trip up to Central Park. That's where the real money plays," stated David.

"That's what I've heard. How about some Winston Vineyard Chardonnay? I've also got an excellent Chianti if you'd rather…"

"No, let's do the white," said David. "I've never seen you at Central Park—must be hard to get uptown in a wheelchair."

"Tell me about it," said Ken, using the slang phrase that translates, "You have no idea how hard it really is."

"How high are the stakes uptown?" inquired Ken, as he rolled to the refrigerator for the wine.

"It fluctuates a lot, but I've played games for five large," replied David.

"Large, is that five hundred or thousand?"

"Thousand."

"I hope you won," chuckled Ken as he proceeded to apply his state of the art cork screw to the cork.

"You know I did—all three games," laughed David. "That fish paid off my van."

"Beth, why don't you and David relax in the living room, while I fetch the glasses and pour the wine."

"No way, dude," responded Beth. "I'll pour the wine, while you two choose some tunes."

"I heard there were a couple of games in June for twenty-five large. I'd sure like to grab a piece of that action!" exclaimed David.

Ken led David to his cream-colored entertainment center.

"Touch select on the screen for an alphabetic index of everything in stock," suggested Ken. "How can you trust a stranger to pay up after the game?"

"You don't. When you play for that kind of green you pay a 'terminator' to hold the stakes, always in cash of course."

As David reviewed the index screen, he said, "I don't suppose you have any rap music in stock."

"No," said Ken, "I used to but it makes the cat's hair fall out!"

David laughed, "Cool. I'll stay with some of this elevator music."

David called out to Beth in the kitchen, "Ken's got some Ethridge, Sting, Nestor, Adele, Carlyle..."

"Play Brady Carlyle," Beth shouted back.

"Carlyle it is."

David selected Carlyle's and Tracey Chapman's albums, sighing, "I guess we're flowing mellow tonight."

"Who's the terminator, the guy who holds the money?" asked Ken, leading David across the living room where he sat beside Beth on the sofa.

"A terminator is one of the big bad bodyguards for hire who hang at the chess tables. They charge four percent to hold the wager and make sure the winner gets paid. For another two percent they'll escort you home or to the bank," concluded David.

Beth poured the wine saying, "If you're going to talk about chess all night, I'm going to watch the tube!"

"Cool, babe," said David, turning to Ken, "She never would. She hates the tube!"

"I guess you heard about Duncan, the black guy in the Spider Man show..." related Beth, changing the subject.

"What about Duncan?" queried Ken.

"He got maced. He's in the hospital," replied Beth.

"Maced?"

"That's that pepper spray that burns," interjected David.

"I know what mace is," corrected Ken coldly. "How did it happen?"

Before Beth could reply, David jumped in.

"The fool was hanging out with the Occupy assholes on Wall Street when the police broke up their stupid protest."

"Not really," Beth corrected. "He just stopped to rap with one of the protesters. His face is really burned pretty bad."

"It's his own dumb-ass fault! The dude rakes in three large a week in Spider Man. What's he doing even talking with those losers!"

"I don't think they're losers. I think they're just people fed up with the system," stated Beth.

"Because they can't hack the fact that Darwin was right. The strong survive and the weak protest!" laughed David.

"Is he going to be all right?" asked Ken.

"He thinks so. But he's out of the show until his eyes heal up." "She visits the dufus in the hospital! The last of the bleeding hearts," mocked David, as he leaned over and kissed her on the cheek. "I love this girl, but she just doesn't get it. That loser in the hospital calls her, not his roommate—not his mother or father, or anyone but—"

"He called his roommate first," interrupted Beth.

"Why did he call you at all, babe—that's my point," argued David.

"Because I'm his friend."

"See," said David, who was becoming more and more obnoxious in Ken's eyes. "She doesn't get it! 'Because he's my friend,' bullshit! He wants to jump your bones, babe—am I right, old buddy?"

"No, I think you're dead wrong," responded Ken, fighting the urge to unleash a flurry of his newly mastered expletives. "Beth really does care about people and they respond to her accordingly, as a friend."

"Duncan is gay. I told you that!" concluded Beth.

"There's no such thing as a truly gay man," sniggered David. "When I get around to writing my book, that's one of the fallacies I'm going to expose!"

The oven buzzer sounded, not a moment too soon, as Ken was about to lose his shit on the insufferable Shark.

"Dinner is ready," announced Ken. We have vegetarian lasagna and a Greek salad. It's team effort time. I'm going to grab the salad. David, capture the Lasagna. The pot holders are hanging right on the oven door. Beth, snag the Chianti and three fresh glasses on the drain board."

The trio followed their orders impeccably. Dinner was on the table in minutes. Throughout the process all Ken thought about was Beth in a relationship with this arrogant jerk.

Both men were surprised when she suggested, "I feel like we should say grace."

"To who?" chuckled David.

"To whoever God might be, and if you fool around, David, I will impale your nose on this fork."

Thus, Beth prayed.

"Oh, God of many names, whoever you might be, we are thankful for this food, and the friendship we share at this table. Amen."

David couldn't resist. He genuflected with a fork full of lasagna.

The dinner conversation started out with a short discourse from Beth citing a recent research project which revealed that people who feel and express appreciation suffer fewer and less chronic illnesses. David immediately ridiculed the research, "The people they cull for these idiot projects are the retards who couldn't make the cut on the Jerry Springer show! My mother was a loving, appreciating person. She was a tireless volunteer for the Special Olympics her whole life. She died at forty-two of cancer. Case closed!"

"Dude," said Beth, "that's one unfortunate example. And you use it to justify your anti-God philosophy. Ken, you are dining with the kindest, most considerate atheist you will ever meet!"

"Open your eyes, babe. The hospitals are overcrowded with people who are all fucked up, pardon my French! I guess none of them exuded enough appreciation. What about Ken here—he seems like a decent dude. What fucked you up Ken, a car accident, Thalidomide, what?"

Not wanting to support the Shark's logic, Ken joked, "Who's fucked up? The wheelchair is a dodge, dude! I use it to get girls."

David and Beth rendered a self-conscious laugh. Ken poured fresh glasses of Chianti and said, "My paralysis is congenital. Therefore, it doesn't resolve the appreciation debate, unless you believe in reincarnation. What it does prove unequivocally is shit happens!"

"So David, where are you from originally?" asked Ken.

"Phoenix, Arizona—born there."

"Do you still have family there?"

"Not really. My father is a Colonel in the Army—so Phoenix was just a two year stop over. We lived all over the country and a few years in Europe—until my mom checked out."

"Excuse me, guys. I've got to tinkle," said Beth as she retreated to the bathroom.

Ken's game plan required him to extract as much personal information as possible, to find out just how to lure the Shark into the most expensive chess game he would ever play. However, the fact that David lost his mother who worked with mentally challenged kids triggered Ken's memory of his mom, and began to dampen his enthusiasm for skinning the Shark.

"How old were you when you lost your mother, David?"

"Nineteen."

"It must have been devastating."

"Yeah, kind of… We weren't close. It's all such bullshit you know—the whole family guilt trip thing. I didn't attend the funeral—fuck all that ritual. I sent flowers. 'Like, she's dead,' I told my brother. 'What's the fuckin' point!'"

"You have a brother?"

"Jesus, dude, are you writing a book?"

"No, I just find you fascinating. Usually, young, free-wheeling dudes like you take up sports betting or poker. What turned you on to chess?"

"My father, he loved the game—taught me and my brother to play when we were kids. Though he never dreamed I'd turn his hobby into a profession."

"Have you ever thought about turning pro?"

"I might when I'm old. Right now chess affords me a great life, without the hassles that come with being a registered pro."

"You mean the IRS hassle, right?"

"There's that, yes, but it's also the exposure. I don't need the exposure. I travel man. I've been hustling fish all over the world! Going to San Diego when it gets cold, with Beth. And next summer we're going to France, Italy, and Spain. I've got the life, dude! And Beth, well, she's the icing on my cake!"

"Tell me about it," said Ken. "Hell, I might try the life of a traveling chess hustler, for the fun of it, of course. Or maybe I'll buy a couple of race horses, now that I've got the money."

David's reaction to the money line was so big you'd think he did it for laughs.

"Sounds like you hit the mother lode, dude!"

"Yeah, close to four hundred thousand—an inheritance from a dear friend."

"I'm sorry to hear about your friend, but hello money!" exclaimed David.

Beth returned holding Top Gun and let Ken know, "You're overfeeding this bum. He weighs more than me!"

"It's Ken's cooking!" exclaimed David, who held up his glass and proposed a toast. "To the man and his amazing lasagna!"

Everyone tapped glasses and said "Here, Here!"

"Wait until you taste my Greek salad," exulted Ken as he slid the large serving bowl toward Beth." Will you please serve the salad, Beth."

"I also need to toast you, Ken, for being instrumental in bringing Beth and me together. To Ken!"

Ken reluctantly tapped the extended glasses. He had to look away when David and Beth embraced.

CHAPTER THIRTY

A FISH FIT FOR A KING

"It's time to fall upon my award winning Greek Salad, boasted Ken. In deference to the vegetarian in our midst, I kept these lovely anchovies on the side," said the host as he raised the lid of a small bowl containing anchovies.

"No," shrieked David, "get them away from me!"

Beth and Ken reached for the bowl of anchovies, accidentally knocking it across the table and spilling it all over David's lap. The young atheist leaped up, brushing the fish from his clothing as though he just caught fire. Then he expelled a horrendous sneeze that rocked the chandelier above the table.

"Fucking anchovies!" wheezed David, fighting back another sneeze.

Beth grabbed a wet sponge from the sink and attempted to remove the anchovies stuck to her boyfriend. Ken sped to the computer desk, retrieved a box of tissues and returned it to David, who was wheezing and sneezing uncontrollably.

"It's really psychological, babe," suggested Beth softly. The anchovies were on the table all the time. You didn't—"

"Save the—ahhchoo—psychobabble for your—ah-ahh-ahhchoo— illiterate girlfriends," shouted David, struggling to catch his breath.

Beth, massaging his shoulders, suggested, "Just think about it, babe. You really didn't start sneezing until you saw the anchovies." "Just shut the-ah-ahh-ahhchoo—fuck up!—ahhchoo!"

"Ken, have you got any of that peppermint oil I left you," pleaded Beth.

"Fuckin'—ah-ahh-ahhchoo—idiot!—with the—ah-ahhchoo—pep

per—ah—ahh—pepper—ahhchoo—FUCKING PEPPERMINT OIL—AHH CHOOO!"

Retrieving the tiny bottle of oil from the kitchen drawer, Ken tossed it to Beth. David was on his feet, doubling over with every sneeze.

"I need air!—ahhchooo—I've got—I've got—ahhchooo—to get out—ahhchoo—" Beth put a couple of drops of peppermint oil on her finger and dabbed it under David's nose and on each of his cheekbones. The smell of peppermint filled the room. Instantly, David stopped sneezing, the allergic reaction completely subsided. After a moment Ken offered David a glass of water but he chose a couple of swallows of Chianti.

"Jesus, that shit really works! This is unreal," exclaimed David, as he took deep breaths through his nose, looking baffled. "I have suffered from this goddamn fish allergy forever—spent a ton of money on specialists—this is un-fuckin' believable!"

"You want to call it a night, big guy?" asked Beth.

"No. I'm just getting started here. Let's test this shit," declared the atheist, holding up the tiny bottle of peppermint oil." Have you got any anchovies left?"

Ken answered, "In the fridge, dude. But let's quit while we're ahead."

"No way, man! I'm telling you, there's a fortune to be made marketing this stuff!"

"It's already being marketed," stated Beth. "Let's call it a night."

"By who?"

"Some company in Utah."

"Do you really want the anchovies?" asked Ken, not wanting to risk his evening with the girl whose presence enchanted him.

"Bring on the fish," ordered David, like a king summoning a conquered enemy.

Ken rolled to the refrigerator, picked up a small plastic container of anchovies and waited for the young king to give a final confirmation for the test. David, still in his kingly demeanor, dabbed a couple of drops of peppermint under his nose and on his cheeks. Then in true kingly fashion he summoned his enemy with a flourish of his hand, spilling some of the wine in his glass. He was obviously quite tipsy.

"Bring those fish to me. I wish to peer upon those little devils. For on this day, My Lady, I will break their hold on me forever!"

Laughing at the absurdity of the scene, Beth cautioned, "Perhaps you should apply a lot more peppermint before you try this, David."

"No, my lady. Such caution bespeaks a cowardice that finds no place in this noble heart," slurred the inebriated king. "Bring me those anchovies!"

Dutifully, Beth took the canister of anchovies from Ken and ceremoniously bowed while holding them out to the atheist king.

"Me thinks they quiver in my presence, Lady Beth," slurred the king as he took the canister of anchovies and raised it to his face. Then holding the anchovies up in true kingly fashion he declared, "These devils are nothing! Thus, I shall eat one now and silence forever the superstition of their power!"

In spite of Ken's overall impression of David, he had to admire his gutsy sense of humor.

Then the tipsy king lifted a single anchovy from the container and held it high in the air before lowering it into his open mouth. With his enemy between his teeth, the king turned slowly in place as though he were displaying the conquered fish to a stadium full of faithful subjects. As he completed the turn Ken and Beth blanched at the sight of David, whose eyelids were fluttering wildly, out of sync with each other, while his face drained of all color before their eyes. Spitting the fish across the room, the ex-king sucked in a monstrous breath and heaved a volcanic upchuck filled with lasagna, wine, and morsels of food that hadn't seen the light of day since his childhood. The mess exploded out over everything, including Beth. The atheist king entered a convulsive state of sneezing and puking simultaneously. The upheaval in David's body was so violent he could not maintain his footing and lunged-sneezing-puking-choking to the floor—heaving- sneezing-choking-puking-crawling-screaming help—convulsing and pissing himself, the king struggled out the door into the hall. A minute later he stumbled gasping down the ramp, out into the street, sneezing and struggling to regain his equilibrium. Beth followed him all the way tossing drops of peppermint oil at him.

Ken came out last and shouted, "Should I call 911?"

"No!" shouted David who was beginning to recover.

When they were certain he was breathing normally they helped him down the hall to Beth's apartment. Under his own power David stepped into the shower, removing his clothes as the water ran over him. Upon observation it was clear that Ken somehow escaped the puke storm, but Beth didn't.

"Ken, is it all right if I use your shower?" requested Beth.

"Of course," he replied, nodding his head.

In a flash Beth grabbed a bathrobe from her bedpost and rushed past him down the hall. Upon entering Ken's bathroom Beth became aware that there were no towels on the rack or in the linen closet. She was half out of her clothes, and searching his kitchen when Ken entered his apartment. Naked from the waste up, without a hint of embarrassment, she inquired, "Where do you hide your towels?"

Ken was literally struck speechless. He wasn't four feet from her, staring at her magnificent bare breasts, and totally dumbfounded. He knew it was wrong, horribly indecent, but try as he may he couldn't stop staring at her bosom. His mind raced madly through lists of words and phrases for a reasonable explanation, an excuse, but he had none, there was none. He didn't really want one. He was entranced by her breasts, captivated by them in some kind of dream-like state. He was out of his mind with sheer delight and he couldn't stop himself from wanting more of her, like a kid eating forbidden candy, resolved to face the consequences later. His initial delight expanded into heart-throbbing affection, an ever-increasing passion until he was on the verge of fainting from the love he felt for the half-naked angel before him. Never in his life had he experienced such transcendent love. In those blessed moments he realized the love his mother must have felt for him, to bear the burden of him for all the years that she did. He was experiencing love as he never did before. He was, as the poets exclaim, "Out of his mind in love."

Through it all Beth didn't try to turn away, or to cover herself. She didn't move. She had no reason to. She lived a life without shame. She sensed Ken's predicament. When she spoke, her voice was soft, flowing with tender concern.

"Are you feeling something?"

"Yes, Yes," Ken whispered, barely able to speak.

"Do you want me to help you?"

"Yes..."

Beth stepped close to her friend and reached her hand down between his legs. There was nothing there to feel.

"No, Beth," Ken managed to whisper, "not that. Please just hold me."

Beth leaned into her friend, gently pulling his head into her breasts. Immediately she felt a rush of passion course through her, exciting her reproductive organs. The sexual energy so quickly ignited her young body she had to fight back an orgasm…but her passion persisted, surging up into her heart. She felt a wonderful churning in her breasts, which she instinctively knew was milk flowing into her breasts. Her mind racing with strange unbearable desires, Beth fought to stifle an orgasm but couldn't pull away from the man in her arms. Hot pulsating waves of sexual passion shot up her spine, flooding her head and breaking her will to resist. She gasped with ecstasy as her whole body gave in to an orgasm that drained the strength from legs, forcing her to her knees and helplessly to the floor. The orgasm didn't stop exploding through her until it rendered her helpless and groaning with pleasure on the carpet.

Supposing Beth was in the throes of a seizure, Ken freaked out, grabbed a vase of flowers filled with water and dumped it on the fallen angel. In the confusion, Ken didn't notice Attos Albaniack standing in the doorway, the apartment door having been left open.

"What happened? What you doing here?" shouted the panicked landlord.

Unhinged himself, Ken shouted back, "I don't know! Epilepsy! Does she have a history of epilepsy?"

"I don't know this thing! Is like leprosy? Should I call doctor?" babbled the landlord.

"No," Beth yelled, pulling herself up with the wet flowers clinging all over her. "Don't call anyone! I'm fine, no problem—no problem…"

Ken and Attos, dumbfounded, just stared at Beth as she marched, bare-chested, head held high past the bewildered Attos out the door. Her final words as she made her exit, "I just slipped."

Ken thought Beth fainted or suffered some kind of seizure. It never occurred to him that she was in the throes of a sexual climax, a release he himself did not have, could not have.

CHAPTER THIRTY ONE

WHERE STARS SHINE LIKE THE REAL THING

Joel was relieved that Julian wasn't around when Sonia pulled up to the YMCA. Getting into the car he kissed her on the cheek. She was wearing a form-fitting black dress slit down the middle to her navel. Her raven hair with the red streak was brushed back over her ears which were adorned with five delicate diamond studs outlining each ear. Her perfume hinted of lilacs and coconut. She was hefty and hot!

"Good evening, Princess Sonia. You look sensational!"

"You're just saying that because—well, tell me something, and I want you to be dead honest about it. I'll know if your bullshitting—so tell me. Are young guys turned on by full-bodied babes like me, or do they prefer these anorexic waifs with no tits to speak of?"

"I don't know about other guys but you turn me on."

"Just the way you said that makes me want to pull over and do you! But I don't want to mess you up, at least not till after the party. Hey, check the glove compartment."

Joel did as she suggested and discovered a black bottle etched in gold with the signature, "Richy Blaze." Removing the gold cap, he sniffed the cologne of the stars.

"Wow, amazing! Is everyone at this gala going to be wearing this?"

"No, just a few, the ones who have 'arrived,' as they say. Spray it on the hair around your ears and chest. Your hair will hold the scent all night. Be careful though, every nymph at the rodeo will be grabbing your junk tonight. Remember, you can score nymphs any night of the week in tinsel town, but a party like this could launch your movie career. Don't get hung up—savvy?"

"I'm down with that, coach."

"Your business cards are in that black plastic case with your name on it. There's twenty in there. That should be enough."

Their conversation consisted mostly of what to expect, who to corner and what to say, for she wanted him to travel solo at the party. When he asked why, she told him she had some schmoozing to do on her own. The entrance to the Celestial Convention Center parking lot was lit up with flashing lights that spelled out "ARCTIC STORM." Beautiful female valets wearing black miniskirts and tank tops checked IDs on their hand-held smart phones before parking the cars. The guests walked under a gold canopy to the arched entry way where large flat screens were showing scenes from Arctic Storm. A team of gorgeous men and women checked people's coats just before they walked into the huge center ballroom where "Phase In," the hottest new band in the states, was rocking out selections of their hit album, while people gyrated on the dance floor below the stage. It was the only area in the immense room that received a continual stream of changing colored lights. The rest of the room, which was half the size of a football field, received only diffused light from the moon and stars in the high dome ceiling, which replicated the night sky, like a planetarium. Occasionally different stars would nova unexpectedly, surprising everyone in the selected areas with a blast of colored light. In the center of the immense ballroom was a square bar with high-back velvet stools. In several other places against the walls were smaller wet bars next to long banquet tables lavished with finger food: shrimp cocktails, chicken legs, salads, assorted fresh fruits, meats, cheeses, dips, and desserts. Waiters, sworn to silence, kept the tables supplied. If management saw a waiter conversing with anyone he was fired. That was the law which kept the waiters, most of them actors, from schmoozing the guests.

Periodically projected on the surrounding walls were huge images of seascapes, mountains, wild animals, outer-space visuals of Saturn, Jupiter, and a whole assortment of recording and movie stars. With all that was going on there were still some secluded alcoves with posh lounges where people could talk privately or grope each other in the pitch blackness.

Fifty or sixty people were already holding drinks and getting absorbed in the party spirit when Sonia walked hand in hand with Joel to the center bar. She ordered a gin and tonic, kissed him on the cheek, picked up her drink and deserted him. Joel just started sipping the Samuel Adams he ordered when Martin Steikes walked up beside him.

"Hey, dude, are you down with this groove?"

Steikes was decked out in an all white suit with satin lapels. Beneath the jacket he wore a black turtle-neck, with a sparkling crystal attached to a solid silver chain. He was about Joel's height with Hollywood spiked black hair. Joel didn't recognize him until he pulled off his rose colored glasses and held out his hand.

"Martin Steikes! You're looking killer, man!" exclaimed Joel as he shook the actor's hand.

"Yeah, these are my money threads. You're looking pretty nasty yourself, Josh."

"Joel."

"Joel. Sorry dude."

"No problem. I suck at names too."

"It's because we're too self-absorbed. That's what that TV psychologist says."

"Dr. Phil?"

"No, the other dude. He's on that morning show—fuck, I can't remember his name," said Steikes, laughing at himself.

Joel laughed politely, as Steikes waved to the bartender and ordered Johnny Walker Black on the rocks, side of 7 Up. Then, surveying the fantastic room, Steikes said, "Man, have you ever seen this much glitzola in your life? Is this the ultimate fantasy or what!"

"Tell you the truth, I'm like hot to get to New York—you know, shake off all this glitz and get into the show."

"Bask, dude, bask in the glitz while you can," said Steikes. "A straight play on Broadway is a scary deal. You ever do Broadway?"

"I don't know. I mean, no, it's all new to me."

"Sure, no pressure on you really. But me, my career will be on the line opening night! Makes my balls quiver."

"I feel for you, man. Tell you what, I'll open for you."

Steikes chuckled, and placed his glass on the bar.

"Hey," Stiekes said, "there are two sizzling babes on that dance floor who absolutely need our attention."

"How do you know?" joked Joel.

"They're dancing with each other."

"What if they're gay?" laughed Joel.

"Then it's time someone rescued them," laughed Stiekes as he took Joel's elbow and attempted to lead him to the dance floor. Joel gently pulled back.

"I can't. I'm with someone else."

"Well, help me out, dude. Just dance with one of them while I move in on the other."

"Okay, but I thought you were here to schmooze."

"We've got all night for that!"

Joel and Stiekes made their way through the room until Stiekes halted at the sight of a group of people circled in light, which included Zack Taylor. Someone at the bar against the wall must have triggered a particular star to beam down on the group.

"That's Zack Taylor talking to Clint Eastwood, and I'll bet some of the people in that crowd are reporters."

Steikes immediately started to shoulder his way into the crowd toward the movie stars. Joel followed him in with his heart racing, eager to get a close look at the body he once inhabited. Joel was still a few feet back when Steikes shot his hand out to Zack Taylor and gushed, "Great flick, Zack! I saw it like four times!"

Zack held out his finger for Steikes to shake, an obvious put-down for the intrusion. Zack turned back to Eastwood to continue his conversation as Steikes shrank back into the crowd. Joel didn't retreat with Steikes but was suddenly attracted to a cute chick with a pixie haircut, gem-studded jeans and a designer t-shirt that let you know she didn't need a bra. She brushed past him as she was leaving Zack Taylor's side. The scent of her perfume and the accidental contact of her body with his triggered the memory of her, a vivid flashback of the two of them on New Year's Eve in Times Square just as the giant ball dropped. The cheers resounding in his head, he pulled her to him and kissed her moist, enticing lips. The flashback of her in his arms evoked the same intense feeling of love he felt on that New Year's Eve. He followed her out of the circle of light as she made her way to the small bar next to the wall. The bar was deserted, most of the guests having rushed into the circle of light like desperate moths. Joel took a stool one space down from the girl whose name he thought might be Kylie. As the bartender approached her, Joel said, "Kylie will have a Pina Colada and I'll have a Sam Adams."

Kylie turned to him and responded, "Do I know you?"

"Yes. Way back when, we shared New Year's Eve together in Times Square."

"No, we didn't," said the dark-haired beauty, "Nice try, though."

"You don't remember the walk back to our apartment? The Buddha Truth you sprang on me?"

Kylie appeared stunned by Joel's last question. The "Buddha Truth" was a personal game Zack and she contrived to force each other to be painfully honest. If either partner thought the other was bullshitting he could call out "Buddha Truth," which meant, if you don't confess now that you've been bullshitting but persist in the lie, then you will forfeit any good karma that was due to you this lifetime. Each of them swore to honor the Buddha Truth as long as they were together. It was some serious fun they used to indulge in when they first met. The game faded from their relationship as Zack became more and more involved with other women. The last time she called the Buddha Truth on Zack, he told her to get lost and stay the fuck out of his personal life.

"Are you a friend of Zack's? Did he tell you about the Buddha Truth?"

"Tell me you don't remember that night when I said, 'Sex in public is phenomenal,' and that I had sex in public with two chicks in high school. You called the Buddha Truth and I said it really took place. Remember what happened next?"

"Hey, man, drop it! You're beginning to creep me out!" demanded Kylie.

"I apologize. Can we just talk?"

Kylie was intrigued by the handsome stranger, supposing he was some kind of psychc. But she also knew that Zack's bodyguard, Riggs, would be watching her, and everything she did would get back to her boss. While Zack could screw every nymph in tinsel town, she was restricted to polite conversation with men. Her job was on the line when she wrote on a coaster, "Wait a couple of minutes and meet me in the alcove closest to the entrance."

Kylie picked up her drink, letting the coaster fall from the bottom of her glass as she walked away. Joel waited a full minute before he picked up the coaster from the floor.

Kylie kept her eyes on Riggs as she disappeared into the crowd. Keeping an eye on Riggs wasn't hard. He was almost a head taller than everyone at the party. She made her way through the subdued light close to the wall, all the way to the alcove near the entrance. The alcove was secluded by a thick velvet drape. As soon as Kylie parted the drapes, motion sensors turned on the step lights and Kylie stepped carefully down the two steps into the cozy sunken room. Once her feet left the steps the lights went out, leaving lit only a single electric candle with a blue white flame. Dark blue lounges surrounded the room. Above each lounge was a round dimmer switch which controlled the candlelight. Kylie sat in the empty room and sipped her Pina Colada. A couple of minutes later Joel joined her. He attempted to sit beside her and she pointed him away.

"Please sit over there."

Joel complied with her request, saying, "I don't bite."

"What's your name? How do you know things about me?"

"Joel Ellendorff. And I need your help."

"You need my help, for what?" asked Kylie, who thought the handsome guy was just putting a move on her.

"I don't want to freak you out, so let me relate it to you as if I were a writer pitching a movie script. Will that work for you?"

"Honestly, Joel, if that's your name, I don't freak out easily. If you're just putting a move on me we can save us both some time."

"I'm not trying to put any moves on you. Not that I wouldn't like to, but there's something more important I need to talk to you about."

"All right, what's your movie about?"

Joel began, "Fade In: A strange apartment in downtown Chicago. A young man, my age, wakes up gasping for breath. He thinks the other man in the room poured acid down his throat, but it was only some kind of hot Tabasco sauce. The young man escapes into the night and comes to discover that he is in the body of a stranger. At first he thinks he's gone insane. But in the ensuing days, weeks, months, he realizes that his real body is in Hollywood, that he himself was a movie actor before someone hijacked his body."

"Man, that's a weird plot—but hey, Sci-fi flicks are big box these days," interjected Kylie. "Sorry, I'm not hooked up with anyone who could help you," said Kylie getting up to leave.

"You're not going to let me finish?" asked Joel.

"Dude, there's a room full of producers out there. Try your pitch on them. Maybe one of them will love it. Worse movies have been made for sure!"

"It's not a movie, Kylie. It involves a girl who has a scar on her left breast from a burn she got in college."

Joel struggled to bring up facts that wouldn't be hurtful but all that came to mind were these disjointed flashes about her. Kylie was stunned by what the strange man just said. No one but Zack knew about that scar. She was indeed freaked out and began to cry. All she could think was that Zack divulged her personal information to this stranger. But for what reason? There wasn't any. Maybe the guy is psychic or something, she thought. But what does he want? Why did he tell her the ridiculous story? Joel reached out and took the crying girl's hand just as the curtain parted and Riggs stepped into the alcove. Riggs was an ogre of few words.

"This motherfucker hurt you, Ms. Bolinger?"

Kylie immediately stepped in front of the ogre to protect Joel.

"No, Riggs. He's an old friend. How could you leave Zack unprotected in this crowd?"

"He sent me to find you," snapped Riggs, pushing forward toward Joel, who was wondering how he was going to pay his hospital bill when it was over.

"He's a friend from my college days. We were just reminiscing," stammered Kylie, wondering if the huge bodyguard even understood what the word meant.

"About what? Why was he holding your hand?" demanded Riggs, who hadn't broken anybody in pieces for a while and lusted for the opportunity.

Sensing the ugliness in the ogre's voice, Kylie shouted to break through his adrenalin high.

"No, Riggs! You touch him and you'll be fired! He's an old friend from college, goddamn it!"

"Zack don't want you talking with no strange men in private. You know that."

The threat worked. She felt Riggs easing back off the balls of his feet.

"I know, Riggs," sighed Kylie, while patting the bodyguard's arm, "but this is just an old friend. Thanks for watching out for me."

Then turning back to Joel, Kylie said, "Hey, nice to see you again. Good luck with your movie."

Joel said nothing, as Kylie led Riggs out of the alcove. But she knew the strange episode wasn't over. Riggs was certain to relate the incident to Zack, who would demand a detailed explanation. Kylie hated having to put up with Zack's male chauvinist bullshit, but her lucrative job was at stake. She chided herself for not having a legal contract, but back when her job became official she and Zack were in love. All that had changed radically since then, their relationship having become so strained that she thought Zack might have set up the bizarre incident just for an excuse to fire her. "Let the bastard fire me," she thought. "I'll share some shit with the press that will bury his career!" On the way back to Zack's entourage she hoped that he had already sniffed out his fuck-mate for the evening and wouldn't waste time with her minor indiscretion. Zack was on the dance floor with a cub reporter from *Teen-Top* magazine. She had to be eighteen but looked younger. Riggs had the rare common sense not to interrupt his boss while he was in heat. From the star's ridiculous attempts to keep time with the hip-hop music, she surmised he was quite stoned.

Kylie didn't know the guy who said his name was Joel, but she didn't want Zack to have him thrown out or do something to damage the young man's career. Zack was that jealous and that unpredictable, so she had to defuse the situation before it got out of control. Kylie invited Riggs to join her for a drink at the small bar.

"You know I don't drink on the job," was the bodyguard's response.

"Yes. You're a good man, Riggs. What say we don't bother the boss tonight, with what happened? It's a big night for him. And we can tell him tomorrow. What's the difference?"

"Tomorrow's my day off. Tyrell's on tomorrow."

"Why spoil the evening, Riggs? Nothing really happened. We were just talking about a movie he wrote."

"I got nothing against you, Ms. Bolinger. But if I don't tell the boss, I'll get fired."

When "Get Wet With Me," Phase One's platinum tune, concluded, lead vocalist Alicia Grange announced that her band would be taking a twenty-minute break. She requested that no one ask for autographs during the break and said their CDs were on sale right by the entrance. Zack remained on the dance floor with his teenage partner, sharing a friendly parting hug as the lights dimmed and the stars came out. It was obvious to even the most naive onlooker that it wasn't just a "friendly parting hug." Zack finally left the dance floor and walked to Kylie and Riggs.

"Is that band the shit or what?" exclaimed the movie star.

"Absolutely, the shit! Cost a small fortune too," commented Kylie.

Then Riggs chimed in, "Mr. Taylor, we got a situation."

"Oh, fuck, Riggs, it's not a situation," interjected Kylie, who sought to cheat the ogre out of his petty, ass-kissing pleasure of exposing her.

"I ran into an old college friend and we did some catching up. No big deal!"

"They was in one of them secret rooms behind the curtain, sir."

"We wanted a quiet place to talk, for Christ's sake!"

"I take it you were with a guy," probed Zack.

"She was holdin' his hand and crying, Mr. Taylor." Even the callous Zack Taylor, stoned out of his mind, had to stifle a laugh at the unfolding situation. Watching the overgrown idiot Riggs ratting out the pixie was too much to stifle. Zack Taylor just started howling with laughter. People in the vicinity turned to behold him doubled over, holding his sides, tears running down his face laughing. Kylie and the people nearby all started laughing at or with the movie star. Only Riggs didn't laugh. He had that old feeling that the joke was on him. Finally, Zack laughed himself out and sensed the imposition of his bodyguard.

"I'm sorry, man. It's just hilarious how foolish she is, trying to pull a stunt like that around your watchful eyes," explained Zack. "And that was it? Did the guy say anything?"

"No, sir. Not when I walked in on them," replied Riggs.

"I'll bet he shit his pants," laughed Zack. "Did he shit, Riggs?"

Now Riggs chuckled.

"Not sure, sir. He be a strange dude, though."

"What was strange about him?" inquired Zack.

"Well, Mr. Taylor, I listen at the curtain before I walk in. This weird faggot is telling Ms. Bolinger about someone stealing another asshole's body—or some such weird shit."

The blood drained from Zack's face, as though the bodyguard's words sliced through his aorta. There was no mirth in his voice when he turned to Kylie and croaked out, "Is that what he said? Is he crazy or something?"

CHAPTER THIRTY TWO
GOING TO THE MAT FOR LOVE

Joel stationed himself back at the big square bar, out of sight from anyone down at the far end of the room by the dance floor. He sensed that he sparked the interest of the lady he once loved but was really worried about her. He had no idea what kind of demon stole his body, or what evil he might employ to keep it secret. Joel only knew that he had to get back with Kylie somehow. He was certain she wasn't party to the demon's evil deed. Yet, she was the closest person to him. If she didn't know how the demon orchestrated the takeover of his life, she might be able to find out. On the back of a napkin Joel wrote, "Please call me when you can, 661-314-3335, Joel." Then he left the bar and caught up with one of the younger female waiters carrying a tray of food to the banquet tables.

"Excuse me, miss—can you do a favor for me?"

"It depends, sir. I can't fraternize with the guests."

"I know. But here's a tip for you," said Joel, as he placed a fifty dollar bill on her tray. "Do you know the lady with the pixie haircut, who works for Zack Taylor?"

"I know who she is, yes."

"Can you slip her this note secretly? No one must see you give it to her. Think you can do that?"

"I can do it, but it might take some time."

"Pull it off and I'll give you another fifty. Don't even try it, if there's the slightest chance of Zack or his giant bodyguard seeing you."

"I got it already!" exclaimed the young waitress, who took the napkin and scurried away.

Joel returned to the square bar where he checked his cell phone to make sure it was operating. He ordered a Sam Adams and tried to relax. The crowd massing in the Celestial Convention Center prevented Joel from visually tracking the waitress on her mission. Besides that, there had to be a hundred people swarming around the bar and the banquet table where he hoped to reconnect with the young waitress he gave the note. Then Sonia came squeezing through the crowd and gave him a big drunken hug.

"Hey, gorgeous, why are you hanging alone? You should be out scoring contacts."

"I'm just taking a short break, babe."

"Come on," said Sonia, "I want to introduce you to Tom Hands. He's in the process of producing a movie for HTO."

Joel followed Sonia along the wall where there were fewer people to get through. The closer they got to the dance floor the more uneasy Joel felt. At last they found Tom Hands and his entourage. Sonia waited for Tom to sign a young actress's autograph book before she stepped up to him.

"Tom, I want you to meet a very special actor and friend of mine, Joel Ellendorff—booked to do a Broadway show in the fall. Joel, this is Tom Hands, the most brilliant producer-director in the business." Sonia watched Tom and Joel shake hands.

"I saw *The Mercenary*. It was riveting."

"What show are you doing, Joel?

"*Don't Call Me Son*, a straight play, written by Stanley Sorrenson," replied Joel.

"That's my brother," added Sonia, "Stanley Sorrenson. Clay Abbot is directing, Russell Crowe has the lead."

"Hey," said the famous Tom Hands, "I'd like to see it. When do you open?"

"October 26th. Call me if you come to New York. I'll get you a ticket," said Joel, as he handed the producer a card from his black box of business cards.

Joel hung with Sonia for another hour, while she took him to meet a number of Hollywood directors, producers, and actors. Joel would have enjoyed the schmooze tour if he wasn't watching out for the waitress who took his note. He was also spooked by the fact that Zack Taylor, Kylie, and the bodyguard were nowhere to be seen. At one point his phone rang and he withdrew to the wall to answer it, but there was no one on the other end. Instantly he checked his "incoming calls" but no number came up. That increased the tension in his bones, as he considered the many possible reasons no one was on the phone when he answered. With all the noise it was hard to tell if it rang three or four times. Maybe Kylie had to hang up before she could talk. Or maybe it was just some random call, a wrong number or something. Determined not to miss the next call, Joel made sure vibrate was on and held the phone in his hand. However, the phone caused his hands to sweat and he had to put it back in his pocket. Fed up with the escalating tension, Joel excused himself from Sonia's schmooze tour to go to the men's room and went in search of the young waitress. Ten minutes later he found her restocking one of the banquet tables close to the dance floor. Getting close to her he whispered, "Hey, what's going on?"

Keeping watch of the people all around, she held up a different colored napkin. "This is from her. Place the fifty on my tray."

"Okay, but what did she say?"

"Fifty bucks first, mister."

When Joel placed the fifty dollars on her tray, she handed him the note and sped off, disappearing into the crowd.

The note read, "I caught a break. Meet me in the smoking area out back at midnight—Kylie."

It was almost midnight. How long the waitress had the note he didn't know. He didn't want to make Kylie wait, so without excusing himself from Sonia's care Joel walked directly to the left of the dance floor and pushed open the exit door beneath the sign that read, "Smoking Area Outside." Checking to make sure no one was watching, he stepped outside. The designated smoking area was just the back alley with four metal folding chairs around several standing ash trays. The area was lit by a single fluorescent light high up in a lamp post. He checked his watch as he started to pace back and forth to a nearby dumpster. Suddenly sharp pain pierced his back, followed by brain-stunning bolts of electricity, which sent him sprawling to the pavement. The electric bolts from the taser, controlled by Riggs, caused Joel's body to jump and twitch uncontrollably. The pain raging through him was excruciating. He thrashed and struggled wildly but couldn't dislodge the tormenting darts buried in his back. Heart pounding erratically and vomiting beer, Joel was rendered senseless before Riggs finally turned the juice down on the taser. The young actor just lay there with beer foaming from his mouth as the ogre stepped into the light.

"Listen up, asshole. Don't bother Zack Taylor or Ms. Bolinger no more—or you be a dead motherfucker! Mr. Taylor says, forget that movie you wrote. Forget it forever. If you don't I will break all your bones. Are you down with that, asshole?"

Joel was too disoriented to respond immediately. Riggs turned up the taser and watched his victim scream and thrash around for another fifteen seconds.

"Was that a 'yes,' motherfucker?" laughed the ogre holding the taser.

"Yes," gasped Joel. "Yes…please stop."

"Cool," grimaced the ogre. "Now, we gonna shake on it. Give me your hand…give me your 'fuckin' hand!"

Joel lifted his hand and the ogre forced his thumb back until it broke, laughing as his victim wailed in anguish.

"Just a reminder, asshole. Get lost and stay lost!"

Riggs pulled the darts from Joel's back, reeled them in and stepped back into the night. The disabled actor just laid there quivering, moaning, waiting for his faculties to stabilize. Finally, he got his cell phone out of his pocket and attempted to call Sonia. He had to dial her repeatedly before she answered.

"Sonia, please don't ask questions now. Just come to the smoking area outside right away."

"You sound weird. Are you in some kind of trouble?"

"Please, just come to the smoking area now," pleaded Joel and hung up.

When Sonia entered the back alley Joel was on his feet but his face was bloody and his clothes torn and stained with vomit.

"Jesus Christ, what happened to you?!" shrieked Sonia.

"I got mugged," replied Joel.

"Oh my God, they stole the watch and the ring!"

"No," interrupted Joel, "They didn't get the watch and ring. I fought them off!"

"Did you call the police?"

"No. They didn't get anything."

"What! They busted you up—your face is a bloody mess!"

Joel touched his face. He hadn't realized it got scraped up on the pavement.

Sonia pulled her phone from her purse, but Joel grabbed her hand, "Don't call the police. Let's just go to a hospital. He broke my thumb."

"He broke your thumb? He broke your thumb and left the watch! What kind of sadistic—?"

"No, my thumb got broken somehow in the scuffle. Please, let's just get out of here!"

CHAPTER THIRTY THREE
CHASING THE GOOD LIFE

Ever since the evening of his ill-fated dinner with Beth and David, Ken hadn't seen or heard from his next door angel. The day after the seizure he called to see how she was. When he mentioned her seizure, she said, "It wasn't anything like that. I fainted, that's all. And please don't tell David, okay?" When Ken asked another question, she just said, "Gotta go. I'll catch you later," and hung up. That was four days ago. Ken suspected that she was purposely avoiding him and that it had something to do with her half-naked embrace with him. It was all so foolish, he chided himself. How could he let himself get so carried away! She just wanted to help her pathetic friend in the wheelchair! How stupid and pathetic! Wanting to apologize and clear the air between them, he called several times but she didn't or wouldn't answer her phone. One morning he stationed himself at his door and listened for her in hopes of intercepting her on the way out, but she never passed by. As the week progressed his life became so impacted with things he had to do that he put his relationship with Beth on hold. He spent most of the week dealing with the Shark and the banking procedures required to withdraw his money in cash from seven different banks. Having accomplished that, he had to focus his attention on other critical issues related to the switch.

There was close to a hundred thousand dollars in a large attaché case under his stereo console for which he had to find a suitable hiding place. Tomorrow morning he was scheduled to play David Heightly a game of chess for fifty-thousand dollars, and the day after that he would be picking Timothy Gales up at the airport. Everything was lining up perfectly for the advent of his new life. Once the switch was completed, Ken considered just walking away from his dead body with the attaché case full of money. However, he couldn't be sure Timothy Gales wouldn't be seen going into the apartment or leaving with the attaché case. There were too many possible mishaps that could implicate Gales in a murder case. After some deliberation, it seemed wiser just to have Gales call 911 and report Ken's death. Gales would wait around as a bereaved friend until it was all over and pick up the hidden money elsewhere. Tomorrow's game with the Shark came about as though it had been scripted.

While he hadn't seen Beth since the ill-fated dinner party, he encountered David every day at the park. Ken knew these encounters were not by coincidence because David preferred playing at Central Park where the fish were much larger. It was obvious that the young hustler was concentrating all of his energy on one gigantic fish, Ken, the guy with the four hundred thousand dollar inheritance. At their first encounter, just two days after the dinner fiasco, Ken asked David how he was feeling, to which he responded, "Great, man. Hey, I'm really sorry for messing up your crib."

"No problem. My cat wanted me to extend his thanks for the anchovies."

"Any time," laughed David. "Are you up for a game, dude?"

"Sure," said Ken, as he wheeled up to a table and emptied the ivory chess pieces from his velvet-lined case. "Haven't seen Beth around. She working today?"

"No, man," answered David. "Her dad is sick, cancer or something or other. She grabbed a bus to Albany last night. She asked me to go with her, but I told her I've had enough of that horror for one lifetime!"

Ken was pleased to hear that Beth wasn't necessarily avoiding him. He was also pleased that David's inconsiderate nature was showing up in their relationship.

"What's the stakes?" asked Ken, as he held out two fists, one concealing a black pawn and the other a white pawn. David tapped the fist with the black pawn, which meant Ken had the white pieces and the first move.

"Let's keep it friendly," smiled the young hustler. "Two hundred?"

"Cool," said Ken, as he moved his queen's pawn two spaces forward.

Two hundred was the highest stakes Ken ever played for in the park. In the games leading up to his phony inheritance, his games with the Shark never exceeded a hundred dollar bet, because in all of those matches the hustle was on, and Ken purposely lost most of them. Now the hustle was mutual, and Ken had to be very shrewd at playing below his potential while observing the Shark's hustle in action. The Shark so obviously threw three out of the four matches that Ken was reassured of beating him at any stakes. The young hustler simply lacked the mental skills to convincingly throw the games. Ken's face registered naïve delight at each victory. As part of the Shark's con, he congratulated Ken on how much he had improved as a worthy opponent, and went on to say, "Wow, am I off my game today! Shit like this doesn't happen when I'm playing for real money!"

To which Ken responded like a complete bumpkin, "I suppose everyone plays better for high stakes."

"No," chuckled the younger hustler, "most people tank under the pressure when playing for heavy green."

"So, heavy green is like what, five, ten, twenty thousand a game?" inquired the older hustler.

"Or more," added the young hustler. "Like I said the other night, the game gets really exciting at those levels."

"I think I might try my luck up there one of these days," lied the old hustler, whose recent life philosophy embraced lying as a necessary evil when employed for a greater good. In this case, bankrupting the Shark, which was Ken's original intention, would have provided the young Shark with a much needed lesson in humility. However, giving him his money back was no longer an option, as scuttling the Shark's travel plans with Beth was now the priority, and the greater good.

Several subtle hooks were baited and cast out by Ken during their subsequent chess games and the negotiations leading up to their scheduled hundred thousand dollar game. Ken kept saying that he needed David to spot him a knight or bishop if they were going to play for such high stakes. David agreed on condition that they play a five game tournament at twenty thousand a game, with the bishop spot being dropped upon Ken winning any game. Ken complained that his physical condition prevented him from committing to a day-long tournament of five games. He informed the young hustler about his everyday bathroom requirements and the effects his mind-numbing medications had on him in the afternoon. They finally decided to play two games in the morning at twenty-five thousand each. The Shark would spot Ken a bishop for the first game. But if Ken won the first game, the second game would be played even, with no spot. Only if each man won one game would there be a third game with no spot. What seemed most surprising to the young hustler was Ken's request for a terminator to hold the money. At first, David joked about it, "What, you don't trust me? A devout, anchovy-hating atheist like me! What's happening to this wonderful, trusting world!"

"I trust you David, but it's a lot of money and I would feel safer with a terminator around."

"Can do," said David. "I'll contact Rufus Carter, who makes most of his living cage fighting. He's the main terminator in Central Park. We may have to pay him a little more for coming down to Washington Square."

"That's all well and good, but can we trust him?"

"I don't know," chuckled David, "Can we trust an ex-Marine who sometimes preaches salvation at the Riverside Baptist Church?"

After all the negotiations, all the phony posturing, the endless back and forth hustling, Rufus showed up at the Washington Square Park chess tables at 9 a.m. the next morning. He carried a large aluminum case with a chain connected to it. Rufus received the agreed upon stipend of two thousand dollars with a nod of his massive mangled head. He then counted and stuffed fifty thousand in cash from each player in his case. The terminator then chained and locked the case to his waist. Ken considered the last procedure sheer theatrics because one look at this tower of tattooed muscles with the cauliflower ears would send any would-be mugger home to consider a new vocation. The games began at 9:35 a.m., and at 10:25 a.m., following a minor argument, Rufus placed the case full of money on the winner's lap and escorted him home. Ken's cell phone rang all the way. At the door to his apartment Rufus once again advised his client in the wheelchair to deposit the money in a safety deposit box at the bank. Rufus was so concerned about the cash that he offered his escort services at half price. Ken declined, but asked the terminator to hang out a minute while he answered his phone. He knew that David would be on the other end.

"You rotten fucking prick! You cheated me out of my life's savings!"

"I didn't cheat you out of anything," responded Ken.

"No, you hustled me, you motherfucker!"

"I'm sorry you feel that way David. You yourself said to a college kid whose tuition you hustled, 'Fuck off, crybaby! I just gave you a valuable lesson. Don't gamble with money you can't afford to lose.' Didn't you say that?"

"What the fuck! That's exactly what I said—like two months ago! Did you record it or something? Is that what this is all about? Are you some kind of freak-o crusader—a defender of the meek or some such shit?"

"Not really, David, but I must admit that your callous disregard for others is something you should deal with!"

"And what about your disregard for me, you freak-o-hypocrite! What about your disregard for Beth? You know this fucks her plans too!"

"You may have a problem understanding this David, but I hustled you for her sake. You're not right for her."

"Who the fuck are you, you shriveled up old prick! What if I come over there and kick your self-righteous ass?!"

"If you do, you will never get your money back. Do you want your money back?"

"Don't talk to me like a fucking retard! What's your angle?"

"Hold on a second."

Ken covered the phone and looked up at the terminator. "It's okay, you can take off. Oh, and could you leave me your phone number?"

"Sure," replied the terminator, as he handed him a business card embossed with a gold cross and the words, "RUFUS CARTER— CHRISTIAN PREACHER AND BODY GUARD. I WILL CONVERT YOUR ENEMIES! 212-757-7638."

"Thanks," said Ken as he shook the terminator's giant hand and turned his attention back to the angry Shark on the phone.

"Here's the angle, David. I will place fifty large in an escrow account at the Chase bank with instructions to send you five large each month, if you leave this state and never see Beth again."

"Man, you are one twisted motherfucker! I knew you had the hots for her! But really asshole, what are you thinking—that you're going to be able to seduce her in my absence? Look in the mirror, dude—you ain't me! In fact, you—"

Ken broke in, "Are you interested in the deal or not?"

After a pause, David answered, "Maybe. Let's put that deal on hold a minute. What if we settled up like gentlemen? We play one more game for fifty large, winner take all. If you win I'll even leave town without Beth."

"And where will you get the money?" asked Ken.

"I'll get the money. But as a gentleman who professes to be fair-minded, will you spot me a bishop?"

"Okay, I'll spot you a bishop. We play one game for fifty large tomorrow, 9 a.m., winner take all."

"I'll contact the terminator," said David, and hung up.

Of all the certainties in Ken's mind, the one most certain was that David the Shark had no intention of leaving town without Beth. Of course, any plans he had of traveling the world with her would certainly be ruined if he lost the final game. He didn't have fifty thousand dollars, of that Ken was certain. The Shark had a monstrous ego. When he bragged about having seventy-five thousand in winnings set aside, he was probably exaggerating by at least ten grand. So, as Ken calculated it, David may have had five or ten thousand left under his mattress. Ken knew the young hustler would either have to borrow another forty thousand or get backers to invest that much in him, a doubtful scenario. Thus, if the young hustler lost the big game, which was a good possibility, he would be deep in debt. Ken believed he could win tomorrow's chess game, even with the bishop spot, and he believed he could win Beth's heart once he inhabited the body of Timothy Gales.

The Rascal was licking his empty bowl, shoving it around the floor when Ken came down from his calculations. While he fed his furry roommate, he resolved to put him on a diet after the switch.

CHAPTER THIRTY FOUR

YOU'VE GOT TO KNOW WHEN TO FOLD THEM

Joel spent the last three days hanging out at Sonia's apartment in a Japanese kimono. She had taken up caring for him, which as Julian would say, costs more skin. At first she refused to let him get out of bed, which led to more skin than any injured body should have to endure. The young actor, whose thumb was splinted and taped was at the mercy of Sonia who was an insomniac. What made things worse were the wheatgrass energy shakes she forced him to drink. Her insatiable sex drive was proof that the drink worked. To be fair, she was not a nymphomaniac, just a person who had memorized all of the love- making techniques in the Kamasutra and wanted to share them with her friend.

The second afternoon, when he demanded a shower, Sonia insisted on personally sponging him down, which culminated in Kamasutra position six. There was just no way to say no to his patron-friend. His encounter with the evil ogre at the party cost her an additional five hundred bucks, which she had to pay Mr. Martinelli because the silver watch got a miniscule scratch.

Sonia never completely dropped her inquiry into the mugging. When they weren't involved in Kamasutra, which meant they were eating or sleeping, she would delve into the attack, which to her made no sense at all.

"So these two bastards, white guys, right—?"

"White, Asian, I don't know—they grabbed me from behind."

"But they didn't hit you over the head—the pricks just threw you down."

"Yes. Maybe they hit me on the head, I don't know. It all happened so fast…"

"You were face down on the pavement, probably about to shit your pants."

"I wasn't about to shit my pants. I was scared but my bowels were tight. Unflinchingly brave bowels run in my family."

"I just can't grasp the logic here," exclaimed Sonia Ammonia. "You're face down on the ground and they don't grab your wallet or your watch! They just break your thumb!"

"I probably broke it when I hit the ground. It doesn't matter. Let's talk about something else."

"Just one other thing, the snake bite on your back. Did they have a fucking snake with them or not?"

"It's not a snake bite, for the fifteenth fucking time!"

"But you can't be sure because you were face down!"

"No, I can't be sure!" shouted Joel. "But if it was a snake wouldn't I be dead right now?"

Sonia shouted back, "How the hell should I know! Like I'm some kind of expert on reptiles! Those fang holes in your back are like four inches apart! And that's one big fucking snake, bigger than the snake in that movie with Michael Douglas! I just don't know why you won't report it to the police!"

"Because the police don't know shit about big snakes either. Maybe I'll call Michael Douglas, he'll know what to do. Pass the pasta, please."

Sonia laughed, "Joel Ellendorff, you are one mysterious dude!"

On the afternoon of the third day, with Joel's penis in full retreat, Sonia decided to go out for some groceries, which gave him time to re-evaluate his situation.

While his gut feeling told him that it wasn't Kylie who betrayed him at the party, he couldn't be sure. He called the Celestial Convention Center in an attempt to acquire the phone number of the waitress who carried the notes, but the manager had no idea who she was. With the rehearsals for *Don't Call Me Son* a week away, he had to decide whether he would go to New York or remain in L.A. If he stayed in L.A. he could try to follow Kylie, or do something to get alone with her, maybe find a way to get to her boss. It would mean giving up the show in New York and risking another encounter with the star's giant bodyguard. If it wasn't for the disproportionate response of the bodyguard, Joel still wouldn't be absolutely sure his body had been hijacked. There was no doubt now, but there wasn't much he could actually do about it. If he went to the authorities they would laugh him down, or have him committed to some psychiatric hospital. Then, if he got caught spying on the star's secretary, the giant would be within his rights to kill him. Getting his body back from the evil impostor seemed hopeless under the present circumstances.

When Sonia returned from the store, she had a copy of "The Hollywood Reporter." On the front page was a photo of Zack Taylor and Barry Mendelson signing a contract with Disney Studios for the Arctic sequel. Joel smiled, "At least my career is thriving."

Sonia also brought him new underwear, jeans, and two shirts. His party suit was being repaired by a tailor, who once upon a time studied acting with Sonia.

At dinner Joel informed his patron-friend that he had to get back to the Y, to get his affairs in order for his move to New York. Sonia unexpectedly knelt down by his chair and cried on his knee. Through tears she whimpered, "Oh, babe, why is life so mean? We have something special together…don't you think our relationship is special?"

"Yes, babe," responded Joel gently patting her head. "Hey, it's not like I'm going to the moon. You can visit me in New York. You're coming to see the show, right?"

"Yes, when you're in it," wept the lady who truly loved feeling younger than she was.

"Oh, Joel, let's just get crazy together! Let's fuck conventionality once and for all! This duplex is worth three million dollars."

"What are you talking about?"

"I could sell this place. We could travel the world together."

"Whoa, babe! I've got a show to do, your brother's show. I can't just run out on everything!"

"Why not? You're the understudy. He could replace you in a heartbeat."

"I can't do it, Sonia."

"Am I just an old cougar to you?" wailed the distraught woman. "No, no. You're my friend," responded Joel, as he pulled Sonia up and sat her on his lap. "I wouldn't have this great opportunity if it wasn't for you. Do you think I'll ever forget that, forget you?"

After a moment Sonia stood up, wiped her tears and touched her young friend's cheek.

"Forgive me for acting like a fool. It's just been a long, a long time since I've had the company of a man—or anyone to come home to—to cook for, care for..."

"Oh, babe, I understand," said Joel, getting up and taking her in his arms.

Sonia, weeping again, "You probably think it is all about the sex but it isn't. Believe me, it isn't! It's the friendship, the company—just someone to talk to. Have you ever been lonely, Joel?"

"Yes. I was lonely, not a friend in the world when I got to L.A. Then I found a real friend—you, Sonia—and we'll always be friends, no matter where I go or what I do. Know that," whispered Joel as he wiped her tears away.

"What if I moved to New York? What if we share an apartment—no strings attached—just friends, roommates—you doing your groove and me doing mine?"

"You don't want to uproot your whole life here!" exclaimed Joel. "You're feeling lonely now, but it won't last. You have your career, your contacts, your acting school."

"I can get all that going in New York. In fact, there's more stand-up work in that city than any city in the world."

"You're serious!" exclaimed Joel, who didn't know how to escape hurting the feelings of a friend who really did care for him.

"Please...come on, Joel, I'm reaching out here," cried Sonia. "I'm not asking for us to be an item, a couple—no commitment, just friends. If it doesn't work out we call it off, go our separate ways."

"No strings. We're just friends sharing a pad," stated the young actor.

"No strings," repeated Sonia. "Of course, if we decide some night to jump each other's bones, it will be as friends—no drama attached."

"Okay, but we have separate bedrooms and we each pay half the rent."

"Done deal," stated Sonia ecstatically, as she held out her hand for a hand shake.

"Done deal," repeated Joel, shaking her hand.

Sonia went to the refrigerator and extracted a bottle of plum wine and a bottle of sake.

"This calls for a farewell L.A. celebration."

The next morning after breakfast, Sonia drove her roommate-to-be to the Y and dropped him off. Over breakfast they had discussed their plans, which entailed Joel going directly to New York while Sonia remained behind for three weeks to finish up her classes and other business. Joel would rent a modest hotel room until Sonia arrived and they could shop for an apartment together.

When she pulled up to the YMCA, Joel gave Sonia a kiss on the cheek and exited the car. He watched her drive off before entering the dilapidated brick building. He stopped at the desk and picked up an official looking letter with a New York return address. Opening it in the elevator, he was delighted to find a check from the producer of *Don't Call Me Son*. When Joel entered his room on the fifth floor, he immediately pulled off his boots, looked into the dusty mirror on his closet door and said, "It just keeps getting better!"

CHAPTER THIRTY FIVE

LIFE IS WHAT HAPPENS TO YOU WHILE YOU'RE MAKING PLANS

N ow that the switch was but a day away, it commanded the ex-priest's utmost attention, though he didn't suffer the nagging guilt that assailed him when he attempted the switch with Joel Ellendorff. Wanting to avoid a lot of emotional introspection, he purposely crowded his final week with personal tasks that required his attention. Hiding the money was the priority, so he picked up his cell phone and dialed information, requesting the number for Grand Central Station, to find out if they had personal storage lockers in the terminal. When he was informed that they didn't, he called the Port Authority Bus Terminal which did.

Ken immediately called for a handicap cab and taxied to the Port Authority to make sure he could get a private locker. Making his way through the crowded terminal for fifteen minutes, he finally found the bay of lockers. Just two were available to rent and low enough for him to reach. He thought better about inserting his credit card. Instead he inserted twelve singles, which allotted him the maximum rental time of 72 hours, three days. According to the engraved notice on the locker, he had that amount of time to reclaim the contents of the locker. After that the key would no longer work, and he would have to have Port Authority Security open it for him and prove the contents were his, at a cost of twenty-five dollars.

The alchemist informed him that it might take time to learn how to walk after the switch, but how long he didn't know. When the alchemist switched in Las Vegas he was up and around immediately. Certainly, Ken thought, he could get the young healthy body of Gales walking in a few hours. Then he would have plenty of time to retrieve the cash from the locker. Even in a worst case scenario where he had to lose the money, he could still play chess for a living as Timothy Gales.

It was 5:30 p.m. when he taxied away from the bus terminal. He still needed to buy the oranges to make the juice he would serve Gales tomorrow afternoon. In the taxi on the way to the small supermarket close to his apartment, he saw a street vendor with a cart full of fruit. He bought the oranges right out the window of the cab and headed home. Just as he entered his apartment, Top Gun hopped in through the open window. He realized he left over a hundred thousand dollars in the apartment with an open window. The gun was loaded and ready in the console drawer, but he forgot to close and lock the window. The tension was obviously messing with his concentration.

After selecting Cheryl Crow on the CD player, he prepared an oriental chicken salad for supper, which he ate with crackers and two glasses of Kendal Jackson chardonnay. He then proceeded to cut the oranges and place them in the automatic squeezer. He made exactly one pint of orange juice and decided to review his handwritten notes for the switch. This was hardly necessary for a man with a memory like his, but it was part of his to-do list. He chanted the alchemist's incantation several times into his pocket tape recorder to make certain he had the cadence perfect. Satisfied, he erased the tape and removed a butane lighter from the kitchen drawer. At the sink he burned the notes to ashes, watching them swirl around beneath the running water and disappear into the drain. They symbolized for him the end of his life in a wheelchair.

He was resolved to never enter another night as Ken McAlister. After tonight he would never go through the exhausting process of carefully stripping off his clothes to avoid spilling his urine bag before getting it to the toilet. After tonight he would never again have to scrub the scales from his dead legs, never again suffer the pains in his crippled body, never have to take the mind-numbing medications before going to bed. He would never again have to suffer the ongoing fear of befouling himself in public. This would be the last night for all of that and a hundred other indecencies that accompanied his handicap. He would either complete the switch tomorrow or end his life with a bullet through the brain.

There was no self-pity in the thought of ending his life. From the time he first contemplated suicide, before ever meeting the alchemist, it never evoked sadness in him. It was just such a logical decision for someone in his situation. Well, not exactly, he thought, for no one in the world had ever experienced his unique situation, which included the option to take a new body. Of course, the alchemist had that unique option lifetime after lifetime for centuries. Unlike Ken's situation, though, taking another life by the alchemist was more like picking out a new suit; there was no internal struggle with the right or wrong of the process. Actually, Ken's struggle with his own conscience had subsided almost to extinction since his failed episode with Joel Ellendorff. Presently, he was thoroughly convinced that a totally benevolent God did not exist, thus alleviating the need for any guilt associated with betraying "the Father," as Jesus personalized the deity. But that bit of logic did not close the door completely on his denial of a supreme creator. It was still possible that there was a God, who did in fact create the world and everything in it, but for a different purpose. It's possible that the motives of this creator were diabolic, that he took pleasure from suffering, a cosmic sadist. However, such a sinister God would have to be considered irrational. Would a sadistic God also create beautiful flowers, birds, trees, oceans, and humans capable of making and enjoying music, theatre, art— humans capable of laughter, friendship, compassion, and love? Another possibility Ken pondered once upon a time was that God is benevolent, but his creation went bad, or, as it's stated in the Gospel of John, *"The light came into the world, but men loved darkness rather than light."*

"And why shouldn't people turn to their own diabolical devices," mused the ex-priest, "considering the long absence of God from his creation!"

While he washed the dishes, Ken recalled a homily on the passage in John given by a Jesuit priest who declared that, *"True goodness could not exist without some entrenched evil to overcome. That entrenched evil is one's own ego-centered view of life. Such a view, stated the Jesuit, is the original sin we inherit at birth, a perception that separates life into a duality of 'Me' and 'All that is not Me.' This sin of separation is the underlying sin of all sins, of all evils, of man's inhumanity to man! For this view of life permits one to embrace evil thoughts and commit evil acts on all living things while supposing he is not simultaneously doing evil to himself. While under the illusion of separation, of 'Me first-and-foremost,' we are incapable of true goodness. For goodness to be truly good, it must be devoid of the motivation for personal advantage. The Jesuit concluded, 'Only when we become disgusted with the lies we tell ourselves to justify our selfish thoughts and actions will we enter the brotherhood and sisterhood of mankind. Only then, will we realize that all of our suffering is self-imposed, for we are always reaping what we are sowing!'"*

Ken also recalled quoting that homily in several of his own sermons, when he tried to believe that life was fair, that everyone in the world was in fact reaping what he sowed. In denial of his own congenital condition, he preached such falsehoods. If one thing in life was perfectly clear to the ex-priest now, it was that life was unfair, bestowing wealth, health, and blessings on some, while bestowing poverty, disease, and unwarranted suffering on others. How could any disadvantaged soul, born in abject poverty, or with a debilitating disease or who suffered inhuman abuse ever come to suppose he should do good in order to avoid bad things coming to him? Perhaps the thought of going to hell forever persuaded some to check their evil intentions, but with most people the thought of Heaven or hell fades and fails to hold any sway over their dark desires. Such calculations hardly ever concerned the servants of the church, who gave their sermons and performed their altar rituals by rote, never seriously questioning the obvious absence of God. No, the ex-priest philosophized, for goodness to be a meaningful endeavor for everyone, it would require that everyone be born and raised with absolute equality—no one having less or more personal advantages or nurturing love than any other. Then suffering and happiness could be honestly measured and explained as the results of each adult's personal choices. No such world ever existed, for no such fair minded God ever existed!

"God vanquished-game to Ken McAlister!"

Ken showered and went to bed knowing that tomorrow he would start a new life of untold blessings. He was awakened at 7:10 a.m. by Beth singing "Fields of Gold," his cell phone ring tone. It was David calling to tell him it was raining

"What do you think about playing under a tent at the park?"

Ken chuckled, only to realize David was serious.

"What's with the laugh?" questioned David. "I've got a tent we can throw over one of the tables and play."

"What are you smoking, dude! We can play at my apartment," stated Ken.

"I won't play at your place. It might kick off my allergies."

"I'll put the cans of anchovies and cat food in the back yard—no problem."

"No," stated the young hustler emphatically. "The rain is supposed to clear up by this afternoon. Let's reschedule for three o'clock at the park."

"I can't play this afternoon. I'm picking a friend up at the airport," stated Ken.

"What time, dude?" pressed the young hustler.

"His plane gets in at three, but I'm leaving at one-thirty to run some errands beforehand."

"You're leaving at one-thirty?"

"Yes."

"Okay, let's reschedule the game for tomorrow morning at nine."

"Okay, tomorrow morning," said the elder hustler, knowing he would be dead by then. "See you at nine."

Blowing off the final game meant nothing to Ken. In fact, he felt relieved. With the switch just hours away, his razor sharp concentration wouldn't necessarily have been up to par for the game. And spotting the young hustler a bishop would have required his utmost concentration to win. Now he could sleep a little longer and have plenty of time to store his money in the locker before picking up Gales. The elder hustler, ex-priest, didn't close his eyes until he brought up the video of Beth on his iPhone singing, "We Walked In Fields of Gold."

CHAPTER THIRTY SIX

WHEN ALONE THE WORLD FADES AWAY SOME

"Life is beyond complicated," Joel thought as he plugged in his cell phone, took two prescription pain killers for his thumb, and laid down on his lumpy bed. Staring up at the broken ceiling fan, his attention was drawn to a tiny spider spinning a web. He fell asleep ruminating on ways to stop Sonia from uprooting her life in L.A. and complicating his life in New York.

At seven in the evening he awakened to a knock on the door. It was Julian with a cold six pack.

"Come in—hang a minute," said Joel, as he went to the bathroom. When he returned to his room, Julian was settled into a chair drinking a beer and smoking a cigarette. Joel immediately opened the one and only window and sat on the bed. Julian tossed him a beer, but he placed it down on the end table unopened.

"Okay, tell uncle Jules all about your adventures in glamour-land."

"My life is a train wreck!"

"As I can see from your broken hand. Don't tell me you demanded your body back from the ghoul," suggested Julian.

"Not exactly. I confronted his personal secretary, the lady I once loved—will always love," sighed Joel.

"And she ratted you out to the man," interjected Julian. "Life is just a bowl of pits!"

"She didn't rat me out. The ghoul's bodyguard overheard us and he worked me over with a taser."

"He worked you over with a taser!"

"Yeah, before he broke my thumb."

"Zack Taylor's bodyguard broke your thumb?"

"Told me, if I went near his boss or Kylie again he would kill me."

"That's some serious shit, dude! Was he black?"

"Who?"

"The bodyguard. Was he black?"

"What the fuck difference does it make?"

"Just curious—read an article that white people hire black bodyguards like two to one over dough boys."

"Yes, he was black. You want to hear the whole story?"

"Have to, if I'm going to continue as your life coach," chuckled Julian. "Drink that beer, dude. It will heal your thumb."

"I don't need a beer. I need coffee. Let's move this session down to Starbucks."

"I can't drink beer in Starbucks."

"Did you ever try coffee, Jules—or tea—or just a glass of water?"

"I tried water once, in Kindergarten. It did nothing for me," laughed Julian.

"Put the beer in this bag. Nobody will give a shit if they don't see it!"

Joel and his life coach took the elevator to the main floor and walked to the coffee shop. Joel ordered a double espresso, and Julian, always a gentleman, took a straw for his bag of beer. In detail, Joel related the tsunami of events that swept over him the last four days. When he finished, Julian finally stopped sipping.

"You know what, I believe you," commented Julian, who had no way to reconcile the irrational response of the movie star.

"Thanks," said Joel dryly. Do you believe just the events at the party, or do you believe that fucking ghoul stole my body?"

"I believe he stole your body, my friend. This is some dark shit! I'm really feeling creeped out dude! And I'm outta beer, for God's sake!"

"Now you know what I've been feeling like for the last six months!"

"What's your game plan? What are you going to do now?"

"Get out of Dodge."

"Reasonable choice, my man. But if I were you I'd pack iron from here on out."

"I plan to. I got a check from the producer of my show, enough to ship my shit to New York and hop a jet. As soon as I hit the city I'm going to buy a gun."

"You ever use a gun, even for target practice" asked Julian?

"Never. But it's not that complicated."

"Target practice, no — killing somebody, yes. But don't sweat it, I've done both. I also know a few thugs who can get us the iron."

"Forget that. I'll never get on the plane with it."

"No shit, Sherlock—that's why we'll be taking the bus to New York."

"'We'll? Who's we'll?'"

"You and me dude, and the iron makes three."

"I can't bring you to New York!"

"You need me to watch your back."

"No, I don't," protested the young actor.

"You have had more evil shit come down on you than that dude in the film 'Zombies From The Moon!' You need a bodyguard."

"You know why I'm hesitant regarding your offer? You actually went to see a movie titled, 'Zombies From The Moon.'"

"Thank your lucky stars I did. I learned a lot of occult mojo—for dealing with zombies and shit."

"From watching that idiot movie!"

"I shouldn't even tell you this, but since we're going to partner up we need to be open with each other. I had a role in that highly underrated film."

Joel, going hysterical, "Say you didn't."

"I did. But I'm done talking unless you stop laughing like a fucking hyena!"

"What role?" howled Joel. "I swear—I swear—I'll never tell a soul."

"I played a zombie who suffered from epilepsy—in white makeup no fucking less! And I rocked it!"

Joel, overcome with laughter, clung to his chair to keep his balance. Julian was also hysterical, spilling his empty beer cans on the floor. A pasty-faced teenager wearing a green apron rushed up to them and asked them kindly to leave.

On the way back to the Y, Joel tried to reason Julian out of going to New York. He revealed his agreement with Sonia, to which Julian responded.

"Two bedrooms. She has her bedroom and we have ours."

"Please don't take offense, Jules, but I really prefer a bedroom by myself."

"You can forget that fantasy, son. That cougar's going to be all over you unless I'm there. Tell her I'm your brother or something, which I am. Hell, I can service the lady every night while you're getting some sleep!"

After dinner at a health food restaurant, and two more hours of discussion at a bar, Joel and Julian compromised. Julian could be his bodyguard in New York, but they would live in a three-bedroom apartment. Joel would tell Sonia that Julian was his bodyguard, which he needed because he was attacked again in New York before she arrived.

That night, while lying in bed, Joel pondered the completed web of the tiny green spider on the ceiling fan. Such a perfect design, he thought, affording the spider a simple, problem-free life. He could just hang out until some fly or moth got caught in the web. Then he would party. After the party he would repair his web and hang out or hook up with a spider of the opposite sex. A clear and simple lifestyle, nothing like human existence. In America humans are always chasing some imagined success they don't have yet, and most of them are merely stuck in some 9-to-5 job working to survive— all of them believing that with enough money their problems would be solved. Still, mused Joel, the concept of "enough money" was itself a delusion, because humans appear to have no faculty for discerning what "enough" means. They could never let go and just hang out like the spider because their minds existed in a state of never-ending comparison and wanting.

If a spider contracted the ego disease of humans, he could never be satisfied with one fly, or two, or a hundred, because he would always suffer the nagging thought that some other spider had more. The ego-driven spider would surrender his spare time for the purpose of spinning more webs, piling up and storing his cache of flies, and devising mechanisms to protect and defend them. Throughout his anxious existence, he would continually justify his madness with the thought that one more web would be "enough," just one more fly and he would kick back and relax. Then the day would come when it dawned on him or her that you don't live forever. That thought caused Joel to laugh. Likewise, humans seldom noticed that old age was moving in on them, until it was too late and their failing health prevented them from experiencing any kind of real freedom or happiness.

How difficult could it be to escape the accepted madness of the world, Joel wondered. How hard could it be to fashion a life truly worth living? Almost impossible, he thought, as he considered the circumstances of his life. Here he was, trapped in a body not his own, in a business driven by ego, success, and outrageous excess! The woman he loved was totally out of reach for him. How could he possibly manage the absurd circumstances of his life in a way that would afford him some peace of mind? That question led Joel to realize that peace of mind was the essential element in any life worth living. Sure, Joel concluded, one had to be free of worry and fear to truly enjoy life. And such freedom was not the by-product of money but of a certain innate wisdom. No one was free who didn't fashion a life that facilitated peace of mind.

In his bedtime speculation, the young actor came to understand that his peace of mind didn't hinge on getting his body back; it hinged on his accepting fully his new life as Joel Ellendorff. Yes, it meant sacrificing any hope of getting Kylie back, but that hope was already gone. Still, he loved her. Could he learn to live a worthwhile life without her? It was a fact, though, before the *Arctic Storm* party, he had no memory of her, no feelings for her at all. "Perhaps," he thought, "I could forget her in time. I could just become focused on my career, become totally absorbed in the play, in the character of Elliot Tidwell, the angry young man in *Don't Call Me Son.*"

There was a lot to keep him busy when he got to New York. Even before rehearsals began, he would have to find cheap digs for him and Julian, that was, if Julian still wanted to go when he woke up sober. Joel also would be required to join Actor's Equity, the stage actors' union. He still had to buy a gun and get some practice with it at a firing range. The whole gun thing just didn't seem to fit with creating a peaceful state of mind, Joel realized.

"What if I completely forgave the ghoul inhabiting my body," speculated Joel. "I could possibly write Zack Taylor and explain that I had no hard feelings about him hijacking my body—that I sought no retribution or revenge—that I would never expose him because I was perfectly content living my new life as someone else." The idea didn't bring him much peace because there were still too many unanswered questions and contingent dangers to afford him peace of mind. Who was the evil dude in the wheelchair? Where did the body of Joel Ellendorff come from? More than likely it was the ghoul's body before he traded it for Zack Taylor. Perhaps Ellendorff's dispossessed soul in some other body was seeking revenge on him? "No," he thought, "I will need a gun."

One thing at least became clear, he had so much to get done in New York, he would take the bus to the Big Apple that evening, with or without Julian.

CHAPTER THIRTY SEVEN
THERE'S NO FOOLING YOUR PERSONAL SECRETARY

The digital clock in the coffee maker blipped to 7:12 a.m., setting off a beeping sound. Kylie, clad in a black silk robe, was seated in a Teak wood love seat with zebra skin cushions reading the *Los Angeles Times*. When the beeping started she placed the paper down on the polished slate coffee table and padded barefoot across the immense living room to the kitchen. With her mug of java in hand she stood in the archway that separated the kitchen and living room and gazed out at the lavish Beverly Hills estate Zack purchased. Against her desperate pleas, Zack bought the furnishings along with the estate. He did agree to remove the rhinoceros, leopard, and ibex heads from the walls, but insisted on keeping the zebra skin settee and the large slate coffee table cradled in four elephant tusks. Hanging on the two walls separated by the wall of windows that lead onto the palatial deck was a warrior shield with crossed spears painted black, yellow, and red. The African motif also ended at the white marble staircase that led to the upper level of five bedrooms, a game room, and three master bathrooms. The maroon carpet with the gold designs flowed down the marble stairway into the living room making the only connection the two floors shared décor wise. "Thank God!" Kylie thought as she went back to reading the paper. The star was still asleep in their upstairs bedroom, having played online poker until 3 a.m. Since the party at the Celestial Convention Center, Zack wasn't sleeping well. Kylie knew it had something to do with the strange young man named Joel. What about this odd, possibly crazy character still caused Zack concern she wondered. Why would he extend the bodyguard's hours to include all night duty at the estate? She herself was still worried about the handsome stranger. By the way Zack and Riggs talked in secret, she knew the situation wasn't resolved in the star's hotel room the night at the party. As she recalled, that whole evening was weird. And that waitress delivering a daiquiri to her that she never ordered, what was that about? It created more trouble because Riggs thought it was sent over by the stranger, causing him to chase down the waitress like she was a thief or something! Then the "tell all" session with Zack, followed by the march to his suite above the Celestial Ballroom. She felt like a child about to be punished for misbehaving. She was never more angry at Zack than on that night in the Celestial suite when she told him to "shove" the job. When Zack scribbled a note on a hotel napkin and gave it to Riggs, she really started to lose it. Abandoning her usual level of subservience, she confronted her boss, "What's that?"

"That, is none of your business," snapped the star, who turned to his bodyguard, "Go on—get it done!"

Riggs left the suite, and her concern for the stranger became heart-pounding dread.

"Where's he going?"

"What do you care?" replied the stoned movie star.

"He's not going after that guy, Joel, is he?"

"Why? Is he more than a friend of yours?"

"No, you're misreading the whole thing, babe. He's just some nobody-actor who made a pass at me."

"Then why are you so concerned about him?"

"I'm concerned for you, Zack—and the bad publicity that might result if Riggs hurts that idiot."

"Hey, the asshole had a chance to get lost and he didn't."

"What do you mean, he didn't?"

Zack reached into his lapel pocket and produced a napkin with some writing on it. Kylie felt droplets of sweat run down her back. She recalled that the waitress tried to give her a napkin even when she refused the drink. Why didn't she take it, she chided herself! Fucking monster Riggs got it! She wouldn't want anybody to experience the wrath of Riggs.

But it was more than that with this Joel guy. There was a quality about him, something in his voice that touched her deeply. In spite of his odd come-on about a body-snatching script, she sensed he was a decent, sincere person.

Dangling the napkin before her, like bait before a hungry animal, Zack continued. "He wrote you a note, told the waitress it was for you only. He didn't get lost, but he will," said the star, as he stuck the note back in his pocket.

"Zack, you're stoned. You're about to do something really stupid, something that could screw your signing the sequel with Disney."

"Do I work for you, or do you work for me, bitch!"

"Fuck you and the job if you can't see I'm trying to save your stupid ass!"

"Chill out, for Christ's sake! Riggs is just going to scare him—what's his name?"

"I don't remember—you can't be sure Riggs won't hurt him! He's a fucking pit-bull! He has no control, no stops! Call him off before he fucks up your career, goddamn it!"

"All right, all right! I'll call him off," relented the star, as he pulled his cell phone out and hit the R which dialed Riggs' phone.

While the star waited for Riggs to answer he said, "You are so hot when you're wild! How about we take a bubble bath right now?" suggested the star as he ran his free hand up between her legs. "Run the water will you, babe?"

Kylie didn't leave, but seductively pressed her body into Zack, stalling until he spoke to Riggs.

"Riggs, did you find the asshole yet?" said the star into his phone. "No. All right, forget about him. Leave him alone, even if you see him. Come back to the room...of course, I'm sure. Just leave him the fuck alone and get back here!" shouted the boss, as though he was actually talking to Riggs, as though his phone was even turned on.

Kylie breathed a sigh of relief, kissed her boss on the cheek and went into the plush bathroom to run the water for their bath. She also prepared her body with some lubricant for the anticipated seduction. As was his custom when he was angry, foreplay lasted about twenty seconds before he ravaged her. This man she once adored had become such a creep it defied any logical explanation. It didn't matter, she was saving her money for a grand exit, someday in the near future, she thought, concluding her flashback.

Sipping her coffee, Kylie's thoughts shifted to the stranger she encountered at the *Arctic Storm* party. Sure, he was hot, but hot guys made passes at her on a regular basis since she was fifteen. There was something different about this guy with the golden hair. His eyes, his voice, even the touch of his hand made her tingle, the way she tingled when she first fell in love with Zack. She contemplated looking him up several times, but talked herself out of it. She knew that was dangerous territory, because she wasn't fiscally secure enough to leave Zack yet. Besides that, she could put the golden haired stranger in jeopardy. Her thoughts were interrupted by Zack Taylor calling down from the second floor landing.

"Honey, I'm like, starving. Is the cook in?"

"No, she won't be here for another forty-five minutes. What are you doing up so early?"

"Hunger. That's no shit, babe—hunger woke me up! Can you rustle me up something—some scrambled eggs and bacon—and a ton of pancakes?"

"Do you want orange, or tomato juice?"

"Orange, and a pot of coffee."

"I'm on it, babe."

"Thanks. You're the best! Bring me the *Times* too, okay?"

"Okay, babe," responded the woman to the man she really had no feelings for anymore.

CHAPTER THIRTY EIGHT

ONLY THE DEAD KNOW AN END OF TROUBLE—MAYBE

It was still raining at 10 a.m. when Ken pulled himself out of the bed into his chair. He took his time dressing for the last day of his handicapped life. When he was done, he looked in the mirror to behold his face, something he did more and more since meeting Beth, something he seldom did except to shave when he was a priest. Now he was looking at the face of a man he would never see again.

The lines on his face were deeper and more extended than they should be for a man his age. It was a face that related forbearance and tolerance, but not necessarily kindness. In the final analysis, he realized that his face betrayed his attempts to veil the agony of his life, despite all the years he spent as a priest extending heartfelt compassion to the people he ministered to.

Leaving the bathroom mirror, Ken rolled to the living room where he set up his chessboard for the final game with Timothy Gales. He paused to speculate on his death:

While playing chess with his student and friend, Timothy Gales, ex-priest Ken McAlister suffered a fatal stroke. Having no surviving relatives, his remains were given to the Catholic church he once served. Father Henry Dorcus will preside over McAlister's funeral services.

Timothy Gales would certainly attend the funeral, and possibly Beth, if she could leave her ailing father. Ken's speculation was interrupted by a call from Timothy Gales.

"Hey Ken, it's Tim. Did I wake you?"

"No, I've been up for hours. How are you hanging?"

"Fantastic. Did you get my last e-mail?"

"Probably not. My computer's getting repaired," lied Ken, who purposely neglected the student's last e-mail.

"That sucks. Well, I'll clue you in when you pick me up."

"Continental at 3 o'clock, right?" asked Ken.

"Yeah, cool. Give yourself some extra time. The passenger pickup at Kennedy is a bitch to find!"

"Thanks for the heads-up. Hey, are we on for a game this afternoon? I've devised a simple opening strategy that will blow your mind!"

"I'm down with that. Man, I've got to tell you, I took those Texas boys to school! I swear to God, they subsidized my stay in the Lone Star State!"

"Way cool, my friend. Hey, I've got someone at the door. I'll catch you at three."

"Cool. Bye."

Ken actually read Tim's last e-mail, as he had all of his e-mails. He didn't respond to the last one because it involved a new relationship Tim was in with "the girl of his dreams!" Tim was relating to Ken like he was his father. Ken blew it off, concluding that it was nothing serious—probably some co-ed just looking to have fun.

In accord with his to-do list Ken retrieved the attaché case of money from under the stereo console. He checked to be sure that the keys to the case and the locker were on the hooks beside the door. Next, he checked his wallet to make sure he had plenty of money to cover his expenses for the next few days.

The crucial preparation of the potion Ken saved for last. He motored to the kitchen pantry, slid open the door and surveyed the shelves crowded with all kinds of bottles, cans, and containers. He retrieved a small metal box from a container of Quaker Oats. Returning to the kitchen, he retrieved the orange juice from the refrigerator. At the table he opened the fireproof box and withdrew the bottle of aspirin that contained the potion. Ken stared at the bottle and thought, "I am looking at the most amazing drug on earth!" Opening the aspirin bottle, he peered in and saw that there was approximately two tablespoons of the yellow powder remaining. He shook the bottle gently. The powder was dry, loose and without any apparent lumps. The alchemist said it would never degenerate or decompose until it entered a human body. The Master also said that a teaspoonful to eight ounces of any liquid would do the trick, and a tablespoonful would be sufficient for a pint. Ken removed a tablespoon from the silverware drawer, carefully tapped the powder onto the spoon. and dropped it into the pitcher of orange juice. As he anticipated, the liquid foamed up. Ken stirred it several times until it foamed no more. He sniffed it—perfect. It looked and smelled just like orange juice. Ken returned the aspirin bottle to the pantry.

Everything was ready. Ken called for a handicap cab. After depositing the attaché case in the locker at the bus terminal, he had the cab driver drop him off at the "Pay and Stay" parking facility where he picked up his van.

Driving through the city was such a hassle, he had to give it his utmost attention. Once out on the highway to the airport he was free to think. He felt good. Hitting the scan button on the radio, he selected a station playing current hits. The familiar tunes made him feel younger already. He passed a hitchhiker soaking in the rain.

"On any other day," he said to himself, "I would pick you up. In fact, when I am Timothy Gales I will pick up every hitchhiker I see." Yes, his journey through life was coming to a beautiful conclusion. There was no reticence in his intentions today. The years of Catholic conscience, guilt, and fear had been dissolved by personal intention—yes, by clear reasoning, yes—but mostly by the discovery of love.

There was no God beyond man, Ken conjectured as he drove, no "caring father" waiting to embrace the soul after death. And all those sages and saints who spoke of morality, truth, Heaven, hell, faith, and salvation, what was their motivation? If not money, some sincere, all too human pity—to give people hope, a reason to go on—to be good and not give in to the evil all around them. The truly wise ones were the alchemists, like Master Zack Taylor, who knew the only life worth living was a life free of the fear of death—a life in which you could pursue personal pleasure in all things without guilt or the absurd fear of hell. Master Zack Taylor was possibly the last alchemist—the last alchemist, whose only fear was that of falling into the hands of ordinary human beings who could not tolerate the thought of someone who transcended their superstitions, suffering and death.

Today he would join the alchemists. He would claim a life worth living and bask in the pleasure of it. It didn't mean that he couldn't also pursue goodness. It just meant that there was no God keeping score.

"And what happens when I reach the end of this new life as Timothy Gales?" Ken pondered. "I will die satisfied that at least I had lived. What then happens to my soul in this godless universe, no one knows, not even Master Zack Taylor. Perhaps, as the Buddhists believe, souls take a short break in dreamless sleep and then reincarnate. Or perhaps souls released from the body cling to their memories of the world until at last they give them up and evaporate into the mindless ethers.

The rain slowed down the highway traffic, but the ex-priest wasn't concerned, for he had allotted an extra half hour to get there. About three miles from Kennedy airport he passed a billboard advertising Florida orange juice— which depicted a gorgeous babe picking oranges in an orchard. It keyed Ken on the fact that he had forgotten to put the orange juice back in the refrigerator. It really presented no problem, thought Ken, for he could serve it at room temperature or with an ice cube.

Ken had no trouble following the airport signs to the passenger pickup lane. He nosed the van in behind the line of cars sitting beside the pickup landing. It was only twenty after three, and Ken's perfect day continued, as he spotted Timothy Gales waving to him thirty feet away. Gales hoisted his red canvas duffle bag onto his shoulder and walked to the van. He looked bigger in his khaki shorts and black form fitting t-shirt. His blue eyes shone like sapphires set in his tan angular face. His brown hair was longer and streaked with blond.

Ken hit the remote button that slid the back bay door open. Gales threw his duffle bag in and waited for the passenger door to open. Jumping into the passenger seat, the young man gave Ken a friendly punch on the shoulder.

"How you be, dude?"

"I'm hanging tough, dude. You look like you grew a couple of inches. What did they feed you in Texas?" asked Ken as he drove out of the airport.

"Mostly Mexican food and steak of course. I got into working out regularly with the football team. Man, am I in shape! I can bench press 225," said the inspired medical student, as he brushed back his brown hair with his hand.

"That's about what I'm bench pressing these days." quipped Ken, "Of course I do it one pound at a time throughout the year."

Gales, used to his friend's humor, laughed easily.

"You look like you caught some serious sun."

"Texas dude. Check my hair, I'm going blond."

"I can see! And you're like bigger—broader."

"I told you, I was working out, like four times a week!"

"You look cool, dude. The babes are going to be all over you," quipped the ex-priest.

"Hey, what's with the new lingo?"

"The new lingo?"

"Yeah dude. You're talking different—using words like dude and babes..."

"I'm changing my groove dog—taking a class in hip jargon."

"Cool, my man!"

"Yeah, way cool! Tell me about those cowboys you hustled."

Ken immediately brought up the subject of chess, hoping to keep the conversation on a trivial level. Tim was happy to oblige, and went on about his many victories, mostly over a couple of football players and the assistant coach. Ken chimed in about his recent victories online and how he was thinking about challenging the top chess pros in the game. They discussed strategies and gambling in general most of the way back to the city. Then Ken stumbled, asking the future doctor about the nutritional value in Mexican food.

"It's surprisingly high in the necessary vitamins and minerals—low in cholesterol by comparison to the average American food diet."

"But of course, as a sports doctor, you wouldn't recommend it for athletes."

"With some modifications I would. But that's not my major anymore. I'm changing it, going to specialize in pediatrics."

"Wow! Big move, Tim. What made you change your mind?"

"God."

"Oh, shit!" exclaimed the ex-priest. "Those raving Texas evangelicals got their hooks into you!"

"No, not really. I met this girl—"

"Uh-oh, even worse!" interjected Ken

"Her name's Maria Sanchez."

"Ah ha! The Mexican food!" teased Ken.

"Those Latin ladies know the way to a man's heart and other vital organs!"

Tim laughed, and held out his cell-phone for Ken to check out Maria's photo.

"Is she to die for, or what!" exclaimed Tim.

"You're not really serious yet, are you? I mean, dude, you've only known each other a few weeks," said Ken, hoping he wouldn't have to deal with some hot-blooded chick with his name tattooed on her neck.

"We're in love, dude. Our meeting was an act of God!"

"Let me guess," interjected Ken, steaming at the intrusion of this babe into his grand scheme. "You went out for Mexican food. She was your waitress. You didn't have anything in common, until she bent over to pour your Margarita and you checked out her cleavage."

Tim burst into laughter. Ken didn't let up joking to keep from venting his anger.

"After five Margaritas and eight tamales you pinched her ass and asked her to join you under the table, where you made out. She said, 'I love people who eat out, Tim, but I can't marry a man involved with sports medicine.' You, in the throes of passion, replied, 'No problemo seniorita, let's open our own Mexican restaurant and have a hundred kids.'"

Tim was hysterical, choking on his words as he tried to respond.

"You're psychic Ken! How else could you know all that—down to the raw details! But you missed the clincher. She picked up the check."

"She has mucho money!" concluded Ken.

"Yes, I'm ashamed to say. She has thirty-four dollars in her piggy bank."

Ken laughed politely, as Tim waxed serious, "She's an amazing person, Ken—a nurse at St. Mary's Children's Hospital. She works with handicapped kids. Wait till you hear how we met."

"I'm all ears dude," sighed Ken, who was beginning to feel sick.

"I'm riding with the team in the bus when this little kid on a bike gets hit by the car in front of us."

"A typical act of God," interjected Ken sarcastically to himself.

"I grabbed the first aid kit, jumped out of the bus and started treating this mangled little boy. He was losing a lot of blood and it looked like his neck was broken—"

"Oh, nice work, God!" interjected Ken to himself.

"Well, I apply a tourniquet to his leg. Meanwhile, he starts to choke on his own blood. I can't move his head so I start sucking the blood out of his mouth."

"Jesus, Tim. Spare me the details. Just tell me you saved his life."

"Well, I guess I did. When the ambulance arrived, I immediately yell at the medic rushing to him with the oxygen mask. 'He has internal bleeding in his head, he'll choke! Just suck the blood from his throat.' They apply a suction device and we slide him onto a gurney. Here's the God part. The little guy is out cold and so badly broken I think he's not going to make it. The lead medic turns to me and says, 'Thanks man, we got it from here.'"

"I'm about to leave when the kid spits out the suction tube and says, 'Stay with me.'"

"It was so freaky, I actually said, 'What?'"

"'Please,' whispers this totally unconscious kid, and that was it!"

"That's quite a story. Did the little guy make it?" asked Ken.

"Wait. The ambulance blazes to the children's hospital. We rush him in, right through the emergency room into an operating room. His blood pressure is imperceptible on the gauge. He needs blood, type O. And they are all out! My blood is type O. Is that a miracle, or what!"

"Do you mind telling me if he lived?"

"Yes, and they think he might be able to walk again. I know he will."

"You do?"

"Yes, because he said that God didn't save him for nothing."

Ken was already in the city driving toward his apartment, and cursing the very thought of God.

"So, Tim, you want to help children?"

"Yeah. I spent some time with Maria at the hospital with handicapped kids. In the little time I was there, I jerry-rigged a bunch of wheelchairs and braces that worked better for them."

"I despise you, God," Ken thought to himself, as he pulled up to the entrance of the Port Authority Bus Terminal. Handing the locker key to Timothy Gales, he said, "Do me a favor, Tim. I've got an attaché case in locker 28. Could you run in and grab it for me?"

"Sure," said Tim, leaping from the van and rushing into the terminal.

People were already leaning on their horns for him to stop blocking traffic. He pulled away and drove around the block. Tim was waiting outside with the case when he returned. The young man hopped into the van, placing the case down between Ken and himself. Ken turned the van down 42nd Street and turned again on Ninth Avenue. The rain had stopped, but the sky was still a smoky gray, as he drove the van straight down Ninth toward the Columbia University dormitory building. Whatever Tim said along the way Ken just nodded to in response. When he pulled the van up to the University dorm entrance, his prime candidate asked, "What about our chess game?"

"Some other time, my friend. I'm not feeling too cool."

"Hey, come in with me. I'll get you fixed up, pronto."

"No thanks, doc. I just need to get back to my place and take my meds."

"Are you sure, Ken?"

"I'm sure, Tim. I'll call you tomorrow."

Tim stepped out of the van, waited for the back bay door to open and grabbed his duffle bag. Ken called to him, "Tim, Tim."

Tim came to the passenger door which was still open.

"Yeah?

"Take this with you."

Ken tossed the case containing the money on the passenger's seat.

"What's in here?" asked the young doctor to be.

"It's a gift. I want you to have it. But you can't open it until tomorrow."

Ken tossed him the keys.

"A gift, for what?"

"For your practice, or your wedding—whichever comes first."

Ken closed the doors and drove away, not noticing that the sun had broken through the clouds and a double rainbow crossed the sky.

CHAPTER THIRTY NINE

IF I CAN MAKE IT THERE, I CAN MAKE IT ANYWHERE

The first thing Joel did when his cell phone alarm started chirping at 7 a.m. was to call the Greyhound Bus terminal. There was a bus leaving for New York City at five o'clock, and with plenty of available seating.

Joel showered and dressed in a half hour. He took the elevator to the third floor and walked down to Julian's room. He knocked gently on the door but got no answer. He could hear snoring, so he knocked louder. After several attempts, each one increasing in intensity, Julian came to the door in his underwear.

"Shit man, do you know what time it is?"

"Hey, if you're going to be my bodyguard, you'll have to improve your response time."

"Don't be spouting that shit in the hall, you'll wake the roaches! Come in."

Joel stepped in and closed the door. A single light bulb hung in a socket dangling from a chain covered with years of old paint. Jules sat on the single bed jammed in between the three walls of the room.

"I'd offer you a chair," said Julian, "but as you can see there's no room for one."

"Jesus, man, how can you live in here? You don't even have a window!"

"Luxury's not my thing these days."

"You don't have a bathroom! They can't rent a room with no window or bathroom! It's not legal!"

"I have a chamber pot."

"Get out!"

"No, really. It's under the bed. And it works for me. I live a Spartan life. What does a man need to be happy?"

"Fresh fuckin' air!" exclaimed Joel, while opening the door. "Get dressed, let's go."

"No way, dude. I've got another hour left before I have to be out," stated Julian.

"What do you mean, 'Have to be out?'"

"My roommate gets in at nine. He works the night shift at Taco Bell."

"You're shittin' me!"

"Yeah," laughed Julian, "Okay, wait for me in the lobby. I've got to shower."

"Where?"

"I've got some wet-wipes under my pillow," quipped Julian.

Laughing, Joel said, "This isn't your room, is it?"

"No, Elmer Fudd, it's not. They're peeling and painting my room."

"Okay," said Joel. "Meet me at the Table Top. And don't go back to sleep."

At the Table Top coffee shop, a hangout for actors and writers, Joel sat down at a computer on the back wall counter. He ordered a black coffee, a bran muffin, and paid five dollars for a half hour of computer time. He logged on and perused the furnished rooms available in New York. He tried to find something near the Belasco Theatre, where his show would open, but the rents were through the sky. After searching for twenty minutes, he found a reasonable two-room apartment way downtown being subletted on a monthly basis. He called and was able to rent it on faith because he told the landlord he was in the Army. He promised the landlord he would be there in three days, cash in hand.

Julian showed up at the Table Top wearing perfectly pressed gray Dockers, a neat pullover golf shirt, and a clean pair of white sneakers.

"What's the occasion?" asked Joel.

"I'm New York bound, dude. When are we splitting?"

"Five tonight, but we best be at the terminal by four to be sure we get seats. How much luggage do you have?"

"Two, maybe three shopping bags."

"No, Jules. No shopping bags. We'll get you a duffle bag at the Army and Navy Surplus."

"Better bury that white pride, dude. I'm also bringing a banjo and a straw hat."

Joel erupted with laughter.

"Have you got three hundred for the iron?" asked Julian.

"No way. With the bus tickets, rent and food till I get paid—can't swing it!"

"I can cover my ticket and food. How much is the rent?" "Twelve hundred, plus utilities."

"A month, right?"

"Yes."

"That's six hundred to me. My social security will cover my end."

"Then we can buy the iron," stated Joel, who really wanted some protection, as little as it might be, from the evil forces at work in his world.

CHAPTER FORTY

LIFE IS A CRAPSHOOT

After dropping Tim off at his dormitory, Ken drove back to his apartment. His back was aching, but the bitterness he felt toward the unseen forces, whatever-the-fuck they were, was subsiding as he drove. After all, life is a crapshoot, just as David Heightly described it. Some win, some lose. What determines who wins and who loses, no one knows. Karma, luck, sin, the configuration of your stars—all attempts by ignorant mortals to explain the disparity between the fortunate and unfortunate—a cosmic crapshoot, that's all! At least everyone has the option to quit the game.

He thought of Beth, his friend and one true love. Of all the people he ever knew, she alone inspired him. She deserved to be physically perfect because her childlike innocence brought joy to everyone around her. She revealed the message of the Buddhist monk, Boccti, who saw the world as a vale of tears, where every person is called to do whatever he can to alleviate suffering, not because he believed in some deity, some benefit beyond the grave, but because he was a caring human being, part of the human family.

Ken drove up to his parking space and just nudged the handicap cones out of the way as he parked the van. His journey was over. The loaded gun rested cold and silent in the stereo drawer inside his apartment. There was no one to call—no suicide note still to write. Anyway, who would question why a man bound to a wheelchair for forty-six years finally killed himself!

The Rascal was sitting on the windowsill waiting to be let in. The ex-priest maneuvered his wheel chair to the pavement and motored to the outside door. He stopped to pet his cat, who was still wet from the rain. The chubby Rascal hopped into his friend's lap and purred.

"You'll be going back to Beth, old buddy. I know, I know, you love her. Don't jump for joy just yet. She's going to put you on a diet, might even try to make you a vegetarian."

Giving his furry friend a final kiss, Ken placed him on the ground. "You stay outside for a while. This is goodbye for us."

Ken opened the outside door and entered the hallway leading to his apartment. He remembered his angel girl who lived at the far end of the hall. He would have liked to say good-bye, to see her face one last time—but it wasn't in the cards for him, the man who once believed there was a Divine purpose at work in life. He placed the key in his apartment door and descovered it was open before he turned the key. He must have neglected to lock it. As he rolled into his apartment, he was shocked to see the entire place in shambles. All the living room furniture was turned over, drawers pulled out and their contents scattered all over the floor. He'd been robbed. "Oh shit," he thought, "did they get the gun?" He rolled carefully through the overturned computer equipment, chairs, cushions, books, to the overturned stereo. All the drawers were out, lying empty on the floor. CDs, wires, and stereo components were snarled in a heap on the floor. Using a wood yardstick, he searched through the debris but couldn't find his gun. Disgusted, he plowed through the rubble of the living room into his bedroom and found his bed turned up on its side and the rest of the room looking bombed.

Ken was angry and confused. What kind of idiot breaks into an apartment and leaves five thousand dollars' worth of computer equipment behind? Ken maneuvered his chair back into the living room, making a more thorough search for the gun. Not finding it, he fought back the impulse to scream out in rage. Then he remembered the potion sitting on the kitchen table.

"Let it be there!" his mind shouted. Pressing the control switch on the wheelchair forward, he plowed full throttle through the mess into the kitchen where he ran into the body of David Heightly sprawled out on the floor.

Ken maneuvered his wheelchair around until he could reach the fallen man's arm. Using the yardstick he maneuvered David's arm enough to reach down and feel his pulse. He held the young man's wrist a full three minutes until he was certain that he was dead. Ken sat stunned in his chair, trying to figure out what happened, when he spotted the gun on the kitchen table beside the empty bottle of orange juice. Now the mystery began to clear up in his mind.

David Heightly came here to steal the hundred thousand dollars he assumed Ken had stashed in his apartment. Of course, why else would he be wearing gloves? He didn't want to leave his fingerprints behind. Ken recalled the phone conversation he had with the young hustler that morning. It was obvious why David tried to get Ken out of his apartment to the park for the game. Logically, the Shark assumed Ken would only bring fifty thousand for the game and leave the additional fifty thousand back at his apartment. The Shark even tried to persuade him to play under a tent rather than play the final game in his apartment. Sure, the young Shark was broke. He didn't have the money for the final game and couldn't borrow it. How excited the devious Shark must have felt when Ken said he was driving to the airport in the afternoon. Now he could steal the entire hundred grand. And it would be a perfect crime because it would be Ken's word against the Shark's as to who won the final game. The cunning young gambler probably assumed that Ken wouldn't even report it to avoid the legal ramifications. What a surprise ending it all had for David Heightly. He came to Ken's apartment probably around two, knocked to make sure Ken wasn't home, and used the apartment house keys Beth left with him in case of any emergency. He came in feeling confident he would leave a richer man. No doubt he searched slowly, methodically at first, but became frustrated and just started tearing through the place, working up a thirst. When he got to the kitchen, he couldn't resist the fresh orange juice on the table. Five minutes later he was gasping for breath, convulsing. Then the darkness closed in around him and he faded into death.

Ken picked up the gun, and thought about the pain that all this would cause Beth. He considered postponing his own suicide so he could be around to comfort her in grief. But, how long would he wait before he took his own life—just a short while and then Beth would have to deal with his suicide. No, Ken thought, it would be better to get it over with here and now. As he slid back the cocking mechanism of the weapon to make sure there was a bullet in the chamber, an odd thought occurred to him.

"It takes a while for the body to completely die, even after the heart stops. Medical journals are filled with reports of people who were pronounced clinically dead but came back to life. What the hell," he thought. He had nothing to lose. Ken placed the gun down on the table and rolled back to David's body.

He struggled for a good five minutes to position the young man's body so that he was lying face up and flat on the floor. Ken had to move the table and chairs out of the way for there to be enough room for him to lie down head to head with the dead man. At last, aching all over from the effort, Ken went to the pantry and fetched the remaining potion from the Quaker Oats container. He placed it in his sweater pocket and swung back to the other side of the kitchen where he eased himself out of his wheelchair to the floor. Dragging himself in proximity to the dead man's head, he pulled his legs into position with his hands. Satisfied they were straight enough, he leaned back until he was face up and almost head to head with the corpse. He had to use his hands to hike himself up a few inches until his head was touching the head of the man whose body he would attempt to inhabit. In the process his catheter separated from the bag, spilling his urine all over the floor.

Ken removed the aspirin bottle from his sweater pocket, unscrewed the lid and wet his finger. Dipping his finger into the bottle, he carefully picked up a few granules of the powder. He put his finger to his tongue. The potion was tasteless. Bringing his hand back down to his side, Ken began to chant the incantation.

> "Eeeloli, Eeeloli David Heightly Has Died.
> Eeelolee, Eeelolee, David Heightly Is Me.
> Eeeloli, Eeeloli, David Heightly Has Died.
> Eeelolee, Eeelolee, David Heightly Is Me.
> Eeeloli, Eeeloli, David Heightly Has Died.
> Eeelolee, Eeelolee, David Heightly Is Me."

CHAPTER FORTY ONE

LIMBO

There was no delay, no interval. Something went wrong. There was no delay, no interval, was all Ken kept thinking as he tried to force his eyes open. His near perfect memory repetitiously delivered the image of Taulb switching into the body of Zack Taylor. There was no delay, no interval between the time Taulb chanted the incantation and his rising up in the movie star's body. Something went wrong, terribly wrong, for him to be immobilized like this for over an hour—unable to open his eyes or move anything at all.

Reasoning that the switch may not have been completed, he tried to resume the incantation several times but couldn't move his mouth or utter a sound. Ken's greatest fear had become a reality—he was totally paralyzed. Now, even if he wanted to he couldn't end his miserable life. Then a greater fear swept over him—maybe he was dead. Maybe he put too much potion on his tongue. Maybe he had no eyes, no vocal cords, or fingers to move. Maybe his soul was in limbo—suspended in nothingness.

"OH GOD, NO! OH GOD! OH GOD! HELP ME! HEELLLP!!!" the ex-priest raved on and on in the dark silence. Then he thought amidst his soundless screams, "Maybe all I will ever experience anymore are my memories."

Though pain was no stranger to him in his life, it couldn't compare to the ice cold aloneness that gripped him now. After a while, the futility of trying to scream sunk in and he just surrendered to his horrible fate. Just as he surrendered, he felt something—an almost imperceptible thump. He couldn't be sure his mind wasn't playing tricks on him, so he focused intently and felt another thump, several thumps, a repetition of thumps. It was his heart beating. The realization restored some small hope.

"I can't be dead," he surmised. If his heart was beating, he had to be breathing he thought, as he felt for a sign of his breath. Yes, he felt it, a slight cool feeling of air moving up through his nostrils and out again. Instinctively, he continued the incantation in his mind, visualizing the sounds.

"Eeeloli, Eeeloli David Heightly Has Died.
Eeelolee, Eeelolee, David Heightly Is Me.
Eeeloli, Eeeloli, David Heightly Has Died.
Eeelolee, Eeelolee, David Heightly is Me."

The visualization created a gentle vibration, a soft buzzing in his head behind his eyes, a pleasant most welcome feeling. Suddenly his eyes opened, but tears blurred his vision. Blinking away the tears of joy, he could clearly see the pewter light fixture on the kitchen ceiling—a star shaped fixture whose points spotlighted every area of the room.

Feeling the wet tears rolling down his temples, Ken concluded that life may slowly be returning to his body. Perhaps the switch process was taking place, albeit much slower than the one he witnessed in Taulb's hotel room. So he continued to visualize the incantation, remaining keenly alert to any signs that the switch was in progress.

Indeed it was. Slowly, warmth and feeling returned to his body, like a wave rolling in slow motion from the top of his head down through his face, neck, and chest. He was already moving his fingers when feeling returned to his mid-section. He waited breathlessly to detect even the slightest feeling below his waist. When he could wait no longer, he moved his right hand to his penis and pinched it. The pain of it was sheer delight.

Fear no longer held him in its grip. He realized that he was fully alive and without a doubt in the body of David Heightly. He wiggled his toes in celebration and sat up and looked at the pyramid clock on the kitchen wall. Over two hours had elapsed since he began the switch. Ken could comfortably move every part of David Heightly's body, but his legs were stiff. Clasping his gloved hands on his right knee, he pulled the leg up toward himself. Then he pushed it down, then up and down and up and down—over and over again—slowly releasing his grip until he was able to continue the exercise without the use of his hands. It wasn't long before he had both legs working on their own. He marveled at the power he felt in his new legs as he worked them up and down and side to side scissor fashion. Like a child enthralled with a new toy, he kept moving his body parts every which way until he was on his hands and knees crawling around the body of Ken McAlister. Finally, clinging to a chair, he pulled himself up to a standing position. Using the chair to steady himself, he took his first step and wobbled forward. Then he took his next step and almost lost his balance. Continuing to step and hold, he made his way unsteadily across the kitchen floor. Confident, he attempted two steps in a row and stumbled sideways before tripping over his old body and crashing to the floor. Laughing, he pulled himself up to continue his practice. Soon he was able to discard the chair and walk slowly from wall to wall, using the wall to keep his balance each time he turned around. After fifteen minutes he was striding carefully back and forth without needing the wall to turn around. Ten minutes later, in a state of mind approaching euphoria, he walked out of the kitchen and stepped unaided through his disheveled apartment. Stopping in the bathroom, he took his first normal pee, marveling as he did at the size of his penis. Limp as it was, it was still a lot bigger than he imagined it would be. While relieving himself, it dawned on him that he hadn't thrown up the potion after the switch, as the alchemist did. And he thought that the extended period of time he spent in the unconscious state may have occurred because he put too much of the potion in his mouth.

Stepping to the sink, he bent low to study his face in the bathroom mirror. Brushing his hair back with his right hand, he beheld his strikingly handsome face with the dark almond shaped eyes and long slightly curly hair. But to him it was still the face of a stranger—and the eyes especially seemed cold and devoid of empathy. He smiled and tried on several facial expressions before leaving the john.

Ken practiced walking late into the night when he was startled by the sound of rap music coming from the cell phone on his belt. The leather gloves on his hands made it difficult to remove the phone from the belt pouch, but he knew better than to take them off. If, for any reason, the police suspected foul play in McAlister's death, and they found Heightly's fingerprints around the apartment, he could wind up spending his new life in prison, or on death row. Beth's name appeared on the phone's screen. Tempted as he was to hear her voice, he knew he couldn't answer. He wasn't ready. He had so much to figure out, so much to do before he could speak to her as David Heightly. He waited patiently for the rap music to stop. A few moments later he pressed the phone message icon and listened to her voice, "Hi babe. Dad is doing better. The doctor said the surgery was a success. They think they removed all the cancer but he will have to do radiation. I'm going to hang here till Thursday when I'll grab a bus for home. I miss you. Call me. Love you."

Ken delighted in the sound of her voice. But he couldn't call her back for a while. First, he had to restore his entire apartment and return to Heightly's digs uptown—to get better acquainted with his new identity. Possibly tomorrow evening he would discover the body of Ken McAlister, contact the police and call Beth.

He wasn't tired, but he knew he should get some sleep. Then he remembered Top Gun. He walked to the bedroom window, let the Rascal in and led him to the kitchen where he fed him a can of cat food. Ken watched Top Gun eat while he himself drank two glasses of water. When the Rascal finished eating he hopped onto McAlister's corpse and started licking his face. In the process of chasing the cat away, Ken became aware that the corpse was already getting stiff. He had to return McAlister to his wheel chair at once. By morning rigor mortis would have made it impossible to sit the corpse back in his chair. While wrestling his old body into the wheelchair, he thought of his tiny mother and how she would struggle to get him into a park swing—how she would tie him in with rope. He wondered if she might somehow be aware of him now, in his amazing new body. It was almost midnight when he finished positioning the corpse of McAlister in his wheelchair and attaching a clean catheter and liquid collection bag to his leg. In the morning he would situate the wheelchair in the living room, where McAlister would be found dead from a sudden and unexpected heart attack. Exhausted now, he undressed and settled into bed for his first night's sleep as David Heightly.

In the morning, he showered and brushed his teeth before putting the apartment back together. Though he was hungry, he didn't take time to eat. He was concerned that the police just might launch a thorough investigation, and he didn't want to leave any traces of himself around.

The restoration of the apartment took longer than he had anticipated. He heard a number of tenants come down the stairs and exit the building while he worked. It was about noon when he went to the front door to leave. At the door he listened carefully to make sure no one was coming in or out before he dashed out of the building. Once outside, he removed the sweat-drenched gloves and set about finding David's Chevy van, which was parked just two blocks away. Since it occupied a legal parking space, he decided to leave it there until he picked Beth up at the bus terminal. Still, he had to learn to drive it. He spent ten minutes getting used to the gas and brake pedals and bucking in and out of the parking space. Then he drove it around the block several times before returning it to the parking space.

Famished, he stopped to eat at Quiznos before walking to Heightly's apartment on the upper Westside. The walk uptown inspired such joy, he wondered why any hardy person would opt to take a bus or cab. About a mile into the walk, he decided to jog. Ken discovered that jogging in midtown Manhattan wasn't easy. He had to dodge this way and that through the throngs of people and stop at almost every street corner to avoid being hit by the oncoming traffic. He was hardly breathing heavy by the time he reached Central Park. Feeling more alive than he ever did, he paused in the shade of a huge maple tree to take in the magnificent scent of the foliage.

Suddenly the rap music from his cell phone broke in on his thoughts. It was Beth. Intoxicated with the health of his new life, he just answered it.

"Hey babe, what are you up to?" he asked.

"Hanging out with my mother mostly. Did you get my message last night?"

"About your father, yes. Glad he's on the mend. You still coming back tomorrow?"

"If my brother and his wife decide to stay another week. If not, I'll hang here until my dad's up and around."

"How's your mom handling things?"

"She says she's cool but she's not. You know, bearing up…she's drinking a lot of wine with her meals though…"

"Yeah. Yeah, my father hit the vino when my mother got sick," responded Ken, recalling Heightly's story of his mother's bout with cancer.

"How are things at the apartment? I talked to Albaniack on the phone yesterday. He wants me back soon or he's going to hire out the cleaning job and add the expense to my rent."

"Honestly babe, the place doesn't look that bad. And don't sweat the rent! I've got—"

"Did you check in on Ken?"

"No, I spaced it out. I'll check him out, later."

"I've gotta run. Mom's waiting in the car. Love you. I'll call you tomorrow."

"Love you too."

Tossing the cell phone high in the air and catching it, Ken exulted in his first successful impersonation of David Heightly.

He trotted the remaining twenty-one blocks to Heightly's digs located in a yellow brick high rise off of West End Avenue. He paused in the lobby of the moderate rent building to empty his mailbox. Placing an electric bill in his pocket, he discarded the remaining junk mail in a shiny brass receptacle beside the elevator. He pressed the "up" button and watched the indicator above the door light up the floor numbers as the elevator descended to the lobby. When the door slid open, a beautiful "twenty-something" with a blond and black punk hairdo stepped out and greeted him.

"David! I missed you last night. Wuss up…"

Ken looked behind him to see who she was talking to before it hit him.

"Oh, yeah—sorry about that—had a meeting, got delayed—I mean, got hung up," he stammered.

"I hope it was a good meeting, because it was a rockin party!"

Ken smiled, "My loss. Maybe next time."

The punk-haired beauty hugged him, pressing her thigh gently into his groin and whispering in his ear, "We don't need a party to enjoy each other's company, do we? You've got my number—see ya…"

Ken watched the girl exit the lobby before he entered the elevator. As he rode the elevator up, the ex-priest ex-paraplegic contemplated the unexpected encounter.

"She could be a problem—might have to move," he pondered. "Does everyone in this modern age think that sex is the goal of their existence? Was I supposed to get sexually aroused when she put her thigh between my legs? Of course—'turned on' is the hip expression. Was I turned on? No, I wasn't—no, not in the least. I wasn't—shit! I might have a problem—David Heightly would have been turned on—would have responded—how? What's the appropriate response to a come-on like that? In India, if a girl places her bare foot on a young man's foot that means she desires him. The young man is supposed to put his foot on hers if he's interested. That helps, Ken. Try it next time you're turned on—in India, idiot!"

Ken's mind raced on as the door opened on the tenth floor and he stepped out and walked down the carpeted corridor to apartment 10F, Heightly's "digs." Neatly stenciled in red above the peep hole in the door was the phrase from Dante's Inferno:

Abandon all hope, ye who enter here.

Ken tried several keys on Heightly's key ring before finding the one that opened the door. Evidently, Heightly joined Beth's keys with his own. Upon entering the apartment, Ken realized that the young man whose body he now inhabited harbored a mite of good taste. The living room was purposely designed in a modern motif that revealed a financially well off occupant, who also enjoyed maid service. Situated on the posh gray carpeted floor was a settee and matching love seat, sporting white cushions in black frames. A coffee table of clear glass shaped like a painter's pallet rested on a piece of bleached white driftwood and separated the settee and love seat. A silver laptop computer rested on the coffee table. The mauve wallpaper maintained the artist theme, bearing delicate brush strokes of brown, green, sky blue, and cloud white, suggesting a mountain landscape. One wall was a bank of tall windows overlooking the river and the New Jersey skyline. Beside a white flat screen TV, the walls held three large framed photos and a white book shelf. One photo depicted David Heightly standing with his arms thrust victoriously up in the air over a stone chess table where an elderly opponent sat surrounded by a group of onlookers. It might have been taken in Central Park. The second photo was of Heightly running with the bulls in Spain. The third photo was taken in Hawaii and depicted him doing a fire walk, while dressed in white and wearing a lei of flowers around his neck.

The item of greater interest to Ken than anything else in the room was the white, double tiered bookshelf which held the "Complete Works of Plato," and "The Works of Herman Hesse." The collection of books also included Friedrich Nietzsche's "The Twilight of Idols," "The Antichrist," and "Beyond Good and Evil." Not surprising at all were, Ayn Rand's classics, "The Fountainhead," "Atlas Shrugged," and "The Virtue of Selfishness." The lower shelf contained "Tax Law for Dummies," and ten or so books on chess, including a collection of Bobby Fisher beside the classics "Winning Chess Strategies," and "Secrets of the Russian Chess Masters," volumes 1 and 2. Ken spent a half hour scanning through the books on the top shelf and was happy to discover that they weren't just decor. All of them had been well handled, dog-eared, and highlighted in numerous places. The investigation confirmed Ken's personal observations of Heightly, as a young man of above average intelligence with a good command of the English language. This confirmation of Heightly's intelligence allowed Ken to relax and not be overly concerned about "youth speak," which he only heard the Shark use when he was hustling the student fish. But it made him wonder all the more how a young man of such obvious intelligence and advantages could resort to deceitful and criminal activities. Cynicism and selfishness could be justified in the young self-proclaimed atheist, but criminality just didn't fit his profile. Ken continued his research into the personality of the man he had to resemble.

There was a small kitchen off the living room, and one bedroom with a king bed piled high with white and red pillows. A few feet from the foot of the bed stood a sizeable dresser with a huge mirror. Two white ivory lamps shaped like King and Queen chess pieces adorned the black end tables on either side of the bed. Ken sat on the bed running his hand over the satin sheets. There was so much to learn about the mannerisms of this self-possessed soul. The ex-priest wondered if he could ever mimic him convincingly enough to fool Beth. Pondering this concern was absurd and Ken knew it, for failure wasn't an option. He could never tell the love of his life the truth. If the David Heightly he presented to her lacked some wonderful, exciting, compelling qualities, then Beth, never one for pretense, would simply end the relationship.

Ken continued his investigation in the bathroom, specifically to see what cologne, aftershave and other toiletries Heightly used. He was amazed to discover all the different hair products the hippie Shark had on hand. Returning to the bedroom, Ken opened the closet door. Automatically a light went on revealing a sizeable walk-in closet with hangers and racks full of colorful shirts, sweaters, jackets, trousers, jeans, and footwear for a man who could be a stand out at any occasion. This also was good news to Ken, who was just about strapped for cash.

In his quest to know David Heightly, Ken searched through every cabinet and drawer in the apartment. In a locked shoe drawer beneath the bed he found buried treasure—several thick ledgers containing Heightly's personal journals. The handwritten journals would prove invaluable in culling the nuances of character that Ken would have to replicate in his new life. With the journals in hand, Ken went to the kitchen, made a pot of tea, and began reading the personal reflections of David Heightly. A couple of hours into the reading, it became evident to the ex-priest that the man whose body he now inhabited was only a chess hustler by default. The Shark was first and foremost just a hustler, who pursued a number of different scams to con people before he became a chess-shark. Leaving his parents when he was seventeen, David worked in a traveling carnival where he learned the secrets of the shell game, three card monte, the black jack shuffle, the lost dog swindle, and others. Later on in his journey, a college professor he was boning showed him how to pirate and sell term papers and final dissertations online. At the age of twenty he got involved in a real estate scam that landed him in jail for eight months. It was in jail that he learned to play chess, exposing the lie he told Beth that he was taught the game by his father. That his mother died of cancer when he was nineteen was about the only truth the journals verified so far. From the information Ken gleaned, the young hustler was an atheist who believed the Ayn Rand philosophy, that the only meaningful quest in life was to pursue and fulfill one's own personal happiness. Speculating on this, the ex-priest realized that he wasn't far from embracing Rand's philosophy himself.

Checking the microwave clock, Ken had to forego his reading and get on with the necessity of reporting Ken McAlister's death. After taking a quick shower and donning some fresh threads, Ken headed downtown on a subway. When he arrived at the brownstone that used to be his abode, he knocked on the door to McAlister's apartment. Then as planned, he called McAlister's cell phone. Next he called the building owner.

"Mr. Albaniac, this is David Heightly, Beth Burton's boyfriend."

"Yes, what is it?" came Albaniac's gruff voice through the receiver.

"Well, Beth wanted me to check in on Mr. McAlister, the man in the wheelchair."

"Yes, yes. Is there some problem?"

"Well, he doesn't answer the door when I knock."

"Knock louder. I think he's a little deaf too."

"No, I banged on his door. I called his cell phone. He doesn't answer."

"What am I supposed to do—he doesn't answer?" was Albaniac's perturbed response.

"I have Beth's keys. Maybe I should just let myself in and see if he's okay, what do you think?"

"Sure, sure. Let yourself in. But holla loud at the door in case he's sleeping."

"I will."

"When does Beth come back?" asked Albaniac.

"Tomorrow I think."

"She better come tomorrow. You tell her that. My building looks like shit!'"

"'I'll tell her, Mr. Albaniac."

Ken's plans unfolded flawlessly. Two hours later the coroner finished his preliminary report. Howe's Funeral Home picked up the body, and the police placed their yellow tape across the entrance to McAlister's apartment. The police gave David Heightly permission to take McAlister's cat until some relative showed up to claim him. David took the Rascal to Beth's apartment and called her. Their phone conversation consisted mostly of her crying and David consoling. He hadn't realized how much she cared for her wheelchair bound friend. The call concluded with Beth reminding him to pick her up at the bus terminal at 6 p.m. the following day.

David ruminated on his situation as he sat in Beth's apartment petting the Rascal. "Now the chips are down. Tomorrow, less than twenty-four hours from now, I will have to meet and make love to a nineteen-year-old girl—not David Heightly—me—the soul and mind of an ex-priest, handicapped from birth, will have to make love to her." In her kitchen of pastel colored walls and oak furnishings, he sat healthy and fit but fearing the possibility that he might not be able to muster an erection. All he knew about sex was abstract biological knowledge, psychological perspectives he studied in school—nothing experiential. Of all the concerns that accompanied the switch, this one involving sexual intercourse never seemed to be that big a problem, until now. Now it loomed as a real and horrible threat to all of his hopes and dreams. He just didn't have a clue how to make love, not just make it, but make it convincingly as David Heightly. He realized he could go online and Google some instructions, but he didn't have a computer. His computer was unwittingly left in McAlister's apartment. He couldn't risk going back in and using it now. Beth had her computer with her in Albany. David's laptop was on the coffee table up town but he didn't have the password. His palms wet with sweat, he stopped petting the Rascal and washed his hands.

While starring at himself in the bathroom mirror it came to him, as things often do when you're starring in a mirror, that he should attempt to arouse himself, at least find out if he could get a hard-on. The idea seemed so foreign to him that he left the bathroom in search of a bottle of wine, or beer, or something to help him indulge in the sin of masturbation. Finding none, the ex-priest on new legs ran four blocks to a liquor store, purchased two bottles of wine, and ran back.

At Beth's apartment he gave the Rascal a hunk of cheese from the refrigerator and locked him out in the backyard. He opened the red, poured a glassful, and surfed the TV in search of sex. There was romance and murder occurring on just about every channel, but no sex to work with. Finally he found a spate of porn channels advertising sexually explicit films. "Hot Teens Spring Break," "Wet Co-eds," "Steaming Hot

Chicks," "Wild Babes and Boys." The problem with the porn flicks was that he would have to pay to order them and he didn't want the transaction to show up on Beth's cable bill. He sure didn't want to become a pervert, so he rejected the porn and continued to surf the tube. Feeling the wine, he settled for an old movie with Marilyn Monroe, *Some Like It Hot.*

Notwithstanding, all of his attempts to stimulate an erection met with failure after failure. It seemed to his somewhat foggy perception that his problem was the commercials that kept interrupting the movie and his train of thought. The ex-priest chided himself for not doing more research into sex prior to the switch. The alchemist warned him that it might take time to learn how to walk because he never used his legs before. Well duh, he never used his penis before either. How could the alchemist overlook such an important element in his instructions! Frustrated, half drunk, with a sore over-stroked cock dangling between his legs, Ken called the alchemist who was in California where it was only 7 p.m. Fortunately, personal secretary Kylie was out on an errand and Zack Taylor answered his own phone.

"This is six, five, four, seven one three, three one three, four eight, eight, eight. Whose calling?" asked the movie star.

"This is Ken Smith—a fan of yours. You helped me some time back—with a screen play I was writing."

"A sci-fi script involving some guy in a coma," added the star, with no little attitude in his voice.

"Yes, well I have another script, which—"

"How did the first one work out? Did you manage to write that guy out of the coma?"

"Yes, but he ran off before— "

"He fuckin' ran off! Where?"

"The Army I think. I wrote him out of the story, if you know what I mean?"

"Your writing sucks! Did I mention that the first time we spoke?"

"Yes, but this new script is much improved."

"There's no one in a coma is there?" inquired the star.

"Well, no, not really..."

"Not really? Either someone's in a fuckin' coma or he's not—so which is it chucklehead?"

"No coma. My character is out of the coma but he's got a problem."

"What? What's his problem—and don't tell me he ran away, because I'm getting fucking sick of re-writing your shit!"

"He can't get an erection."

"He what?"

"My leading man can't get an erection."

"Jesus H. Christ! Get him a fuckin' hooker. I mean write a hooker into his life!"

"There's no time. He's meeting the girl he loves tomorrow and he needs to be able to make love to her."

"And he's tried to masturbate?" queried the star.

"Yes, but it didn't work. What can he do? He's desperate!"

"I don't suppose you have the shavings of a rhinoceros horn laying around—"

"No."

"Any bat guano?"

"No. Look, my leading man lives in a modern city, not a jungle!"

"What about Viagra?"

"It's too late for Viagra!"

"Your leading man may be gay. Did he fantasize about the girl he loves while masturbating?"

"No, he used an old Marilyn Monroe movie."

"There's your problem. Your leading man has no imagination. Write him kneeling outside the bathroom door of the girl he loves—peeking through the keyhole while she undresses for a bath…she's nude except for her panties…are you there?"

"Yes."

"Are you writing this down?"

"Yes, its riveting."

"She is nude except for her panties. She walks to the door and starts to tease the door knob, not two inches from his eye—"

"Stop! She would never do that, tease the door knob," protested the ex-priest.

"It's a fantasy, Father!"

"Okay, I'll modify it so it jibes with her character," stated Ken. "Thanks for all your help."

"How old are you Mr. Smith?" asked the movie star.

"Twenty-eight."

"Congratulations. Never call me again!"

David Heightly hung up and went to the bathroom, but before he could get his pants down there was a knock on the door. Pulling his jeans up, he answered the door to discover the Spider Man duo, who just heard about McAlister's death. They were looking for Beth but settled for an evening of commiseration with him over a bottle of wine. When they finally left, David took a shower and went to bed.

CHAPTER FORTY TWO

A FIRST

Upon awakening, David Heightly attempted to stimulate an erection but failed and failed again. Bringing to mind erotic visuals of his angel girl just didn't get it. He thought it beyond devious to take advantage of her that way—it just seemed like mental rape. His predicament weighing heavy on his mind, he left Beth's pad, picked up his van in the alley, and drove to Central Park.

It was a sunny day with thick white clouds drifting slowly across an azure sky. There were plenty of fresh fish at the chess tables, and he was able to parlay his bankroll of three hundred dollars into nine hundred. At four in the afternoon, David left the tables, jumped into his van, and drove to the florist shop near his apartment. After purchasing a dozen long-stemmed red roses, he drove to the Whole Foods market and bought wine and groceries that would enhance his first date with the girl of his dreams. In her phone call to him that morning to confirm her arrival time, she requested that they spend the night at his crib. She didn't want to encounter Albaniac until Friday, which was a day of fasting and penance for Muslims like her boss.

When David dropped the groceries and flowers off at his crib, he met the housekeeper, a sturdy Latino woman in her fifties who was just finishing up the windows.

"Flowers," she said smiling—"for someone special, yes?"

"Very special," replied David. "Is there a vase around somewhere?"

"No vase. There is one in the lobby."

"In the lobby?"

"Yes. Is empty forever. We will borrow, yes?"

"Sure."

David shared the elevator down with Juanita, getting her name and some necessary information by requesting her card "for a friend." After capturing the vase, Juanita returned to his crib while he headed out to fetch Beth.

Realizing that he had time to spare, David drove his van through a car wash on Tenth Avenue. The shiny orange and black Chevy blazed in the setting sun as he drove to the Port Authority Bus Terminal. Parking would have been impossible, so Beth agreed to meet him outside at the Ninth Avenue entrance. He circled the block six times before she appeared outside with her rollling suitcase. For the last fifteen minutes he had been a nervous wreck, but when he saw her he thought he might actually throw up. She was dressed in jeans and a cobalt blue shirt with signatures of rock stars scrolled in white all over it. Waving as he pulled up, she appeared even more beautiful through the new eyes of David Heightly. Throwing her suitcase into the back, she stepped up into the passenger seat. Before she said a word, Beth leaned over and kissed him full on the mouth, her sweet tasting tongue sliding gently through his lips before she eased away. Dizzy and sorting through a barrage of new feelings, the new David Heightly just stared at the beautiful girl that kissed him. He just couldn't find a cool response and had to restrain himself from saying thank you. After a pause too long, Beth said, "What?"

"I've missed you," responded David Heightly as he leaned over and kissed her on the cheek. The sound of a car horn behind him made him aware of the traffic, and he drove away.

As they traveled, Beth wanted to know the particulars of Ken McAllister's death. She went on a bit about how difficult it would be to rent his apartment which was renovated to accommodate a person in a wheelchair. It never registered with the new David that every closet, cabinet, sink, and countertop was lowered for McAlister. He responded saying, "Albaniac can't be too happy about that."

"He's a sharp dude. He'll figure it out," Beth concluded.

David's mind wasn't really into the conversation. He was inwardly frozen with the fear that he might be impotent. He wondered if he wouldn't have been better off trying to score some Viagra. Of lesser concern were the vegetarian dishes he selected at the Whole Foods Market. Would they be to Beth's liking? The idea of cooking for her was out of the question because it seemed like something the male chauvinist David would never do. He thought about eating out on her first night back but wondered if they had a favorite restaurant he didn't know about. While he was still second guessing every decision he made for the evenings encounter, Beth shot a question at him that caught his attention.

"Do you think it's possible that he killed himself?"

"Who, Ken?" David responded. "No way."

"No way! He was lonely, babe," stated Beth. "He had no relatives—no friends to speak of, except me—"

"The police told Albaniac it was a heart attack."

"But Ken was a crafty dude."

"Like he induced his own heart attack! Hey, even if he did, what difference does it make?"

"I think that Ken loved me—and I told him—just before I left, I told him there was no way we could—you know, be anything but friends—was that cruel? I mean—"

"Beth, Beth, it was the truth. The truth is sometimes hard to take but it's never cruel —" consoled David.

"I don't know," Beth conjectured almost to herself.

David reached over and took her hand.

"Honestly babe, he was a very unhappy dude. Who wouldn't be? Spent his life in a wheelchair—believe me, you had nothing to do with his death."

After a moment Beth asked. "Where's Top Gun?"

"Back at your place, with plenty of food and water."

"Cool. What about us? I had a rice cake for breakfast."

"I thought we'd fork up some delectable veggies at my crib—with a bottle of chilled Chardonny."

"Yum—and dessert?"

"Greek yogurt and fresh figs."

"Yum, yum. And I have something for you," said Beth in an exaggerated sultry voice while placing his hand between her legs.

With that gesture, any concern about getting it up was eliminated, for it rose up and stayed up until he parked the car. While pulling into a parking space across the street from his apartment building, he spotted his punk neighbor talking to a couple of girlfriends outside the entrance. He had no little concern escorting Beth through the punk posse but had no choice. With Beth's suitcase in one hand and Beth in the other, the new David Heightly crossed the street. The posse parted to let him through, with merely a wink from the punk girl. Unfortunately Beth caught the wink and stepped menacingly into the girl's face.

"Did you just wink at my guy?" Beth hissed in a voice so chilling, so out of character for her that it shocked David.

The punk girl also registered shock as she stepped back from the taller girl starring her down.

"No girl," responded the punk girl weakly, "Got something in my eye, that's all."

Beth hissed, "Better keep that eye to yourself, girl! Because if you ever come on to my guy here, your eye is going to the hospital with the rest of your slutty body parts!"

Beth waited for the punk girl's response. When there was none, she turned from the punk girl, took David's arm and strolled through the entrance to the waiting elevator. David managed to stifle his laughter until the elevator door closed. Then he howled with laughter, Beth joining him all the way to the tenth floor.

Upon entering the apartment Beth went immediately to the roses in the crystal vase on the table, taking in their aroma as she brushed her cheek gently against them.

"What's the occasion?" she asked, while continuing to admire the flowers.

"You," responded David, "You're the occasion."

Turning to him she teased, "This is a first!"

"Of many," said the soul who adored her from the moment they met.

Putting her arms around him, she kissed him passionately. This time David pulled her into him, kissing her back and tickling her lips with his tongue before sliding it gently into her mouth. The thrill, the sheer ecstasy of the prolonged kiss caused their hearts to pound with passion, dissolving every second thought, every inhibition of the once paralyzed priest. His hands did not hesitate to move down to her ass and pull her pelvis into his rock hard manhood. The angel girl gyrated in his embrace as she drew him gently down to the carpet where they pulled off the rest of their clothes and made love. Their simultaneous orgasm left them groaning with pleasure in each other's arms.

Together they showered, donned terrycloth robes, captured the food and wine from the kitchen, and retreated to the king bed with the satin sheets. The once-paralyzed priest and his angel girl ate, drank, and made love through a timeless night; a rare and perfect night in which David realized that his soul must have always known how to make love, while Beth realized that something unexplainable, weird and wonderful had come over her boyfriend.

THE END

Joel Ellendorff was seated in the wings of the Belasco Theater, following the dialogue in his script, while the actors on stage rehearsed, *Don't Call Me Son*. Julian was sitting a short distance from Joel, drinking a beer and reading the New York Times. Sonia Ammonia was on a United flight headed to the "Big Apple." Joel felt his phone vibrate on his belt. He got up and walked into the darkness backstage before answering.

"Hello."

"Is this Joel Ellendorff?"

"None other."

"This is Kylie Bolinger...Zack Taylor's personal secretary. I don't know if you remember me—"

"I remember you."

"I'm in New York this week...I really need to talk to you...in private. Did you know a man named Ken McAlister?"

READ THE LAST ALCHEMIST II

READERS OF THE LAST ALCHEMIST

I invite you to relate any comments you may have to me on my website:

thelastalchemistnovel.com

This novel is the first of two involving this group of characters. This first novel merely hints at the alchemical power that shapes the circumstances in which we find ourselves, while the sequel will expose just how it operates 24/7 in our lives.

When the sequel is finished, it is my intention to share information which will help people transcend any personal problems blocking their happiness in the here-and-now.

Sincerely,
Poe Hawkins

CPSIA information can be obtained at www.ICGtesting.com
Printed in the USA
LVOW11s0315111115

461937LV00001B/1/P